PROMISED KINGDOM

Stele Prophecy Pentalogy
Prequel I

Promised Kingdom

Randy C. Dockens

Carpenter's Son Publishing

Promised Kingdom

Published by Carpenter's Son Publishing, Franklin, Tennessee

Published in association with Larry Carpenter of Christian Book Services, LLC
www.christianbookservices.com

Cover and Interior Design by Suzanne Lawing

Edited by Robert Irvin

Printed in the United States of America

978-1-946889-73-7

CHAPTER 1

The situation seemed impossible.

Edvin pressed his head and back against the cement column. Its coolness sent relief to his sweaty back. He looked up and tried to calm his breathing. The warehouse had windows near the ceiling, but they were all closed. *Just my luck.*

He wiped his forehead and peeked at the gunman attempting to kill him.

In Arabic, Edvin replied, "You don't have to do this, Raheeb. I'm sure we can come to an agreement."

"I'm willing to die. Are you?" the gunman said.

Edvin closed his eyes and shook his head lightly. No. He wasn't willing to die. *Edvin Isakson, how did you get yourself in this mess? There has to be a way out of this.*

The mission seemed simple enough: save the girl. Well, he reminded himself, the original assignment was to secure the needed information. He had passed the first test and discovered the girl *was* the needed information. The information existed only in her head. Now he had to save her or the mission would be completely blown.

"I have the grenade and I'm willing to use it," Raheeb said. "It's either you or oblivion."

Think, Edvin, think. He quickly glanced around the column. Raheeb had the woman as a human shield with a gun to her head and his other arm around her with a pin-pulled grenade.

Edvin quickly looked around to see what he might be able to use. It looked like a warehouse of rejected stuff. Nothing useful seemed close at hand. To his left a steel filing cabinet stood on a platform with casters. Farther over lay an old iron bathtub. In front of it were a row of doors with vents on the bottom. Nothing else looked close enough to access. What could he do with those? Even MacGyver would be challenged with that list. If he only had more time to think.

"Can we talk about this?" Edvin asked. "Surely we can come up with a deal we can both accept."

"You're out of deals," Raheeb said. "You come out, I shoot you. If you don't come out, I blow all of us up. Which of those deals do you want?"

Lousy deals. Edvin really needed to change the odds. He looked at his gun—only one bullet left. Raheeb should have about six left. Again, not good odds. He first needed to get Raheeb to discharge all his bullets, but not get himself shot in the process. He then needed to kill Raheeb and save the girl. If Raheeb escaped and gave away his position, the mission would be a bust.

He looked around again. For some reason, which he couldn't understand, a plan suddenly popped into his mind. A nutty plan, it seemed to him, but anything was worth trying at this point.

He dove and rolled behind the filing cabinet only a few feet away. The action apparently took Raheeb off guard because he fired and missed. *OK, one down. Five to go.* Edvin took off his boots. He didn't know if it would work, but he gave a quick look over the top of the cabinet and threw his boot at Raheeb. He wanted to make Raheeb mad enough to fire his gun, but not drop the grenade. His boot hit the girl instead. She screamed. Raheeb discharged his gun. *Success.* Thankfully, with Raheeb holding the girl, he did not aim well.

Would this guy continue to fall for this? This time he aimed from the side with his other boot and almost hit Raheeb in the head. This apparently made Raheeb even more angry and he discharged twice more. One went through the top of the filing cabinet near his head. Edvin ducked by reflex, even though it was actually too late at that point. But a miss was a miss. *OK, two more to go.*

Edvin walked behind the cabinet and rolled it over to the doors. This elicited another bullet. The cabinet stopped the bullet, but his thumb took some of the force of impact. He shook his hand fiercely because of the pain. His thumb immediately began to swell. But if that was the worst he got from this exchange, he would be fine. *Only one shot to go.*

Edvin examined the doors. Not all had a vent on the bottom. He kicked the first door over and the captor took another shot and nearly hit his foot. Edvin fell but quickly scurried to safety behind the cabinet, now breathing hard. Before he had time to think, he grabbed the second door and turned it upside down to place the vent on top. The captor shot again, and the bullet went through the door vent. *Wait! That was seven. Did I miscount?* At any rate, Raheeb should be out of bullets now.

Edvin quickly took off his shirt, split it in two down the back, tied one piece to the doorknob, the other to the vent of the door, and leaned the door on the end of the tub. One final piece of the plan was left. He found a brick and a small clay pot under the tub. He hurriedly took off his pants and put a knot in the end of each leg. He put the brick down one leg and the clay pot down the other, then put another knot in each leg. He was glad he decided to wear boxers today.

Edvin knew he had to now get the captor to drop the grenade. He was counting on Raheeb bluffing. He noticed Raheeb sweating heavily—too much for a guy already resigned to die no matter what. He felt sure if Raheeb saw the grenade on the floor, a flight response would kick in. He knew with only one bullet left, he had to make it count.

Edvin looked over the filing cabinet. "You have no more bullets. But I do. This is your last chance to give up."

"Your bullets are no match for my grenade! Throw down your gun, or it's over for all of us!"

Edvin tried to envision the best way to manage this. Unfortunately, the grenade remained in the guy's left hand with his left arm wrapped around the girl. Shooting the guy's elbow to make him drop the grenade seemed the best plan. He hoped that would cause the guy to then run and try to escape. He could think of no better plan.

Edvin aimed and took the shot. The bullet grazed the captor's arm just above the elbow. The grenade dropped to the floor as the guy grabbed his arm, yelling in pain while letting the girl go. She screamed. Raheeb's eyes widened. He looked at Edvin, at the grenade, and then bolted for the door holding his arm.

Edvin knew he only had about ten seconds to finish his plan. He ran to the grenade and stuffed it in his pants pocket. Then, like an Aborigine hurling a bola at prey, he hurled the pants, letting them fly toward Raheeb. Edvin wasn't sure if it would work like a real bola, but it was his only hope . . .

It worked well enough. One of the pant legs wrapped around Raheeb's foot as he fled, and the other pant leg hit the other foot, causing him to stumble, trip, and fall.

Wasting no time, Edvin grabbed the girl, pulled her quickly to the bathtub, pulled her inside with him, and grabbed his shirt, causing the door to fall on top of them just as the grenade went off. Edvin held tightly to the arms of the shirt to hold the door in place. The grenade's blast caused the steel cabinet to forcefully hit the tub and deflect some of the blast.

And then . . . sirens and a mechanical voice over a loud speaker. "Simulation over. Simulation over." He pushed to get the door off the tub so he and Ranata could climb out. The first thing he saw was Captain Andreasson standing over him. He expected a "congratulations," or something of the kind, but her expression made it clear that wasn't forthcoming.

"So, do you do all of your operations without clothes?"

Edvin gave a weak smile. "I do my best operations that way. Right, Ranata?"

Andreasson rolled her eyes and walked away.

"One date does not an 'operation' make," Ranata grunted as she climbed out of the tub, rubbing the back of her head. "You could've broken my neck." She sounded irritated. "And you can refer to me as Corporal Edstrom, thank you."

"Well, excuse me for saving your life."

Saeed Amari, the former Raheeb, came over and helped Edvin from the tub. He was covered in yellow die, indicating the grenade had done its dirty work.

"Congratulations, Isakson. I think you finally beat the system. However, I for once would like to be the good guy. Just because I'm of Iranian descent doesn't mean I have to play the terrorist all the time."

"But you look so good in yellow." Edvin tried to look serious.

Saeed laughed. "Not quite as good as you in white skivvies."

Edvin shrugged. "A treat for Ranata."

At that, Ranata walked off with a huge eye roll and her arms raised in frustration. Saeed and Edvin laughed even more.

"Sorry about your arm, Amari."

"Oh, it will smart for a while, but no major damage. I've

had worse paintball injuries." Then, pointing his finger into Edvin's chest, he said, "But you do owe me—big time."

Edvin smiled, but seeing Sergeant Larsson in the distance in heated discussion with Captain Andreasson caused his smile to vanish. "Well, I don't think Larsson will be pleased with my accomplishment," Edvin said.

"Likely jealous. He now has to come up with another program. He's used the same program for over five years. I think he thought it unsolvable. Get prepared. I bet he's going to make you out to be the bad guy. He's not going to admit his defeat without a fight."

"Well, I don't see why I should get slammed for succeeding. Shouldn't that help instead of hurt my chances to qualify for Swedish Special Forces?"

"Stay calm, Isakson. Here comes Andreasson."

"Debriefing in fifteen minutes," she said with a grunt. Captain Andreasson looked him up and down. "Seeing how you're dressed, you can't afford any more debriefing."

Edvin laughed but saw the captain didn't crack a smile. Her look remained stern. He turned somber quickly.

"I hope you can find something appropriate to wear between now and then."

"Yes, ma'am. Right away, ma'am."

Edvin headed out, giving a quick look at Saeed, who flashed a grimace. Exactly. This was not off to a good start. He hoped this didn't keep him from getting into Special Forces.

When Edvin arrived at the debriefing room, he sensed the meeting would be more like a trial. Andreasson and Larsson were present as expected, but two other officers he had never seen before also were there. Larsson and the other two were seated; Andreasson stood behind them. Edvin remained standing; no one asked him to sit.

Sergeant Larsson spoke first. "The mission was to negotiate for the information. Yet you killed the man with it."

"Yes, he had the information—the girl," Edvin said. "I accomplished the mission because I saved the girl and, in essence, retrieved the information. Therefore, sir, the mission was a success. So why am I on trial about this?"

"Your methods were unconventional," Larsson said.

"What? A terrorist is about to shoot me or blow me up, and you're worried about me using unconventional methods?" Edvin looked at Andreasson and pointed to Larsson. "Captain, are you hearing this?"

"You will answer the questions asked of you without the emotion. Is that clear?" Andreasson answered him a stern look.

Edvin took a deep breath. "Yes, ma'am." *Unbelievable. Whose side is she on?*

"So," continued Larsson, "please tell us how you came to believe you should save the girl, and why you killed her captor."

Edvin rolled his eyes. He could tell this was going to go downhill fast. "One, the girl had perfect memory."

Larsson interrupted. "And how did you come to that conclusion?"

"She was supposed to be an artist captured to copy the motherboard design of a classified computer. Yet I discovered her drawing it from memory and not from looking at the design. Then, when confronted, the captor-turned-psycho fled with the girl and used her as a human shield. If he had the information, he wouldn't need the girl at that point."

"But how did you surmise the girl drew from memory?" Larsson asked.

Evidently, Larsson wasn't going to let up. *Oh, well, it's just my career,* Edvin thought. "For one, because you haven't changed your program in over five years."

Larsson gave a hard stare but didn't say anything.

"And I happened to hear others talk about their experience in the program."

Larsson started to say something, but Edvin held up his palm to stop him.

"I didn't *try* to overhear, and the others didn't know I was in hearing range. But I heard one say it seemed odd she could draw so quickly, and another say the captor accidently covered the motherboard, but she kept drawing without moving the paper covering it. During the simulation, I removed one of the memory chips from the motherboard, but her drawing still contained it."

Larsson maintained his stern look. "So, you cheated."

"No, I verified my suspicions. At one point, the captor held up the motherboard to explain something to me. Even though he looked at it, he didn't notice the missing memory chip. Yet when he gave it back to the girl, I saw her eyes get wide, but then quickly recover. That led me to understand she, and not he, understood the circuitry design and knew it so well she didn't have to look at it. When he kept her captive rather than just escaping himself, that confirmed it for me. He was no longer a needed part of the equation."

"You should have reported what you heard." Larsson looked as if he was about to boil over.

Edvin couldn't hide his irritation either. "Yeah, and you should have more than one version of your program. Who's to say I wouldn't have figured it out anyway? Besides, saving the girl was all my thinking and doing. Not your program. That should count for something."

Edvin looked at Andreasson, but she remained emotionless—at least on the outside.

"Captain," Larsson said, "this should totally disqualify his results, and I suggest he not be allowed to pass this test."

Edvin felt heat rush through him and his pulse quicken. "I would have mentioned what I heard if it would have allowed you to alter the program, but you don't have a different version of the program, do you? If you do, then please tell us."

Edvin looked at his captain. "Sorry, ma'am. But I shouldn't be blamed for Sergeant Larsson not being thorough in his operation planning."

"Isakson, I suggest you go home and let us come to a final decision. Go straight home. I do not want you talking to either Corporal Amari or Corporal Edstrom. Is that clear? We'll deliver a verdict to you on Monday."

"Yes, ma'am." Edvin saluted and walked out.

Outside the room, Amari and Edstrom waited. He glanced at them but kept walking. He was in too much trouble to look like he was disobeying a direct order. So, if he had told what he heard, would that have changed anything? And even if it would have, it didn't change his success in the warehouse. That had nothing to do with what he learned before the simulation. He hoped the captain understood that.

Edvin could feel a long weekend awaiting him.

*****

Edvin headed back to his flat on Lidingö Island, not far from the center of Stockholm. Well, technically, his girlfriend's father owned the flat. With Stockholm being part of an archipelago, this island was located in the northeast corner of the city district. The area was too expensive for him to afford, but he really liked this part of Stockholm. Before meeting his girlfriend, Claire, he lived in various places for people who were out of the country. He moved many times, and not having many possessions made it easier to do so.

Edvin was glad Claire was out of town right now; he wanted

to be alone. The closer to home he got, the more exhausted he felt. He wanted to eat, shower, and go straight to bed. Hopefully, the morning would give him a better outlook on things—but he wasn't optimistic. He hoped this didn't jeopardize his chance to qualify for Special Forces. Surely the captain would see through Larsson's wounded pride.

His future was now out of his hands.

CHAPTER 2

Edvin woke with a start as his alarm beeped. He reached over, hit the snooze button, and fell back on his pillow. He was glad his fitful sleep was over. He couldn't stop thinking about what ruling Andreasson would give his performance yesterday. Maybe he should have said something before the simulation. Hopefully, his overall performance would allow him to pass or be allowed another simulation test—if Larsson developed one.

Calm down, Edvin. Don't speculate. He knew he would have to wait for the outcome before he could make plans to move forward. Being on call this weekend, he told himself, should help take his mind off this worry. He turned off his alarm and headed for the shower. As he passed the full-length mirror, he studied himself. He flexed his biceps and scrutinized. *Not bad. Still a ways to go.* His six-pack was visible, and his V-lines were forming nicely.

As he looked at his muscle definition, Edvin realized he owed these changes to his potential father-in-law, who had placed demands on him to be with his daughter. He was protective of Claire and wanted the best for her. Rightly so. She was a blonde bombshell. To Edvin, she was perfect in every category: gorgeous, smart, articulate, and charismatic—not your average flight attendant. She often traveled the route between Brussels, where her parents resided, and Stockholm, so her father bought this flat for her to stay in when she had layovers. Edvin thought back to the flight when they first met. He couldn't stop looking at her. To his amazement, she kept smiling back at him. Fortunately, she had a long layover in Stockholm that weekend and they spent the entire time together. She asked him to move in . . . and never asked him to move out. That was almost two years ago.

He couldn't wait for her flight to arrive that evening.

He switched on the television and headed for the shower. If the weather was good, he would walk to the subway. If not, he would once again borrow Claire's car. As he finished the shower, he reentered the bedroom to look at the weather as he dried off.

" . . . we have never seen anything like this. Two planes are down within the city, causing several fires and making a mess of Stockholm's subway system. There are also many car crashes making traveling this morning almost impossible."

Edvin stared at the television, frozen.

"Lidingö Island is isolated from the city as the SAS flight crashed into the Lidingöbron. Residents are going to have a challenging time getting anywhere today."

Was that the boom I heard last night? Edvin thought he had been dreaming. He tried calling work to be sure they knew he would likely be delayed getting in, but he couldn't get through. It had to be worse than he thought. He decided he should go in and see if Andreasson needed him. He knew the ferry would be the only way in. He dressed quickly. As he headed toward the door, his phone rang.

A panicked voice was on the other end.

"Edvin? Edvin, thank God I got through. Please, please come to the Karolinska University hospital."

"Lars? What's wrong? Are you OK?"

"It's . . . it's Adelina." Edvin strained to hear. Lars choked up as he tried to talk.

"Is Néa OK? Is she having Adelina now?"

"No . . ." Edvin heard sobs. "Néa's in the hospital. Adelina's gone . . . just gone."

"What? Lars, you're not making sense."

"Just get here, Edvin. I need you."

"OK, Lars. Hold on. I'll get there as soon as possible."

Edvin hung up, confused. His brother was usually a level-headed person. So his sister-in-law was in the hospital, but her unborn daughter was gone? *How is that possible? I must have heard wrong.* He grabbed Claire's car keys and dashed out.

As soon as he stepped from the apartment, however, Edvin faced sensory overload. The smell of burning diesel assaulted his nostrils. He looked toward the southeast and saw huge columns of black smoke. That had to be from one of the downed airplanes. As he looked around, he saw many people in a state of confusion and panic. People were screaming, crying. Many mothers ran around, seemingly frantically, asking others if they had seen their son or daughter.

Edvin turned, slowly. It was all so surreal. *What's going on?* Taking the car was definitely not a good idea today. Edvin hurried down the street to catch the bus to the ferry terminal. All along the route he kept seeing families outside calling the names of their children. It was all so bizarre. Edvin felt sorry for them, but he also knew he had to get to the hospital as quickly as possible.

It took almost four hours to get downtown. There were so many accidents and such intense street congestion he ended up walking most of the way. When Edvin arrived, he found the hospital full—beyond capacity. He eventually found a nurse able to tell him which room his sister-in-law was in.

Edvin opened the door to Néa's room and froze. He saw Lars sitting next to the window and realized he was in the right room. Néa's face looked almost foreign. Her eyes, puffy from so much crying, made her facial features look somehow distorted.

As soon as she saw him, she reached out her hand. Edvin went to take it and Néa grabbed his hand, pulling him close.

"She's gone, she's gone," she kept repeating. She had a wild, crazy look in her eyes.

Edvin wasn't sure what to think. He glanced at Lars, who was crying and shaking his head.

Edvin tried to pull away, but Néa's grip was like a vice. He gave a panicked look toward Lars.

Lars walked to the bed. "Honey. Honey, get some rest and let me talk to Edvin. OK?" Lars patted her hand. She looked at him and then slowly let her vice grip ease on Edvin's hand. Edvin pulled away as quickly as he thought reasonable before Néa would think to grab it again.

Néa closed her eyes but sobbed quietly. After a few minutes, she went into a fetal position and continued to sob.

Edvin and Lars walked to the corner of the room to sit and talk. Lars didn't look much better than Néa.

"Lars, what on earth happened? I couldn't comprehend what you were saying on the phone."

Lars's eyes kept watering, but he managed to calm himself enough to speak. "You know Néa and I already named our daughter and started calling her Adelina?"

Edvin nodded. "I always thought it was a beautiful name."

"Néa only had another month to go before giving birth. Late last night she woke up and started screaming. I asked what was wrong and she kept saying 'the baby, the baby.' I thought maybe her water broke, or she was bleeding or something, but that wasn't it. The problem was her stomach was flat."

"What? What do you mean by that?"

"I mean there was no baby inside her. She didn't look the least bit pregnant."

Edvin's brow furrowed. "But . . . but how's that possible?"

With teary eyes, Lars just shook his head. "I don't know. I just don't know." After a couple of seconds, Lars continued. "I called the ambulance. They couldn't find anything physically wrong with her, and of course didn't believe she had been pregnant. If it wasn't for her hysteria, they probably wouldn't have taken her to the hospital. They were afraid to leave her by herself.

"Again, when we got to the hospital, it was difficult to explain the situation until her gynecologist arrived. He was stunned. The other doctors didn't believe she was almost nine months pregnant. They did an ultrasound and found nothing except an intact placenta. She went into a type of labor this morning, but, of course, only delivered the placenta. The doctor stated this was just a normal body function as the body was treating it as a failed pregnancy."

"But Lars, what was the cause and where did the baby go? It can't just disappear, can it?"

Lars could only shrug. "The doctor should come by soon. Hopefully, he'll have answers. He should have the lab results."

Edvin tried to process all this, but he just couldn't make sense of it. He wondered if this was somehow tied to what he observed this morning—families looking for their children. But how would it be? Their children were born years earlier; Adelina was still in her mother's womb.

Néa's gynecologist entered the room and came over to talk to Lars. "The good news is, all tests came back normal. But that only adds to the abnormality of the situation. Néa's water didn't break until she delivered the placenta. Yet all the tests came back normal. This would have implied a normal delivery, but this was anything but. I have no explanation as to what happened to the fetus. Scientifically, it doesn't make sense."

Edvin jumped in. "Doctor, I'm her brother-in-law. Is this the only time this has ever happened?" Edvin had the memory of the morning's events on his mind.

The doctor shook his head. "This is the first time I have ever heard of something like this occurring, yet this is not the only one that happened. There are three others that occurred last night in this hospital, and I have heard of other instances throughout the city. They are similar to Néa's experience. But all were in different stages of fetal development. I can't give any rational explanation."

The doctor put his hand on Lars's shoulder. "Lars, I'm deeply saddened by your loss. I'll stop by later to check on both of you, OK?"

Lars nodded, and the doctor left.

Edvin sat with Lars, neither of them speaking. He looked at his brother. They had not always been close even though they were only thirteen months apart. Their parents separated when they were young. Edvin stayed with his father and Lars with their mother. His mother changed Lars's last name to hers, Bjorn. Edvin was always envious of Lars's taller stature and that he was more muscular—or used to be, before Edvin started his intense workout schedule. Otherwise, they were similar in facial features, and both had blond hair and blue eyes. They would spend summers together with one of their parents. Once Lars was on his own, he kept in touch with Edvin more often.

Edvin's phone rang. It was a number he didn't recognize.

"I'm trying to reach an Edvin Isakson," the woman on the phone said.

"Yes, this is Edvin."

"Do you know a . . . Claire De Voss?"

"Yes, I know Claire."

"We found your name and number in her belongings."

"What do you mean?" Edvin's pulse quickened, and a knot formed in his stomach. "Has something happened?"

"Sir, I'm afraid there has been an accident."

"An accident?" How was that possible? She was to fly in from Brussels late tonight, Edvin knew. Was this some kind of mix-up?

"Can you come to the Karolinska hospital?"

"I'm . . . already at the hospital."

"Then please meet a Dr. Rosen at the ICU."

"The intensive care unit. Dr. Rosen. OK. Got it." Edvin's knot was turning to nausea.

"Can you arrive soon?"

"Yes. Yes, I'll be right there."

Edvin was in a state of shock and confusion. *Intensive care unit?* That didn't sound good. This day was getting worse and worse.

Lars looked at him when he put his phone down. "Everything OK?"

Edvin shook his head. "Something's wrong with Claire. I need to go check on her."

"Oh, Edvin." Lars grabbed Edvin's arm. "I'm so sorry. Can I do anything?"

Edvin shook his head. "I don't know anything yet. I'll check back with you later, OK?"

Lars nodded. "Let me know what you find out."

Edvin nodded and left the room. He glanced at Néa as he left. She was still in a fetal position, but now at least sleeping soundly. It seemed the meds had finally kicked in. *Poor girl. I can't imagine what she's going through.*

It took Edvin only a short time to make it to the intensive

care unit. As requested, he asked for Dr. Rosen.

A man wearing a white lab coat, who looked not much older than Edvin, approached. For some reason, Edvin felt it odd someone his age could be so official. Dr. Rosen reached out his hand in greeting, and briefly explained Claire was on one of the planes that went down in the city.

"Dr. Rosen, are you sure it's Claire? She wasn't even supposed to be here until tonight."

"We did find her airline ID," the doctor said. He reached behind the nurses' counter and pulled out a folder. He handed the ID to Edvin.

Edvin looked at the picture. He couldn't believe it. Claire. His eyes began to water.

"Can I see her?" His voice was barely audible.

Dr. Rosen put his hand on Edvin's shoulder. "I'm sorry, Mr. Isakson, but she's in surgery. I won't gloss over the seriousness of her condition. She's literally teetering between life and death. A piece of metal pierced her chest and nicked her aorta. The odds are not good. Does she have other relatives you can call?"

Edvin nodded. He was so choked up he could barely speak. He couldn't stop tears from forming. *Why had this happened to Claire?*

"I'll let you know how she is once we know. OK? Why don't you have a seat in the waiting room?"

Edvin nodded again, unable to say anything.

He sat there with tears trickling down his cheeks; he would brush them away, but they kept coming. It felt like the world had gone haywire. Nothing seemed to make sense.

Edvin thought back to a year ago when—out of courtesy—he asked Claire's father for permission to marry her; Claire was always tight with her father. Surprisingly, stipulations were placed on him before he could propose: he had to be extremely physically fit and have a distinctive and honorable job. Neither man told Claire of the arrangement. She thought this whole Special Forces kick was his idea. Yet Edvin took it seriously and now, more than anything, wanted to make the team. He had changed his workout and eating habits to achieve his current physique. If he made the team, then he felt confident he could propose to Claire with her father's blessing. Now, would he get that chance?

Edvin shook his head. *I can't think like this—especially when I have to talk to her parents.* He stared at his phone, immensely dreading the call he needed to make. He sighed, took a deep breath, and punched in the number.

"Dr. De Voss, this is Edvin."

"Edvin? What is it?"

"I'm sorry. I was called to the Karolinska hospital here in Stockholm regarding Claire."

"Claire?"

"Apparently her plane crashed."

"What? How? When?"

"I . . . I don't know, sir." Edvin found it hard to get through a complete sentence without choking up.

"Is . . . is she OK?" De Voss's voice sounded unsteady.

"The doctor said it's serious and asked that I call you. She's in surgery right now."

"Should we . . . " He choked up and cleared his throat. "Come?"

"Yes, I think you should."

"I'll head to the airport as soon as possible."

"OK. Call me when you arrive."

"Call me as soon as you hear—anything."

"Yes, sir. I will. . . . Sir?" Edvin's eyes watered again. "Did . . . did she get an earlier flight or something? I wasn't expecting her until tonight."

"She swapped schedules with someone. She . . . she wanted to surprise you." De Voss was choking up again.

"Oh, I see. That was sweet of her." His voice cracked as he tried to speak further. "I'll . . . I'll be sure and call as soon as I hear from the doctor."

Edvin ended the call. Claire had swapped schedules with another flight attendant to get back early to surprise him. The thought of that overwhelmed him, and the tears began to fall once again. Edvin wiped them away. *Oh Claire, I'm so sorry.*

It wasn't long before Dr. Rosen came back. "Mr. Isakson, she's out of surgery, but in very critical condition. We need to keep a close eye on her. She can't have visitors right now, so I suggest you go home and get some rest."

Edvin shook his head. "No. I should be here in case something happens. Her parents should be here soon."

Dr. Rosen nodded. "Hopefully, I will have better news tomorrow. But . . . " Dr. Rosen put his hand on Edvin's arm. "I can't really say her chances are good. We'll have to stay optimistic until we know more. Understand?"

Edvin nodded. Rosen patted him on his shoulder. "I'm truly sorry."

As the doctor headed back to the intensive care unit, Edvin decided to go back and check on Lars. There was no change with Néa. They sat together, and he filled Lars in on Claire. Lars gave him a sympathetic pat on the back.

"Edvin, there's no need for you to stay. One of us should get some rest. Go home. I'll see you tomorrow, OK?"

"No. I need to stay in case Claire gets worse."

Lars put both hands on Edvin's shoulders and looked him in the eye. "Edvin, one of us needs to be coherent tomorrow. I need you. So, please, get some rest."

Edvin shook his head. "Rest? There's no way I'll be able to get that. I have to stay."

Lars nodded.

Edvin's phone beeped. It was the station. Edvin read the message and rolled his eyes.

"Anything wrong?"

"I'm on call—and I've been called in."

Lars put his hand on Edvin's shoulder. "Maybe it's best. It'll keep your mind occupied. I'll keep checking until you get back and call if anything changes."

Edvin sighed. "OK." Under other circumstances, he would try to get out of this duty, but with so much chaos he couldn't ignore his responsibility. Thankfully, the office wasn't far from the hospital.

When Edvin arrived, he found the station an absolute zoo, and extremely shorthanded. The police force had to respond to nearly countless calls, yet not all shifts could get into work. Due to phone disruptions, the station was unable to call many into the office.

When Edvin arrived, Captain Andreasson was there, and she motioned him over. "Edvin, thank goodness you're here."

Edvin quickly filled her in on his day.

"Edvin, I'm very sorry to hear this news. However, we're extremely short-staffed. I haven't been able to send anyone into Lidingö. Since you live there, I thought you could follow up. That will save us a lot of time, and you can still be in your own neighborhood."

"Ma'am, can I do something closer to the hospital?"

Andreasson shook her head. "Already covered. I really need you in Lidingö."

Edvin's shoulders dropped. That would take him farther from the hospital. But what choice did he have? He nodded, reluctantly. "Sure." He turned, paused, but then turned back. "Captain, any word on my Special Forces results?"

"Let's worry about that on Monday, OK?"

Edvin nodded. "I'll see you on Monday. I'll file all my reports into the system from home—assuming the website is still working."

Andreasson nodded. "Very good. Sorry, but I have to go."

Edvin watched her head down the hall. Well, it seemed he'd find out what all the commotion was from the morning after all. He headed outside to find a way to get back home. He thought about Lars, Néa, and Claire. *What's happened to the world?*

CHAPTER 3

Edvin woke slowly even though his alarm was beeping incessantly. He reached over to shut it off and sat up. For a few moments, he tried to understand if all his memories were simply from a dream. Reality set in. His heart went heavy with the thoughts of Claire and Néa. He looked at the clock again. He had slept only a couple of hours after filing his reports. He had wanted to get back to the hospital at that point, but knew his body needed at least a couple of hours of sleep to function.

He remembered his interviews from yesterday evening. He must have investigated fifty homes in his neighborhood alone. It seemed almost every interview was a carbon copy of the previous one. Each parent woke unable to find their child—anywhere. Only their child's clothes remained where the parents expected their child to be. No one had any idea what happened to them, or how it could have happened.

Edvin turned on the television and headed for the shower. He needed the hot water to help him wake up and function. While drying, he watched to see if the news reports had any logical explanations.

" . . . Authorities also have no answers to the dilemma of the missing children. In addition, it seems this phenomena is not just in Sweden, but has happened in all countries around the world. Many theories are popping up. The main theory is alien abduction, but the question is why children would be targeted."

Edvin changed the channel.

" . . . This reporter went to several churches today that have an early service. It seems every one of these churches had very few attendees. Several had no pastor show up. We interviewed one pastor. Be prepared: he was very distraught in this interview."

The scene shifted to a church in an urban environment. Edvin couldn't place its location.

"Minister Sorenson, you say you know why many of your members are not at church today."

"Yes." The minister's voice sounded panicky. His eyes looked puffy and red. "It's the Receiving of the Messiah's bride. The rapture is upon us. I was wrong. We all need to repent."

"Minister, does this explain both the disappearance of the children and selected adults?"

"Yes, yes. Don't you understand?" His eyes were now wide. "Both the innocent and those who have trusted in their Messiah have been taken. There's a lot of trouble awaiting the world."

The scene shifted back to the reporter in the newsroom. "Well, it seems one explanation for the disappearance is one of a religious nature. Does it make more sense than alien abduction?" She shrugged. "You decide."

Edvin turned off the television.

There were children *and* adults missing? There had to be a rational explanation for these disappearances. He never thought of religion as anything more than esoteric beliefs to help people feel better. *Could religion really be something more concrete?* He shook his head. Nonsense.

Edvin quickly dressed and headed to the hospital. Claire's

parents would likely be there soon. Her father was arriving on his own plane, so he wasn't bound to regular airline schedules.

Edvin found mass transit to be a little better. He arrived at the hospital an hour later than he wanted. He first went to check on Néa and Lars. As he entered, he saw Lars asleep in the chair. Néa looked at him and smiled. *She must be better.* She waved him over.

"Hi, Néa. How do you feel today?"

"Oh, I'm good." She pulled Edvin closer. "I saw Adelina last night."

Edvin jerked his head back. "*Really?* How . . . did that happen?"

"Oh, she visited me, and we had a long talk. She's very happy—and very beautiful."

Edvin tried to think of what to say. "Well, that's understandable. She comes from a very beautiful mother."

Néa beamed. "Thanks, Edvin. I knew you would believe me."

"Well, I . . . "

Lars approached, and her disposition changed.

"But some people . . . " She looked at Lars, eyes glaring. " . . . don't—won't—believe me."

"Now Néa," Lars said. "Let's not get too excited."

Clearly agitated, she let go of Edvin's hands and started pushing Lars away. The more she spoke, the more restless she became.

"You don't believe me. Some father you are. You don't care about her. You don't care about me. Just get out—get out! Leave me alone. Adelina and I don't need you anyway."

Edvin was shocked to see her this way. She had always adored Lars.

Lars pushed the button for the nurse. A nurse entered and put something into Néa's IV line, and she slowly calmed and drifted off to sleep.

"Lars, what just happened? What's wrong with her?"

Lars pressed his lips together and his eyes watered. "I'm afraid she's become mentally unstable. The doctor says she may snap out of it, but it could be quite a while before she does."

"Lars, I'm so sorry."

Lars approached and put his arms around Edvin's neck—something Edvin had not experienced from Lars in quite some time. Edvin slowly reciprocated the hug and they stayed that way for several seconds.

After Lars gained his composure, he asked, "How's Claire?"

"I'm not sure yet. She's next on my list. If you're OK, then I'll go and see how she's doing."

"Yes. Yes, Edvin. Please. By all means, go and check on her. I did go by last night, but they couldn't—or wouldn't—tell me anything." Lars waved his hand. "Go, go."

"OK. I'll check on you later."

When Edvin reached the intensive care unit, Claire's parents were seated in the waiting room.

"Dr. De Voss, Mrs. De Voss. I'm glad you made it here without incident."

Mrs. De Voss gave a weak smile. Edvin bent and kissed her on the cheek.

De Voss stood to shake Edvin's hand. "Well, I wouldn't say without incident. Everything is in such chaos. I was unsure if we would actually make it. We only got here about an hour ago."

"How's Claire?"

De Voss turned solemn. "They let us see her when we first arrived, but she didn't know we were there. Within fifteen minutes, her vitals became unstable, and they rushed her back into surgery."

Edvin remembered what Dr. Rosen said yesterday. Her condition could deteriorate rapidly. He hoped this wasn't the case. He looked up and saw Rosen coming down the hall. For some reason, he had a bad feeling. The knot in his stomach returned. The time in surgery seemed too short.

When Rosen arrived, his face was hard to read. He asked all three of them to sit.

"Dr. and Mrs. De Voss, I am so very sorry. We did all we could do."

Mrs. De Voss started sobbing. Edvin felt confused.

"Dr. Rosen? Why . . . what happened? I thought the surgery yesterday was successful."

"Mr. Isakson, I'm sorry. I did say she was still in critical condition. It seems the wall of her aorta was weaker than was needed to handle the delicate surgery. Again, I'm truly sorry."

As Dr. Rosen left, Edvin felt numb. Tears came, and he didn't try to stop them. He leaned back and closed his eyes, the tears starting to flow freely now. *Claire. Oh, Claire. What am I going to do without you?*

Edvin opened his eyes and saw De Voss comforting his wife and also crying. With Claire in his life, Edvin felt like he was finally going somewhere. Now, he felt totally lost. He decided to leave and give the De Vosses privacy.

De Voss grabbed Edvin's arm. "Edvin, please stay."

Edvin nodded and took a seat. After a while, Mrs. De Voss calmed down. She said she wanted to walk for a while and would return momentarily. This gave Edvin and De Voss a few minutes to talk quietly.

De Voss wiped tears from his eyes. "Edvin, I would like for you to come back to Brussels with us tonight. I want you at Claire's funeral. She cared so much for you, and I see that by your commitment to changing yourself, you were very sincere in your devotion to her." He gave a weak smile. "Actually, you were not the first man to ask for her hand in marriage. Yet you were the first one willing to change yourself because of your love for her. Once you started, I knew you were the right man for Claire. It was more about your devotion to her than about really changing yourself. And I can see you took it seriously. Your physique looks much more muscular than the last time I saw you."

Edvin gave a weak laugh as he pulled out a tissue and wiped his eyes and nose. "Well, I did think the request a little strange—at first. But when I started, I realized it was the best thing for me, and it helped me focus on what I wanted for my future."

De Voss nodded. "It was to serve a dual purpose. I knew you would also benefit, but my main concern was Claire's happiness." He choked up again, but quickly recovered.

Edvin nodded. "About coming back with you. I need to talk to my brother and my boss. My sister-in-law just lost her baby, and there is utter chaos at work."

"You talk to your brother and boss. If you have any issues, let me know. I have some pull. You should be back by Wednesday."

Edvin looked at him, unsure how to respond. He simply nodded and said, "Yes, sir."

* * * * *

Surprisingly, Captain Andreasson was very accommodating. She told Edvin to report next Friday. When asked why not until that date, she seemed ominous, and said, "Things are developing." Edvin wasn't sure what that was supposed to mean, but she wouldn't say anything more.

Néa wasn't better, but Lars was insistent he go with the De Vosses.

The funeral ceremony was simple but emotionally charged. Edvin found it hard to focus on anything but his loss, but he tried. He couldn't remember seeing so many people at a funeral before, but then, many could have been there mainly because of De Voss's governmental importance. Claire's friends seemed very warm, genuine.

Then, in another surprise, De Voss offered Edvin to return home by use of his private jet.

While in the limo on the way to the airport, De Voss turned toward Edvin and handed him an envelope. "Edvin, here is the deed to the flat."

Edvin's eyes widened. "What?"

"Edvin, I want you to keep the flat. It was going to be yours and Claire's anyway."

Edvin shook his head, but De Voss stopped him. "No, I really want this for you. I only bought it so Claire would have a place to stay in Stockholm. We don't need a place there, and I would only sell it, so I want you to have it."

"Dr. De Voss, this is most generous. I will certainly make payments on it."

De Voss shook his head, "No, Edvin. It's already paid off. It's my gift to my would-have-been son-in-law." He smiled. "I really want to do this."

"I don't know what to say."

De Voss smiled. "Just say yes. I hope you don't mind if I keep in touch occasionally."

"That would be my honor, Dr. De Voss. Again, thank you for everything."

"No, Edvin, thank you." He gave Edvin a brief but heartfelt

hug. "I know my daughter died happy, and that was all due to you."

Edvin was overwhelmed; he didn't know what else to say. They shook hands as Edvin boarded the plane. He had never been treated so royally. In any other circumstance, he would have loved the attention.

* * * * *

Edvin spent the next day at home—now *his* home. That change was yet to sink in. De Voss gave him the car also. It was all so hard to comprehend. He called Lars at the hospital and found that Néa's condition was worse instead of better. The doctors were beginning to make suggestions of a psychiatric hospital.

That night, Edvin had a tough time sleeping. He thought about Claire, about Néa, and about what may happen at work the next day. While his marriage to Claire was no longer on the line, he still greatly desired to be in Special Forces; he felt achieving that position would honor her memory. But he wasn't sure what to expect. A week had passed since the simulation, and he had heard nothing.

Edvin arose well before his alarm went off.

He stuck to his usual routine, turning on the television and heading for the shower. As he was dressing, he listened to the morning news broadcast.

" . . . We should be very grateful to our city's workers who, in less than a week, got the city back to nearly normal working order. And a big thank you to our citizens, who banded together in this time of crisis. Now, some are advocating all procreation be suspended until we know more of the reason for the children's disappearances. It has been confirmed there are no children left in the world. That is a very odd statement, I know, but something we all should consider very seriously."

Edvin shook his head. This was now a very different world. He thought about this on the way to work. He and Claire never seriously talked of having children. Just having her in his life would have been enough for him.

When he arrived at work, Andreasson immediately called him into her office. "Isakson, I hope things are better with you now," she began.

"Getting there, I guess. Not so much for my brother."

"I'm sorry to hear this about your brother." She gestured for him to sit. "Please sit. We need to talk."

Edvin sat and prepared himself for the worst.

There was a short pause, then: "Edvin, I want you to lead a Global Special Forces mission."

"What?" Edvin sat up straighter. "Really? I made it into the GSF? Why . . . I mean, what changed your mind?"

"Changed? What makes you think I *changed* my mind?"

"Well, after the simulation, you didn't seem very pleased."

"I wasn't. I wasn't pleased with you, and I wasn't pleased with Larsson."

Andreasson was quiet for a minute and looked at Edvin. That made him uncomfortable.

"You should have come to me after hearing the conversation about the simulation."

"Yes, ma'am." Edvin's tone was now apologetic.

"And Larsson should not have been so smug in his past laurels. He's rectifying that mistake now."

Edvin smiled to himself. He would love to have heard the conversation between Andreasson and Larsson.

"But," Andreasson continued, "a lot has happened this last week. I need someone who can think on their feet, and you certainly demonstrated that during the simulation." She paused again. "I want to bring you into a global concern. I'm going to send you, Amari, and Edstrom for a special debriefing. The leaders of the European Union have a plan to help restore calm from the chaos. The Supreme Commander wants Sweden to be a part of that. It's too bad we don't know someone on the inside to get Sweden a more prominent placing."

Edvin quickly pondered if he should say what was on his mind—then decided to do so. "I know Dr. De Voss," he said.

Andreasson whipped around and looked at Edvin. "You mean Dr. Ivan De Voss, president of the European Council in Brussels?"

Edvin nodded. Andreasson stared at him. "This is a person you could just pick up the phone and call?" Andreasson sounded doubtful.

"His daughter was my girlfriend. And the one whose funeral you gave me permission to attend."

Andreasson gave a wry smile. "Are you willing to make a phone call?"

CHAPTER 4

"Isakson, you're unbelievable." Saeed smiled as he raised his glass. "What other country representatives get to ride first class to Brussels?"

Ranata nodded as she took another sip of her wine.

Edvin smiled. "When I asked for Dr. De Voss's help a few weeks back, I didn't intend for such accommodations. Just for him to put in a good word."

"Well, you must be on his good side." Saeed laughed.

"Apparently," Edvin said. He was exhibiting levity on the outside, but inwardly, he wanted this to work out more than anything. It had been about a month since Claire's funeral. This was just the mission for him to make good on his promise to De Voss and let him know how much he loved his daughter.

All three laughed and talked during the short flight to Brussels. A limo waited for their arrival and dropped them off at headquarters, where other country representatives were staying in their attempts to qualify for the newly formed Global Special Forces. Because of De Voss, Edvin and his two friends didn't have to prequalify, but that didn't mean their qualification would be any less strenuous than that of any other applicant.

* * * * *

Reveille sounded early. Edvin awoke but was discombobulated for several seconds. His memory slowly returned as he saw all the activity of his bunkmates also responding to the blaring sound in his ears. He quickly jumped from bed as Lieutenant Farrell entered the room. Everyone stood at attention in various stages of dress.

"OK, recruits! You're supposed to be the best of the best. Do you really expect me to believe you're the best when you can't even get yourselves dressed?"

Farrell stopped in front of Edvin and looked him up and down. Edvin tried to look directly ahead, but couldn't miss the disapproving look in Farrell's eyes. As Farrell turned, he simply said, "Mess in five minutes, or go without."

As soon as Farrell left, everyone jumped into action, dressing quickly and making their bunk. No one wanted the lieutenant on their bad side. Edvin met Ranata and Saeed at breakfast.

"Farrell is going to be hard to impress," Ranata said. "He made Phillips over there make her bunk three times, like she was some kind of rookie."

"Yeah, he caught me undressed this morning," Edvin grunted.

Ranata and Saeed looked at him with raised eyebrows.

"Relax." Edvin's tone was defensive. "Everyone was in the middle of dressing."

Ranata laughed and then said sarcastically, "I thought that was how you did your best work."

Edvin gave a half grin. "Very funny. OK, let's go and do our best before we get chewed out for eating too long."

* * * * *

The next three months were grueling. There were tests of tactics, physical strength, strategy, and endurance. Many of the candidates turned it into a competition, but Edvin remembered Captain Andreasson's warning and advice: "You forget about the other guy. You do your best and then keep improving it. When you think you've done your best, treat that as your next baseline. Remember, the Global Special Forces are looking for the very best. *Become* the very best."

Each night over dinner, Edvin, Ranata, and Saeed assessed the tactics and abilities of everyone they competed against, outlining each person's strengths and weaknesses. When in personal competition, they used their opponents' weaknesses against them, but they utilized the strengths of others when competing in group efforts.

In the end, Saeed and Ranata made it on the GSF with a promotion. Edvin spent another month in further officer training.

At the end of the four months of training, De Voss invited all three for dinner—an invitation they readily accepted. All were in awe of the De Voss' accommodations. They entered a gorgeous, oversized foyer: stained glass windows with outside lights casting colorful shadows on opposite walls, a miniature statue of Europa riding Zeus transformed as a bull prominently displayed on an ornate wooden table, and an elegant chandelier with crystals reflecting the light. Edvin had been in this house only once—at Claire's funeral. He hadn't really been in a frame of mind to notice much of anything at that point, so it all seemed just as new to him now as it did to Saeed and Ranata. Meanwhile, the aroma of a cooking roast made their mouths water.

Mrs. De Voss welcomed them and invited them into the dining room. "I do hope you like roast. I wasn't sure what would be a favorite."

"No worries," Saeed said. "It smells wonderful."

Ranata nodded. "Mrs. De Voss, your place is exquisite."

Mrs. De Voss smiled. "Thank you. Both my husband and I are somewhat of what you might call collector junkies."

Ranata laughed with her. "Well, you're a junkie with good taste."

"Thanks, Ranata. We're happy to have people over to share them."

Over dinner, each of the three thanked De Voss for his help.

"No, I gave you the opportunity," he answered, looking at each of them. "You each took it from there. And Edvin, I hear further congratulations are in order." He looked at his wife. "They all received a promotion, and Edvin received further officer training and will be a lieutenant."

Mrs. De Voss smiled and nodded toward Edvin.

Edvin smiled back. "Yes, I'm very fortunate."

"I think the congratulations should go to us," Saeed said with a wry smile. "After all, we trained him first, and look how well he turned out."

Everyone laughed. Edvin held up his glass. "A toast to Saeed and Ranata."

"Seriously, Edvin, you deserve it. I've never seen anyone with such sharp instincts as you seem to possess," Ranata said. "Although you'll likely get a big head about my statement"—she too had a wry smile—"I found your training sessions very impressive."

"Thanks, Ranata. Coming from you, that means a lot."

"Edvin, I guess my instincts were right about you," De Voss said.

Edvin held up his glass to toast De Voss as well.

"So, Edvin," he continued. "I also invited you here to let you know I have requested you for a special assignment. Actually, all three of you ranked very high, so, although it's up to Edvin, I'm assuming he would pick both of you."

Edvin nodded.

"I'm stepping down as president, and another will take my place."

Edvin had a hard time believing what he had just heard. He had such respect for this man. De Voss must have seen the shock on his face.

"Don't worry, Edvin. I'm not retiring. I will be advisor to the president. But I need a team to watch the new president and my family as well. You can pick four others to help you."

"Are you sure our trainer, Lieutenant Farrell, will approve of this?"

"Well, who do you think recommended the three of you?" De Voss asked.

Edvin's eyebrows shot up. "So, who will we be protecting?"

"You may not believe this. But his name is Malach Ebano Sahir Shen Ignado Ahmed Hatim."

"You've got to be kidding me."

De Voss gave a short laugh. "That's only the half of it. He also has doctorates in both political science and molecular biology."

"That's remarkable," Ranata said. "It's odd he would be so diverse in his expertise."

"Exactly. But that's what makes him such a great candidate for leading, well, all of earth at this time in its crisis. He understands people, he understands technology, and he knows how to incorporate the two together. And yet, he's perhaps the humblest man I have ever met." He paused. "I've made arrangements for our new president to talk to the United Nations in three weeks. You'll need to get your team together—pronto."

Edvin nodded. "I have four people in mind. I'll talk with them tomorrow."

"Very good. In the next week, I'll send you more instructions over a secure line. We can further debrief everyone on the flight over—and you can meet the man who may be the most intriguing person in the world today."

At the end of dinner, all three thanked Mrs. De Voss for such a delicious dinner and said their goodbyes. Once back in his bunk, Edvin thought about how quickly things seemed to be changing. He was extremely pleased the man he respected most would still be in his life. It was like a touch of Claire remained with him.

CHAPTER 5

Over the next three weeks, Edvin made preparations. He conferred with Saeed and Ranata on his choices for the other four assignments, and they agreed. Phillips was a friend of Ranata's; Edvin had observed her performances during their training and was impressed. Not only were her muscles toned, her red hair and smoky-colored eyes made her striking in the beauty department as well. Her strengths certainly outweighed her weaknesses. Cortez was another impressive choice. He was as tall as Edvin, but more muscular than Edvin and Saeed combined. But he wasn't arrogant—just confident—and he had become a good friend of Edvin's. Then there were Masaki and Chong, two of the few Asian participants in this round of trainings. They were nimble and quick in tactics, but also keen in strategy.

Edvin met with all six a few days before their mission. "Both here and in New York, Phillips and Cortez, you two will ride ahead of the limo. Masaki and Chong, you two will ride behind the limo. The three of us will ride in the limo with the De Vosses and the President."

Each nodded.

Phillips got his attention. "What about after we get to New York?"

"Amari and I will flank the podium. Chong, you and Phillips patrol from the back. Cortez, you and Masaki guard Dr. De Voss. Edstrom, you guard Mrs. De Voss wherever she stays. I'm not sure she will be attending the UN meeting."

Cortez cocked his head. "What exactly will we be looking for?"

Edvin looked at each of them. "We need to keep our eyes peeled for anything out of the ordinary. We need to be prepared for anything. Dr. De Voss wants the new President protected at all costs."

"OK," Masaki said. "We get that. But what about the agenda and travel routes?"

"We'll get more detailed plans on the way to New York."

After a bit more exchange of information, they disbanded for the night.

* * * * *

Over the next couple of days, Edvin made the transportation arrangements to the airport. Once the day arrived, he had no time to talk with either the President or De Voss before the private jet took off from Brussels—all seven of the guards were in constant communication to be sure all was clear while en route.

Once the jet was in the air and everyone settled, De Voss asked Edvin to join him in the conference room to meet the President.

"Hello, Lieutenant Isakson," Hatim began, "Ivan has told me much about you."

The President motioned for Edvin to sit near him. Edvin thought Hatim looked a little on the tall side but well proportioned. His features looked somewhat middle eastern, but his skin tone looked lighter, like he was just well tanned. His hazel eyes had a youthful twinkle to them. Just from this brief encounter, Edvin could feel his charisma. It just seemed to emanate from him. After Edvin took a seat, Hatim continued. "And he has been very complimentary of you as well." Hatim smiled while looking at De Voss.

Edvin smiled but decided he should get down to business. "So, President Hatim, what is the agenda in New York so we can make plans?"

Hatim looked at De Voss, who nodded.

"We'll be staying at ONE UN hotel. We need to be at the UN by ten o'clock day after tomorrow. However, the remainder of our stay is really dependent on the reception we receive at President Hatim's presentation."

Edvin nodded. This at least gave him a plan for the next couple of days.

"OK," Edvin said. "We'll regroup at the end of the day of your presentation, sir, and decide what to do from there."

De Voss nodded.

Hatim smiled. "It seems, then, that all is in order."

Edvin rose to leave, but Hatim held up his palm to stop him. Edvin settled back into his chair.

Hatim pulled out a large silver briefcase and laid it on the table. Edvin watched him with raised eyebrows.

As he opened the briefcase, Hatim said, "I think you and the others will find these unique—and useful."

He turned the case around, and Edvin saw seven handguns displayed before him. Edvin opened his mouth to say something, but then closed it. He didn't know what to say—or ask.

Hatim continued. "These are made from one of my factories utilizing a 3-D printing technology. They are made from a special material and have no metal in them at all. To my knowledge, no one else has been able to achieve anything like this."

Edvin picked up one of the weapons. The handle had a quite different feel from any gun he had held before. "What type of material is this?"

"Well, I can't say until my patent has been approved. It's unusual. Although it's fire resistant, if the heat gets very high, it will burn and serve as a catalyst for the material to continue to burn. It's nice because it's lightweight but can be remolded when one wishes."

"President Hatim, I'm very impressed. But why do you want us to use these—we're already sufficiently armed." This seemed odd, but if De Voss respected the President, Edvin was going to give him the benefit of the doubt.

"I want to take no chances," Hatim said. "There could be some who will want you to relinquish your handguns due to their policies. You can have these hidden on your body without fear of detection. Yet they are as deadly as any metal gun, and they're highly accurate."

"I see." Edvin laid the gun back inside the briefcase. He began to wonder what exactly he and his teammates were getting themselves into. If the threat against them was this serious, then they would need to double-check all their protocols. *And if this guy is the savior De Voss believes him to be,* Edvin thought to himself, *why would he be in such danger?*

Hatim handed Edvin another small case. This one was clear, and Edvin could see several earpieces placed into the foam. Also inside it was another smaller, clear case with only two earpieces in it.

"The smaller case," Hatim said, "is for you. Each has a different frequency: one to communicate with your team and the other to communicate with me and/or Ivan. Of course, the others are tuned only to one frequency, the one for your team to communicate with each other. A tap to your ear will alternate between the frequencies."

Edvin nodded. *This guy leaves nothing to chance.*

"I expect you to keep your earpieces in almost 24/7. They fit within the ear canal and will not be noticed by anyone."

Edvin nodded again. He waited another minute to see if further instruction would follow, but none did. "If you'll excuse me, I'll go distribute these," he said. "Thank you for the details."

Hatim nodded. "Lieutenant Isakson. I'm expecting great things from you. Ivan assures me you're the man for the job. He's never wrong."

De Voss smiled.

Edvin gave a slight bow before exiting. "I'll do my best, sir."

Later, when Edvin distributed the nonmetallic guns to the others, nearly everyone met him with raised eyebrows.

"This is our insurance policy," Edvin said. "This gives us the ability to protect under any circumstance."

Amari took his. "I see. So even if others think they've disarmed us, we stay armed." He nodded. "Impressive." The others looked their pieces carefully over as well.

* * * * *

Once they arrived in New York, the team followed the same protocol procedures from airport to hotel as they had observed in Brussels. At the hotel, they made arrangements for the De Vosses and Hatim to have side-by-side suites, and for rooms on either side and directly across the hall for Edvin and his comrades.

Edstrom kept watch within the De Voss' suite and Phillips in the President's. Edvin and Amari took point within the hallway. They would rotate with Cortez, Chong, and Masaki every four hours until time to head to the UN.

"So, Isakson," Saeed asked when they had set up in the hallway, "what do you think we're really facing on this stakeout?"

"I'm not sure. It's hard to imagine someone against President Hatim if he's really the savior for the whole world that Dr. De Voss portrays him to be." Edvin shrugged. "Maybe they're just being cautious."

Edvin did a double take to his right. Everything looked quiet, but his muscles tensed.

Saeed turned up his brow. "What's the matter?"

Edvin shook his head. "Nothing, I guess. I thought I saw movement. But I guess not."

"Don't get jumpy on me."

Edvin laughed. "Don't wor—"

He turned with a jerk and saw an arm disappear around the corner of the hallway.

"What's wrong?"

"Stay here and guard the door," Edvin barked to Saeed. "Someone's around the corner."

Edvin brought up his gun and slowly turned the corner, prepared for whatever he might find. When he got close to the corner, he whipped around it with gun pointed. No one. He talked into his earpiece. "Chong, Masaki, Cortez. Get out here now and guard the door. Someone's out here."

"Roger," he heard back from Chong.

He must be around the next corner. Edvin walked quickly. Before he reached the next corridor, he had a distinct feeling of someone behind him. He turned, but before he could focus on the figure before him, his gun was knocked from his hand and a blow headed for his midsection. His reflexes were quick enough to block the punch, and he managed an uppercut to the guy's chin. *What's with the ninja suit?,* he asked himself in that split-second. But the eyes of this ninja looked more Mideastern than Oriental. He didn't have time to contemplate this any further, though.

Edvin's opponent flew backward and Edvin dove to retrieve his gun. By the time he turned to shoot, the ninja had disappeared around the corner. Edvin followed. A star dart flew by so close to his head that it nicked his ear. He jerked his head back out of reflex, but it was too late. He felt a sting, and a sharp one, but ignored it. Before he knew it, the ninja had knocked his feet out from under him, turned, and was gone.

Edvin looked around. Nothing. He had to return to his post and see how Saeed was doing. He ran as fast as he could. The door to the suite was open, and Saeed was lying in the hallway.

"Amari! Amari!" Edvin yelled as he ran and bent over to feel for a pulse in Saeed's jugular. Amari moved, then moaned. Edvin pulled a dart from Amari's shoulder.

Edvin entered the suite. Phillips and Masaki were in the same state as Amari. The door to the President's bedroom was open. He noticed a note tacked to the door with a janbiya dagger. As he peered in, Chong was holding a prisoner, having pinned him to the wall. Chong had the guy's arm behind his back and was pushing it upward to inflict pain so he wouldn't move. Hatim was standing on the other side of the bed.

"President Hatim, are you all right?"

Hatim nodded.

Edvin looked around. "Where's Cortez?"

Chong motioned with his head toward the door. "He chased dart man as he escaped out of the room."

Saeed entered, still a little groggy. Ranata also was waking. Edvin heard Masaki moan.

Edvin pulled the notice from the door and studied it.

"I think it reads, 'You are not as safe as you think. Decide wisely.'" He handed it to Saeed. "It's in Arabic. Do you agree with my translation?"

Saeed gave Edvin a stare with a furrowed brow. "Edvin, I was raised in Sweden just like you. Your Arabic is better than mine."

Cortez entered.

Edvin met his gaze. "Where's the other guy?"

"Got away, I'm afraid."

"At least we have one of them," Edvin said. "Let's find out what he knows."

All entered the bedroom. Chong had his prisoner tied in a chair, his gun drawn on him.

"What have you found out?" Edvin asked.

"Nothing. He refuses to talk."

"Well, I think we can help with that." Ranata stepped forward cracking her knuckles.

"No."

All eyes shot to Hatim. "I don't think their intent was to harm. Otherwise, the darts would've been poisoned."

Hatim turned to the prisoner. "I want you to go back and tell Youssef he needs to reassess his thoughts. And he needs to have faith in me."

The prisoner's eyes widened for a moment. It was obvious he knew what Hatim was talking about. All eyes turned back to Hatim.

Edvin stepped forward. "President Hatim, what's going on?"

Hatim smiled. "No need to worry. It seems some of my leaders wanted to make a bold statement."

Confused, Edvin replied, "Bold statement? It seemed like a lot more than that."

"Let the man go so he can deliver the message," Hatim said.

"But President Hatim . . . "

Hatim held up his palm.

"Sir, let us at least question him. He obviously knows something."

"Lieutenant, my decision is final."

Edvin nodded to Chong, who shook his head, shrugged, and untied his prisoner. Once untied, the man bolted from the bedroom and out the door.

"I thank each of you for your service tonight," Hatim said. "I do need to get some sleep now. We have an early day tomorrow."

"Sure thing." Edvin headed for the bedroom door. "Let's head out, everyone."

They all looked at each other and shook their heads. Each headed back to their designated station.

Edvin lingered behind. "Dr. Hatim, I can only protect if I know what you apparently know."

"You know all you need for now, lieutenant. Good night."

Edvin paused but knew he would learn nothing more—at least not tonight. As he left Hatim, Edvin pondered what he had just experienced. He really needed his team to step up its game. They couldn't afford to get caught off guard again.

CHAPTER 6

Morning came too quickly. No one got much sleep. Edvin had everyone meet at 6 a.m. to coordinate what to expect that morning.

"Edstrom, I want you to continue watching Mrs. De Voss."

Ranata nodded.

"Don't let your guard down, because whoever wants to get to Dr. De Voss or the President—well, that makes Mrs. De Voss a predictable target as well."

"Understood. We've established a good rapport, so to change who stays with her at this stage may not be the best."

"You'll be able to hear what's going on in your earpiece." Edvin looked at each of them. "OK, guys, all is as we discussed on the plane ride over. Any questions?"

There were none. Each nodded. The team seemed ready.

Edvin and his team first went to the De Voss suite. Edvin knocked, and De Voss answered.

"Ready?" Edvin asked.

Ranata entered. De Voss kissed his wife goodbye. "Don't worry, honey. All will be OK."

Mrs. De Voss nodded. "I'll treat this as girl time," she said with a smile.

Ranata laughed. "Sounds good to me."

The team next collected Hatim and flanked Hatim and De Voss to the limo. Each took their respective places. Although it was a short drive, it was important to maintain protocol. Edvin hoped that small step, in itself, would deter anyone wanting to take action.

Once at the UN, each member of the team went through security and had to relinquish his or her firearm. Edvin was relieved that their nonmetallic weapons went through without detection. Again they flanked Hatim and De Voss as they were escorted to a room off the UN assembly chamber until the time came for Hatim to be introduced. Chong and Phillips went ahead, to the back of the assembly room. From that point on, Cortez and Masaki flanked De Voss while Edvin and Saeed flanked Hatim.

Shortly after ten o'clock, one of the UN aides entered and announced that it was time. All entered from the right of the podium and stage. Saeed and Masaki walked in on the opposite side while Edvin and Cortez entered with the two speakers.

The UN president was at the podium. "Delegates, Dr. Ivan De Voss needs no introduction. While not a voting member of the UN, he's well respected by each of us and has always provided great insight into many of the issues the world has faced. We all consider him one of us, and he has a very important announcement for all of us today. I have to say I was both surprised and impressed when he first approached me."

The UN president turned toward De Voss. "Dr. De Voss, please step to the podium and address us."

All the delegates applauded. De Voss smiled and then waved for an end to their applause. As the noise dissipated, he began. "Mr. President and respected delegates, thank you for the honor of addressing you today. I have thoroughly enjoyed my position as president of the European Union and my interaction with the UN on many important matters. However, as you know, our world has come to a crisis in more ways than one, and we must have the correct leadership to guide us to a better tomorrow. I think we have such a man in our midst. Many of you already know him. He has both the training and the experience to lead us all in a positive direction. For that reason, I'm stepping down as president of the European Union and have yielded my position, quite willingly, to the man I want to introduce you to today."

There was stirring in the audience and many whispered comments among the delegates.

De Voss held up his palms for silence. "Let me first introduce you to this man's credentials before introducing him. He earned a doctorate in political science and international government from Oxford University and became a key resource to the European Union in various issues we endeavored to solve. Therefore, he understands the issues we face today and the worldwide significance of the solutions we need to implement."

Edvin scanned the delegates for their reactions to De Voss's words.

"In addition, he received a doctorate in molecular biology from Harvard University. He used that knowledge to develop a company whose sole purpose is to increase the food supply to hard-hit drought areas by genetically engineering plants to flourish in harsh conditions."

Edvin noticed some of the African delegates quietly conversing.

"He has a passion for the world and wants everyone to flourish to their full potential. Not only this, but he's an extremely humble person who often puts others' wishes ahead of his own. He works tirelessly to ensure the best is accomplished for a solution to any crisis. Because he understands both science and people, he's uniquely qualified to lead the world through our current substantial issues. Please, allow me to introduce to you Dr. Malach Ebano Sahir Shen Ignado Ahmed Hatim, new president of our European Union. Colleague. Advisor. And the best hope for our world today."

De Voss stepped back and raised his right hand toward Hatim, who approached the podium. He joined the delegates in their applause. Edvin studied the audience. Several were giving Hatim a standing ovation. Obviously, these delegates knew him, or at least *of* him. Edvin looked to see who stood. Most were European.

As the applause died, Edvin checked in with his team.

"Philips, all OK in the back?"

"All looks fine. Nothing out of the ordinary."

Hatim waited until the applause subsided. He didn't make any effort to stop the applause early, as De Voss had. At the same time, Hatim gave a hearty smile and looked genuine in his response to the audience.

"Thank you for that warm welcome. I know some of you well, but not all. For those of you who do not know me, let me get to the first puzzle in your minds—my name."

There was light laughter throughout the audience.

"I never knew my parents, and I lived at several different orphanages around the world over the course of my young life. As you can tell, my name is derived from several different ethnicities in our world.

"I think that, growing up, my name allowed me to develop a special attachment to the people of our world and made me want to help it be a better place for all to live. That's what drove me to my studies—not only of politics, but also science. After our last disturbing crisis, strong and precise action must be taken. Despite our struggles, pain, and hardships, I believe there is a way out of our crisis that can move us into an optimistic new world."

Many of the delegates renewed their applause.

"Let me outline a path forward I feel is needed for all of us—and one that is achievable if we all work together."

Hatim delivered a charming smile. Edvin could see he had nearly everyone captivated already.

"First and foremost is to understand, and deal with, the huge loss of our innocent population. Children have always been our most precious achievement, as well as resource. However, we must approach our loss rationally. We don't want to keep whoever—or whatever—is responsible around so they could ever reap such a harvest again. I do believe it is best for our world to restrict the urge to have children in our near future. Doing so will deter such an event from happening again. Soon, the threat will be gone, and we can continue our lives in an uninhibited way.

"Second, to plan for that glorious day, we want to make the world a welcoming place, a place we can leave to the next generations so they can live better lives. To that end, we need to provide sufficient food and nutrition for all. This means we need to utilize areas of our world to raise crops and foods—areas we have not used to date. Yet, I'm glad to report to you the science to achieve this objective is here today, just waiting to be used. We're on the verge of eliminating poverty and starvation which, unfortunately, happens in our world. I'm here to say . . . " He struck the podium with his fist. " . . . No more!"

Another round of applause rose from the audience.

"Third: we need to rethink our political agendas. We can no longer think as separate countries. We must think globally if we're to save our world. You're to be commended for already thinking in this way. Through your key insight, you have considered how to divide our world into ten manageable divisions. We now need to fulfill what you've started. Joining these sections of the world into a more cohesive unit will only build better unity for our world. Although the European Union is not a voting part of the UN, we have a great deal of experience in helping to rule across regions and ethnicities. We can certainly help in this regard. The leaders of the original ten-member countries of the Western European Union, which was rightly dissolved into the larger European Union, have a vast amount of experience and can help the leaders chosen for these ten territories succeed. We are on the verge of new greatness—and you all are a part of it."

The audience exploded with applause. Edvin scanned the large room. It seemed almost everyone was enthusiastic in his or her applause—but not quite everyone. Edvin took out a notepad and quickly wrote down the names of the nations whose delegates didn't seem enthusiastic. Edvin looked at Hatim. He had to admit he was impressed; Hatim certainly had huge crowd appeal.

"Everyone," Edvin said into his comms. "Are you noting which delegates are not enthusiastic in their response?"

Edvin heard each respond in the affirmative.

"I want each of you to watch those in your area at the end of Dr. Hatim's speech—see what they do and to whom they talk. This may help us assess where our next threat might come from."

Hatim continued. "However, we must not forget the human touch. We need to care about the emotional needs of our citizens. Religion is an important aspect of human civilization, one that meets most of those needs. There's a group pioneering work in understanding how all the magnificent religions of our world can be united through understanding the foundational root of all religions. The Interfaith Congress identified the best plan of unification at the Shrine of Fatima, and it has already become a positive symbol for many of almost every faith. Moving forward, we should promote this further, and I suggest the shrine's rector, Bishop Mateus Duarté, be our leader in helping unite our world's people and helping us all to heal. I believe the unification of our emotional state and our physical state provides great hope to the people of our world."

Another thunderous round of applause erupted. This time Hatim motioned for everyone to become calm.

Hatim smiled. "As always, there are exceptions to every rule. I would propose the same here. I would suggest both Israel and Jordan be exempted from the rearrangement of the world's new ten territories."

There were hushed murmurings, and even a few gasps, among the delegates.

Edvin noticed the delegates who didn't previously applaud enthusiastically were the same ones now making the most comments to their neighboring delegates. And it was interesting that most of these were from the Middle East and North Africa.

"My dear colleagues, don't be offended by this. I will work with the leaders of these two countries personally. As we all know, both sides have been at odds for centuries. I say this not to offend anyone. I have a deep respect for both sides. Yet, I'm convinced there's a solution to every problem." He smiled reassuringly. "We need to think outside the box. I look forward to meeting with both delegates and leaders of these impressive nations."

The delegate from Israel removed his glasses and shook his head. The delegate from Jordan looked solemn.

"In summary, we're on the verge of a new era. We can't afford to stay with our current way of living and moving forward. For our sake and that of our future generations, we must embrace the challenges before us. In generations to come, they will look upon this day and celebrate that we, their ancestors, had the courage to bring the world into a new and brighter future. Come with me. Let's begin that journey."

Hatim received a standing ovation. But not by everyone; pockets around the room had little or no reaction.

"Phillips, Chong, eyes alert. Not all delegates are thrilled. Keep your eyes peeled."

"Roger that," Chong answered.

Edvin looked up and saw the two of them roaming the back, eyes moving.

Hatim stood at the podium for several minutes, a huge smile on his face. He then stepped away from the podium area. The applause grew louder, into a roar.

The UN President approached the podium. The applause slowly ended.

"Delegates, I, like you, feel we've found someone to lead us into a bright future. Thank you, President Hatim, for visiting and sharing with us. I do hope you can stay for a few weeks. I believe we have a great deal of work to do. I will set up several meetings for further discussions and negotiations."

Hatim smiled and bowed slightly. Edvin and his crew escorted Hatim and De Voss back to the room behind the assembly chamber. Cortez, Saeed, and Masaki guarded the outside while Edvin remained inside with the two.

"Congratulations, President Hatim," Edvin said. "It seems your speech was well received."

"Yes," De Voss said. "I don't think it could have gone better. They were all very receptive."

"A lot of the credit goes to you, Ivan. You set the stage with these delegates. Their respect for you allowed them to be more receptive to me. You're the key to this success."

"That's kind of you to say."

"Lieutenant Isakson, you're going to be overhearing a lot

of sensitive discussions," Hatim said, turning to Edvin. "I need to be sure you'll be OK with what must be done. Do you understand the significance of what Ivan and I are trying to accomplish?"

"Well, I certainly think so. I can say I'm definitely onboard with what I heard today."

Hatim smiled. "Well, that's good to hear. There may be things I'll require of you that you'll likely not understand. I have a good reason for all I'll do, even if those reasons are not readily apparent. Can you follow directions you don't understand?"

"Yes, sir. I've done that most of my life."

Hatim laughed. "I guess that's true. And then, one other thing. The details you'll hear can't be communicated to your team."

Edvin nodded. From what he had seen and heard so far, he agreed with De Voss that Hatim was a leader the world should get to know. At the same time, it sounded like things could get complicated.

There was a knock on the door. Edvin answered.

"Lieutenant, can you come outside for a minute?" It was Phillips with a somewhat urgent look.

Edvin looked back toward the room behind him. Hatim and De Voss were talking.

Edvin nodded. "What's up?" He stepped out and closed the door behind him.

"Amari heard something."

Edvin turned to Saeed. "What did you hear?"

"Well, nothing earth-shattering, but I overheard several delegates talking. None of these seemed to be swayed by Dr. Hatim's speech. One mentioned the name Youssef. I don't know if that name is connected to the name Dr. Hatim used last night, but it could be."

Phillips entered the discussion. "Not only that, but did you notice the relation between those who didn't applaud for Dr. Hatim and those who attacked us last night?"

Edvin and Saeed just looked at Phillips.

She looked back. "Really? Lieutenant," she went on, "you said the ninja looked to be from the Mideast, and Cortez, you said 'dart man' had dark skin. Do you see the connection? Those that didn't react well were from the Middle East and Africa. That seems to be a direct correlation to me."

Edvin put his hand to his chin. "So, what are these countries afraid of?"

Phillips shrugged. "I don't know. But something's not sitting well with them."

"Lieutenant Isakson." Edvin heard the words through his earpiece.

"Sergeant Edstrom, anything wrong with Mrs. De Voss?"

"No, all is OK. But . . . "

"What is it?"

"A note was shoved under her door. It said, 'Talk is cheap.'"

"What's that supposed to mean?"

"I think it means whatever Hatim and De Voss are saying there at the UN is not resonating well with everyone."

"Thanks, Sergeant. Keep your guard up."

"Roger that."

"Phillips, Chong, head back to the hotel and get some rest. You can relieve some of us later. I'll need to fill in President Hatim and Dr. De Voss." Edvin turned and headed back in the room.

Once Edvin had spoken with the two, he expected a stronger reaction. Hatim, however, didn't seem alarmed.

"Hmm," was his entire reaction.

Hatim turned to De Voss. "Ivan, it looks like it's time to start our next phase."

De Voss nodded.

"Lieutenant Isakson," Hatim said. "I need you to take this list to the UN President and begin setting up necessary meetings. The intimate ones we can have in my hotel room. The larger ones we can have at the UN building."

Edvin looked at the list and then back at the two of them. "It looks like you'll be very busy."

Hatim chuckled. "Well, that's why we're here, isn't it?"

Edvin smiled. "I guess so. I'll have Cortez, Amari, and Masaki take you back to the hotel while I set up these meetings for you."

Edvin gave quick instructions to his team outside and then headed to speak with the UN President. It seemed a new dawn was rising. Although Edvin was definitely uncertain about what tomorrow would hold, if De Voss was certain of the future Hatim was promising, he was going to do all he could to be a special forces agent Hatim could count on.

CHAPTER 7

Edvin opened the door and welcomed the Israeli Prime Minister.

"Prime Minister Afrom, do come in." Hatim had great enthusiasm in his voice. "I'm so pleased you agreed to meet with me."

Hatim stuck out his hand to Afrom, who paused but then shook it. Hatim motioned for Afrom to sit opposite him on the hotel room settee. Edvin stood at the door along with Afrom's bodyguard.

Hatim smiled. "Prime minister, I noticed you weren't as impressed as others with my speech yesterday. May I ask your concerns?"

Afrom didn't return Hatim's smile. He removed his glasses and ran his palm from above his right eye over his short-peppered hair and around his ear to his neck as he sighed. "What am I supposed to think when you single us out and want to treat us as *special*?" Afrom asked. "Mankind has been doing that to my people for millennia. Why should I think you're any different?"

Hatim smiled again. "My dear sir. That's because your people *are* special. You have never followed other religions or their practices. Yet, I do feel there's some compromise which can be reached."

Afrom's frown accentuated the wrinkles around his mouth and eyes. "There's no compromise my people will accept unless it includes a temple back in Jerusalem."

"But, Prime Minister, who's saying that's not a possibility?" Hatim gave a wry smile.

Afrom's eyes went big and he opened his mouth to speak, then closed it again. He seemed unsure what to say.

"This is why I want Israel and Jordan to be exempt from the rest of the world. It's then just a matter of working something out between the three of us."

"But others have tried over the years—to no avail," Afrom said.

"Yes, but both sides have been vying for the same plot of ground. I'm a believer that the ground you seek is not the ground revered by Islam."

"What makes you think you know that when the best scholars in my country believe otherwise?"

"Often, I've found when arguments occur over prolonged periods of time, the reality of the beginning of the argument is lost," Hatim, quite collected, said.

Afrom looked at Hatim with a confused look. "What are you saying? Are you trying to say we don't deserve the temple mount?"

Hatim gave a small chuckle. "For a religious man, I'm surprised you would follow traditional history rather than the words of your own prophets. I fear you've let tradition speak too loudly. Go back and search your prophets and realize all can be achieved inside your own territory."

"Are you trying to patronize me?" Afrom had scorn in his tone.

"My dear Prime Minister. I wouldn't insult your intelligence. I can't say I necessarily believe in the divine as you do, yet I have read your scriptures and see the truth of some of those who believe in other alternatives as to the site of your historical temple."

Afrom squinted, tilting his head slightly. "You are a peculiar man, Dr. Hatim. Something tells me you're not all you seem to be." He paused and simply stared at Hatim. "I will look into this matter."

"Yes, please do. Once you find what you're looking for, come back to me. Once I receive the backing of the UN, I assure you I can back you in your new endeavors."

"There are those who would still oppose such a resurrection of a temple."

"Indeed." Hatim nodded and then gave a small smile. "But has that ever stopped great men from achieving great things?"

Afrom stood. He smiled and cautiously stuck out a hand. "Dr. Hatim. I look forward to getting to know you better."

Hatim returned the handshake. Afrom and his bodyguard left the president's suite.

Edvin closed the door and pondered what he had just heard. *Is Hatim on Israel's side?* He thought it best to withhold judgment until Hatim's talk with King Nazari.

Hatim headed toward his bedroom. "I think I'll get some rest now. We can take up with this tomorrow."

"I'll have Cortez be with you until then, sir," Edvin said.

Edvin went back to his room and took a shower before retiring. As the warm water relaxed his tight muscles, he wondered about his position. It felt like he was involved with more than just protection. For some reason, he had an unsettled feeling.

Sleep came, but not easily.

He awoke to a sound in his ear. "Lieutenant. Lieutenant Isakson . . . Edvin, can you hear me?"

At first, he didn't process what was happening. Groggy, he looked around to see who was talking. Reality set in quickly. His hand flew to his ear. "Sir? I'm here. President Hatim, do you need something?"

"I need Colonel Cortez to run an errand for me. Can you send someone else over?"

"Sure. I'll be right there."

Edvin sat on the edge of the bed for a minute, rubbing his hand behind his head and glancing at the clock on the nightstand. *Nine-thirty?* He usually didn't sleep that long. He certainly didn't feel like he'd slept that long. He washed his face, shaved, and was ready within ten minutes.

When Edvin arrived, he heard the shower and saw Cortez eating a banana.

"Morning, Lieutenant. Thanks. I should be back in a few hours."

"Sure. Anything you need help with? I can have Phillips go with you."

"No. I'm good."

As Cortez left, Edvin noticed his belt had missed a belt loop. *Strange*. Cortez was usually extremely meticulous about protocol.

Hatim peeked into the living area from the bedroom. It looked like he had just stepped from the shower. "Good morning, Lieutenant Isakson." He smiled and pointed to the table. "Feel free to partake of the bagels and fruit."

"Thank you, sir. What's on the agenda for today?"

"Ivan has arranged for King Nazari to visit before lunch. Give me a few minutes and I'll be out."

"Take your time. I have no place to go."

Hatim laughed and returned to his bedroom to change.

De Voss arrived shortly before King Nazari arrived.

Hatim gestured for De Voss to sit. "How well do you know King Nazari?" Hatim asked.

"Youssef and I have worked together for some time," De Voss said. "I thought he was trustworthy, but after the stunt he apparently pulled the other night, I'm not so sure."

"Can you win him over?"

"I can certainly do my best."

Hatim nodded.

Edvin answered a knock at the door. There stood a Middle Eastern man, in his mid-thirties, wearing a checkered keffiyeh held in place with an agal around the top of his head over the headdress. He had a handsome face with a neatly manicured pin-striped beard. Next to him stood a muscular man dressed in more modern, but conservative-looking, clothes. De Voss and Hatim stood.

"Your Highness," Edvin said. "Welcome. Please come in."

"Youssef, I'm so glad you came." De Voss gave a slight bow and shook his hand. "I believe you remember Dr. Hatim—now President Hatim?"

Nazari nodded but didn't extend his hand.

Hatim smiled and motioned for him to sit. Nazari sat in one of the chairs, Hatim in the other, and De Voss on the settee. Edvin stood with the king's bodyguard at the door.

"Thank you for your message," Hatim said, smiling. "I trust you received our reply?"

Nazari held his silence.

"We really meant 'our reply,'" Hatim continued. "You can trust us. I do feel we're all on the same side."

"Really?" Nazari said flatly. "Singling me out from all other Middle Eastern countries and tying us to Israel is to instill my confidence? Forgive me if I don't sing your praises."

"Youssef, please hear him out," De Voss said. "I think

you'll find it interesting."

Nazari sighed. "President . . . I mean, Dr. De Voss. I'm only here because you're here. Our paths have been strong in the past, but I question our future road."

De Voss leaned forward. "I understand your sentiment. I truly do. Yet I think we're closer to each other's view than you may now realize."

Nazari gave a short shrug. "We shall see."

Hatim smiled. "I singled you out, as you put it, because you are a key player in the future of our entire world."

Nazari gave a confused look, even turning up his brow.

"Being a neutral party removes you from the official politics and allows you to act unencumbered."

"Care to elaborate?"

Hatim smiled again. "Let's just say you can encourage those likeminded to continue with their pursuits without ramifications on your part. After all, anyone can travel through neutral territory. Wouldn't you agree, Your Highness?"

Nazari gave a slight smile. "Maybe you're beginning to grow on me."

"I'm pleased to hear that." Hatim raised a finger as if to make a point. "Yet, as you know, to encourage a response one must supply the impetus for the right response and right intensity. You've found that to be true, I'm sure."

Nazari nodded.

Edvin couldn't help but be impressed with Hatim. By hearing his words in context and tone, it would seem he was working against Israel. But even if his words in this meeting were repeated by someone, they would never be able to prove that as fact.

Hatim leaned forward. "Both of us should speak with Prime Minister Afrom. Israel is looking for a temple. Surely, we can compromise on that point?"

"Well," Nazari said, "that's an interesting request. Agreeing to that request could get some people very worked up. Some might even become violent."

Hatim nodded. "We can't always control what others do. The real question is: are we going to be strong enough to do what has to be done?"

"Yes, I can see we need to rise to the occasion to accomplish what needs to be done. When do you see this discussion with the prime minister taking place?"

"Well, part of it is dependent upon your support. If you can use your influence to help me secure the support of other UN members, it would really help the process along."

Nazari smiled. "I think you can count on that." He then turned to De Voss. "I must say, Ivan, when you're right, you're right."

De Voss smiled back. "I thought you would see it that way."

"I'm sure," Hatim said, "Prime Minister Afrom would love to receive confirmation on Rosh Hashanah, as it would mark not only a new year but a new era. You can now help bring in that era. I think your guests would like to know at least a week earlier."

"I like your plan, President Hatim. I guess I really did misjudge you earlier. I think we'll make an effective team. And, Ivan, I owe you an apology. I should not have doubted you."

"I'm glad we're all on the same page now," De Voss said with a small smile and nod of the head.

Nazari stood and the others followed. "Consider my support endorsed. I think my afternoon is now full of phone calls." He gave a slight chuckle.

"Thank you, Your Highness." Hatim bowed slightly.

Nazari held up his palm. "Please, call me Youssef. We are now close friends, are we not?"

"Absolutely. I look forward to future conversations with you."

"As do I."

Edvin opened the door for Nazari. As he closed the door, Edvin wondered what had just happened. Did he know their plan?

"Ivan," said Hatim, "come to the table. Let's discuss our plan of attack further to get all the support we need. Oh, Lieutenant Isakson, please have a seat. You've stood for a long time."

"Thank you, sir."

As the two of them discussed matters, Edvin thought more about the conversation he had just heard. He reached for a mint and popped it in his mouth. It should prove interesting to see how Hatim would attempt to pull the negotiations between these two rivals together as well as pacify the rest of the Arab world. Yet, from what he had seen, if anyone could do it, it would be Hatim.

* * * * *

The rest of the week was a flurry of activity. There were several meetings at the UN, where Hatim and De Voss met with the UN president, various members of the ten divided world territories, and the original members of the Western European Union. Edvin was surprised at how quickly Hatim won over nearly everyone. Of course, De Voss was instrumental in influencing all of Europe, including Eastern Europe and other allies. The UN president won over many of the third world countries. Prime Minister Afrom won over many of Israel's supporters, including the United States. King Nazari achieved the support of many countries in the Middle East. It was also evident, however, that some countries in Eastern

Europe, the Middle East, and North Africa were not entirely on board with the plan. But, in truth, Hatim didn't seem that concerned. He kept repeating that he had a plan.

Edvin was even more surprised at the media frenzy and support for Hatim by the populace. It seemed, as if overnight, that throngs of people would gather wherever Dr. Hatim went. He was treated like a rock star by both the media and the people.

In only a few weeks, Hatim received invitations to appear on many different American-produced television spots: *The Today Show, Good Morning America, The View,* and others. One network did more and set up an entire show around him.

He was more than willing to oblige its request.

As Hatim arrived for the broadcast, there was a mob of people already present carrying signs and banners and shouting his name. Once inside the building, he was greeted by various studio personnel.

"President Hatim. It is my honor to meet you," said a beautiful woman with long blonde hair pulled to the left side of her head and draped over her shoulder. Her red dress was evidently a power statement, and it also set off her curved figure. "I'm Anna Bonfield, host of our show, *The Politically Influential.*"

Hatim held out his hand to shake hers and then placed his other hand on top of hers. "It's my honor to be here." He smiled broadly. "I look forward to our discussions."

She gazed into his eyes for a moment. It was obvious she was enthralled with meeting this man. "We're on the air in thirty minutes. Come with me and we'll get you ready."

The two sat next to each other as makeup specialists did their work. Anna gave a brief outline of what would occur and the topics of discussion. Hatim nodded and said he was ready.

The studio was packed. Bonfield told Hatim that people had stood outside all night to obtain a seat for the show. As the lights went up, both were in place on stage, standing next to high-backed chairs, waiting for a stagehand to give the countdown. He counted down from ten, mouthed beginning from five, and then pointed to Anna when he reached zero.

"Good evening, America—and the world. We are pleased to have with us this evening Dr. Hatim, who is the new President of the European Union. There are some who are calling him the world's president."

The video screen cut to Hatim and the audience roared in applause. Hatim smiled broadly and gave a slight bow as he sat.

"President Hatim. Let's get right to it," Bonfield said. "What do you think of the term World President? Is that how you think of yourself?"

Hatim continued to smile. He turned a light shade of red. "Well, Anna, I must say I'm honored many think that highly of me. I truly want the best for our world, and I do feel I have a lot to offer. That term may be a bit of a stretch. Yet, I do feel it does convey a sentiment I hold dear."

"And what is that sentiment?"

"I truly believe we have to do away with our territorial view of the world, embrace the fact we are all world citizens, and not think of ourselves as citizens of a specific country." Hatim laughed. "Before I receive criticism for that statement, let me say I'm not against patriotism. But I think we need to break down all the walls that people tend to build to divide us. We need to break down those walls and see each other as equals."

Applause filled the studio. The cheers from outside the

building were so loud they could be heard inside the studio as well.

Anna laughed. "For those tuning in, I'm not sure if you can hear that, but we heard the cheers and applause from those outside the studio as well as here inside."

She turned back to Hatim. "It seems you have quite the following. Did you happen to see the signs and banners displayed outside?"

Hatim shook his head.

"Let's see if we can get an outside shot."

The monitors in the studio cut to the crowd outside cheering and clapping. Several of the signs said, "President Hatim, our Savior." The camera panned a banner that read, "President M.E.S.S.I.A.H."

"So, President Hatim, what do you think of those messages?"

"Well, it's quite an honor people feel that way."

"Do you think it coincidence your initials spell the word *Messiah*?"

Hatim smiled. "If you're implying I was born to fulfill this role in which I now find myself, I'm not sure I can go that far. I feel my passion for politics and science has led me to where I am today. I have to say, though, I've always felt an obligation and commitment to the betterment of our world."

Anna turned to the audience. "So, everyone, are you like me? Do you feel it's no coincidence President Hatim's initials spell Messiah, and that's an indication that he can lead our world into a better tomorrow?"

The audience produced thunderous applause.

"And I don't think it hurts that our savior is a very good-looking savior." She turned to the audience. "Am I right, ladies?"

There was applause, whistles, and laughter.

Hatim chuckled. "I'm not sure how to respond to that."

"So, President Hatim, in all seriousness, as our savior, what are your plans for our new world?"

"Let me preface my statement by saying we have a lot of work to do. And it all depends upon everyone getting behind the plan."

Anna laughed. "Well, I think you've already seen we're all behind you."

Again, more applause and a few whistles.

"And," Anna said, "I can tell you from my research, there's an unprecedented change in majors by many college students now choosing political science or molecular biology."

"Well, that's certainly encouraging." Hatim smiled broadly. "I will say, though, our new world will need more than politicians and molecular biologists, so I wouldn't want everyone to follow that direction."

More laughter from the audience.

"From seeing those outside, it's encouraging there's a diversity there," Hatim said. "As stated earlier, we need to put down our differences and think of our neighbors as equals. We need to embrace innovative technology to abolish poverty and hunger. If we take care of our world, our world will take care of us."

The audience burst into more applause—and Anna herself joined them.

"President Hatim, it is an honor having you on our show. If the audience, both outside and inside this studio, is a representation of those around the world, you can be assured you have the world on your side. It would seem the title World President is indeed apropos."

"Thank you, Anna. I feel our world has a bright future."

After a warm handshake, Anna turned to the camera. "Join us next week as we more greatly explore the direction of our new world. We will host the UN President and ask his view of where the world is heading."

The stage lights and cameras went off. Anna turned to Hatim.

"Thank you so much, President Hatim, for being here today. It's really an honor to meet you."

Hatim smiled at her. "It was my honor, Anna."

He stood and turned to head offstage, to circle up with his entourage, but then turned back. "Do you have plans tonight?"

She froze briefly, but her shocked looked turned into a seductive smile. "Not especially. Why?"

"I need someone to publicize my ideas and help promote them. I was impressed with how you handled yourself and the audience. I'd like to discuss possibilities. Care to do so over dinner?"

Anna's eyes grew large. She opened her mouth to say something, but stopped short. She nervously moved some of her hair behind an ear. "Really? I mean, absolutely." She was beaming.

"Great." Hatim smiled back.

"I have a few more obligations here," she said. "Can I meet you somewhere?"

"Just stop by the ONE UN."

"OK. I can be there by seven."

Hatim kissed her hand and left.

Edvin looked back; Anna was nearly floating across the floor as she headed offstage in the other direction.

Outside, the crowd remained, and it was still very much in a frenzy. There were various shouts above the crowd noise.

"Messiah, we love you!"

"We're on your side!"

"The world is in good hands!"

Hatim smiled and waved, but Edvin and those with

him hurried him to his limo, blocking those begging for an autograph.

As they headed to the hotel, Edvin watched Hatim; he seemed contemplative. Edvin knew he had to prepare himself for what would surely be a roller coaster ride.

CHAPTER 8

Edvin sat on the edge of his bed reading the letter a second time that morning. He found it waiting for him the night before when he returned from the studio with Hatim. He read it, then thought of its contents throughout the night. Not only had Captain Andreasson asked him to return for a promotion, Hatim wanted him to lead a mission in Israel. Going home would be good. Not hearing from his brother the entire time he'd been in America had made him worry.

Edvin headed to Hatim's room; the letter had stated to stop by before he left. As he opened the door and entered, Edvin stopped short. Cortez was walking out of the bedroom tucking his shirttail into his pants.

Cortez smiled. "Good morning, Lieutenant."

Before he could say anything, Edvin noticed another man buttoning his shirt as he walked by the bedroom door. Dumbfounded, he just looked at Cortez.

Cortez smiled. "Don't worry, sir. Nothing's going on that the President isn't in control of."

Edvin turned and his jaw nearly dropped to the floor. Coming out of the bedroom was Gwen Sheridan, the hottest recording star—ever. Then, just behind her was Ken Colston, the actor every woman on the planet drooled over.

Gwen smiled. She put her purse over her shoulder as she tossed her long, straight black hair over her other shoulder. Her stylish black leather outfit accentuated every curve.

Before Edvin could recover and say anything, Colston stepped forward and reached for a handshake. "Hi, you must be one of the President's bodyguards. I'm Ken Colston."

Edvin couldn't help but notice his muscular forearms and biceps. His six-pack was visible through his tight pullover. "Yes, I recognized you—both of you." He gave a smile to Gwen. "I'm Lieutenant Isakson. I was just surprised to see you here."

Hatim entered the room. "Thank you both. Please stay in touch. Gwen, when your current tour ends, call me and we'll set up the African benefit to destroy hunger and poverty. And, Ken, thanks for being willing to emcee the benefit."

"My pleasure, President Hatim. The cause couldn't be more important."

"Absolutely," Gwen said. "What you're doing for the world—well, it needs everyone on board, and we want to be a part of it."

"Lieutenant Isakson, would you mind escorting these two to the Columbia University Medical Center and bring back Ms. Bonfield? Ask for Dr. Margaret Lyle. Dr. De Voss will ensure your plane is then waiting for you."

Edvin gave Hatim a somewhat concerned look but responded, "Certainly. It would be my pleasure."

Edvin rode with Sheridan and Colston in the limo to the medical center. "No one is going to believe I rode in a limo with Gwen Sheridan and Ken Colston. This is cliché, but can I have your autographs?"

Both laughed. "Well, of course," Gwen said. "What if I sign one of the test brochures for the African benefit?"

"That would be great," Edvin answered.

As they were signing, Edvin had to ask his nagging question. "I know it's none of my business, but why are you both going to the medical center? Is anything wrong?"

Gwen laughed. "No, we're both healthy." She looked at Ken. "At least I know I am."

"Hey," Ken said. "What are you saying? I'm healthy. Don't I look healthy?"

"Indeed, you do," Gwen said with a laugh as she patted his bicep.

"So, what gives?" Edvin asked.

"Well," Ken said, "we promised not to tell anyone, but since you're already on the inside . . . "

"And he's helping us," Gwen added.

Ken nodded. "So, we have agreed to donate a pint of blood since we have the same blood type as the President, and we agreed to get a biopsy."

"What?" Edvin couldn't believe what he had heard. "A biopsy? Why?"

Both shrugged. "We don't know," Ken said. "President Hatim said it was important, so we're happy to do it. If he says it's important, it must be important."

Edvin nodded, but he didn't understand at all. He wanted to ask more questions about this but knew he probably shouldn't. He had a more nagging question but knew he should probably keep that one to himself as well. What the President did in private was really none of his business. After all, Hatim was good to him and trusted him. *Who am I to judge,* Edvin asked himself.

Once at Columbia Medical Center, the three of them made their way to Dr. Lyle's laboratory. She was busy looking through a microscope. After a few seconds, she looked up and noticed them.

"Oh, hi. Sorry. I was engrossed in some slides. Ms. Sheridan and Mr. Colston, welcome. My assistant will take you to get prepared for your procedure."

Gwen turned and gave Edvin a hug. "Thanks for the lift—and the company," she said.

Ken shook his hand. "Goodbye, Lieutenant. Tell President Hatim, thanks again."

Edvin nodded and watched them follow the assistant down the corridor. He turned back to Dr. Lyle. "Is Ms. Bonfield ready?"

Dr. Lyle looked up from her computer and removed her glasses. They were what Edvin would describe as older, secretary-style glasses but set in a modern-style frame. Each time she looked up from the computer, she let them fall to her chest as the ends were attached to a golden chain around her neck. She then put them on each time she returned her gaze to the computer screen.

"She should be out momentarily."

Dr. Lyle's assistant reentered the room. "Dr. Lyle, the DNA sequencer is acting up again."

Dr. Lyle sighed. "Can't Brian fix it?"

The assistant shook her head.

"Honestly, why did I even hire the guy?" Lyle groaned. "Excuse me a moment."

Edvin nodded and watched Dr. Lyle follow her assistant into an adjoining room. Edvin looked around but noticed the computer screen was showing information about Dr. Hatim. Although only initials were used for the privacy of the individual, the document on screen was clearly showing: M.E.S.S.I.A.H. Edvin nearly laughed out loud. *How subtle do they think that is?* As he looked closer, he noticed there were several individuals who had biopsies performed at the request of Dr. Hatim. From the initials provided, it was obvious that Cortez provided a skin biopsy, Anna Bonfield a liver biopsy,

Gwen Sheridan would be giving a thyroid biopsy, and Ken Colston a bone biopsy. Edvin grimaced as he read the last one. He noticed each person also provided a pint of blood. He knew Hatim was charismatic, but to charm people to willingly take part in biopsies like this was unprecedented. He shook his head.

The screensaver came on just before Dr. Lyle reentered the room.

"I'm sorry for the interruption. You were waiting for Ms. Bonfield, correct?"

Edvin nodded.

Lyle turned and called to a woman passing by. "Jane . . . Jane, would you please go to Recovery and see if Ms. Bonfield is ready to leave?"

The woman nodded and headed in the opposite direction.

Edvin couldn't hold in his thoughts. "Can I ask what this is all about?"

Dr. Lyle smiled. "I'm afraid only President Hatim can tell you that."

Edvin nodded. It all seemed so surreal.

Within a couple of minutes, Anna entered smiling. "I see my ride is here."

Edvin smiled in return. "Indeed. Are you ready to go?"

Anna nodded. They left, but she didn't say much on the return trip. Edvin wondered what Hatim was doing. After all, none of these people were loose characters who didn't have an important public persona. Anna Bonfield had received a Master's in journalism from Yale. All of these people were smart, talented, physically fit—and all had Hatim's blood type. It just seemed bizarre.

De Voss was waiting for Edvin in the lobby at the hotel.

"Hi, Edvin," he said. "We need to get going."

Edvin turned to Anna. She held up her palm. "Don't worry. I'm fine." Anna touched Edvin on his shoulder. "Thanks for the lift."

"Sure. Take care. Keep in touch."

"Absolutely." She turned and gave a short wave.

Edvin watched her walk away. He noticed every other man in the room was doing the same.

Edvin followed De Voss back to the limo. The limo headed to the airport and pulled up to De Voss's plane. Once inside, Edvin was surprised to see others already in the passenger cabin.

"Ranata. Saeed. I didn't know you were coming."

"Oh," Ranata said. "You think you're the only one getting promoted?"

"Really? That's great. I guess we're the three musketeers."

They laughed as each sat and got comfortable. They chit-chatted over various topics for quite some time. Eventually, they settled into their own thoughts.

Edvin picked up a magazine which, of course, had Hatim on the cover. It seemed his picture was everywhere. Edvin turned to the main article, an interview between the magazine's reporter and Hatim that described Hatim's major emphases regarding food production.

***Reporter**: So, President Hatim, what is the purpose of these modified foods?*

***President**: These foods are not only able to grow in currently inhospitable places, they will help individuals' personal needs as well. In addition to drought-resistant foods, we have developed two major brands of certain fruits: one for women and another for men.*

***Reporter**: And why is that?*

***President**: Both have unique needs. The Radiant brand is composed of grapes, kiwi, and cherries. They are not* *only nutritious but help produce more supple skin and help give a radiant complexion.*

Reporter: *And what woman doesn't want that?*

President: *Exactly. And then we have the Masculine brand, composed of apples, bananas, and mango. Each will aid in one obtaining a better muscle-to-fat ratio.*

Reporter: *And, again, what man wouldn't want that? So, are there any side effects to people eating these fruits?*

President: *There is only one side effect we've observed.*

Reporter: *And what is that?*

President: *They seem to increase one's libido.*

Reporter: *I have only one thing to say: who doesn't want that? [Laughter] But, seriously, President Hatim, some claim this is just to put more money in your pockets. After all, you have become a wealthy man.*

President: *Well, I can't deny that fact. Yet, as you know, all progress requires funding and we offer these at prices no different from the cost of most other fruits and vegetables. The profits, as you call them, really go back into production, research, and providing the drought-resistant products to those who are in extreme need.*

Reporter: *Thank you, President Hatim. I for one wish you even more success. It seems we are on the verge of eliminating world hunger. This allows everyone to be a part of that. I think your plan is brilliant.*

Edvin had listened to De Voss and Hatim discussing these facts before. The so-called side effect was in place to, in a way, bribe people to continue eating these fruits. What was not mentioned in the article was the fact these fruits also contained some type of contraceptive to prevent women from getting pregnant, and an agent to decrease men's sperm count to further decrease the odds of a pregnancy. Hatim's position was that it was important to prevent pregnancy until the world's crisis was stabilized. It would allow people to focus on the planet's immediate needs. *Perhaps he's right,* Edvin told himself.

Edvin looked up and saw De Voss combing through e-mail. "Dr. De Voss, do you have a place to stay in Stockholm? You're more than welcome to stay at my place."

De Voss smiled. "That's nice of you, but I have a lot of work to do, so I don't want to impose."

"Oh, it's not an imposition. There's an extra bedroom, so you can be as isolated as you need to be—when you need to be."

"Well, if it's not an imposition, I would like that."

Edvin shook his head. "Not an imposition at all."

De Voss smiled and went back to his work; Edvin went back to his reading. The next thing he knew, the pilot announced their arrival.

* * * * *

Once back at the apartment, a wave a familiarity and calmness washed over Edvin. He helped De Voss get settled and then headed to his own bedroom. The bed felt like being in the arms of an old friend. Sleep came effortlessly.

The next day was a whirlwind of activity. It was good to see all the guys Edvin had worked with. Most were happy for him, but Sergeant Larsson didn't fall into that category.

"So, Isakson, I guess the old saying is true: 'It all depends on who you know.'"

Edvin opened his mouth to respond but heard De Voss's voice from behind. "Actually, I've heard that only gives you an opportunity. It's hard work and aptitude that creates the success."

Larsson looked stunned, mumbled something, and walked away.

Edvin smiled. De Voss patted him on the back and walked to where Captain Andreasson was standing. A few who had been standing around chuckled under their breath at the De Voss-Larsson exchange.

Someone said, "Finally, someone to whom Larsson can't make a comeback. That was priceless."

Edvin nodded. He just smiled, did a fist bump with the officer who made the statement, and then walked over to where Captain Andreasson was standing.

"Hello, Captain." He saluted.

Andreasson gave a half laugh. "I guess that's the last time you have to salute me. In a few minutes, you'll be the same rank as me."

"And how do you feel about that?"

"Edvin, it's an honor to see you advance. This isn't a competition, even though Larsson may think it is. I see this as a win-win-win. It's good for you, it's good for our department, and it's good for Sweden."

The ceremony was small but meaningful. The commander of Swedish Special Forces was on hand to congratulate them. De Voss gave a small speech praising all three of them, and the commander gave his appreciation for how they had advanced the Swedish notoriety to the world. It made Edvin feel extremely special, but it also seemed odd at the same time to think that he, Ranata, and Saeed had advanced so quickly.

After the ceremony, Edvin tried to call Lars, but he couldn't get an answer. This worried him and only heightened his concern.

It wasn't long before he received a cryptic text message from Lars: *Meet me at Claire's favorite restaurant and come alone.*

Edvin was concerned.

He headed out immediately to the restaurant, and once there, Edvin asked to be seated near the front so he could watch for Lars. However, another text came nearly as soon as he was seated: *Order only water, ask where the restroom is, and then leave through the back door. Turn left, go two blocks, then turn right and go three blocks. Enter the small bistro restaurant next to the bookstore.* Edvin stared at the text in disbelief. This seemed more like a joke, and it was only making him more irritated.

The waiter approached Edvin. "May I get you something to drink?"

"Just water, please." The waiter nodded and turned. "Excuse me," Edvin said, stopping him. "Where's your restroom?"

"Down the hallway next to the kitchen," the waiter said, turning back.

"Thanks."

Edvin rose and glanced around; no one seemed to be paying him any attention. He headed toward the restroom, went through the kitchen itself, and exited. If this turned out to be a joke, Edvin thought to himself, he was going to kill his brother—after he hugged him.

Edvin followed the instructions Lars had given him. As he entered the small restaurant, it took his eyes time to adjust; it was very dark in the interior. He glanced around and saw someone near the back. He saw a hand shoot up and give a short wave. *It must be Lars.*

Lars stood. "Hi Edvin. It's great to see you." Lars gave him a hug.

Lars didn't look well. He looked exhausted and had dark circles under his eyes.

"Lars, what's going on? I thought you were playing a joke on me, but seeing you, I'm . . . well, I'm concerned."

"Have a seat. We'll talk," Lars said.

The waiter came over. Both men ordered tea and a danish.

"OK, Lars. What on earth is all this clandestine activity about?"

Lars first took a deep breath. "As you know, Edvin, Néa was in bad shape when you left."

"Yes, and I've been worried about both of you. How's she doing?"

Lars shook his head. "Not much better, I'm afraid. She's now in a psychiatric observational facility. Physically, she's fine. But she becomes very upset with me when I visit. Either she's mad because I can't see Adelina, or she's mad because I try to talk to Adelina, but I'm not looking at her. She then yells at me and demands I leave. She feels I'm not being sincere, that I don't care about our daughter." Lars's eyes began to water, although no tears formed. "I don't know what to do about her, Edvin. Sometimes I think I shouldn't visit. I keep hoping she'll get better, but it doesn't seem that will ever happen."

"Lars, I'm so sorry. Is there anything I can do?"

Lars shook his head. "No." He paused. "And I'm here to tell you I will not be able to see you anymore."

"What?" Edvin's head jerked back. He then leaned forward. "Lars, what are you talking about?"

"It's because of Adelina's blood work."

Edvin gave him a bewildered look, furrowing his eyebrows. "What do you mean?"

"For some reason, the hospital did genetic testing on the blood from the delivered placenta. I was able to get a copy. It stated Adelina would have been 17 percent Israeli."

"Lars, I still don't understand. What does that even mean, and what difference does it make?"

Lars looked around as if he expected someone to be observing them. "It seems the new administration forming under

President Hatim is requiring testing when a person has to give a blood sample for other reasons. So far, they're not mandating individual blood testing, but I wouldn't be surprised if that would be implemented in the near future."

Edvin tried to process what Lars had said. *Is he talking about being partly Jewish?* He remembered the conversation Hatim had with the Israeli Prime Minister. But was that even remotely connected to what Lars was talking about?

"Lars, are you talking about being partly Jewish?"

Lars shook his head. "There's a difference. I didn't understand the difference until a few weeks ago."

Edvin shook his head. "I don't understand."

"Well, I did a lot of Internet searching. It seems a *long* time ago—and I mean a long time ago—Israel split into two nations. One kept the name Israel and the other took the name Judah. Both were taken captive by other nations, but this happened more than one hundred years apart: Israel by the Assyrians and Judah later by the Babylonians. Those from Judah were termed Jews. It seems some believe the descendants from Israel at some point were scattered throughout Europe, and many within various countries today are descendants from these ancient ancestors."

"And you believe this to be true?"

Lars stared at his brother. "Did you hear what I said? Adelina would have been 17 percent Israeli."

"But why is that important?"

"The word on the street is the new administration will be against Jews and Israelis."

"And you think 17 percent constitutes significance?"

"I'm hearing anything above 5 percent will be considered significant."

"So, what do you think will happen?"

"I will be executed."

Edvin sat back. "Lars, come on. Why would you think such a thing?"

"Well, not today," Lars said, also sitting back. "But that's the direction I'm hearing it will go."

"Who's saying such a thing?"

"It's on the Internet."

Edvin began to say something, but Lars held up a hand.

"The person who wrote these articles was one of the taken ones. He wrote this more than ten years ago."

"What? How could he possibly know that?"

"I don't know. He was some type of 'last days' theorist. I never put much stock in those types of guys, but it's as if what he said is now happening. I believe we need to take precautions."

"What are you saying?" Edvin asked. "How do you plan to do that?"

"There may not be any hope for me—but there is for you."

Edvin tilted his head and turned up his eyebrows but didn't say anything. *Has my brother gone off the deep end? Has Néa's insanity started to affect him?*

"Néa's blood is negative for Israeli DNA. So that would mean Adelina's Israeli DNA came from me, and mine, of course, would be higher than hers. That means yours would be high as well. We can't have that."

"Lars, I'm not following you. You're not making sense."

"Edvin, look. If my Israeli DNA is more than 17 percent, then so is yours. Our last names are not the same, so it will buy you more time. It will take some digging for them to connect us via paper trails. That's also why we can't see each other anymore. I have to keep you safe. I couldn't help Néa. I couldn't help Adelina. But I can help you." Lars's eyes were watering again, and this time tears were brimming over his lower eyelids and trickling down his cheeks. "It may be too late for me, but I will do all I can to protect you."

"Lars, you don't have to protect me," Edvin said quietly.

Lars shook his head. "No, that's where you're wrong, Edvin. When I looked at Néa's blood type, I noticed her type was the same as yours: O-positive. So . . . " he paused. "I broke into the hospital and changed her blood record to yours and yours to hers."

"Lars, why would you do that?"

"As I said, Edvin, I have to protect you. Néa is gone to me . . . to anyone. What can anyone do to her? She's no threat." Tears were now rolling down his cheeks. "But you . . . " He pointed his finger at Edvin. "You are important and can do important things. After all, you're so close to the President. I can't afford for you to be discovered."

"Lars," Edvin said in a hushed voice, "I think you think too highly of me."

Lars shook his head. "No. No, I always knew you were the one to go farther—farther than me. Edvin, I'm so proud of you. Now stand up. Give me a hug. I want to remember this moment forever."

Edvin stood and Lars gave him a tight hug, which lasted for what seemed several minutes. Edvin couldn't stop his own tears from coming. Lars released the hug and looked Edvin directly in the eyes. Lars's cheeks were still wet from his tears. "I love you, Edvin. Goodbye."

Lars walked out and didn't look back. Edvin sat down in a daze. After a few moments, he collected himself, sat back, and thought over what had just occurred. *Is Lars right?* If so, what type of conspiracy was he now involved in?

It was just then that the waiter approached the table with two teas and two danishes. Edvin could only stare blankly at their order.

The world, Edvin feared, was becoming a strange and frightening place.

CHAPTER 9

Edvin stepped off the plane with Ranata and Saeed. Through the entire flight, he couldn't get Lars off his mind. *Will I ever see him again? Was his sacrifice that crucial?* Yet, now landing in Haifa, he had to get his mind in the game. His team was here to assess what was needed, and three squadrons of world soldiers would arrive sometime day after tomorrow. At the bottom of the plane stairs stood an Israeli officer awaiting their descent.

Once Edvin reached the soldier, he extended his hand. "I'm Captain Isakson. I'm looking forward to working with you."

The officer reciprocated. "Captain Mik'kel ben David. Follow me, and we can go over our planning phase."

Ben David had a Hummer waiting for them. Edvin noticed this guy was a little shorter than he was, had broader shoulders, and was more muscular. His face, however, while handsome, had a scar which ran from just above his right eye down to his right ear. There was likely an interesting story behind that scar.

They got into the Hummer and ben David drove off.

Edvin looked over. "Where are we headed?"

"We're going to Ramat David. It's only a little way southeast of here."

The drive was pleasant. The Mount Carmel range was impressive, and the Jezreel Valley area looked lush and green.

"This area is beautiful," Ranata said, looking out the Hummer window on one side and then scanning the other. "Not what I expected to see in Israel."

Ben David laughed. "You'll find almost every type of terrain in Israel. We go from snow on Mount Hermon in the extreme north to desert in the far south—and almost everything in between. There's a large part that's arid, which is what most people think of, but our country is quite diverse."

They passed a sign stating they were entering a restricted area. Yet there were no buildings in sight.

Saeed looked out the windshield. "Where's the base? I don't see anything. All I see is a road ending."

"Looks can be deceiving." Ben David gave a slight grin.

Ben David kept heading down the road and—to their amazement—the road ahead of them descended into a decline and they literally drove . . . into the ground. Edvin looked behind and saw the ramp raising back up; they were now in an underground parking garage.

"Well, that was different." Edvin looked at ben David, eyebrows raised.

"When you live with all your neighbors wanting to wipe you off the map, you try not to make it easy for them," ben David coolly replied.

"Impressive," Saeed said.

Ben David parked and they entered a hallway that led to a large room with many people at various desks. It surprised Edvin to see everything looking modern and neat. On the far wall was a door with a sign reading: Special Forces.

Edvin pointed. "And through that door?"

Ben David glanced where he pointed. "Well, I can show you. But then I'd have to kill you."

Edvin laughed, but ben David didn't, his face remaining stern. He headed for the door, opened it, and walked in.

Edvin looked at Ranata and Saeed, mouth open. "What just happened?" Both shrugged.

After a few seconds, ben David opened the door. "Well, are you guys coming?" He burst into laughter. "Sorry. But you must admit. Got you there."

Edvin smiled. "Yes. Yes, I guess you did."

They entered another corridor and then a conference room to the right. Again, everything appeared modern and technologically advanced.

In the room were several other Israeli military leaders. After introductions, all took their seats. Edvin addressed the officer who was clearly in charge.

"So, Commander, how do you see the World Forces helping you when the treaty is signed to allow Israel to build its temple?"

The commander looked at ben David. "Captain, care to elaborate for our visitors?"

Ben David pressed a button and the wall lit up; a map displayed Israel and all surrounding countries.

"As you can see, we have Syria to our north, Jordan to our east, Saudi Arabia and Egypt to our south, as well as other countries which don't like us very much adjacent to them. So, we're pretty much sitting ducks. We can expect retaliation from any of these countries. We probably need you to add additional strength in Golan Heights, around Jericho, and around Eilat."

"I see," Edvin said. "The three of us can help deploy the arriving three squadrons to each of these areas."

"I hope that's not all the forces you plan to supply." The commander leaned forward, removing his glasses. "We probably need at least three times that."

Edvin nodded. “This is only the first wave. Certainly; more will be coming—including weapons. We first wanted to see where you would need them.”

“Roger,” the commander said. “I’ll make preparations on our side as well and be sure we have sufficient accommodations for them.” He paused. “Having you here helps us know President Hatim is sincere in his efforts.”

Edvin nodded. “We’re happy to help.”

The commander stood. “I’ll let you get to your hotel and get some rest. We’ll talk more tomorrow.”

They all shook hands and dispersed. Ben David drove the three to their hotel in Haifa.

“Captain,” Ranata asked, “where are they in knowing where to construct the temple?”

“Call me Mik’kel when it’s only us,” ben David replied. “I like to be informal when possible. It’s been a touchy situation ever since the Prime Minister returned from seeing President Hatim. There are those extremely adamant that there’s no place for the temple other than on the temple mount. As you can see . . . ” He pointed to the scar on his face. “Some opponents are adamant about their resistance.”

Edvin just looked at Mik’kel, unsure what to say.

“So, what happened?” Ranata paused. “If I’m allowed to ask?”

Mik’kel grinned, nodded. “It’s no secret. While putting down a riot on the temple mount, one of the rioters cut me with the jagged end of a piece of pipe.”

Ranata grimaced. “Ouch.”

Mik’kel shrugged. “A memento of what’s important.”

Ranata sat back and shook her head.

Mik’kel glanced at her in his rearview mirror, then at Edvin. “Anyway, Prime Minister Afrom has insisted scholars look more closely at Scripture to see if there’s any indication the temple should be closer to the City of David. Some archaeologists are looking there, but not to everyone's approval."

"Wow," Edvin said. "You have so much external pressure—and now a lot of internal pressure."

Mik'kel shrugged. "Seems to come with the territory. Lived with it so long, I'm not sure what it feels like otherwise."

The ride was quiet the rest of the way to the hotel. They said their thanks and goodbyes; Mik'kel said he would stop by the next day to pick up Edvin for a meeting with Prime Minister Afrom.

* * * * *

Edvin had not planned to meet the Prime Minister, but it turned out to be an excellent meeting. For some reason, Afrom seemed to like Edvin. He went on and on about Hatim's brilliance in getting him to think about the temple differently. When Edvin asked questions about the temple, Afrom talked—for a couple of hours—about how important finding the temple would be for his nation. Edvin nodded and smiled at the discussions; this seemed to feed Afrom's ego. Afrom ended the meeting thanking Edvin profusely for Hatim's pledged military support.

That same night, Edvin felt unsettled. He wasn't sure if he was helping Mik'kel and his countrymen or preparing them for the inevitable. Hatim had said Edvin would have to do things that may not make sense. Perhaps supporting an invasion was one of them. He hoped not. He was beginning to like Mik'kel and Afrom. After some time, exhaustion took over; he drifted into a restless sleep.

Edvin dreamed he was at Fettisdagen, the Swedish Mardi Gras, with crowds, noise, and celebration. He slowly woke and yet still heard the same type of noise and celebration—only more muted. He sat up, still listening to some type of celebration taking place. *Where is that coming from? Outside?* He went to the window and looked out. The entire street was packed with people dancing, singing, and yelling. Before he had time to process what he was seeing, there was a knock at the door.

Edvin walked over and looked through the peephole. It was Mik'kel. He opened the door and Mik'kel opened his mouth to say something, but then began looking Edvin up and down. Edvin realized he was wearing only boxers.

"Sorry. Just got up. Come in. So, what's going on outside?"

"It's the temple."

Edvin looked at Mik'kel as he put one leg into his pants. He couldn't help but smile. Mik'kel was practically bouncing up and down.

"What . . . about the temple?" Edvin finished putting on his pants.

"They . . . the archaeologists . . . they found it." Mik'kel seemed excited.

"What? They found the temple?"

"Well . . . " Mik'kel cocked his head. "Not the actual *temple*, but where the temple used to be."

"Already? How did they find it so quickly? How can they be so sure?"

"You can read it in the paper." Mik'kel held up the morning newspaper. He handed it to Edvin.

Edvin took the paper and rolled his eyes; everything was in Hebrew. "Mind giving me the English version?"

Mik'kel laughed. "Oh, sorry. Well, what it says is archaeologists found a tunnel leading from the City of David out toward the original Gihon Spring. There were several places where the tunnel caved in, but there was one intact section containing some implements used in the temple—things like snuffers, trimmers, and a vial of olive oil."

"Well, that's pretty amazing."

Mik'kel smiled. "But not as amazing as what else they found."

"What was that?"

"It's something those wanting a temple had wondered how they could ever start rituals again. It's the find of the century—no, of the millennium."

"OK, Mik'kel, you have my interest. What did they find?"

Mik'kel smiled again and answered excitedly, "Ashes of the red heifer."

Edvin's shoulders dropped. "I thought you had something spectacular in mind."

Mik'kel just gave Edvin a blank stare. "You don't get it, do you?"

"Get what? Ashes from a dead animal mean something?"

"Edvin, it's like finding the Holy Grail. Our Scriptures state only the ashes of a red heifer without blemish, mixed in living water, can be used for cleansing and purification. There are those who have looked for such a red heifer, for decades or more, with no success. Now, on the verge of the treaty with President Hatim to help secure a temple, it means sacrifices can be started immediately."

"That's incredible."

"That's not all."

Edvin's eyes widened. "More?"

"Some of our scientists believe the ashes may contain some traces of DNA that may still be viable. If so, they can clone the heifer and then have a perpetual source."

"Wow. Amazing. It looks like you want to go celebrate. Do you want to go celebrate?" But then Edvin's smile vanished quickly.

Mik'kel's expression followed suit. "What's wrong?"

"I need to call President Hatim."

"Is that really such a downer?" Mik'kel laughed.

Edvin shook his head. "No, Mik'kel. What this means is this: if anyone is going to attack, this announcement just sped up their timetable. We may not have time to get more troops here. You had better put everyone here on alert."

Mik'kel's face turned quite serious. "Are you certain about this?" He paused. "Yes, of course you are." He pulled out his phone. "You make your call. I'll make mine."

Edvin dialed Cortez; he thought this would be the fastest way to get in touch.

"Cortez, this is Isakson."

"Captain. Good to hear from you."

"Has President Hatim heard the news from Israel?"

"Yes, he just got off the phone with Prime Minister Afrom, who was ecstatic. He kept thanking Hatim for the tip of looking in other locations. However, the President didn't look too happy. He's now on the phone with King Nazari—trying to convince him plans must change. It's one thing to attack before the temple is located, but now it becomes an image problem. If they attack now, all Hatim's credibility will go down the drain. He's trying to convince Nazari they must seek another alternative. It's a hard sell, though."

"From what I'm hearing here, this may be the match that fell into the tank of kerosene," Edvin said. "How quickly can we get the other forces here—and the weapons?"

"Captain, the forces were never supposed to arrive before the treaty signing. The troops coming tomorrow are all that's on the docket."

Edvin's heart sank. So it was true. The President wanted to have Israel destroyed before the treaty signing. Deep down he knew this—and Edvin had told himself he was OK with it.

Edvin glanced at Mik'kel, who was still on his call. He walked a little farther and lowered his voice. The less Mik'kel knew, the better.

Edvin turned curt with Cortez. "Well, that's changed now, don't you think? This will be a political nightmare if we don't get more troops and weapons here. Otherwise, we can only assist and not be of much help."

"I know, Captain. But it takes time to muster something not planned for—more time than we have, I'm afraid. Our only hope right now is for the President to convince the King to delay the invasion."

"Well, do *everything* you can to make that happen. Keep me posted."

"Roger that."

Edvin disconnected. He looked at Mik'kel, whose face didn't look encouraging either.

"What did you find out, Edvin?"

"Just what you don't want to hear. If the attack comes early, then all you're going to get are the soldiers arriving tomorrow. No more manpower. No further weapons."

"The weapons aren't arriving with the soldiers?" Mik'kel just stared.

"No, they were to arrive next week. That may be a few days too late." Edvin hated to lie to Mik'kel, but he couldn't let him think Israel had been totally abandoned. "What did Afrom say?"

"He said he believes he can trust you. If I can trust you, then so can he."

Edvin nodded but felt horrible on the inside. Hopefully, he could continue to earn their trust.

Mik'kel let out a big sigh. "Having extra bodies is good. But no additional weapons . . . " He shook his head.

Edvin nodded. "I know. We can deploy a squadron to each

of the locations you mentioned yesterday, and you can integrate them however you see fit. Amari can go to Eilat, Edstrom to Jericho, and I can accompany you to Golan Heights."

Mik'kel nodded. "Sounds like the best we can do."

They headed back to Ramat David. As the vehicle traveled slowly through the jubilant crowd, Edvin felt disconnected, as if he was in a different plane of existence. He thought he would be OK with being a double agent. After all, he had found Hatim extremely politically savvy when he had talked to Afrom and Nazari. He thought he would be on board with the President's plan to destroy Israel shortly before the treaty signing. Now . . . he looked over at Mik'kel. Now he wasn't so sure. It was hard to not care about someone after you've met them and become, at least on some level, friends. Then, suddenly, the information Lars had found shot back into his mind. *Am I also betraying myself?*

Edvin knew the news of finding the temple location had turned into a face-saving nightmare for Hatim. The treaty was to have been sold as an attempt at peace. Now it was a matter of protecting what the treaty was supposed to offer. Edvin couldn't think of any winners in this scenario.

CHAPTER 10

Edvin stood with Mik'kel on the edge of the lookout facing Syria. The precipice on which they stood overlooked the valley below. In the distance, no more than a ditch marked the border with Syria stretching out beyond them, an almost perfectly flat area—at least here. It was rumored an attack would occur tonight, two weeks earlier than expected. So far, no sign of movement.

Edvin shook his head. Four days. It had been only four days since the temple location was announced. The opposition must have been calculating its best, quickest way to attack. "How sure are you of your intel, Mik'kel?"

"It comes from a reliable source," ben David said. "It should definitely happen sometime tonight. Having your extra soldiers is a help. Not ideal, but certainly a help."

Edvin's SAT phone came to life. "Captain Isakson, this is Corporal Masaki. Come in."

"Masaki, what is it?" Both Masaki and Chong had arrived with their troops, Edvin knew. Edvin had placed Masaki to accompany Saeed, and Chong had traveled with Ranata.

"Calling to report we've already had some flybys. Probably looking to see what they'd be up against. None have penetrated Israeli air space—yet."

"Roger that. Can you tell from which country they originated?"

"Can't tell for sure. But they looked Libyan to me."

"Roger. Keep us posted."

"Yes, sir. Over and out."

Mik'kel looked at Edvin. "And so it begins."

Edvin nodded.

As they stood on this precipice, Edvin suddenly felt the air change. The wind picked up slightly and the temperature dropped a few degrees. In the distance, dark clouds gathered. *Oh, great. A storm and an invasion.* Something glistened briefly against the dark clouds. Edvin held up his binoculars for a better look. *Tanks.* He handed the binoculars to Mik'kel. After a brief look, Mik'kel turned to alert the others.

As evening approached, more and more troops were observed just on the other side of the border, and the storm grew closer and closer. Everyone braced themselves for the worst.

* * * * *

Near sundown, the action began—in full fury. Two MiG jets flew over at low altitude at the same time several missiles were launched from Syrian territory. The missiles hit a few Israeli vehicles and caused large explosions. Apparently, this created better visuals for the MiGs; they returned though the airspace and dropped their payloads. Edvin felt the heat of the blasts, but thankfully, the explosions didn't lead to any human casualties, according to quick reports. Two supply trucks and three unmanned tanks, though, were no longer.

This time, the Israelis began firing back, but without inflicting any apparent damage. Edvin looked through his glasses again and saw tanks and infantry advancing rapidly. It looked to be thousands of the enemy. *Were they really prepared for this?* How were they to keep all these troops from getting deeper into Israel? The horizon looked full of the approaching army; they were coming from as far north and south as he could see. It reminded him of army ants advancing across a forest floor.

Two missiles launched from the Israelis took out several Syrian tanks but didn't affect the overall advancement. Two F-16 jets in tandem flew low and bombarded the Syrian advancement—this was the first real impact, taking out an entire flank of infantry. The two Syrian MiGs pursued them. The Syrian tanks continued their bombardment and took out an Israeli tank and several soldiers.

The Syrian army, now in Israeli territory, kept advancing and showed no signs of stopping despite the bombardment of the Israeli military. Then, once again, the weather changed suddenly. A strong wind gust came from the west and, in the distance, Edvin saw something falling from the sky. He looked through the binoculars and was astounded to see hail falling to the east of where they were standing. He handed the glasses to Mik'kel for a look.

"Can you believe what you're seeing?"

"Is that hail?" Mik'kel lowered the binoculars and handed them back to Edvin while cocking his head with raised eyebrows.

"Is that freaky or what?" Edvin asked, mouth agape.

Edvin looked again through the binoculars. As if by providence, as soon as the F-16s reentered Israeli airspace and directly out of the way of the hail, the size and intensity of the hail increased. The hail, strong and large, caused the MiG fighters to lose control and crash as they crossed into Israeli airspace. Cries and screams from the Syrian infantry could be heard as well; they were pummeled with the huge hailstones and seemed to fall like dominos. Only the tanks were able to continue advancing. Both sides kept firing; rain now came down in sheets. It came so hard and so fast the ground became soggy quite quickly. The Syrian tanks now had difficulty moving forward. Their drivers seemed to lose focus and their bombardment decreased; this gave the Israelis more time to inflict their damage. The F-16s now flew north to south, avoiding the hail, and still accurately hit their marks.

Edvin saw more tanks coming, and these formed rows for an intense onslaught of firepower. He could *feel* the vibration of their advancement through the ground due to the vast number. The vibrations then felt . . . different. They now felt more like a rumble that penetrated from his feet up through his legs. He looked at Mik'kel, who also seemed to notice something different. It became undeniable. The ground quaked and became violent. It would have been easy to panic, but Mik'kel signaled his men to maintain their positions. The precipice on which they had stood earlier now collapsed and fell toward them. Edvin dove and pushed Mik'kel out of the way as boulders fell into the foxhole from which they had watched moments before. Edvin found himself looking into Mik'kel's eyes.

"Thanks for that," Mik'kel cracked, "but I prefer to dance standing up."

Edvin chuckled. "You're welcome." He stood and pulled Mik'kel to his feet. As they looked toward Syria, they could not believe their eyes. The ground opened and swallowed up every Syrian tank in position. Once the quaking stopped, only one tank and a few soldiers remained. Two F-16s then flew over and annihilated them. A shout of victory sounded from the Israelis. The F-16s returned for a flyover, dipped their wings, and flew south, likely to help at other border fights.

Everyone shouted and gave hugs and high-fives. Edvin

gave Mik'kel a hug, patting his back. He turned and looked at the horizon again. Everything was ablaze or . . . nonexistent. Nothing was moving forward any longer.

"That was incredible," Edvin said. "A full battle starting at sundown and ending before midnight. I wonder how the other groups fared."

"Probably the same," Mik'kel answered.

"What makes you say that?"

"Come on, Edvin. The freaky hailstorm, the earthquake, the torrential rain. I wouldn't call that coincidence. I would call it divine intervention."

"Well, I'm not sure I can go that far, but it was remarkable."

Mik'kel smiled. "You'll see. Once you talk to everyone, you'll be hard-pressed to explain it any other way."

Edvin started to respond, but his SAT phone beeped.

"Edstrom, what's up?"

"You won't believe it, sir. The battle's already over."

"Same here."

"Really? Amazing. All I can say is, it was amazing."

"Meet back at Haifa by dawn. We'll debrief."

"Roger. Over and out."

Edvin turned to Mik'kel, but his SAT phone beeped again; once again he quickly answered.

"Amari. Is all OK?"

"More than OK. It was incredible—already over, and very few casualties. You won't believe what we experienced."

"Save the details for the debrief. We . . . had something similar here. Meet us back at Haifa by dawn."

"Roger. Out."

As everyone around them celebrated, Edvin and Mik'kel walked the battlefield. After all the bombs and gunfire, it was nearly an eerie quiet—except for the background celebration, which settled over the battlefield. Some tanks were still burning, but most everything now only smoked as the torrential rain had extinguished most of the fires. Bodies lay in mud, many bent in unnatural positions. Edvin couldn't help but feel partly responsible. He bent down and picked up a rifle. The feel and look of the handle reminded him of the handle of the gun Hatim had given him in New York. All these weapons were likely made from similar 3-D printing.

And then a hard realization sunk in. Hatim had engineered all of this. Maybe not the timing, but definitely the design. And Edvin had willingly participated in it.

Edvin found this hard to process. Agreeing to a plan from a distance had been easy. Now that he knew Mik'kel and some of his countrymen, willingly following through was much harder. He had to admit to himself: he agreed with Hatim's overall plan, but not his methods. Not anymore. *What should I do? What can I do?* For now, perhaps, seeing how things would play out was best.

"Mik'kel, these are unusual weapons," Edvin said, turning to his Israeli friend. "I think you want to have these gathered and processed. They may come in handy as fuel someday."

"What?" Mik'kel had a furrowed brow. "What are you talking about?"

"The material of these weapons is unusual. If it gets extremely hot, it will burn and be a catalyst for the material to burn."

"Really?" He took the rifle from Edvin and studied it closely. He looked back at Edvin. "How do you know that?"

Edvin could only give a small smile. "Let's just say I've encountered it before."

Mik'kel raised his eyebrows to question, but only said, "I'll alert my superiors."

On the way back to Haifa, Mik'kel appeared in a good

mood—just not a talkative one. He seemed to have a lot on his mind. Edvin let him remain in thought; he was deep in his own. Could he really support Hatim's desire to get rid of Jews? Since the invasion failed, would that change his plans? Edvin hoped so. He truly liked Mik'kel.

Edvin was unsure how, but when he and Mik'kel arrived at the hotel, everyone else was present. They looked excited, ready to explode to tell their stories. All gathered in Edvin's room to debrief. Though cramped, they made it work. Edvin and Mik'kel took chairs. Saeed took the ottoman with Masaki and Chong sitting on the bed. Ranata took the floor despite offers to sit elsewhere. A few other officers were also in attendance for support.

"OK, Edstrom," Edvin said. "You and Chong go first."

"It was freaky awesome," Edstrom said. "We were getting nervous because we saw what looked like thousands of troops and tanks approaching and crossing the Jordan River. We felt the air change and dark clouds roll in. Several planes flew over and about a hundred soldiers parachuted in."

"Yeah," Chong said, jumping in. "Then the worst weather of the century kicked in. It was odd because it only occurred east of us, but it wreaked havoc on the enemy."

Mik'kel's eyes blazed with anticipation. "What happened?"

"The worst hailstorm of the century happened, that's what. The smallest hail must have been the size of baseballs. The planes flying troops in crashed all around us due to hail damage, and some even crashed into those planes that had already made it over successfully."

Ranata jumped in. "Then the rain started. Not any rain. It came hard and fast—like pure sheets of rain. The river swelled in a matter of minutes. It got so swift even the tanks couldn't cross. The soldiers on our side were able to do a great deal of damage to theirs." Ranata just laughed. "Their confusion was massive."

"Then," Chong said, jumping in again, "the weather stopped almost as fast as it started. Our pilots took advantage and swept in and devastated every soldier and tank left."

"That's awesome," Saeed said. "But Masaki and I can top that."

Ranata's eyebrows shot up. "Really?"

"Trust me," Saeed said. "This will blow you away."

Masaki nodded.

"Right at sundown, jets flew over and started dropping their payloads. Our jets engaged them, and the dogfights began. Thousands of troops and hundreds of tanks crossed the border and engaged us. We fought back, but we had to keep withdrawing. We got pushed back to just below the Dead Sea."

Masaki jumped in. "That's when the miracle happened."

"Miracle?" Edvin asked.

Masaki laughed. "I have no other way to describe it."

Edvin glanced at Mik'kel, who seemed jubilant listening to these reports.

"Exactly," Saeed said. "It was incredible. The ground began to quake and huge crevices between them and us opened. The smell of sulfur filled the air. Out of these large crevices exploded huge plumes of molten . . . something. Some of our men later told us it was sulfur. You've heard the expression 'fire and brimstone'?"

There were nods all around the room.

"Well, we saw it up close and personal."

"Yeah," Masaki said. "We literally saw balls of burning sulfur fall from the sky. As it burned, it turned red and had a blue flame. Although we were freaked out of our minds, it was . . . well, it was amazing to look at."

"But the most amazing part," Saeed went on, "was the wind

that blew to our favor. All the noxious fumes were blown over our enemy and asphyxiated the majority of them. The tanks in front stopped dead in their tracks and blocked others from moving forward. Our planes took advantage of that and took out the tanks in the back. The burning sulfur fell on other tanks and, for some reason, they also burned. I think their whole advancement became massively confused—and we were able to take advantage of that."

Mik'kel looked at Edvin. "And what is your assessment now?"

"Well . . . " Edvin paused and tried to keep a straight face, but smiled and then laughed despite himself. "OK, yes. I have to admit this is more than just coincidence."

Mik'kel fixed him with a hard stare.

"And . . . it's very unusual."

Mik'kel cocked his head.

"And . . . yes. I have to concede it falls into the definition of a miracle."

Mik'kel threw his hands in the air. "There now. That wasn't so hard, was it?"

Edvin laughed. "Harder than you know."

Mik'kel laughed and nodded.

"OK, everyone," Mik'kel said. "I'll give you all four hours of sleep, and I'll be back here at thirteen hundred to take you to our official debriefing."

All nodded and filed from Edvin's room. He sat down and gave a long sigh. He felt tired and wound up at the same time. *Had it been a miracle? Could such things still happen?* If it *was* a miracle, then what did that mean? He had always heard the Jews were God's chosen people, but he always believed that was just nationalistic bravado. *But is this proof?* And if it was true, where did that place Hatim and his plans? *Where does that place me?* He shook his head. This was too much to contemplate right now.

He headed for the shower. After stepping in, he realized he hadn't yet called Hatim. After a moment of internal debate on whether he should call now or after a quick shower, he shut off the water, wrapped in a towel, and headed back to the bedroom to find his phone.

He called Cortez again. Edvin wanted to get a pulse of the atmosphere around Hatim before talking to him.

"Hey, Cap. You guys OK?"

"Yeah, we're all fine. The Israelis had few casualties. Has President Hatim heard about the Israeli victory?"

"He just hung up with Prime Minister Afrom. He doesn't look happy. I'm pretty sure he'll want to talk with you. Hold on."

Edvin waited anxiously. What was he going to say? All he knew was to say the truth.

"Captain Isakson. Give me details."

"Hello, sir. Well, all I can say is we won the battle despite ourselves."

"What do you mean?" Hatim sounded more than a bit irritated.

"Well, sir, there were freaky gigantic hailstorms, rainstorms, earthquakes, and even, well, something like fire and brimstone. These were of biblical proportion. These natural disasters obliterated the enemy. Our side didn't have to do much."

"And how did the Israelis fair so favorably with these disasters taking place?"

"That's the other freaky thing, sir. All these things occurred on the enemy, but not on us. But we did get some of the rain."

"So you're saying all this happened on the fringes of Israel, but not within Israel?"

"Pretty much, sir."

"Hmm. Well, I guess we have a lot of work to do."

"Sir?"

"I'll do damage control from here until the treaty signing."

"Is it still on?"

"I'll make sure of it. I have more work to do with Nazari, but I'll get him there. Meet me when I arrive, and we'll discuss how to move forward. Keep me informed of all developments there."

"Yes, sir."

"I'll give you back to Corporal Cortez." Edvin heard the phone shuffle between the men.

"Hey, Cap. It's been pretty crazy here."

"I don't think it compares to what's going on here."

"Well, no. I just mean the President's been meeting some very important people."

Edvin didn't care to talk about Hatim's private meetings; he changed the subject. "What happened between Hatim and Nazari?"

"Apparently, Nazari couldn't get the attack cancelled. Now they're having heated conversations as to how to do damage control. I'm sure the President will pull this through to his favor—somehow."

"Well, that will be interesting to hear. I assume you'll be coming with the President to Israel?"

"Yeah, I'll be there. I guess we'll see you in a couple of weeks."

"See you then."

Edvin disconnected and tossed his phone on the bed. In the shower, the warm water soothed his body but not his mind. He contemplated his role in all of this. *What would Hatim do?* Could he live with that decision, whatever it was?

No matter which side he took, he would feel like a traitor. He let out a long sigh and shook his head. Maybe clarity would come after a nap.

CHAPTER 11

Edvin awoke, sat up, and stretched. For the first time in weeks he had a chance to sleep in a little and wake feeling rested. Since the invasion, a week earlier, he had spent large amounts of time with the Israeli brass and the Prime Minister doing his best to convince them Hatim hadn't initiated the invasion. After all, that part was true. The invasion, at the time it took place, was not Hatim's idea. Lying to one person was one thing, but to so many influential people . . . Edvin was just glad he could be truthful with at least some amount of information.

Now it was time to meet with Hatim and prepare for the treaty signing. He got dressed and opened the door to leave. He jumped back—eyes wide. There stood Mik'kel, fist up, ready to knock.

"Oh my God, Mik'kel. Scare a man to death, will you."

Mik'kel laughed. "Well, it wasn't intentional. I thought I would drive you. I want to show you something before you meet with Hatim."

For some reason, Afrom and Nazari had chosen the temple mount for the signing. Edvin could only guess: since it had been the most disputed spot for so long, it seemed the appropriate place to initiate a peace treaty.

As they headed out, Edvin tried to act mostly disinterested about where they were headed. After a short while, however, he couldn't hold back his curiosity.

"So, where are you taking me? I can't be late to meet President Hatim. I'm supposed to meet with him at the King David Hotel before the signing."

"Relax, Edvin. I'll have you there on time. I want to show you the *new* temple mount."

Edvin raised his eyebrows. He looked at Mik'kel with a questioning gaze.

"Prime Minister Afrom has been extremely busy getting things prepared for the new temple. Once the treaty is signed, the priests will have their first sacrifice—this evening."

"How is that possible?" Edvin asked. "Isn't there too much to prepare?"

"Preparing is what many have been doing for decades," Mik'kel said. "The Hassidim, the orthodox Jews, already have a tent prepared to erect in short order. All the furniture has been ready for a long time. They just needed a go-ahead to put it all in place. Prime Minister Afrom has been preparing the groundwork since the day the caved-in tunnel was found."

Edvin looked at Mik'kel in disbelief. "You guys waste no time, do you?"

Mik'kel just smiled. "We Jews tend to seize opportunities. They seem to be taken away from us so often that we feel we can't afford to wait."

Edvin nodded. He sat back in his seat and stared out the windshield.

"But there's more."

"What?" Edvin turned back to Mik'kel. "And that means what?"

"All the stones for the temple are already formed. They just have to be assembled."

Edvin was in disbelief, all but speechless. "How . . . how?"

Mik'kel laughed. "Sorry, Edvin. Your look is priceless. As I said, the orthodox Jews have been making plans for a long time. There's an architect who worked at Dr. Hatim's 3-D printing factory. He used an alias rather than his Jewish name, and since leaving there has spent his time with the orthodox Jews to design a formula for 3-D printing stones for the temple."

Edvin found all this fascinating.

Mik'kel smiled and went on. "He built his own 3-D printer and has been cranking out stones ever since the new place for the temple was found. I heard he's nearly complete. The other interesting thing is, they plan to build the temple like Solomon did."

"How was that?"

"Without tools. He's forming each stone so they will stack precisely and go together in record time. Yet, different than Solomon, they plan to build the temple in just a little more than three months and have its dedication on Hanukkah. Fitting, don't you think?"

Edvin didn't know what Mik'kel was talking about; he could only give a blank stare.

Mik'kel laughed again. "You've heard of the Maccabean Revolt, right?"

Edvin nodded. "I think so."

"Well, it started when the ancient Jewish temple was defiled by a ruler named Antiochus Epiphanes, and it ended the day Judas Maccabeus rededicated the temple. There was just enough oil for the light of the menorah to last a day, but it lasted eight days—a miracle."

Edvin shook his head. This time, it was his turn to laugh. "Not another miracle."

Mik'kel joined in. "Face it, Edvin. Jews and miracles just go together."

Edvin shook his head. "But really, Mik'kel. Erecting a temple that quickly is almost too much to comprehend. How widely known is this?"

"Well, it isn't being advertised. But it isn't a secret either."

Edvin was glad to hear this last part. He didn't want to release information considered secret. But he didn't want to have to lie about anything either. Knowing something and not telling Hatim wouldn't be a pleasant conversation once it was known he hadn't completely informed.

Once they reached Jerusalem, Mik'kel did a quick drive-by near the City of David. Edvin could see, in the background, fill had been brought in and laid to form a flat area to support a building. The speed of this building project was amazing. The activity reminded Edvin of bees in a hive. Everything looked chaotic, but everyone seemed to know exactly what they were doing and what was needed.

Next, Mik'kel dropped Edvin off at the King David Hotel. "I'll see you at the signing. I have some prepping to do with the Prime Minister as well. See you there."

Edvin stepped from the car, nodded, and watched Mik'kel drive off. He realized he admired the guy for his open but matter-of-fact manner. Despite their differences, they seemed to, somehow, click. He hoped he could keep his friendship with Mik'kel. Edvin took a deep breath and let it out slowly. He would find out soon enough. He turned and walked into the hotel. The expanse and beauty of the lobby impressed him. He took the elevator to Hatim's floor.

After catching up with everyone—briefed on what they knew, debriefed on what he knew—Hatim told Edvin he wanted him present as he met to debrief both Afrom and Nazari. Edvin wasn't sure why he was always in the middle of everything, but he was glad he was. He didn't like being in the dark.

The next several hours reminded Edvin of the time spent in New York. Same agenda, different setting. This time, the order was reversed. There was a knock on the suite door. Edvin opened it and welcomed King Nazari and his bodyguard.

"Youssef, please. Do come in," Hatim said.

Nazari did so, but he didn't appear pleased.

"I'm beginning to believe I extended the courtesy of addressing me in this informal way much too early," Nazari flatly said.

"Oh, no no. Don't say that." Hatim's voice was reassuring. "Please take a seat, and let's discuss. We have much to talk about."

Nazari sat on one end of a very ornate sofa. Hatim took the nearest chair.

"I regret our earlier conversation got a little . . . heated," Hatim said. "It was all such a shock, and not according to our previous plans. Yet, I believe we can still accomplish much."

"You called me a traitor." Nazari's tone was curt.

Edvin grimaced slightly. It appeared Hatim would, for once, have to eat crow.

"Oh, please accept my apology." Hatim's tone seemed sincere and he placed his hand on his chest in a gesture of sincerity. "Those were unfortunate words spoken too hastily. At the time, I didn't understand your sincere efforts to keep our original agreement. I now understand the difficulty of the situation you faced."

Nazari nodded. Apparently, the apology was working. Edvin was amazed at how Hatim seemed to be able to talk his way out of anything—and still get what he wanted.

Nazari looked at Hatim in a completely deadpan manner. "So, how do we 'accomplish much,' as you put it?"

Hatim's tone was soft but sounded sincere. "Well, it will not be good for some, I'm afraid. But it will be best for all."

Nazari didn't change his expression. He continued to listen.

"Don't worry, Youssef." Hatim smiled. "You come out as the good guy."

Nazari didn't return the smile. He merely nodded, as if those words were expected.

"Because of your neutral status, you were taken advantage of where so-called friends—without your invitation, I might add—marched through your territory to attack Israel. You are the innocent bystander in all this."

"And?" Nazari had anticipation in his voice.

"And. . . . and the others will have to face the music, as the expression goes."

"I'm not sure I follow."

"Well, with the world in political disarray, everyone is looking to me to restore order," Hatim said. "I'm afraid I will have to ask the leaders of these three territories to step down and relinquish their power to me."

Nazari was good at keeping a straight face. But Edvin saw his eyes grow large with this last statement from Hatim.

"I'm not sure I'm comfortable with that arrangement," Nazari said.

"Well, I agree it's not the way I wanted things either. Our original plan was to be swift and decisive. That plan can no longer work because of their hastiness. This is the only plan where we—both you and I—come out in a good light. There's no other option in which that can happen. I can't afford for all our efforts to unravel from this fiasco. Our gains must be preserved at all costs. It will now take longer. That's all. Those who would have been praised must now be punished. That's the price for rash actions."

Nazari sat in thought for a few moments. He nodded slightly. He looked at Hatim with a weary look, then sighed. "Yes, I can see your wisdom here. It's unfortunate. Yet, I can see no way to salvage the situation." He paused again and looked down at his hands as he pressed the fingertips of one hand against those of the other. He looked back at Hatim with an expression that could only be described as sorrowful. "I will support your plan."

Hatim nodded to Cortez, who nodded back and disappeared into the bedroom. Edvin wondered what had just occurred, until Hatim responded to Nazari. "Thank you, Youssef." He smiled weakly. "We must do difficult things at times. I'm alerting the UN President now. He will call a meeting of the ten territories to relay the decision. I'll go right after signing the treaty to take control."

"Be sure you state my role correctly in all of this." Nazari's voice was forceful, but at the same time seemed to contain more than a hint of trepidation.

"Absolutely, Youssef. You have nothing to fear." Hatim gave a reassuring smile. "This also gives me a solid reason to establish my headquarters in Babylon. Since the territory will now be mine, it's fitting, don't you think? We'll practically be neighbors."

Nazari looked up quickly but without expression. Edvin wasn't sure what Nazari thought of that statement. His look didn't give anything away, but Edvin felt his eyes did. Nazari didn't seem to consider this a positive move. Hatim continued to smile.

Nazari stood; Hatim followed suit. "Well, I must go and prepare for the signing ceremony," Nazari said.

Hatim nodded. "Your presence and signature as a witness will lend stability and credibility to the treaty. Thank you for agreeing to participate."

Nazari nodded and exited.

Hatim turned and headed into the bedroom. "Captain Isakson, please call me when Prime Minister Afrom arrives."

"Yes, sir."

Edvin let out a breath. He didn't realize he had been holding it in. That meeting seemed a little more intense than the earlier one between Hatim and Nazari that Edvin had witnessed. Edvin wasn't convinced Nazari's support was totally genuine. But then, he thought, Hatim probably doesn't truly trust Nazari either. Before he could put all this together in his mind, there was another knock on the door. Edvin opened it.

"Prime Minister, welcome. Please come in. I will let President Hatim know you've arrived." Before Edvin could reach the bedroom, however, Hatim entered.

"Dear Afrom, I'm so glad you could stop by before the ceremony. This is a great day." Hatim sounded enthused and extended his hand.

"It is indeed." Afrom accepted the handshake.

"Please, do sit down." Afrom sat where King Nazari had sat earlier; Hatim sat in his same place. Edvin was curious as to how amicable things would be during this talk.

"Let's go over our terms again to be sure we have no surprises at the signing," Hatim said, starting the talk.

"Agreed," Afrom said. "There are a few additional requirements I would like to ensure."

"Oh?" Hatim leaned back, obviously playing it cool.

"It's not anything huge. We want to start on the temple immediately after signing."

"Oh." Hatim sounded relieved. "Of course. That would be expected, now wouldn't it?" Edvin wondered, though, if Hatim's tone would be so amicable if he knew what Afrom meant by "immediately."

"And we need access to the hydraulics underneath the current temple mount."

This was the first time Edvin saw Hatim speechless. The President had his mouth open, but no words were forthcoming.

"It's a simple request, really." Afrom smiled. "No one is using them today. This will allow us to wash away the blood of sacrifices, as Solomon did in his day. Is that such a difficult request?"

"Well, Afrom, as you know, what's physically easy and what's politically easy are not synonymous."

"You can't expect us to have sacrifices without a means of cleaning and cleansing, can you?"

As if a light bulb had come on, Hatim's countenance went from one of worry to one of satisfaction—cunning satisfaction.

"Well, if I agree to that, there are a few things you also need to agree to," Hatim said. "I hope you understand the global importance of what I need to say at the signing."

Afrom's smile faded. Now it was his turn to look apprehensive. "What do you mean?"

"Well, I don't want this to be the focus of the meeting, for certain, but it's important the world sees my administration restoring peace to the world. I want you to agree my troops in Israel were instrumental in securing the defeat of those who invaded your great land."

Afrom began to speak, but Hatim did so first.

"These three invading world territories need to relinquish their control to me, and this will be the rationale that will help to secure that. You see the logic of this, surely."

Afrom paused. "But we consider the victory a miracle."

"Well, of course you do. And you should." Hatim's tone had strong affirmation. "But let me ask you. Did your troops do anything more in conquering the invaders than mine?"

"Well . . . no. But . . . "

"There. You have it. It really isn't a lie then, is it? My troops were instrumental in helping your troops, and it was a miracle that even with so few troops, victory was won."

"But that makes it appear as though your troops provided

the miracle."

Hatim shook his head. "I will not directly say such. But . . ." Hatim smiled. "If the rest of the world believes that, then should we stop them?"

Afrom once again started to respond, but Hatim cut him off once more. "Of course, Israel can—and should—celebrate this as a miracle. I will certainly not deny you that."

Afrom was quiet.

"Come now, Afrom. Is it wrong for both of us to get what we want? That's what we call a win-win, isn't it? You get your hydraulics, I get your support."

"Yes." Afrom was hesitant. "I suppose you are right."

"And what better way for me to help you secure the future of your people than for the rest of the world to accept me as the peacemaker? We need this just as much for your country's sake as for mine. Surely you see the wisdom in this."

Afrom thought a moment and slowly nodded. "Yes. Yes, I can see where you're coming from. I will allow you to support that premise."

"Excellent." Hatim gave a reassuring smile. "I knew you were a man of wisdom and clarity. Your people are fortunate to have you as their leader."

Afrom smiled broadly. "Thank you." He stood. "Well, I still have much to prepare. I'll see you in a few hours."

"Very good."

They shook hands and Afrom left the suite with his bodyguard.

Hatim looked quite pleased. "Well, Captain Isakson, we're off to a good start. Wouldn't you agree?"

"Yes, sir."

"I'll take a nap until time to go. I need to be one hundred percent for this."

"Yes, sir. I'll be certain to wake you in time."

Hatim nodded, entered the bedroom, and closed the door.

Edvin had to admire Hatim. He took a tough situation and came out smelling like a rose—to most, at least. The three territories he was pulling authority over likely would not be thrilled with this outcome.

CHAPTER 12

The limo pulled up as close to the Wailing Wall as possible. Edvin stepped out first and looked around. The entire site was packed with people. Ensuring absolute protection would be impossible, but Hatim was very popular, so the crowd should, on the whole, be friendly. The Israeli forces enforced an open path to the Wall. Cortez exited from the limo's opposite side and also looked around, scanning the area to be certain nothing looked suspicious. Edvin nodded toward Hatim, who stepped from the limo while Edvin and Cortez flanked him on the walk to the Wailing Wall and then up the ramp to the temple mount.

A huge screen, erected atop the Wailing Wall, was provided for onlookers below. No other Jews were allowed on the temple mount except for Prime Minister Afrom and his entourage. Between the al-Aqsa Mosque and the al-Kas Fountain, a canopy awaited them, and Afrom and Nazari were already present, along with what seemed dozens of reporters and news crews. Anna Bonfield was near the front of that crowd, and she gave a big smile when Hatim's eyes met hers. She was dressed in a plain black dress that flowed with her every move. Almost every man around her noticed her. Next to the canopy was a lectern that displayed the new world logo Hatim had designed: a Pangaea color coded into the ten new world territories. Around the logo were these words: One World Undivided.

Hatim shook hands with both Afrom and Nazari and headed directly to the lectern. He delivered a large smile before he started his talk.

"My dear friends, this is a most momentous day. A lot has happened over the last few weeks—and we are here today to ensure it doesn't happen again."

There was much applause from the large crowd.

"Our new world must be a place of order, and today we will help ensure that. The leaders who instigated the attack on this great country have been removed from office, and I will oversee these three territories myself." Hatim paused and smiled.

"When I created our new world with our ten world territories, Israel was kept separate for a reason. To preserve that promise, I had military personnel deployed to help Israel in its defense during the recent attack. Some have called the victory a miracle. Maybe it was, as we were certainly outnumbered. And yet, we still prevailed."

Again, another large round of applause. Hatim held up his hand to quiet the crowd.

"I now promise that the signing of this treaty will guarantee a seven-year protection by my new world order. As you can see by our new logo, as Pangaea was once one continent, my new world order will unite us as one politically. I am confident how Israel will integrate into our new world will be worked out in that seven-year period. Therefore, all those living in Israel will be able to live without fear or threats. Now, Prime Minister Afrom will tell of other good things to come." Hatim turned and gestured toward Afrom. "Prime Minister, the podium is yours."

The crowd again applauded, though some whistling was

interspersed.

Afrom walked to the podium. He smiled and nodded at Hatim. "Thank you, President Hatim." He looked forward and addressed the cameras. "My fellow countrymen, today is a momentous occasion. This will be the first Rosh Hashanah in millennia that will be commemorated with an evening sacrifice."

A thunderous applause erupted, and it took some time for Afrom to get control again.

"Although our temple today will be a tabernacle, it won't be long until we have a fully functioning temple complete with a flushing system from the very hydraulic system underneath where I currently stand. We will have a new temple functioning like the one from the time of Solomon."

Again, thunderous applause. Afrom, along with almost everyone else, smiled deeply. Edvin noticed Nazari was not smiling, however, and instead shot a hot glare at Hatim. Evidently, Hatim had not considered it important to let Nazari know of this promise to Israel.

"We are also pleased to have King Nazari with us today. I look forward to working with him going forward to achieve increased harmony between our nations." Afrom looked toward Nazari, who nodded and smiled in return. As soon as the cameras turned, his smile vanished.

"Once the treaty is signed, Rosh Hashanah will begin with the setting up of the tabernacle, the offering of the evening sacrifice, and the sounding of the shofar. Those here will be able to see the event on the large screen provided."

Afrom left the podium as the crowd applauded. He took his place beside Hatim. As Hatim picked up a pen to sign, cameras flashed furiously. After signing, Afrom picked up the other pen and the same flurry of activity was repeated. Nazari, as a witness, signed last. While his signature was not binding to the agreement, it did imply his knowledge and implicit agreement. All three posed for photos, then shook hands. A shofar at the new temple site could be heard; the crowd once again went wild. There was clapping, whistling, and some even started dancing the Hora.

On screen, the erection of the tent near the temple site occurred in short order, followed by another shofar blast. The flurry of activity stopped—all eyes were now glued to the screen. Items of furniture were carried on the shoulders of the priests just as ancient Scripture prescribed. Once everything was set up, and all appropriate items correctly placed in the tabernacle, the cleansing ceremony for the priests and all items to be used in the ceremony was started.

Shortly before sunset, the sacrifice was lit. The slaughter of the chosen animal, however, was not shown on the large video monitor. Several more shofar blasts sounded. The reaction of the crowd made things clear. Celebrations would continue late into the night.

Once the sacrifice ended, Hatim nodded to Edvin. Edvin nodded to Cortez, and both escorted Hatim back to the limo. All three were jostled by the crowd as they struggled to get Hatim back to the limo; the Israeli military no longer had maintained a clear path back. Many of the Israeli soldiers were dancing with the crowd! Edvin couldn't blame them, but it did make his job more difficult.

Once in the limo, Edvin leaned back and sighed, nearly melting into his car seat.

Cortez laughed. "That was something, wasn't it? Mr. President, did everything get accomplished as you wished?"

Hatim nodded but gave no comment.

Edvin cleared his throat a bit, then jumped in. "King Nazari didn't seem to know of your agreement with the Prime Minister to let Israel use the existing hydraulic system under the temple mount."

Hatim smiled. "My dear Captain Isakson, King Nazari needed to understand I don't need his permission for what I do. It was a subtle but important point to make."

Cortez laughed. "I love how you practically choreograph every move you make."

Hatim chuckled. "You can take the word 'practically' out, and your statement would be a true one."

Cortez raised his eyebrows. "Nothing is ever spontaneous?"

"I go for controlled spontaneity." Hatim smiled. "Yet, this doesn't decrease the sincerity of my actions."

Cortez seemed satisfied with that response and seemed to smile to himself.

Hatim turned to Edvin. "Captain Isakson, how are you?"

"Sir? I'm fine."

"Well, you've been through a lot over these last months. I want to give you a month off."

Edvin wondered what led to this. "I'm fine. Really."

"Perhaps you are, but we still have a lot to do, and I want you to get recharged and not lose your mental edge. Why not go back home for a while? Cortez will accompany me to Babylon. The time you are away will give me time to get things started there."

Edvin paused, but knew he shouldn't oppose Hatim. "Well, thank you. I guess a little downtime would be nice."

Hatim smiled. "See? I just had to get you to admit it to yourself."

Edvin laughed. "I guess so."

When the limo arrived at the hotel, Edvin noticed someone waiting for them. Once they stepped from the limo, Edvin realized it was De Voss.

"Dr. De Voss, what a pleasant surprise."

"Hi, Edvin. It's good to see you again." They shook hands,

but De Voss then pulled him in for a warm embrace and pat on the back. "Edvin, you've been doing such an excellent job. I need to talk with President Hatim for a while, so I'm letting you use my jet to go back to Stockholm."

Edvin's eyes widened. "Dr. De Voss, you don't have to do that."

"Nonsense. It's the least I can do. As a matter of fact, I want you to leave now." As if he knew what Edvin was going to say, he held up a hand. "You don't even have to pack. You have plenty of clothes back at home, and I have ensured your apartment is clean and ready for you."

"I . . . I don't know what to say."

"Nothing is necessary, Edvin. You can sleep on the plane and wake up rested to start your vacation."

De Voss reopened the limo door and gestured for Edvin to enter.

Cortez walked over and shook Edvin's hand. "Don't worry about anything. I promise to let you know if anything important happens so you will be in the loop. Go. Enjoy yourself."

Edvin entered the limo and gave a short wave to everyone as Cortez closed the door. The limo pulled away and Edvin leaned back into the seat and closed his eyes. It was hard to believe this had happened. In one sense he was certainly glad for it, but everything seemed quite sudden.

Yet, was it? Maybe De Voss planned this. Edvin smiled. It would be like him to do something like this. *But why now? Do either he or Hatim feel I'm losing perspective?* Edvin turned his head and stared out the window, lost in thought. He even closed his eyes to think more deeply.

This break *would* allow him time to perhaps regain some perspective. He wasn't as on board with Hatim's agenda as before, but he didn't want to lose his position either. Was there a way to keep his job with Hatim and still help Mik'kel and his people? He suddenly opened his eyes, realizing he needed to let Mik'kel know where he was going. He texted him, wrote that he was going back to Stockholm for several weeks, and would catch up later.

He closed his eyes again and waited for the driver to tell him when they had arrived at the plane.

CHAPTER 13

Edvin woke and stretched. Now, three weeks back at home, he never felt more relaxed. That hadn't been true of his first week. Not hearing from Lars since that last uncomfortable meeting made him desperately hope to talk with his brother. But Lars was nowhere to be found. His house still looked in order, but neighbors said they hadn't seen him in months.

Edvin went to the institution to see Néa, but discovered she had committed suicide a month earlier, having become extremely depressed and emotionally disconnected. Not knowing where else to look for Lars, he nearly came to terms with letting him go.

He strolled into the kitchen, which had been fully stocked upon his arrival, to find something for breakfast. At this point, there wasn't much food left. It looked like shopping would be on his agenda for the day. He made some tea and took a few sips before heading back to the bedroom to get ready for the day.

As usual, he watched the news as he dressed. Hatim was still a hot item with the press. He seemed to have a nearly magical way of knowing how to keep the world's attention. His new Babylonian headquarters quickly became a popular place for those of influence, and a scientific mecca of knowledge as well.

The city seemed to blossom overnight, something like a blend of how Las Vegas and the Silicon Valley, in the United States, had once grown. The press was always fascinated to know who Hatim was with or having dinner with. It was usually one of "the beautiful people": men, women, or both, people of influence who were making a name for themselves or had already done so. Either way, their popularity would skyrocket along with the President's.

Edvin's tea only held his hunger at bay for a brief time. He finished dressing and headed out. He walked to the nearest store, got his few groceries, and headed for the checkout. As he waited in line, a tabloid headline caught his eye: "Disturbance in the Force." Under the headline was a picture of Luke Skywalker, Han Solo, and Chewbacca from the old *Star Wars* fame, with three big differences: Hatim's face had been photoshopped onto that of Luke, *his own* onto Han Solo, and Cortez's onto Chewbacca! When he studied the picture more closely, he laughed aloud before he caught himself. Looking more closely, he noticed the picture had been taken at the new temple in Jerusalem, and it contained two other individuals he didn't recognize.

Edvin heard a voice behind him. "Your line is open, Han."

Startled and embarrassed at the same time, Edvin turned to the voice behind him. His jaw nearly hit the floor. Facing him was one of the most beautiful women he had ever seen. She had olive-colored skin, long dark hair that glistened in the light, and a smile he found captivating. Rather than being annoyed, she had a little smirk on her face. His embarrassment quickly faded, but he was still tongue-tied.

"Oh, sorry. I . . . I was intrigued by the photo on the tabloid." He stumbled forward and pushed his items toward the cashier.

She picked up the tabloid and put it with her items. Edvin's eyes widened. "You're buying it?"

"Hey, I have to have proof I met Han Solo."

Both laughed. Edvin paid for his items and waited for the woman to get through the line as well.

"By the way, I'm—"

"Captain Isakson. Yes, I know." She smiled.

Edvin was stunned. "How do you know me?"

She laughed. "You're probably not quite as popular as the President, but people often see you when they see him."

Edvin laughed. "Well, I guess that's true. But this puts me at a disadvantage. I don't know *you*."

"Well, I can remedy that." She gave an intriguing smile. "My name is Elsbeth Cohen."

Without thinking, Edvin responded. "That's one of the most beautiful names I've ever heard."

Elsbeth blushed slightly. "Well, my mother thanks you."

Edvin laughed. As they walked from the store, Edvin could feel his heart beating faster and his hands getting clammy. He knew he couldn't let this woman go and never see her again. He made himself respond by trying to keep his voice nonchalant and keep it from cracking. "Care to get some breakfast?"

Elsbeth paused before answering. Edvin's heart skipped a beat. *Will she turn me down?*

She turned and smiled. "That sounds great. What did you have in mind?"

"Well, there's a great deli only two blocks from here."

"OK. Can we take the long way and stop by my apartment to drop off these groceries?"

"Sure."

Rather than turning left, they turned right. Edvin couldn't explain it, but he already felt comfortable with her. For some reason, her personality put him at ease.

"So, what's your story, Elsbeth? How did you arrive in Sweden?"

"Well, my grandfather came here to escape persecution. He was very conservative and kept waiting for the day when the temple would be restored. He passed away five years ago, so he didn't get a chance to see it happen."

"I'm sorry to hear that." After a pause, Edvin went on. "Forgive my ignorance, but why was he so interested in the temple being restored?"

"Well, he always told us he was from the lineage of Zadok."

Edvin could only stare blankly. He didn't understand.

Elsbeth chuckled at his look. "Sorry. I guess that does sound strange. Levi was the Jewish tribe from which priests came and, after the time of King David, the descendants of Zadok were given the high priest position because of Zadok's faithfulness to David." Elsbeth gave a half laugh. "Grandpa was always adamant his descendants would one day be priests again."

"Well, it seems that should come true for your father, right?"

Elsbeth nodded. "Yes, my father is there now."

Edvin raised his eyebrows and gave a slight nod.

"As soon as he heard the news of the finding of the ashes, he started packing. He was part of the ceremony at Rosh Hashanah."

Edvin saw her eyes water just a bit, and even a tear start to trickle. He gave her a side hug. She seemed appreciative.

"Your grandfather got his wish, then."

Elsbeth nodded and gave a weak smile; she seemed determined not to cry. Her eyes still watered.

They walked on in quiet for a short time. Elsbeth stopped and Edvin went a little farther, not realizing she was standing at her doorstep.

"Sorry," she said. "Here we are. Why don't you come up and let me fix you breakfast?"

"Really? Well . . . I don't want to put you to any trouble."

"Oh, no trouble. It's just an omelet. I hope that's OK?"

"Sounds great."

As they entered the apartment, Edvin realized the layout was similar to his. He cut up bananas and strawberries while she prepared the omelet. "You have a wonderful view," Edvin said. "Being able to have a waterfront view is really great."

"Yeah, that's what I fell in love with when I first saw it. Why don't we eat on the balcony? Here, take the plates and I'll bring the juice."

The omelet was delicious. The strawberries and bananas were a nice contrast and provided a light ending to the meal. They ended the meal with tea.

"Elsbeth, that was truly delicious. Thanks."

"It was nothing. But thank you for the compliment."

Edvin noticed the tabloid on the other chair and picked it up. He stared at the picture.

"Admiring yourself again?" Elsbeth smiled as she set her teacup down.

Edvin laughed. "No. I'm trying to figure out who these two individuals are at the temple."

Elsbeth had no trouble immediately delivering an answer. "Those are the two Witnesses. Or, at least, that's what people are calling them." She paused a few seconds. "Sorry, but I'm a little surprised you don't know about them."

"Well, I've been here for several weeks. One of my men was supposed to keep me in the loop, but he's been in Babylon and may not know about them either." Edvin looked up at Elsbeth. "So, how do *you* know about them?"

"My father. He says they preach about the Messiah—and protect the temple."

Edvin turned his head and gave her a questioning look. "What do you mean by that?"

"Apparently, a suicide bomber entered the temple area. One of the Witnesses held up his hand and the bomber became paralyzed, transfixed. The Witness blew in the direction of the man and the explosives began to melt and drip on the ground. The man began sweating like crazy. Once the explosives were no longer viable, the Witness allowed him to move again. Everyone thought the guy would turn and run—but no. He pulls out a knife and runs at the Witness. Again, the Witness stands there, blows toward the guy, and the attacker bursts into flames, screams, and falls dead. Can you believe that?"

"That's . . . that's incredible. When did that happen?"

"Just a couple of days ago."

Edvin looked again at the photo. "I guess the headlines make more sense now."

Elsbeth nodded. "Does this change your plans?"

Edvin thought about that. *Should it?* He shook his head. "No. Not yet, anyway."

"So, you'll be around a little longer?"

Edvin nodded. The way she said it sounded like she was glad. His hopes were raised.

Elsbeth looked at her watch. "Edvin, I'm sorry, but I have to get to the travel agency for work."

"Oh, yes . . . yes, of course. I hope I haven't made you late. I didn't even consider that."

She smiled a bit sheepishly. "I may be a little late, but it's OK."

Edvin picked up their plates and took them to the kitchen counter, then headed for the front door.

Elsbeth spoke next. "I'm off tomorrow. That is, if you want to do anything."

Edvin opened the door and turned. "I would like that. Lunch?"

She walked up next to him. “Lunch would be great.” She smiled.

The breeze wafted her perfume his way, and the light orchid scent seemed to suit her perfectly. It was delicate yet intoxicating. He leaned in. She didn’t move. His lips touched hers; it was like electricity flooding through him. He had not felt this since . . . *Claire!* That thought made him pull away quickly.

She gave him a curious look. “Are you OK?”

“Yes. I . . . I don’t want to make you too late for work.” He smiled and touched his finger to her lips. “I’ll stop by around twelve-thirty tomorrow.”

She smiled in return. “OK. See you then.”

He glanced back a few times and saw her lingering at the door watching him. He saw her close the door just as he turned the corner of the block.

* * * * *

That night Edvin couldn’t sleep. His thoughts of Elsbeth excited him, but he couldn’t get Claire out of his mind either. He knew the thought of Claire when he kissed Elsbeth was a knee-jerk reaction. He had nothing to feel guilty about. But he also knew that what got him to this point in his career was the belief that he was doing it for Claire and proving himself to Dr. De Voss. He realized he had to start living his life for himself. Claire was a memory—a loving memory, but he had to live for the future, not the past. After coming to terms with that, he fell into a deep sleep . . .

His first thought when he awoke was Elsbeth. The morning seemed to go too slowly, but noon eventually arrived. His pulse quickened the closer he got to her apartment, and he could feel the thud of his heart as he knocked on her door. He barely got the first knock out before the door opened. There she stood, radiant and beautiful, wearing a dark green sweater and jeans. The color suited her—and her figure. Edvin gave a big smile, and she reciprocated.

He leaned in and gave her a quick kiss. She kissed back. Yes, this was going to be a good day.

Edvin's good day turned into several good days. The time Elsbeth was at work felt like an eternity. He was usually waiting at her apartment when she returned, and they would spend the rest of the day together either sightseeing, dining, or catching a play. He started to realize he was depending on her to always be there, but he only had a couple of days left in Stockholm. What was he going to do? He hoped he would think of something before he had to leave the city.

Edvin took the tunnelbana, the city's metro, and exited at a downtown stop where he met Elsbeth for lunch; she only had to work half a day. Edvin's heart skipped a beat when, a few blocks from the restaurant, Elsbeth's fingers reached for and interlocked with his. Edvin smiled to himself. It seemed things were moving quickly between them, and he didn't mind that at all.

Over lunch, they continued to get to know each other better. Edvin ate slowly to make the time last longer and chit-chatted about everything—though nothing in particular. He ordered dessert because he wanted to be in Elsbeth's company as long as possible, and he still had to broach the subject of them being so far apart after he returned to work.

About halfway through dessert, Elsbeth folded her hands and looked at Edvin with an admiring smile. "So . . . you've learned a lot about me these last few days. What about you?"

Edvin looked at her with raised eyebrows. "What do you want to know?"

"Anything. Anything at all. All I know about you is you travel with President Hatim and some people think of you as

Han Solo."

Edvin chuckled and gave a lighthearted shrug. "What's more to know?"

Elsbeth gave that smile that often made Edvin go weak inside. "Quite a lot, I'm sure."

"Well, let me see. Not much to tell, really. I grew up in Stockholm, tried out for Special Forces, got a shot at the President's World Forces, and got chosen for the President's detail."

"I'm sure there's a little more to it than that." She gave another smile. "How did you get the President's attention?"

"Well, I guess I owe a lot to Dr. De Voss for that."

Elsbeth's eyes widened. "Are you talking about the former European Union president?"

Edvin nodded.

"How on earth did you get to know him?" She cocked her head. "The more I know about you, the more I learn I *don't* know."

Edvin smiled. "Well, it's nothing mysterious. I was almost engaged to his daughter, before . . . " Edvin's voice trailed off; sorrow grabbed at him unexpectedly.

Elsbeth's voice got soft as she spoke. "Before what?"

Edvin's eyes met hers. His eyes began to water even though he tried to keep them from doing so. "She died in a plane crash when . . . the disappearances occurred."

"Oh, Edvin. I'm so sorry." She placed her hand on top of his and gave a slight squeeze.

Edvin nodded. He forced a smile. "That's the downside." He looked into her eyes again. "But without that pain I would never have met you." And he meant that. He missed Claire—a lot—but knew he was falling for Elsbeth.

Elsbeth blushed a little. She looked down and back into his eyes and smiled. "So, tell me more about you. Any other family?"

"I have a brother." He remembered his last conversation with Lars and added, "Well, half brother. Our parents separated when we were young. We spent summers together, but Lars made sure we kept in touch once we left home. He married a wonderful girl, Néa, but . . . " Edvin's voice began to crack. He stopped talking.

Elsbeth looked concerned. "What happened, Edvin?"

Edvin shook his head. "She was pregnant when the disappearances occurred. Losing her unborn child caused her to go insane. She recently committed suicide."

Elsbeth put her hand over her mouth and gasped. "Oh, Edvin." She shook her head. "That's terrible."

"And I haven't been able to find Lars since I returned here." He looked back into her eyes and gave a weak smile. "Sorry for being such a downer."

"No . . . no. I'm glad you told me. I'm glad you feel OK to open up to me."

Edvin felt bad he wasn't entirely honest about his relationship with Lars, but Lars had gone to a lot of effort to protect him—at least according to what Lars said—and he wanted to honor that. Edvin told himself that perhaps it was time to change topics.

"So . . . care to go for a downtown tour?"

Elsbeth smiled. "Sure."

Edvin paid and they stepped outside. The air was cool but pleasant. The sun was low but still added sufficient warmth for an afternoon stroll. As they walked, now hand in hand, Edvin had a desire to go see Captain Andreasson.

"Care to see where I used to work?"

"Sure. I'd like that."

"It's only a few blocks from here."

As they entered the building, he pointed out several features. After a few minutes, he asked if Elsbeth would mind waiting while he went to see his former captain for a few minutes. She encouraged him to go and said she didn't mind waiting.

As Edvin neared Captain Andreasson's office, she stepped out and then came to a sudden halt. "Captain Isakson!"

"Captain Andreasson. Just came by to say hello."

"Well, it's been a while. Come into my office, please." She stepped aside to allow him to enter. "So, how is everything? I keep hearing good things about you."

Edvin smiled. "Thanks. I think things are going well. It feels funny to hear you call me Captain."

"I've seen you come a long way from when I first knew you. You should be very proud of your accomplishments. I know I am. Your doing well has made me look good to my superiors as well." She smiled. "No promotion yet, but I've been given more responsibilities, so I hope that leads to something. So, what brings you back home this time?"

"Just a short break. I'll be heading back in another week."

"I see. Everyone needs a little R&R now and then."

Edvin nodded. "I have a question to ask."

"Yes?"

Edvin cleared his throat. He didn't want to appear out of touch, but he needed to know. "I've heard rumors some police forces are gathering those of Jewish or Israeli descent for detainment. I haven't seen anything official about this, but I thought I'd ask what you've heard."

"Interesting you ask."

Edvin gave an inquisitive look. "Why is that?"

"There's no directive supporting what you said, but we've received specific lists of individuals to be detained. It's not clear why, and we're not permitted to question the action. I assume it's for a good reason. But I've noticed they all have paperwork showing their Jewish or Israeli heritage. Is there something I should know?"

"No. No, I was just curious. I've been on vacation for several weeks, so I didn't know if it was a rumor or not. I guess I'll find out more once I'm back."

"We received our first list several weeks ago and just finished rounding those folks up. We have them in lockup. You probably passed them on your way in."

"Really? What are you supposed to do with them?"

"No idea as yet. Still waiting for orders." Andreasson paused. "I'm sorry, Isakson, but I have to get back to work. It was great seeing you again, though. Don't be a stranger, OK?"

Edvin smiled. "Promise." He stood, shook her hand, and left. On his way out, he glanced at the twenty or so prisoners in lockup. He felt sorry for them, but was unsure what he could do. As he passed by, one of them looked familiar. Looking around, he saw no one, so he went closer to investigate.

To his amazement, one of the men in the back of the cell was Lars.

"Lars!" Edvin looked around to be sure no one heard his loud whisper. The man sitting next to Lars poked him and directed his attention to Edvin. Lars looked up, recognition slowly coming to him. Lars looked terrible, as though he hadn't slept in days. Edvin motioned for him to approach where he was standing.

As recognition came, Lars's eyes got wide. He stood, looked around, and walked slowly to where Edvin stood.

"Edvin? What . . . what are you doing here? You can't be here! You can't be seen with me!"

"Lars, what happened to you? I've been looking for you everywhere."

"Don't worry about me. Take care of yourself. What happens to me is not important."

"What? Of course you're important. You're important to

me. I found out about Néa. I'm so sorry, Lars."

Lars's countenance drooped. He looked exhausted. *What has he been up to?* Edvin thought.

"It was unfortunate." He looked at Edvin, eyes watering. "Perhaps it was for the best." His lips quivered. "She was . . . so far gone." He shook his head. "She wasn't coming back. Now perhaps she can have the peace she deserved."

"What about you, Lars? What have you been doing?"

Lars closed his eyes and shook his head. "Don't worry about me, Edvin. I knew this day would happen." He looked into Edvin's eyes. "It's OK. It's really OK."

"I'm going to do something about this, Lars. Trust me."

Lars grabbed Edvin's hand. Startled, Edvin stared at him. Lars had more strength in his grip than his disheveled frame revealed.

"No. No, Edvin. Don't do anything. Too much is at stake. You can't be seen with me."

A guard came by. "Everything OK, sir?"

"Yes. Yes, all is fine. Where are these prisoners being taken?"

"Nowhere yet, sir. We haven't received orders."

"Can I see the paperwork?" Edvin showed his badge to the corporal.

The corporal saluted. "Yes, sir. I have it right here, sir."

Edvin looked. The prisoners were classified as "research subjects." *What did that mean?* Maybe he could direct their travel before another order came in. Edvin took out his pen and wrote a destination on the order sheet: "Deliver to Tel Aviv on first flight out."

Lars had worked to save him earlier. Now it was time for him to return the favor.

He handed the order back to the corporal. "You now have a destination. Any questions?"

The corporal looked at the sheet. His eyes widened. He

looked from the sheet to Edvin. He nodded. "Very good, sir. I will see to it at once."

When the corporal left, Edvin turned to Lars. "I'll see you in Tel Aviv."

Lars said nothing. Edvin was hesitant, but knew he had to go. As he turned the corner, he looked back. Lars had gone back to where he was previously sitting. *Poor Lars.*

Yet, Edvin hoped, they would be together again soon.

Once Edvin returned to the precinct lobby, he was lost in thought and actually momentarily forgot about Elsbeth.

He felt an arm wrap around his. "Hey, forgetting someone?"

He snapped out of his thoughts. He turned to Elsbeth and smiled. "Sorry, lost in thought." He noticed a worried look on her face. "What's wrong?"

"Let's just go."

They walked out of the precinct and, after a few blocks, Elsbeth let out a deep breath.

"So, what's wrong, Elsbeth?"

"Edvin, I heard some people talking about rounding up Jews. The two men talking began to sound very anti-Semitic. It reminded me of stories my grandfather used to tell. It really shook me up. What's going on?"

"I'm not sure. But it seems those who had recent blood work done are also being genetically tested. Apparently being Jewish has ramifications. I'm not sure yet what that is."

Elsbeth stopped in her tracks and gave a frightened look to Edvin.

"What's wrong?"

"Edvin, I had post-physical blood work done yesterday."

Edvin looked at her. His plans were to leave for Israel the next morning to catch up with Lars. Now, hearing this news, he knew he had to change his plans. He couldn't take chances. "Elsbeth, pack your bags. We're leaving for Israel tonight."

CHAPTER 14

Edvin felt as though he didn't really breathe until both he and Elsbeth were in the air on De Voss's plane. He wasn't sure what he would have done if Elsbeth was taken away from him. Although their time together had been short, he now couldn't imagine his life without her in it.

"Well, I'm very impressed with the perks of your job," Elsbeth said. "Even the head executive of our travel agency doesn't travel like this."

Edvin laughed. "This is only the fourth time I've been on his plane."

Elsbeth repeated his words in a bit of a mocking tone: "It's only the fourth time I've been on his plane." She chuckled. "And how many people can say that?"

Edvin held up his hands. "OK, OK. I concede. My travels are above average."

Elsbeth laughed. She held up her glass of Pinot Grigio and took another sip.

Edvin sat across from her. He felt fidgety and couldn't sit still. He hadn't been totally honest with her, and it was eating at him. She seemed to notice his uncomfortableness and turned up her brow in curiosity.

"What's wrong, Edvin? What's got you so worked up?"

Edvin gave a weak smile. "I . . . haven't been completely truthful with you."

Elsbeth cocked her head slightly.

"I told you I have a half brother. That's not true. He's my full brother."

"That's OK, Edvin. It's not really a big deal."

Edvin shook his head. "No. At the precinct, Lars, my brother, was there—in prison—arrested because his blood work showed him to be of Israeli descent."

Elsbeth's eyes got big and her voice grew quiet. "You . . . had your brother arrested because he's Israeli?"

"What? No! No." Edvin shook his head. "I think you're missing the point. If he's of Israeli descent, then so am I."

"Oh." She sounded confused. "Yes, I guess that would be true." She paused in thought. "So, how is it you are working for someone who's against the Jews and Israelis?"

"That's what I'm trying to explain. I don't quite understand why, but Lars altered the databank's information about my blood work, and, somehow, altered my birth certificate. Our last names had already been legally changed by our parents when we were kids. He has my mother's maiden name and I have my father's last name. He did all this so no one would find out about my heritage."

"How did he know to do that?"

Edvin shrugged. "All I know is, the last time I saw him he kept saying he found out the hospital had tested his unborn daughter's blood for genetic markers and found the Israeli DNA. At the time, I thought he was losing it because of the psychological trauma his wife was undergoing. But he insisted he was unsafe having that genetic marker, and he was going to make sure I wouldn't be detected."

"But you just said he was in prison. You left him there?"

Edvin shook his head, then lowered his voice. "No. I had

the prisoners sent to Israel. I thought that would be the safest place for him. Since his wife Néa is dead, there's no real need for him to stay in Sweden. I had planned to leave tomorrow to meet him, but when you said they may now have paperwork on you, I wanted to get you to Israel as soon as possible."

Elsbeth gave a shy smile. "Does that mean you care about me?"

"You could say that." Edvin smiled back.

Elsbeth jerked upright. "Edvin, you should tell this to Captain Cohen."

"Who? Is that a relative of yours?"

Elsbeth chuckled. "No. His family and ours have always been friends. Same last name, but no relation. At least, not that I know of. Although a captain, he's somewhat close to the Prime Minister."

Edvin gave a shrug. "The only captain I know close to the Prime Minister is Mik'kel ben David.

Elsbeth nodded. "Yes, that's the Jewish name he would go by."

"I've been working with him ever since I came to Israel."

"Really?" She laughed lightly. "Well, that saves me on introductions."

Edvin chuckled as well. "I'm hoping he can help me with Lars."

"I'm sure he can."

Elsbeth changed seats and sat next to Edvin. She put her head on his shoulder. She was quiet for a few minutes. "Edvin?" Her tone was hushed.

"Yes." He put his arm around her.

"I know you care about me—and likely Mik'kel. But how are you going to reconcile friendship with Jews if your employer is trying to get rid of us?"

"Well, I first want to clarify his intent. But, granted, it may become tricky."

After a few more minutes of silence between them, they fell asleep in each other's arms.

When they landed in Tel Aviv, Edvin made sure he knew when the flight from Stockholm would arrive the next day. He wanted to be present when the plane landed. He then called Mik'kel to catch up. Mik'kel was at the temple, and he asked Edvin to come there first.

As they approached the temple, Edvin was surprised at how much work had been done. He estimated at least one third of the temple was already completed. There were so many people there. Looking around, he found Mik'kel near a group of people, including a man who seemed to be instructing those present. The one speaking looked different from anyone else. His clothes looked like what someone from ages gone by might have worn. As he passed one of the onlookers, he heard them call the man speaking an "Old Testament prophet." *What does that mean?* Edvin wondered.

Halfway to Mik'kel, his friend spotted him, came over, shook Edvin's hand, and gave him a quick hug. Mik'kel noticed Elsbeth. His eyes widened and he gave a short gasp. "Elsbeth?" He glanced at Edvin and then back at her. "You two know each other? But . . . how?"

Elsbeth laughed as she gave Mik'kel a big hug. "It's really a simple story. We met at a grocery store in Stockholm and got to know each other." She glanced at Edvin. He nodded.

"Well, I'm speechless." Mik'kel continued to look at them for a few moments and then shook his head quickly as if trying to clear his thoughts and get back on task. "Anyway, I want you to meet one of the two Witnesses, as they've come to be called."

"We have, sort of, already," Elsbeth said.

Mik'kel gave her a questioning look. Edvin wondered what she meant. Elsbeth pulled out the tabloid article from her bag and handed it to Mik'kel, then gave Edvin an exaggerated grin. He put his hand over his eyes and shook his head.

Mik'kel looked at the picture, glanced at Edvin, back at the picture, and then burst into laughter. "I always knew there was something about you I couldn't put my finger on. Now I know. You're Han Solo in disguise."

"Thanks, Elsbeth." Edvin shook his head. "Will I ever live this down?"

Mik'kel laughed again. "I don't think so."

"OK, OK. Can we get back on topic?"

"Right." Mik'kel cleared his throat but continued to smile. "Come this way."

Mik'kel walked them over to one of the Witnesses. He seemed to be praying over two men. Both were on their knees before him, and his hands were placed on their heads.

" . . . The Messiah's Spirit will be in you and will protect you as you spread the good news of why the Messiah came, and what he offers to everyone who will put their faith in his payment for their sins." Both men stood. "James, son of Manasseh, I am sending you to the Americas; you will find many from your tribe there. Many may not even realize their ancestry. You can help not only save them physically but spiritually." Turning to the other man, he said, "John, son of Ephraim, I am sending you to the British Isles. You will find many from your tribe there. Remember, God has sealed you and no one can harm you. Remain faithful and you will bring the Messiah much fruit."

Both men nodded, turned, and left with huge smiles on their faces. Those smiles seemed to say they had a *purpose*, something to live for.

The Witness looked up and locked eyes with Elsbeth.

"Elsbeth, daughter of Zadok, please approach. You are the threshold to the Promised Kingdom. Your faithfulness will be emulated by many."

Edvin was shocked the Witness knew her. He looked at Mik'kel, who gave a slight shrug. *What did that prophecy mean?*

The Witness then locked eyes with Edvin. "Edvin, son of Levi, please approach." *Son of Levi?* Edvin had never heard that before. "Your heart will be pierced by sorrow as you lose your most valuable possession, but it will return to you purer than before. Through perseverance and faithfulness will come happiness."

Edvin was dumbstruck. He had no idea what that was supposed to mean—but was also unsure if he should admit it.

"I know this confuses you, but I can only speak what my Messiah gives me to speak," the Witness said. "I can promise one day this all will make sense."

Edvin didn't know how to respond. He simply nodded.

"And Mik'kel, son of Levi, you have been zealous. But now is the time to challenge your traditions."

The Witness then looked at all three of them. "All three of you have character and morals that have served you well. Yet, realize you missed the gathering of the sheepfold. If you don't get to know the Shepherd, you will not be part of his Promised Kingdom. If you don't listen to me, listen to his other 144,000 prophets—from every tribe of their father Israel. All this is part of the Almighty's holy Scriptures. Whoever has an ear should listen and respond."

The Witness then turned his attention to others in the crowd. The three of them made their way—a bit slowly, looking back over their shoulders at him—to the temple entrance.

Elsbeth was the first to speak. "What was that all about? How am I a 'threshold'?"

Mik'kel shrugged. "He seems to imply the Messiah was the cause of the disappearances. But many of our people abandoned the idea of a coming Messiah a long time ago." He shook his head. "There's a lot about what he said that's mysterious."

Edvin gave a small laugh. "That's an understatement." Edvin's phone beeped. He stared at the text for several seconds.

Elsbeth cocked her head. "Well, what does it say?"

"President Hatim wants me in Babylon as soon as possible."

As if reading his mind, Elsbeth responded, "Don't worry, Edvin. Mik'kel and I can meet Lars and make sure he's OK. Just text me the information on when and where he's supposed to arrive and what we should do."

At that moment, Edvin knew his heart had completely fallen for Elsbeth. She and he were already in sync with their thoughts.

With deep gratitude, Edvin responded. "Thanks, Elsbeth. Please text me as soon as he arrives. I'll be back as soon as possible."

Elsbeth gave him a hug. "I will. Don't worry. I'll miss you, though."

"Me too." He gave her a quick kiss and shook Mik'kel's hand. "I'll see you soon."

As much as he didn't want to, he left them and headed once more for the airport.

* * * * *

In only a matter of hours, the plane was descending into Babylon. By going farther east, darkness fell more quickly. Night had firmly secured itself as Edvin stepped off the plane. Looking around, he noticed a car with someone standing by. As he stepped closer, he recognized the feminine figure: Anna Bonfield.

"Anna, what a pleasant surprise."

"Hello, Captain Isakson. It's nice to see you again."

Edvin got into the limo and the driver headed out—most likely to Hatim's headquarters, wherever that was.

"I can't believe how everything has grown up so quickly," Edvin said to Anna. "How is that possible?"

Anna laughed lightly. "Well, there's always activity wherever the President goes. But, as you know, the President had plans for all this well before he announced it. With him, it's not 'build it and they will come.' It's 'speak it, and they will come build it.'"

Edvin laughed. "Yes, I guess that's true. How is the President?"

"Very well. He left just before you arrived."

"Oh?"

Anna smiled. She apparently had seen the disappointment on his face. "It's really quite the compliment. He trusts you, Captain, and wants you to take over the supervision of all projects going on here. He trusts your judgment."

Edvin nodded and gave a half-hearted smile. This wasn't the type of assignment he thought he had signed up for. "Where is the President heading?" he asked.

"He and Cortez left for Libya. He needs to get the other two territories in order and have them firmly behind his plans."

Edvin nodded. "Well, I don't want to add to his plate, but he may want to stop by Jerusalem. There are two individuals at the temple who are drawing a lot of attention." Edvin thought it best to be forthright; he didn't want Hatim to hear about them on the news and wonder why he had not been told about them. He needed to be open with Hatim but protective of Mik'kel and Elsbeth at the same time. He wasn't sure if that was possible, but knew he had to try.

Anna nodded. "I'll tell him." She shook her head. "There's

so much on his plate right now. It's a shame there's something else for him to contend with."

Edvin glanced out the window and saw the limo approaching a huge building. It looked like a ziggurat, each stage outlined in glass. There appeared to be elevators on each corner that traveled along the angle of the building to near its top, but only one seemed to go all the way to the top. Edvin couldn't help but admire the architecture. Atop the highest tier was a floodlight shining straight up into the sky.

Anna glanced out the window at the same time. "Ah, we're here."

The limo pulled up to one of the corners of the building. The driver opened the door and helped Anna from the limo. Edvin followed. The building was as spectacular up close as it was from a distance. This particular elevator allowed entrance from the outside. Behind it, glass doors opened to a large lobby. Through the glass, Edvin could see the huge Pangaea logo and slogan behind the receptionist's desk. Anna explained this elevator was the only one that went to the top level—the President's penthouse—and it allowed him to come and go as needed without entering the facility. The other three elevators, one on each corner, were for employees. Anna had provided her thumbprint to get access to this corner elevator.

When they reached the top, the doors opened into a luxurious living area. Each wall, full glass, provided a spectacular view of the city and beyond. The furnishings were modern yet extremely earthy at the same time.

"Wow," Edvin exclaimed, looking around. "Quite the digs."

Anna chuckled. "And you expected anything less?"

Edvin didn't respond. He just kept looking around.

"The President has several bedrooms here and wants you to have one while you stay here. You have an early day tomorrow. Go to the receptionist. She will have your agenda. Dr. Tiberius

Moretti will be your guide for the day. He'll show you around."

Edvin nodded; he wasn't sure it was all sinking in.

"I will be in and out periodically." She handed him a note. "This is my phone number. Call me if you need anything."

"Thanks, Anna."

She smiled. "I think you'll be impressed."

"I already am."

Anna chuckled and turned to leave. As she reached the elevator, she paused and turned. "Oh, your bedroom is the last one down this hallway. Have a good night." The elevator door opened, she entered, and she was smiling as the doors closed.

Edvin headed down the hallway to his room. He opened the door and stood there a few seconds in awe. The room, spacious in its own right, looked even larger due to the outside wall being all glass. He looked for curtains. There were none. He noticed a switch on the near wall. Pressing it, the window went opaque. He noticed it also had a timer so it could be set to turn opaque automatically at a desired time. *Impressive.*

The bed looked king-size. A sofa and chair, next to the wall window, allowed a panoramic view of the grounds and Babylon beyond. There was a desk in the corner and a huge plasma screen television mounted on the opposite wall from the bed. A doorway to the side led to an opulent bathroom with a glass-enclosed shower, and the counter displayed every bath and grooming product one could want. Edvin shook his head in disbelief.

It had been a long day; he took a quick shower and jumped in bed. It was extremely comfortable, but sleep did not come quickly.

Lately, it seemed exhaustion was the only thing that allowed him to sleep.

CHAPTER 15

The next morning, Edvin arrived at the receptionist's area as she was booting up her computer. She looked to be in her early twenties, had short copper-red hair, and had a tattoo of Pangaea on her right temple—evidently, she was a big Hatim supporter. She looked up as he approached.

"Captain Isakson, you're definitely an early riser."

"Just want to get things rolling this morning, you know."

She smiled. "Let me call Dr. Moretti. He's expecting you." She donned her earphones and pushed a few buttons. She reached for an electronic tablet and handed it to Edvin. "This has your agenda and all sorts of other information you'll need." Her attention then changed to her earphone. "Dr. Moretti? Yes, this is Donna at reception. Captain Isakson is here." She glanced up at Edvin and smiled. "Yes, sir, he is." She motioned to some chairs. "If you care to sit, Dr. Moretti will be down shortly. He'll have a badge for you which will give you access to everything." She smiled again.

Edvin returned her smile. "Thanks." He went to the nearest plush chair, sat, and began scanning the information on his tablet. Edvin was amazed at everything he saw. Hopefully, Moretti would have many explanations. He didn't understand half the terms on the agenda.

"Captain Isakson?" Edvin heard his name called from behind him.

Edvin stood and turned. "Dr. Moretti?" He held out his hand.

"Call me Ty," the man said as he returned the handshake. "Dr. Moretti is too formal, and Tiberius is what my mom calls me when I'm in trouble."

Edvin laughed. He was certain he was going to like this guy. His features looked familiar to Edvin, but he couldn't understand why. Ty was muscular, but not overly so, had brown hair with lighter brown highlights, and wore wire-rimmed glasses.

"OK. So, Ty, what's first on the agenda?"

"I'll give you an overall tour. It may take a while, and we may even have to continue for a couple of days. As you've noticed, the Ziggurat of Knowledge, as we call it, has seven stories, with President Hatim's penthouse above that."

Edvin nodded.

"The first six stories are where the various scientific projects are ongoing. The seventh story is where President Hatim meets with various individuals and groups for political reasons." He handed a badge to Edvin. "This is your unrestricted badge. You have the highest clearance level—access to all tiers." He motioned toward the scanners. "Let's go in and I can explain the tiers better."

They came to an archway that seemed to be the only entrance to the wall behind the receptionist. It went from wall to wall across the huge lobby.

"This glass wall is made of bulletproof glass and the archway is the only entrance. There is one in each of the three lobbies on this floor since this is the ground floor and largest tier."

The security archway blended in well with the architecture and didn't look out of place. It was cobalt blue and its outline matched other cobalt-outlined arches in the glass; this one was just more open and deeper. Once through, Ty brought Edvin to the center of the tier. This looked to be the building's cafeteria. The ceiling was the floor of the seventh tier, and balconies could be seen on the other tiers overlooking this vast opening. Hung from the seventh tier, like a huge chandelier, was a slowly rotating Pangaea orb.

"This is the ziggurat's main cafeteria. Each tier has break rooms on various balconies above us. This really helps with morale and allows people to meet and brainstorm. We strongly encourage this as this is how innovative ideas are born."

"This is amazing." Edvin looked up and admired the view.

Ty smiled. "Yes, it's a wonderful place to work. This tier and the next are mostly genetics: animal, human, and plant. With the world's environment rather chaotic lately, there has been much work to do to get plants more adaptable to harsh environments."

"Like getting plants to survive drought?"

Ty tilted his head slightly. "It seems you already know a little about our work."

"Not really. I overheard Dr. Hatim and Gwen Sheridan talking at one point."

"Oh, you know Ms. Sheridan? She's here for another project."

"Really? Well, no. I don't know her exactly. I mean, I've met her, but don't really know her. She's here now? Why?"

"It's probably best I show you. It's difficult to explain. I'll be sure we stop by the lab in which she's working."

"I didn't know she was a scientist."

Ty shook his head. "She isn't. But she has a strong passion for this particular project. It's pretty interesting. Anyway, the next three tiers are with various science projects: astronomy, physics, marine biology, geology, tectonics, etcetera. Not everything is set up yet, but it's all coming together rapidly.

Finally, the sixth tier is devoted solely to 3-D tissue printing—a passion of the President's—and it's strictly guarded. Very few people have access to the sixth tier. You're one of the few."

Edvin was impressed—and overwhelmed—at the same time. He couldn't understand why he was being put over all of this. "Ty, why aren't you over all of this rather than me? You seem to understand it all. I understand hardly any of it."

"Don't worry, Captain. The President just wants you to keep track of it and what's going on. There are plenty of people here to help you understand the why behind everything. I'm sure President Hatim will give the final say of what's funded."

Edvin still wasn't sure of this structure, but nodded anyway.

"Let me take you to Ms. Sheridan. I think what she's working on will give you a good clue as to what we're trying to accomplish here."

As they headed down the hall, Edvin saw Saeed coming toward them with a large box on his shoulder. He walked by without saying anything.

"Amari!" Edvin said loudly.

Saeed turned. "Captain!" His tone was one of pleasant recognition. "I didn't see you there."

He turned around to shake hands as he kept the box balanced on his shoulder. "I didn't realize you had already arrived."

"Got in last night."

"Well, I'm glad you're here. I've been helping Dr. J here, but I'm ready to turn it all over to you. Edstrom's here somewhere as well."

"And the others?"

"Chong and Masaki went with Cortez and Dr. Hatim. And Phillips is now with the De Vosses. She and Edstrom swapped assignments."

Saeed shifted the box on his shoulder. "Well, if you'll excuse me, I have to go deliver this to Dr. Creepizoid." He looked at Ty. "Sorry, Dr. J, no disrespect. But that guy gives me the willies. Anyway, glad to see you, Cap. I'll talk with you later."

"Sure." As Saeed walked off, Edvin turned to Ty. "Why does he call you Dr. J?"

Ty laughed. "It's a long story. The condensed version is some of my graduate students said I looked like Dr. Jackson from the *SG-1* TV series when it was out." He laughed. "Some of them were big fans and started calling me Dr. J, and it caught on. Some of them are still with me and still call me that. Probably Lieutenant Amari doesn't even realize that's not my real name."

That explained, to Edvin, why Ty had looked familiar. He remembered Claire used to love watching old *SG-1* reruns. "And what of 'Dr. Creepizoid'?"

Ty's smile vanished. "He was referring to Dr. Conrad Bonn. He has a . . . uh, well, unique project."

Edvin raised his eyebrows. "And . . . you're not going to leave me hanging, are you?"

Ty shook his head. "I'll show you later. Let's see the good stuff first."

Edvin wasn't sure why Ty was reluctant to talk about Conrad. He decided he would pressure him later; he needed to know about all projects.

Ty led him to a room not far down the hallway. "This is it."

Edvin noticed the sign on the door: "Lopion Experiment."

As they entered, Gwen Sheridan stood talking to one of the lab assistants. She was wearing a white lab coat, but it was unbuttoned, and this helped revealed her svelte figure despite her baggy sweater and jeans. Her long hair was in a stylish ponytail. Noticing the lab assistant glance in the direction of the door, she turned, and a huge smile crossed her face.

"Ty. And Captain Isakson! Well, it has certainly been a while."

Edvin could feel heat rush to his cheeks. "I'm surprised you remember me. Call me Edvin."

She approached and gave Ty a kiss on the cheek; he beamed. She turned her attention to Edvin. "But I'm mad at you." She poked his chest with her index finger. "You didn't come to my concert."

Edvin was taken back. "Well, uh, I mean, I . . . uh, didn't have a chance to go." His cheeks were now very hot, and he knew they were likely beet red.

Gwen laughed and patted Edvin on his chest. "Don't worry, Edvin. I know you were busy. If President Hatim couldn't make it, I know you couldn't." She gave him a wry smile. "But it was spectacular."

"I bet."

"The first of the drought-resistant crops had sprouted, and I wanted the concert to be a real celebration of the food that would now be available to that part of the world. Also, Ken did a wonderful job as emcee." Gwen giggled. "He was so funny, and a big hit. And then there was Reverend Duarté. Oh, he was so fantastic. He ended the concert with everyone lighting a candle with all the lights turned out. It was very moving." A frown, though, suddenly came to her face. "But right after, a swarm of locusts came through and destroyed all the crops that had sprouted. I was so upset and explained my frustration to President Hatim. He pointed me to Ty, and voilà, here I am." Her bright smile returned.

Edvin furrowed his brow. "That's awful, Gwen. But why are you *here*?"

She looked at Ty. "I didn't want to spoil the surprise," he said.

She looked at Edvin. "Then come this way and be amazed."

"Well, that sounds intriguing." Edvin followed her to a large glass case.

She reached in and pulled out . . . a creature.

Edvin jumped back in shock, nearly knocking over a chair. "What on earth is *that*?"

"Come now. Don't you recognize a beautiful creature when you see one?"

"I ask again," Edvin repeated. What *is* that?"

Gwen laughed. "This is a *lopion*. It's a chimera—a combination of locust and scorpion."

Edvin's curiosity took over and he approached Gwen and the creature once more. She held the thing tightly while he took a closer look. It appeared to be quite docile even though it looked menacing. It had a scorpion tail and was about the same size as a scorpion. The creature had wings like those of a locust but not the big legs for hopping. The front part of its body appeared dark green in color, and its body curved upward to the head. The creature's thorax looked like it had a breastplate. The genetic manipulation pushed its eyes closer together in front, and instead of two large antennae, it had multiple small antennae, giving it the appearance of having hair. The eyes and "hair" made it look something like a human face—except the mouth opening was jagged and looked like teeth.

"It has a face only a mother could love."

The creature moved in Gwen's hand and Edvin jumped back once more.

"Aw, you're hurting its feelings." Gwen stroked its side with her index finger.

"So, what is it supposed to do?"

Ty jumped in. "These creatures are docile to humans, but they'll kill and eat most anything that has the potential to swarm: locusts, grasshoppers, insects of that sort. The acoustic frequency of a swarm irritates them, and they attack. When released, their breeding habits will be similar to those of insects and should help prevent swarms from happening."

"Then these drought-stricken areas can produce their crops for all those poor people," Gwen added. "It seems like a perfect solution to a devastating problem."

"OK, Captain," Ty said. "I do have a lot more to show you."

Gwen tapped Edvin's tablet. "You can keep tabs on the project with your tablet."

"Oh . . . OK. I will."

Gwen put something in Edvin's pocket. "I'll be doing a concert in Babylon in a few months. Now you have no excuse." She smiled. Edvin could feel his cheeks getting warm again. "Feel free to bring a friend."

Edvin smiled. "Thanks." He turned and left with Ty. When he looked back, Gwen was back at the lopion cage.

Ty took Edvin to several other genetic labs on the second tier, and this ate up much of the morning.

"We have time for one more visit before lunch," he said. "Any preferences?"

Edvin's phone beeped. He looked down; it was Elsbeth. "Mind if I take this?"

"Sure. I'll take a bathroom break and be back."

Edvin walked to one of the balconies as he answered. "Elsbeth, it's great to hear from you. Are you calling about Lars?" There was silence. "Elsbeth, is something wrong?"

"Edvin, I'm sorry. Lars wasn't at the airport."

"What? What do you mean?"

"There was no flight from Stockholm. Well, there was a flight, but no prisoners and no Lars."

"How . . . how is that possible? What happened?" Edvin's mind spun. He felt dizzy and had to sit.

"Mik'kel was able to contact someone in the precinct at Stockholm. Apparently, orders came in before your orders could be enacted, and those overrode yours."

"So, where were they taken?"

"Babylon."

"What? He's *here*?"

"He's apparently been there longer than you. His flight left even before we left for Israel. He's there somewhere, Edvin."

"Thanks, Elsbeth. How are things there?"

"Things are fine. Would be better if you were here. I miss you."

"I miss you, too. I'll talk to you soon." Then, more softly: "Bye."

Edvin ended the call and tried to think. *Where could Lars be?* He remembered the paperwork he had seen in Stockholm that called the prisoners "research subjects." That should mean he was likely in the very building in which Edvin stood. He looked up and saw Ty approaching.

"Decide where you want to go?"

"Ty, do you know of any subjects flown here a day or so ago?"

Ty's smile vanished. "Those were for Dr. Bonn. His research is a little . . . unorthodox."

"What type of research is it?"

"He calls it memory transference."

"What does that mean?"

"He's trying to have one person's memories transferred to another person."

"Is that even possible?"

Ty shrugged. "Anything's possible. But what concerns me is he claims he needs human subjects for testing."

Edvin wasn't sure what that meant—he just knew it couldn't be good. "I want to see his lab."

"Now?"

"You did say it was my preference."

Ty paused and looked at Edvin. "OK. But remember, Dr. Bonn's work is highly regarded by President Hatim. You can't alter what he's doing. Only the President can do that. Understand?"

Edvin nodded. *But what if I find Lars there? What do I do?*

"He's on the fourth tier," Ty said. "Follow me."

As they reached the lab, the sign on the door read "Memory Transference." This time, Ty's phone beeped.

"Sorry, Captain. I have to check on something. Go ahead and enter, but please only ask questions. Don't interfere—even if what you find is disturbing. Do I have your word?"

"Yes. Of course. I'll only observe."

Ty nodded and headed toward the elevator.

As Edvin opened the door, he saw a technician placing and adjusting wires attached to a subject facing away from the door. The technician turned and stopped his activity. A look of surprise filled the eyes of the technician, but this slowly turned to recognition.

"Oh, Captain Isakson. Hello." The man approached with outstretched hand. Edvin shook it. "I'm Sean, Sean McElhaney. I'm a graduate student of Dr. Bonn's. I wasn't expecting you today, but I'm glad you're here. What would you like to know?"

"Just wanted to know what your work entails. Memory transference is unfamiliar to me. I want to know more."

"Certainly." Sean seemed excited, even eager, to explain his work. "Ultimately, we want to be able to transfer memory from one person to another. Currently, we're testing to see if we can transfer thoughts."

"How much success have you had?"

Sean's enthusiasm waned. "Well, not a lot—yet." His voice quickened. "But Dr. Bonn feels we're getting very close."

Edvin nodded toward a man in a chair. "Who's this?"

Sean looked at the man. "Oh, he's a test subject." Then, with excitement in his voice, Sean asked, "Would you like to see?"

Edvin slowly walked over. He saw a chair opposite the individual with some type of helmet with all sorts of wires attached. As he walked closer and turned to see who was in the chair, Edvin's heart leapt into his throat, and he did a small gasp. *Lars*. Evidently, Sean didn't hear the gasp; he kept talking, nearly nonstop. But Edvin had tuned him out at the site of Lars. He walked over and picked up the helmet and looked back at Lars. Lars stared straight ahead and didn't move a muscle.

"Did you want to try it out? Captain? Captain?"

Edvin snapped out of his fog. "What?"

"Did you want to try it out?" He pointed to the helmet in Edvin's hand.

Edvin nodded. Not really sure what he was saying, he answered, "Yes."

Sean nearly jumped with excitement. "Oh, that's great. Just sit there and put the helmet on. I'll be over here working with the frequencies. Let me know if you hear anything."

Edvin nodded. He donned the helmet as Sean went to the machine and turned several switches and nobs. Several lights went on and others began blinking.

Lars's gaze remained transfixed, straight ahead and expressionless. *Is he drugged? Is his mind already mush? What have these people done to him?*

Suddenly, Lars's gaze changed from staring straight ahead to staring directly at Edvin. Edvin gasped. He didn't see any recognition. The blank stare seemed to penetrate his soul. It made Edvin uneasy.

Sean went into a frenzy. "Wow. Oh wow." He put his hands on his head and looked around, apparently not sure what to do. "He's never done that before. Uh, uh, stay right here, OK? I should go get Dr. Bonn. He must see this. OK?" He ran to

Edvin. Edvin nodded. Sean then ran toward the door, but then turned and ran back to the machine. He looked at several indicators and wrote something down. He looked back at Edvin and Lars, then bolted from the room.

Edvin looked back at Lars. He tried to keep his voice low. "Lars! Lars, can you hear me? Are you in there?" *Should I be saying it or thinking it?* Since Lars didn't respond, he tried thinking it. *Lars, can you hear me? Please, answer me. Please.*

Lars blinked. *Lars, does that mean you can hear me?*

Edvin heard something in his thoughts: *Edvin. Leave me. You must continue.*

Was that Lars, or his own thoughts? Edvin wasn't sure! Lars's expression never changed.

Lars, I can't leave you here. Edvin's eyes started to water.

You can. And will. There's no hope for me. Edvin saw tears forming in Lars's eyes.

Don't say that.

Edvin, you must leave me here. And say nothing. There is no coming back for me. You! You must continue!

Lars.

Go! Go now!

Edvin took the helmet off, stood, and placed it on the seat. He walked over to Lars and kissed him on the head. He reached down and wiped away the tear running down Lars's cheek. As he approached the door, he felt all breath leave his lungs. It seemed he couldn't get a breath.

His heart raced. He opened the door and ran for the nearest restroom. He turned the water on and splashed his face with cold water. He grabbed both sides of the sink and took several deep breaths. He felt horrible leaving Lars, but his brother was right. Any other action would undo all the work Lars had done. He wasn't sure Lars should have done all this, but he couldn't let his sacrifice be for nothing. Edvin sobbed uncontrollably for several minutes.

He finally collected himself, washed his face, and gathered his composure. As he stepped from the restroom, he saw Ty approach.

"All done, Captain? Ready for lunch?"

Edvin nodded.

CHAPTER 16

Over the next two weeks, Ty showed Edvin every research project in the Ziggurat of Knowledge—except two. Edvin decided he needed to break the ice on this subject.

"Ty, you've shown me everything except for the sixth tier and your own research. I can check out the sixth tier for myself. But what are you working on?"

Ty smiled and gave Edvin a wink. "I've saved the best for last. Follow me."

Ty led Edvin to the elevator, exited on the fifth tier, and went to the last lab down the left corridor. As they entered, Edvin read the sign: "Teleportation."

"Does that sign mean what I think it means? Like, 'Beam me up, Scotty?'"

Ty laughed. "Yes and no. We're only in the beginning stages of teleportation. My thesis was on its theory and how it's feasible based upon our knowledge of physics."

Edvin was impressed. "So, it isn't just science fiction?"

Ty shook his head. "No, it's definitely possible. Remember, many things once considered science fiction have become reality. I think science fiction sparks the imagination and science allows its reality to take shape. Just think of the replicator on the old *Star Trek* series and our 3-D printers now. Or, video calling on the old, old cartoon *The Jetsons*—and how common that is today."

Edvin smiled. "I see your point. So, what are you doing now?"

"We've attempted to have inanimate objects travel between here and a similar lab in Washington, DC." Ty's voice took on a disappointing tone. "But there have always been . . . mishaps."

"Mishaps?"

Ty nodded. "We've been successful in getting an object to come through, but it never arrives in the same state as when it left. The object is always deformed—like the machine doesn't know how to reassemble the object back into its original design." Ty rubbed the back of his neck. "We still have a lot of work to do. That's why I'm heading back to Washington next week."

"What?" Edvin turned to be certain he wasn't joking. "You're not staying here? Who's supposed to help me?"

"Captain, I'm the acting head until you get established. The head of the facility will be Conrad."

Edvin gave a prolonged "ugghh" sound.

Ty laughed. "He isn't that bad. While I don't necessarily agree with all of Conrad's tactics, he's a brilliant scientist and has great ideas. Besides, you have everything you need in your tablet. You probably won't have to meet with him often."

Edvin nodded, but he still wasn't happy about this news. "So, why back to Washington?"

Ty perked up. "We just employed a new recruit who did his thesis on gluon tagging. He feels this is the key to our reassembly problem. I think he may be right."

Edvin looked at Ty and chuckled. "I have no idea what you just said."

Ty laughed. "Sorry. Let me see if I can give an analogy." Ty looked in thought for a moment. Then: "Let's say you have a jigsaw puzzle, but each piece is shaped exactly the same. You are asked to put the puzzle together—but upside down and without looking at the picture. How would you accomplish that?"

Edvin thought for a moment. "Impossible."

Ty nodded. "Exactly. But that's what we're faced with. What Brad is saying to do is tag the edges of each jigsaw piece and note where each is connected to the next piece. Now, when the puzzle is totally taken apart, one can more easily put the correct pieces in their correct place. When you turn the puzzle over, the picture is exactly as it was before."

Edvin nodded. "Still sounds challenging."

"More than you can ever know."

After a few moments of silence, Ty responded. "Well, Captain, I've shown you everything I know to show you. Everything else is on your tablet—including my number, if you need it. Conrad can also answer further questions. Since I can't go with you to tier six, I'll leave you now. Take care."

Ty stuck out his hand and Edvin returned the handshake. "Thanks. I look forward to seeing your progress."

Ty nodded. "Care to be the first to visit me via teleporter?"

Edvin winced. "Uh . . . maybe second."

Ty laughed. "Fair enough. So long, Captain." Ty headed down the hallway.

Edvin looked at the floor plan on his tablet. Only one elevator other than Hatim's went to the sixth tier, and it was in the opposite direction. Edvin decided to take it . . .

When the elevator door opened on the sixth tier, Edvin had a sense of déjà vu. There was a woman peering into a microscope who would periodically look up at a monitor. She would go back and forth between putting on her glasses and looking at the monitor to having them dangle around her neck as she peered into the microscope.

"Dr. Lyle?" Edvin didn't feel comfortable, at this point, calling her Margaret.

She looked up from her microscope and put on her glasses. Her surprised look quickly turned into one of recognition. "Captain Isakson. I wondered when your rounds would bring you here." She walked forward with a handshake and smile. "What do you wish to see first?"

Edvin shrugged. "I'm not sure. Why don't you give me a quick tour?"

"Glad to. I think this is really exciting stuff. 3-D tissue printing isn't new, but the strides we've made, I think, are revolutionary. Dr. Hatim's interest and funding have really helped us make important breakthroughs."

As Edvin looked around, he saw various organs being perfused in miniature aquarium-looking tanks. The first thing that came to his mind was a lab created by Dr. Frankenstein.

As if reading his thoughts, Dr. Lyle responded. "I know all this looks like something Dr. Frankenstein would have cooked up, but this means we're closer to helping a lot of people prolong their lives. That's what makes me so excited every morning about coming to work." She gave Edvin a broad smile.

"So, why is Dr. Hatim so interested in all this?"

Lyle shrugged. "I don't know, but someone of his stature can't take too many precautions. By being proactive, he ensures any sustained injury or illness he encounters can be corrected efficiently and effectively."

"Is this all for him—or for science?"

Lyle turned and glared at Edvin. "What are you implying?"

"Nothing. I was just asking—"

"Look." Dr. Lyle stood in a defensive stance, fists clenched. "This is my life's work. Yes, Dr. Hatim sped things up and insisted I prioritize his requests, but this is work that will benefit all of mankind. So don't think I only do things for Dr. Hatim."

Edvin swallowed hard. He didn't want to start things off badly. "Dr. Lyle, I'm sorry. I didn't mean for my statement to come across that way. Please accept my apology."

Lyle slowly loosened her fists. "Sorry. I guess I'm a little defensive. Having a tier all to myself gets my peers suspicious—and rumors flying." She smiled weakly. "Maybe we can start again. Let's start by you calling me Margaret."

Edvin gave a reassuring smile. "Absolutely, Margaret. I'll come back another time, and we can talk in more depth."

Margaret nodded. "Thank you."

Edvin let himself out, closed the door, leaned against it, and let out a deep sigh. This job could prove harder than he thought. He decided he had had enough for the day and walked to Hatim's elevator, which was able to stop on any floor. He used his access key and the elevator doors opened. He punched in the eighth tier. The panel requested his fingerprint. He placed his thumb on the pad and the eighth tier button lit. The elevator ascended . . .

Once back in the penthouse, Edvin took a seat on the sofa against the wall window and looked across the valley. It was a magnificent view. It still impressed him this city had grown so fast—and was still growing. He could see construction in many places. Beyond that, desert.

He turned back to the tablet and looked more at Dr. Lyle's work. He found a file that showed all the contributors to Hatim's collected biopsies. It looked like a list from biology class. There were organs and tissues he had never heard of before. How did he get so many people to donate so willingly? When he looked at the list of donors, he couldn't help but grow wide-eyed. These were the most influential and good-looking people from around the world. He thought back to the limo ride with Gwen Sheridan and Ken Colston. They donated without any question. He knew Hatim was extremely charismatic, but to charm people to do *this* was truly amazing. Edvin had to question himself. Was he being manipulated, or was he in full control of his actions? He *felt* in control, but still . . .

His phone beeped and he jumped. He took a deep breath and tried to calm his heart rate. *Get a grip, Edvin.* It was Elsbeth. His heart rate quickened again, but this time for the right reason. He was also glad he had installed encryption software.

"Elsbeth, hi. I'm glad you called."

Elsbeth's voice was calm, soothing to his ears. "Hi, Edvin. It's really great to hear your voice. How's everything?"

"OK. Missing you, though."

"Same here. I have very interesting news."

"Oh?"

"Dr. Hatim was at the temple today confronting the Witnesses."

"Really?" Edvin could feel his adrenaline surging. "What happened?"

"Well, it was quite the show. Somehow, he's always able to be out of the press's limelight at the appropriate time. Anyway, he brought several soldiers with him. He ordered the Witnesses off the property." Elsbeth laughed. "Can you believe that?"

"So, what did the Witnesses say?"

"They basically ignored him. One of the Witnesses said something like, 'To show you the Lord is displeased with you, there will be no rain until one-third of the earth's vegetation has been destroyed by fire.'"

"What? That's actually kind of scary. What did the President say?"

"Well, before he could say anything, the other Witness said much of the earth's water supply would become like blood."

"Like blood? Are you sure that's what he said?"

"Yes, Edvin. I'm sure. At that point, the President lost it. He turned completely red. I never thought he could lose his composure like that. He ordered his guards to seize the two, but they remained frozen where they were.

"One of the Witnesses said, 'The Lord's sword of judgment will cut deep until final decisions are made. Rash decisions will hurt the earth you hope to protect.'

"The President ordered the guards to shoot the Witnesses, but they couldn't raise their arms! Hatim grabbed one of the rifles and pointed it at one of the Witnesses. The end of the gun began to glow red, like it was getting really hot, and the President flung it to the ground. He shook his fist at them and said they wouldn't get away with this. One of the Witnesses said, 'What God has decreed could never be revoked.' The President glared at them and stormed off."

Edvin took a breath. "I'm more concerned about what the Witnesses said than the President's reaction. Do you think what they said will actually occur?"

"I do. And I would like to talk with you about that. Will you be coming back here anytime soon?"

"I don't know. There's lots here I need to get my head wrapped around. Once I do, I hope to convince the President I should work from Israel and come here periodically to check on things. I may not get there for a couple of months, however."

"Oh." Elsbeth sounded disappointed. "Well, be sure you get here for Hanukkah. There will be a big celebration when the temple is dedicated."

"That may be just the event to get the President to allow me to head there."

"Did you ever find Lars?"

Edvin felt his throat tighten. He found it difficult to say anything.

"Edvin? Are you there?"

"Yes, I'm here. He . . . " Edvin swallowed and took a deep breath while trying to keep his voice from cracking. "He's no longer himself, I'm afraid. There was nothing I could do for him."

"Oh, Edvin. I'm so sorry. I wish I could be with you."

"So do I, but please promise me you'll not leave Israel. I can't bear to have something happen to you too."

Elsbeth's voice got quiet. "I promise, Edvin."

"I'm not sure why the President is going against his treaty with Prime Minister Afrom to protect the Jews."

"He isn't."

Edvin's head jerked back. "What do you mean?"

"Mik'kel went back and looked at the wording of his speech. He said he would protect the citizens of Israel—meaning those who are living in Israel. We think he's taking this literally—so persecution of Jews, and apparently anyone of Israeli descent, outside Israel, is not breaking the treaty."

"Well, that's, that's . . . "

"Deceitful. Yes. Mik'kel said the Prime Minister was meeting with the President today and would confront him on this topic. But we think we already know the answer."

Edvin's phone beeped. "Elsbeth, sorry. But I'm getting another call. I'll talk with you soon."

"OK. I'll miss you."

Edvin pressed the bar at the top of his phone. "Hi, Donna. Is something wrong?"

"Yeah, something's wrong if you call me Donna again."

"Uh, I, uh . . . " Edvin looked at his phone. The call said it was Donna, the receptionist. There was something extremely familiar about the voice, though. "Amari? Is that you?"

There was laughter on the other end. "Gotcha."

"Very funny. What's up?"

"It's been weeks, and Ranata and I still haven't had a chance to get together with you. What about tonight?"

"What do you have planned?"

"Nothing yet."

"Let me talk to Donna."

Edvin heard the phone changing hands. "Yes, Captain Isakson."

"Could you have dinner for three brought up here tonight?"

"Sure. But you'll have to come down and take them up."

"OK, tell them I'll be down in a few minutes."

The night was like old times, except with upscale accommodations: wine instead of beer and turkey sandwiches with cranberry aioli rather than pretzels. After many shared stories and much laughter, Edvin turned more somber.

"What do you guys think about all that's going on?" He looked from one to another.

Saeed smirked. "You mean why you get the penthouse and we're in some hotel in the city?"

Edvin chuckled. "No. Come on. You know what I mean."

"I know what you mean, Edvin," Ranata said. "Still, you have to admit we have probably the best jobs of anyone at this time. Granted, Dr. Hatim can be a little eccentric, and he has some not-so-normal views, but he treats us well and we get to travel almost everywhere he does. It's really a dream job from my perspective."

"Yeah," Saeed said. "Plus, Dr. Hatim is having me become a pilot. Isn't that sweet?"

Edvin nodded. He knew it wasn't worth trying to explain what was bothering him. These two were certainly not seeing things from his perspective. It seemed useless to try and convince them otherwise.

"Besides," Ranata said, "your job has more perks than ours.

You can't say you don't like that, can you?"

Edvin chuckled lightly. "You guys are right. I'm sure there are many who would love to have my job."

Saeed elbowed Edvin. "Yeah, and you have two of them right here."

All three laughed. Edvin kept it light after that, and they had an enjoyable evening. They continued reminiscing until about two in the morning. Edvin talked them into staying for the night. They slept on sofas and wouldn't take an extra bedroom; they didn't want Edvin to try and justify their stay without first getting the President's permission.

The next morning, Saeed and Ranata got ready for the day in Edvin's apartment. He offered to have breakfast brought up, but they declined and headed for the first-tier cafeteria to start their day. Edvin planned to stay in the penthouse and go over all the projects on his tablet to try to understand them better. He prepared a bagel and tea and settled on the sofa so he could enjoy the view while he got down to work.

He was quite absorbed in the information when his phone beeped. Irritated, he rolled his eyes, set down the tablet, and picked up his phone. It was Hatim. His pulse quickened as he read the text.

Arriving by ten; prepare for my arrival.

CHAPTER 17

Edvin wasn't sure what to expect or what type of mood Hatim would be in. From the moment he received the text, he tried to focus on his work, but the closer to ten it got, the more anxious he became. He turned his attention to the elevator as it rang its arrival on the top floor. The doors opened and out stepped Hatim, Anna, Cortez, Masaki, and Chong. Edvin rose to greet them.

"President Hatim, welcome back." They shook hands and Edvin greeted his three fellow soldiers, whom he had not seen in some time. They exchanged pleasantries and briefly caught up.

After a couple of minutes, Hatim broke in. "I know everyone needs some rest, so why don't you all go and get some while I talk to Edvin?"

Masaki and Chong returned to the elevator, likely heading to their hotel. Anna and Cortez entered Hatim's bedroom. Again, this seemed strange to Edvin, but he didn't want to think about it. It wasn't his place to judge.

Hatim didn't sit, so Edvin remained standing as well. Hatim walked to the large window and looked out. "So, Edvin, how are things going here?" He turned briefly and looked at Edvin, then turned back to the view.

Edvin walked next to Hatim. "Well, sir, it's quite mind-blowing here. All projects seem to be going well. I have to say, I don't understand all of them, so I hope I can meet your expectations."

Edvin could see Hatim smile through the reflection in the glass. "I'm sure you will do just fine. I'm not trying to convert you into a scientist." Hatim turned to Edvin. "I need someone to help assure everyone is doing what they've been charged to do. Keep track of progress, what they are ordering, and if they are staying within their designed experimental and financial parameters. And if you see anything out of the ordinary, let me know."

"Absolutely, sir. Do you want me to stay in Babylon to monitor things here?" Edvin first wanted to see what Hatim's plans were for him. Then he would determine how to best persuade Hatim to let him monitor from Israel.

Hatim seemed to both ignore his question and look through him. "I came here from Israel."

Edvin wasn't sure where he was going with this statement. "Yes, sir. I saw on the news you were there."

Hatim's attention went directly to Edvin. "What did the news say?"

"Not much. It mentioned you visited the new temple building and were ensuring the treaty was working well."

Hatim smiled. "Anna does an excellent job in getting the right message to the news. And . . . " he paused. "I had an encounter with the Witnesses at the temple." He seemed irritated and paced the length of the window. "What kind of a name is that anyway? 'Witnesses.' They are arrogant nitwits."

"What happened, sir?" Edvin wasn't going to say anything about what he had heard from Elsbeth.

"I need someone to keep an eye on those two." Hatim continued pacing, now mumbling to himself.

Edvin wondered if this was the right time to suggest he could do that task.

Hatim stopped and looked at Edvin. "I want you to go to Israel and keep an eye on them."

Edvin was so stunned that he gasped.

"I know, I know." Hatim held up his hands as if Edvin was about to object. "I ask a lot of you, but I need someone there I can trust. Everyone there mistrusts me, and it seems you're the only one on my staff the Prime Minister even likes. It should be easy to keep track of projects here via your tablet. Feel free to travel back and forth as you see fit. You can use that Israeli captain—Mik'kel, is it? . . . " Edvin nodded. " . . . to help you gain insights into what's going on there politically. And I need to know what these two Witnesses say so I can counterattack as needed."

"Mr. President, I would be honored to serve you there. I know you have important work to do elsewhere, so I could really help be your eyes and ears there."

Hatim paused. Edvin found the pregnant pause unnerving. "Anything wrong, sir?"

Hatim's eyes met Edvin's, locking directly. "Dr. Bonn brought something to my attention."

"Sir?"

"He reported you were seen with the high priest's daughter in a restaurant."

Edvin cringed on the inside as he tried to maintain a calm demeanor. He knew his heart rate had skyrocketed. "Well, sir, I have to be friendly with influential people there in order to be effective. They have to like me to be open to me."

Hatim looked at Edvin for a few moments without expression. This made Edvin nervous; obviously, he wondered if Hatim suspected something. He smiled and patted Edvin on his shoulder. "Just as I told Dr. Bonn. You're quite the servant,

Edvin. I expect updates regularly."

"Yes, sir. Absolutely." Edvin felt his heart rate calm. "When did you want me to go?"

"When do you think you'll be done here?"

"Well, I was assessing that this morning before you arrived. I think I need to be here a couple of months to be sure I know all the projects well. I heard on the news the temple is to be dedicated on the Jewish holiday Hanukkah. I could go right before that time since that may be a time of gaining good intel." In addition to his explanation, Edvin hoped his plan of waiting two months would hide his eagerness to get there to see Elsbeth.

Hatim nodded. "Perfect. I'll leave all that to you. There are other things on which I need to focus."

"Very good, sir."

"I think I'll get some rest myself."

Edvin nodded as Hatim headed toward his bedroom. Hatim turned, smiled, and entered.

Edvin sat on the sofa next to the window and let out a long breath. He looked at the scene below but didn't focus on anything in particular. He couldn't believe this. He wondered, since talking with Elsbeth, how he would get to Israel. Now, in two months, he would be there and, more importantly, be with Elsbeth. Edvin surprised himself at how much his heart ached for her. *You got it bad, Edvin. Really bad.* He smiled to himself. That was fine by him.

The next couple of months went by quickly. Edvin went over all the projects until he knew the basics of each and what each should deliver. He put off meeting with Conrad Bonn until he knew he could no longer do so. He had Donna make an appointment in Bonn's office. He didn't want to see that lab again. If he met Lars again, he knew he would lose it. While he felt terrible about Lars's situation, he knew all Lars had done for him would be a waste if he tried to help him further. In truth, he had no idea how to help his brother at this point.

Edvin entered Conrad's large window-bordered office on tier four. Conrad's appearance matched Edvin's mental picture almost perfectly: beady eyes, sallow complexion, tall, lanky. He shook Edvin's hand and motioned for him to sit. Edvin was uncomfortable as he sat across from Bonn.

"I'm glad to finally meet you, Captain. I'm not sure how our paths haven't yet crossed."

"Well, it's a big complex, and there are lots of projects." Edvin hoped that sounded convincing. "So, how's your research progressing?"

"I think it's going well. Quite well, actually." Conrad put his chin between finger and thumb and propped that arm on top of his other crossed arm. "As you can imagine, this is a very complicated science, and any progress at all is significant. Our latest advancement I actually owe to you."

Edvin was stunned. "How's that?"

Conrad leaned forward. "Well, when you put on the helmet many weeks ago, Sean was able to determine the frequency to which the subject responded. I was sorry you left by the time we arrived back in the lab."

"Sorry about that." Edvin tried to keep his breathing natural and not give anything away. "I had to keep to a tight schedule that day."

"Yes . . . of course." Conrad set back in his chair.

Edvin felt like Conrad was staring right through him. He diverted his gaze.

"Anyway, we've made a few other breakthroughs. We haven't heard thoughts but have found other frequencies where the subject responds in some form or fashion."

"So, why do you need human subjects, and how are you

using them?"

"You're probably thinking of Dr. Rosenberg's work in animals. I do confer with her often, but we feel using human subjects gives us a faster turnaround on results. Results in animals may or may not translate to humans. Since our subjects are deemed noncitizens by the President, we're still within our ethical guidelines to use them." Conrad had a smug, twisted smile.

"I see." Edvin rose and tried to maintain his composure. He wanted his time in this office as short as possible. "Please keep your updates posted, and I look forward to seeing your progress."

"Uh, there is another matter I wanted to discuss with you." He waved his hand. "A misunderstanding, surely."

"Oh?" Edvin sat again, eyebrows raised.

"Yes, the last group of research subjects had apparently been redirected to Israel rather than here. It was a good thing I called the precinct when I did."

Edvin shifted in his seat. How was he going to get around this? "Oh, were these subjects from Stockholm?"

Conrad nodded, giving a look as if demanding Edvin to explain himself. "I thought the precinct was made clear the nature of these subjects."

Edvin gave a half laugh. "Oh, I guess this was my fault. I visited that precinct when I went home, visiting previous coworkers, and was told most of them were of Israeli descent. I knew Prime Minister Afrom was accepting such people, and since I saw there was no destination . . . " He shrugged. "I assumed I was doing someone a favor and speeding up the process. My apologies if I made things difficult for you. That was before I knew the work you did here." He smiled and tried to make it genuine.

Bonn gave a forced smile. "Oh, no. It all worked out in the

end. Like I said, a misunderstanding."

Edvin nodded and rose. "I'll leave all that to you next time." He returned a forced smile. "If nothing else, I must get going."

"Of course. Please stop by as often as you like."

"Thank you. I'll try," Edvin lied. "I may be traveling a lot, but I will certainly keep up on your progress. Thanks for your time."

Edvin let himself out and headed to the elevator as quickly as possible. He let out a long breath and glanced back, hoping Conrad wouldn't continue to remain suspicious. He likely had some relationship mending to do even if he didn't really want to do it. While transferring one's memory was likely an admirable goal, Edvin couldn't justify the methodology Conrad was using.

* * * * *

A week before Edvin left for Israel, Hatim asked him to attend a meeting with Reverend Duarté, whose arrival would happen before Edvin's departure. Edvin knew Duarté's title had been changed from Bishop to Reverend to relate to more types of religions. Duarté conducted many religious meetings around the world, but Edvin had no idea what this meeting would be about.

While visiting with Dr. Lyle, Edvin's phone beeped to let him know Hatim wanted him to come to tier seven. He had not yet visited that tier. When he arrived, Hatim and another individual were sitting at a long table. Edvin assumed this was Duarté. A massive print of a night aerial view of Babylon hung on the wall opposite the outside window. Edvin thought it impressive—and beautiful—with the ziggurat in the middle and the floodlight shining into the heavens.

"Captain Isakson, please come in. I would like you to meet

Reverend Duarté." Edvin stepped forward and shook Duarté's hand.

"I've heard a lot about you, Reverend."

"But you've never been to one of my services, though, have you?"

Edvin shook his head and felt heat rise in his face.

Duarté chuckled. "Oh, no need to be embarrassed. I know you're a busy man."

Edvin wanted to change the subject. "Who else are we waiting for?"

"No one. Take a seat, Captain." Hatim motioned for both men to sit.

Edvin's eyes widened slightly. He assumed he would be listening in on a conversation but not be a participant in any such conversation. He took a seat and looked expectantly toward Hatim.

"So, before we get started, Reverend, why don't you tell us where things are spiritually with the citizens of our world."

Duarté smiled. "Gladly. I feel most people have embraced our one-world religion. My message is one of peace, harmony, getting along, and taking care of our planet. This seems to fit in quite easily with the background of most peoples' religion, and it helps them transition and feel at one with people of all backgrounds."

"Well, 'all' may be too big of a generalization," Hatim said.

Duarté gave an inquisitive look. Realization came across his face. "Oh, you mean the Jews. Yes, it's a struggle to find how to fit them in."

Hatim nodded. "Captain Isakson, this is why I wanted you here. Reverend, the Captain here will be my eyes and ears within Israel. He's been able to make friends there, and even Prime Minister Afrom will give him audience."

Duarté's eyebrows shot up. "That's impressive, Captain.

Maybe you need to teach us some of your diplomacy skills."

Edvin laughed. "I find it hard to believe I can teach you anything. Uniting the world has certainly taken more skill than I could ever possess."

Duarté looked back at Hatim with a surprised expression. "I see now why you have him as a leader in your organization. I think he has taught us something already."

Hatim laughed and nodded. Edvin felt his cheeks begin to flush again.

"Seriously, though, Captain," Hatim continued, "you head-quartering in Israel is very important. Not only can you let me know what's going on, you can help us see if there's a way to integrate the Jews into our new world. I have given King Nazari permission to have Arabs around the temple area in their—what do they call it?—oh yes, Court of Gentiles. This should help the Prime Minister understand he's not in total control and still answers to me. Personally, I don't see how to integrate them. Yet, since this treaty was forced upon us, I'm willing to have an open mind—for a time. I really can't wait seven years to achieve this from them. We have to find a way—soon—to incorporate them, or . . . or else."

"Or else?" Edvin thought he understood Hatim's meaning, but he wanted to see if the President would actually say it.

Duarté interjected. "I think I have a plan for this. A test if you will. Over the next few years, I'll get the citizens of the world to look toward you, Mr. President, as the one to whom they owe their adoration. After all"—Duarté gave a big smile—"you're the one who created our one-world culture." He turned to Edvin. "We can give the Israelis this same time period to come on board. A final test will decide their fate. If they agree to honor the President as the rest of the world does, we'll incorporate them. If not . . . well, we'll do as we must." Duarté held up his palms. "Rest assured, I'm opposed to violence. But there are times when it's in the best interest of all."

"Does that answer your question, Captain?" Hatim asked.

Edvin nodded. Yes, it answered the question—and more. He knew, as they did, the likelihood of Israel joining such a change in focus of worship was extremely remote. Maybe there was something he could do, Edvin thought. Maybe Mik'kel or Elsbeth would know how to change the direction of their people.

"Great. I had some refreshments brought up. Why don't we get some now and, Reverend, you can fill me in on some of your ideas as to how to get the world to alter its focus."

As they got up for finger sandwiches and other hors d'oeuvres, Duarté explained his plans. "While there's nothing complicated about my ideas," he said, "I do think they'll be effective."

He went on for several minutes explaining in detail how he planned to execute his proposal. Hatim seemed interested and kept nodding, giving his approval. Edvin only heard bits and pieces of Duarté's proposal; his mind kept thinking about getting back to Israel, to Elsbeth, as his trip was only a few days away. His attention snapped back when Duarté made a certain statement.

" . . . and I think I'll start this direction with Gwen's concert in a couple of weeks here in Babylon. What better place, or better time, to start?"

The concert. Edvin remembered the tickets Gwen had given him. He felt a little guilty he would again miss her concert, but that paled in his mind compared to seeing Elsbeth again. He decided he would give his two tickets to Saeed and Ranata.

After a while, Duarté left, and Hatim went to his penthouse. Edvin went to find Saeed and Ranata to give them his tickets and say his goodbyes. As he looked for them, Edvin thought of what living in Israel would mean for him. He appreciated his position, and he liked Hatim. But the President's hatred of Jews and his approval of the work Conrad was doing were both hard to accept. Edvin also felt trapped; he couldn't express his real thoughts since that would yield his true position—maybe even end his life—and make Lars's work meaningless.

For now, he just wanted to get to Israel, to Elsbeth. He would worry about the rest later.

CHAPTER 18

Edvin deplaned. He stood there a few moments looking around. He closed his eyes and gave a satisfying sigh. He was finally here. The limo pulled up and he told the driver where to take him. He was to meet Elsbeth at Mik'kel's apartment.

When he arrived, a note on the door said that he should go to the corner apartment on the same floor. He did so and knocked.

Elsbeth opened the door and greeted him with a huge, bright smile. "Surprise!" She gave him a big hug and he returned it eagerly. He gave her a prolonged kiss and, to his delight, she kissed back. He was glad to know she had missed him as much as he had missed her.

Mik'kel stepped forward and they shook hands.

"So, why are we here and not in your apartment, Mik'kel?"

"Because this is *your* apartment. This is your new home," Elsbeth said, displaying a big grin. "What do you think?"

It took a minute for this to register. "What . . . I mean how, who . . . uh, why . . . " The right words wouldn't come.

Elsbeth laughed.

"I think you're only missing 'where,'" Mik'kel said with a chuckle.

"Did you guys do this for me?"

"Uh-huh," Elsbeth replied. "It was actually Mik'kel's idea."

"Well, I was told to get you on my good side and pump you for information, so what better way than to have you in the same building?" Mik'kel cracked.

"Works for me." Edvin laughed. "And I'm supposed to keep an eye on you by getting you to like me."

"Oh, so you're to do whatever I want?"

"Uh, no," Edvin replied. "I can bring it down to 'tolerate you,' if that helps."

Mik'kel laughed. "We'll start with 'like' and see where it goes from there." He put his hands together. "OK. Since you have no furniture, let's go to my place. Elsbeth prepared something for us to eat."

As they headed down the hall, Elsbeth spoke up. "I'll be right back. I need to get the dessert."

"Where do you live? Do you need any help?" Edvin asked.

"No. It's just upstairs. I'll be right back."

"You live here, too?" Edvin looked from Elsbeth to Mik'kel and back.

Elsbeth nodded. The realization of Elsbeth being so close left Edvin feeling a rush of excitement. Elsbeth gave him a quick kiss and rushed up the stairs at the end of the hallway.

As they entered Mik'kel's apartment, he pointed to the table. "Help yourself, Edvin. There's humus, cheese, crackers, fruit."

Edvin prepared a plate and sat down just as Elsbeth entered. "Is that cheesecake?" he said, looking up. Elsbeth nodded. "How on earth did you know I like cheesecake?"

Elsbeth set the cake down and turned to Edvin with a grin. "I have my sources. A woman can't reveal her secrets."

Mik'kel laughed. "She had no idea."

"Hey." Elsbeth slapped Mik'kel on the back of his head. "Anyway, who doesn't like cheesecake?"

Edvin laughed. "She's a smart woman, Mik'kel."

Elsbeth smiled at Edvin, prepared a plate, and sat next to him. The three of them talked for several hours. Edvin was so glad to be with Elsbeth again. Before he knew it, the sun was nearly setting.

"The temple dedication will start after the evening sacrifice," Elsbeth said. "If we're going to go, we better get started. I'm sure the place will be mobbed."

Edvin turned to Mik'kel. "Coming with us, or do you have duties?"

Mik'kel shook his head. "My job tonight is to stay close to Hatim's envoy to Israel."

Edvin laughed.

Elsbeth smiled and took each of their arms. "Good. I always wanted two escorts."

Edvin wasn't sure what to expect, but he found the temple's beauty spectacular. The temple walls were overlaid with white plaster, and with the floodlights shining on them, they nearly glowed. The column capitals in front of the temple and along the roof's edges were of gold overlay, which also glowed brilliantly. It almost took his breath away.

The excitement among the crowd was palpable since everyone could see the priests preparing for the evening sacrifice. As Edvin looked around, he also noticed many Arabs in the outside courtyard. This seemed to go unnoticed by the crowd, however. As long as they stayed in the outer court, they should not pose a problem, Edvin reasoned.

As the priests began the evening sacrifice, the excitement in the crowd grew. Many observed from large stadium seating erected for this special event. Elsbeth dragged Edvin and Mik'kel to some seats atop the bleachers for a good seat. Once there, Edvin could see, even with the seating filling to capacity, that there was still a large crowd standing.

A priest blew the shofar. The crowd erupted with applause and whistles. The Prime Minister went to the podium and waited for the crowd to calm, which took several minutes.

"My fellow countrymen and friends, this is truly a momentous day. Our new year, or Rosh Hashanah, started with a treaty to let us begin our temple." A deafening roar went up and was accompanied by clapping, whistling, and those in the stadium seating stomping their feet. The Prime Minister again waited for the crowd to quiet. "Today, only a little more than three months later, we dedicate this temple to our Creator and God on this day of Hanukkah. Just as Judas Maccabeus consecrated the temple after much adversity, we, today, once again consecrate this temple out of centuries of adversity." Another deafening roar went up from the crowd.

The priests went about the cleansing process for the temple and its various pieces of furniture used in temple worship.

The Prime Minister held up his hands to quiet the crowd once more. "We are pleased to present to you our new high priest going forward from this day. I present to you: Avraham Cohen."

The crowd again applauded.

Edvin looked at Elsbeth. "Why didn't you tell me your father was the high priest?"

"I . . . didn't know until now. I knew he was under consideration, but not that he was the one chosen."

Edvin saw her eyes water and a few tears form. Edvin reached over, wiped away the tears, and gave her a hug.

"I'm very happy for you, Elsbeth."

She smiled. "Thanks."

Edvin kept his arm around her.

High Priest Cohen adjusted the microphone at the podium. "My dear Israelis, many of you were born here, others are visiting, while others were forced here because of persecution. No matter how you arrived, you are welcome here." Another huge round of applause erupted. Once it lowered, he continued. "We now have a temple to worship our God once again. Let's be sure we honor our God by acting in a manner which reflects his character. Let us welcome with open arms those who come to us to worship, whether they be Jew or Gentile. Our God is big enough for everyone." More thunderous applause. High Priest Cohen raised his hands and the crowd quieted. He kept his arms raised and prayed, "God, we thank you and praise you tonight. Just as Solomon prayed millennia ago, so I pray now in his words:

> *Will Elohim really dwell on earth with men? The heavens, even the highest heavens, cannot contain you. How much less this temple we have built. Yet give attention to your servant's prayer and his plea for mercy, O Yahweh Elohim. Hear the cry and the prayer that your servant is praying in your presence. May your eyes be open toward this temple day and night, this place of which you said you would put your Name. May you hear the prayer your servant prays toward this place. Hear the supplications of your servant and of your people Israel when they pray toward this place. Hear from heaven, your dwelling place; and when you hear, forgive."*

High Priest Cohen lowered his hands and stepped down. Prime Minister Afrom returned to the podium. "Please enjoy the rest of your evening. Shalom." He raised his hands over his head and waved. The crowd once again gave thunderous applause before beginning to disperse.

Music was soon heard, and people began dancing in the streets. Many were doing the Hora—or trying to. Others were doing more simple dancing movements. Elsbeth sat down and pulled on Edvin's arm to once again have a seat.

"Sitting here is just as good as sitting anywhere else," she said. "We have a splendid view of the temple and can hear the music. Let's enjoy the atmosphere."

She also pulled on Mik'kel's arm for him to sit. He did for a few minutes, then stood. "Two's company; three's a crowd. I'll meet you guys tomorrow." He punched Edvin playfully on the arm. "Remember, her father is the high priest. And I know where you live."

He looked so serious it took Edvin aback for a minute. Mik'kel laughed and patted Edvin on his shoulder. Mik'kel started down the bleachers, but then came back up. "Since you have no bed yet, stay at my place."

Edvin nodded. "Don't worry." The way Mik'kel used the word "stay," he knew what he was implying. He expected Elsbeth to sleep alone. Mik'kel nodded, descended the bleachers, and slipped into the crowd.

Edvin and Elsbeth sat there for several hours, talking, laughing, and just enjoying the overall atmosphere. He tried to not get too intimate so he could maintain his ruse of obtaining intel from Elsbeth. But it was difficult to do sitting this close to her. Yet, Edvin felt couldn't have asked for a better homecoming. They sat there until the cleanup crew told them they had to start tearing down the seating.

Edvin and Elsbeth went to a nearby restaurant with bistro seating and continued their conversation over tea and rugelach. Before they knew it, the waiter came by and said the restaurant was closing.

"I thought you said you were open late tonight," Edvin said.

The waiter nodded. "We normally close at 11. It's, uh, 2 a.m."

"Really?" Edvin glanced at his watch. "I guess time stands still when you're with a beautiful woman."

The waiter walked away and gave him two thumbs up.

Elsbeth noticed and laughed. "I guess someone liked your lame compliment."

"Lame?" Edvin put his hand over his heart. "You slay me."

Elsbeth giggled. "OK, let's go before your comments get unbearable."

They walked slowly back to the apartment complex. Edvin escorted Elsbeth to her door, then stood, gazing into her eyes. "Thanks for such a wonderful homecoming."

"I'm glad you think of it as a homecoming."

He leaned in to kiss her; Elsbeth reciprocated. He gave a long, passionate kiss. Her hug grew tighter the longer he prolonged it. As their lips separated, Edvin whispered, "You're making me fall for you, Ms. Elsbeth Cohen."

"I guess my magic spell is working," she whispered.

He laughed and put his forehead to hers. "Definitely."

Elsbeth opened the door and looked back. She quickly gave him another kiss, entered her apartment, and closed the door. Edvin lingered, not wanting the moment to end. Finally, he headed to Mik'kel's apartment. He looked at his watch: 3 a.m. He didn't know what time warp he had entered; it felt like they had left for the temple only a few hours earlier. He found some blankets on the sofa, undressed, and pulled the blankets over him. He knew he would have pleasant dreams tonight.

Edvin woke slowly. The sun shone on his face. He turned over and found the focus to look at his watch: 9 a.m. He sat up. The room was empty. He noticed a note on the end table next to the sofa: "Edvin, call me when you are up. Mik'kel." Edvin headed for the shower. He would call after he was fully awake.

After a short shower, he called. "Mik'kel, what's with the mystery note this morning?"

Mik'kel laughed. "No mystery. I didn't want to wake you. Can you come to the temple?"

"Sure." Edvin paused. "But why?"

"I want you to meet someone."

As Edvin walked up the temple steps, he saw both Mik'kel and Elsbeth talking with someone.

"Edvin." Elsbeth flashed a bright smile, met him, and kissed him on his cheek. "Come meet a friend."

A handsome man with black hair and neatly trimmed facial hair stuck out his hand. "Hi, I'm Jeremiah Ranz."

Edvin returned the handshake. "Edvin Isakson."

Edvin looked at Elsbeth and then Mik'kel. "And I'm here . . . why?"

"Jeremiah is one of the prophets." Elsbeth was quite bubbly in her response.

Edvin didn't want to appear clueless—but knew he likely looked as clueless as he felt.

Elsbeth gave a slight nod. "You know, one of the one hundred and forty-four thousand prophets the Witness spoke of the last time you were here."

"Oh, right." Edvin still had no clue what this was about.

"Mik'kel and I have been talking with Jeremiah on and off since that day."

"So, Jeremiah, which tribe are you from?" Edvin asked.

"I'll give you a guess," Jeremiah said.

"I would say . . . Judah."

"You owe me twenty shekels, Mik'kel." Jeremiah held out his hand with a smile.

"I told you Edvin was pretty savvy," Elsbeth said, grabbing Edvin's arm and giving it a squeeze.

Edvin held up his hands. "OK, I give. What on earth is going on?"

"You lost me money," Mik'kel said. "You owe me dinner."

"What? I think *you* owe *me* dinner for not believing in me,"

Edvin said with a laugh.

Mik'kel laughed and patted him on his shoulder. "I'll buy you a falafel."

"Deal. So, why am I here?"

"Jeremiah has been telling us about what's happening today, and what will happen over the next few years," Elsbeth said.

"What are you talking about, Elsbeth?" Edvin felt as though he had entered a twilight zone of sorts. He could not make sense of anything being said.

"Edvin, you do know what I'm a prophet of, right?" Jeremiah said.

"Scripture. But, Jeremiah, that doesn't really apply to me."

"Edvin, Scripture applies to everyone."

"But isn't prophecy just mumbo jumbo words that can be interpreted anyway someone wants?"

"Edvin," Elsbeth said in a quiet tone, "everything that has happened since, and including, the disappearances are stated in Scripture. And there's a lot more to happen. I think you need to hear this."

"Elsbeth, I've never been one to believe in all that stuff."

"Neither was I, but this . . . this is too real to ignore," she said. "All we ask is that you listen."

Edvin rolled his eyes. He couldn't believe he was listening to this. He shrugged. "OK. What've you got, Jeremiah?"

"Edvin, tell me what has happened since the disappearances."

Edvin rolled his eyes, but this time only slightly. "Well, let me see. Dr. De Voss got me to try out for the World Forces, I was selected for President Hatim's detail, he brought the world out of chaos and formed ten world territories with the help of the UN and the European Union's backing, I was sent to Israel when it was invaded by three of those territories, Hatim made a treaty with Israel—but is persecuting your countrymen everywhere else around the world—you have your temple back, and Hatim moved his headquarters to Babylon. And now I'm here talking to a prophet who says he is one of one hundred and forty-four thousand prophets. And, oh yes, there are two Witnesses at the temple who apparently can stop rain and cast fire. How's that?"

"All that is found in Scripture," Jeremiah said.

"What? What are you talking about? There's no way all that is in there. That's impossible."

"And if I show you it's there? What then?"

"If it's all there, I'll give you my falafel."

Jeremiah laughed. "Well, prepare to go hungry."

Over the next hour, Jeremiah went through various Scriptures showing Edvin where all the various events had been prophesied. Edvin found the material overwhelming. Jeremiah showed him other things prophesied that were to happen soon. Edvin was speechless.

Elsbeth touched his arm. "So, what do you think?"

"It's . . . it's a little overwhelming. Not all the passages are exact, but the events are so close to what has happened that it's hard to deny they're what these Scripture passages are referring to."

"But that's not the most important part, Edvin," Jeremiah interjected.

"What do you mean? What's more important?"

"*You* are."

Edvin looked at Jeremiah as though he had three heads. Jeremiah laughed. "Sorry, Edvin. I do understand your expression. We've all been there." Elsbeth and Mik'kel each nodded. "Yahweh is the one who predicted all this, and he is the designer and orchestrator of all that has happened and is going to happen. You missed his first Receiving. He's coming back. Don't miss the second. When you have time, I can show you how wonderful things will be then. But right now, the question is: do you put your faith in him?"

"But even your own people don't believe in him," Edvin argued, though it wasn't convincing—even to him.

"Yes, but that's changing. God's getting their attention again. He's driving them back to their homeland. Even those who don't know they're connected to Israel are becoming aware and being driven back. God has brought the two Witnesses to proclaim his Word and has assembled one hundred and forty-four thousand prophets to preach his truth about the Messiah.

"Edvin, the Messiah came a long time ago. He died a painful death as the sacrifice Scripture predicted. He did this so he could be the ultimate sacrifice for all our sins. He then overcame death and was resurrected. We won't go and be with him on our own merit—only on his. Faith in him, and what he did, is the only way to be one of his upon his return."

"I . . . I need a minute to process this."

"Edvin . . . "

Edvin held up his hands. "Elsbeth, please. Let me think a minute."

All three of them stood back and talked quietly while Edvin thought. His heart started to beat rapidly, and his palms became sweaty. He tried rubbing them on his pants, but the sweat kept coming. Feeling hot and flushed, he kept tugging on his shirt collar. He knew all Jeremiah said made sense, but it was also overwhelming. He never gave any of this a single thought before as he considered Scripture something the mentally weak and feeble used as a crutch to help them through rough times—something to provide a little hope and a good feeling for a time. But now he was living through something apparently predicted thousands of years before. These weren't vague words. They were specific ones, portraying what was now happening in the world. But if true, then the rest of Scripture, Edvin knew, also had to be true. And if all of it was true, then accepting the Messiah for who he claimed to be had to be the answer. It seemed insane—and yet logical.

"Jeremiah, can I talk with you?"

Jeremiah walked over. "Have you made a decision?"

"I believe what you're saying. But does that mean I have to stop doing what I'm doing? For some reason, I can't give that up."

Jeremiah smiled. "Edvin, Yahweh is not worried about what you do, but who you are. It's a one-step-at-a-time deal. I don't know what he has planned for you, but he does have something planned. You need the Holy Spirit, or Ruach HaKodesh, to guide you, but you only get him after you trust the Messiah for your future. The first step has to be faith. He'll give you a lot more after, but only after. Understanding comes later. Only believing comes now."

Edvin found it difficult to breathe. It felt like his heart would literally burst out of his chest. *Why this internal resistance?* He knew it was true—all true. He had to do this. He looked into Jeremiah's eyes. "Jeremiah, I'm ready. What do I do?"

"It's really simple, Edvin. Just talk to him."

"To who?"

"The Messiah, Edvin. The Messiah. You can't see him now, but he's listening. Talk to him like he's right here beside you."

Edvin gulped, smiled, then began. "Yahweh, Messiah . . . I now know there's nothing I can do to earn my way into your favor. Only your death and resurrection can do that. I trust in you and you only for my future and my future inheritance with you."

Edvin wondered if anything had happened. Nothing seemed different. Still, he felt an unseen burden lifted. His anxiety about the future was gone. Now he knew it didn't matter because his future was now secure. It wasn't up to him anymore. He had given up freedom—only to find it.

Jeremiah hugged Edvin. "You are my brother now, Edvin. Not because you're a Jew, but because you and I have the same inheritance with our Messiah."

Elsbeth and Mik'kel also came over and hugged him.

"I'm so excited," Elsbeth said. "Let's go celebrate."

Elsbeth locked arms with Edvin as they began to walk off. Edvin turned. "You're coming, too, right, Jeremiah?"

Jeremiah smiled. "Sure."

"I want to be part of your Scripture study," Edvin said. "Maybe you can tell me more over lunch."

"I'd be glad to."

As the four of them walked, Edvin suddenly felt a trembling through his body—but this feeling was different. He watched in small horror as some tiles fell off the roof of one of the nearby buildings.

Edvin stopped. "What was that?" All four looked at one another.

"Revelation six," Jeremiah said.

CHAPTER 19

By the time they arrived at a nearby restaurant, the earthquake was already on the news. Edvin asked the establishment owner to turn up the TV volume. This was no ordinary earthquake. It went around the world following the Ring of Fire and caused destruction in eastern Asia, the western coast of the Americas, and even Antarctica. It spawned other minor earthquakes in many places around the world. In addition, several volcanoes erupted, causing additional damage and casualties from fire. The earthquakes caused many houses and businesses to burn while the volcanoes started several forest fires. The eruption on Antarctica had many scientists speculating as to the overall effect on the ocean level and its salinity content.

The volcanoes threw ash into the atmosphere and, with no rain occurring, the ash remained aloft longer. That evening, as the sun set, it had a strong reddish tint, and the moon took on a crimson appearance as well.

* * * * *

As time passed, those areas without drought-resistant crops suffered the most, causing deaths in vegetation, followed by animals, and even many humans. This also led to increased disease as areas could not handle all the animal carcasses. Many World Forces were deployed in these areas to help bring relief efforts, but there were more needs than the manpower could assist.

Israel was the only place rain occurred!—though even it had less than normal. This allowed crops to be grown to sustain its ever-increasing population. Prime Minister Afrom was forced to restrict those who came into the country. With few exceptions, only those with Jewish or Israeli descent were allowed to enter—and only if they had sufficient paperwork.

Despite all the world's problems, the media seemed to unceasingly put a positive spin on the changes—and highlight how well Hatim "handled the world's issues." For most, despite the many deaths, the media coverage helped them maintain a positive outlook for the future.

Edvin's job was forced into a routine. In the morning, he reviewed all the ongoing projects at the Ziggurat of Knowledge, made any needed calls to verify and correct any concerns, and then headed out to meet with Jeremiah to review what Scripture predicted would occur next. Elsbeth and Mik'kel came when they could, but often Mik'kel's duties prevented him from joining, and much of Elsbeth's time was spent working at the Temple Plaza giving tours to those visiting. As often as she could, she scheduled her breaks to meet with Edvin and Jeremiah.

Jeremiah showed Edvin where meteors, some likely large, would fall to earth and create more havoc. Every morning as he checked on all the projects, Edvin made sure to look at the astronomy project to review that team's updates.

Conditions seemed to improve over the next several

months. World Forces made a strong dent into getting the diseases outbreak under control. Although some of the volcanoes remained active, they didn't cause much more trouble, except for periodic spews of ash into the atmosphere.

One morning, Edvin read a post from Dr. Lisa Jensen of the astronomy project: "Warning. Déjà vu: a repeat of asteroid 1998 QE2 fast approaching." Edvin had no idea what that meant, but knew it wasn't good. He quickly phoned Babylon.

"Hi, Donna. Captain Isakson. Please put me in contact with Dr. Jensen."

Edvin had to wait a few minutes, and he was impatient. Finally, she came on.

"Hi, Lisa, Captain Isakson. Can you please fill me in on your recent post?"

"Yes, sir. I don't know how we missed it. I was in contact with NASA this morning to see if they were aware. It seems no one saw its approach."

"Forgive my ignorance, but please give me more details. Is the earth in trouble?"

"Sir, back in 2013 there was a binary asteroid which passed close to the earth . . . well, within several million miles. It was about 3 kilometers across and accompanied by a satellite about 600 meters in diameter. This one is more than twice that size and . . . " Jensen paused.

"And what, Lisa?" He worked hard to hide what was a growing sense of panic.

"Sir, our calculations show it will pass between the earth and the moon."

"What does that mean for us?"

"Well, we're not sure. There will be a lot of gravitational stress, so it depends on how solid it is. It could pull apart, with some of it hitting the earth or the moon. Or it could all pass through without any effect at all."

"What can we do?"

"Do? I don't think there's anything we can do. We just found it, and it will be here by Saturday."

"You mean we only have three days to prepare?"

"Sir, I'm not sure you understand me. There's no way to *prepare*. We can only observe and hope for the best."

"So, your assessment is not to tell anyone?"

"I leave that to Dr. Hatim and you."

"OK. Thanks, Lisa. Please update your report continuously so I'll know what's going on."

"Yes, sir. I'll update it by the hour."

Edvin ended the call and ran his hand back and forth behind his neck. He gave a big sigh. What to do? He had to inform Dr. Hatim and see what the official stance should be. *More prophecy coming true before my eyes.*

Edvin made the phone call, but Anna answered. She said she would take care of how to distribute the news internationally. All Edvin could do now was what everyone else would do—watch and wait.

* * * * *

Edvin had Elsbeth, Mik'kel, and Jeremiah at his apartment that Friday night, and they stayed up through Saturday to see what would happen. Like the rest of the world, they remained glued to the television. Obviously, this was all the news being reported. At one point, the four of them focused closely on a new report.

"We are happy to have Dr. Lisa Jensen, a noted astronomer from Babylon, with us tonight. What can we expect tonight, Dr. Jensen?"

"Thank you, Bill. This diagram shows the asteroid will pass between the earth and moon around midnight GMT. It's expected to graze the edge of the upper atmosphere, so the glow should be detected visually. If it's going to break apart, this is the time it will do so . . . "

Elsbeth broke in as the reporting continued. "Edvin, we should go to the roof. We shouldn't be watching this on TV if we can actually see it." She looked at the time. "Midnight Greenwich Time is 2 a.m. here. That's only half an hour from now."

"You're right," Mik'kel said. "Let's go."

The four of them hurried up to the roof of the building for a better look. Edvin brought his tablet so they could follow the newscast at the same time.

A short time later, as they gazed into the sky, the approaching asteroid looked like a comet, only larger. For whatever reason, it had a reddish tinge. Edvin found it quite awe-inspiring.

" . . . If the asteroid stays intact over the next several minutes, it will mean we are out of danger," Jensen told the audience.

"That's not going to happen." All three turned toward Jeremiah. "You know at least part of it is going to fall to earth. The Scriptures don't lie."

As their gaze turned back to the asteroid, they saw a chunk of the big rock separate from the main piece. The smaller piece curved earthward and, as it entered the earth's atmosphere, it shattered into hundreds of pieces, like a fireworks display.

"It's beautiful," Elsbeth said.

"Yes, but deadly." As all three looked at Jeremiah again, he added, "I'm not sure exactly in what way, but I know it won't be good."

Edvin looked back at the sky and directed everyone's attention to the larger piece.

As they looked they heard the newscaster: "We just received word the chunk falling off the main asteroid caused it to become unstable and it slammed into its satellite, throwing both off course. Both are expected to fall under the moon's gravity and impact just behind the visible horizon."

As they continued to watch, there was a bright explosion as the asteroid hit. It appeared almost like a fireworks display, but without the same sound effects. The glow was bright and intense and left behind a slight afterglow on the moon's horizon, which slowly faded.

Mik'kel pointed. "Look at the debris field."

There was so much debris it caught and reflected the sunlight and formed a swirl up and away from the moon. This swirl slowly expanded.

"I know it's awful," Elsbeth said, "but it sure is beautiful. I wonder what all this will mean for the world."

"I don't know," Edvin said. "But we'll find out over the next few weeks."

All four sat on the roof with their backs next to the half wall, which ran around the roofline. They kept looking at the moon as Edvin followed the updates on the chunk that fell to earth.

Edvin raised his tablet to get everyone's attention. "Reports are starting to come in."

Mik'kel raised an eyebrow. "And?"

"It seems sizeable chunks hit Lake Superior and Lake Michigan in North America. One hit the edge of Lake Victoria in Africa, and small ones were scattered over northern Europe and Asia. It seems new forest fires have again started."

"So, all but one hit the northern hemisphere?" Elsbeth furrowed her brow. "How did that happen?"

"Well, that's all they were able to track," Edvin said. "It did split into hundreds of pieces. But this particular astronomer is saying another explosion occurred to one sizeable chunk as it hit the earth's atmosphere, causing part to travel to the south."

Elsbeth directed their attention back to the sky. "Look!

It seems the debris is wiping out the sight of the stars as it spreads across the sky. Only the brighter stars are still visible."

"That is what Scripture predicted," Jeremiah said. "A third of the stars and light would turn dark. Here we see the stars of less magnitude are no longer visible, and you're noticing the amount of sunlight reaching earth has decreased from all the ash in the air. Look at the moon. Even its light is less and has a strong reddish tint, just as Scripture said."

Edvin found it amazing he was living exactly what was predicted millennia ago. It was absolutely surreal. He looked at the time: 3:30 a.m. "Well, as much as we probably can't, we should try and get some rest before morning."

Elsbeth shook her head. "There's no way I can get any sleep tonight. I suggest we stay up and have a sunrise prayer vigil. We need to prepare ourselves spiritually for what's yet to come."

Jeremiah nodded. "I think that's a great plan."

"OK," Edvin said. "I'll go downstairs and get some pillows and blankets so we can stay here and continue to observe and talk."

As Edvin climbed the stairs, his phone beeped. It was a text from Hatim: *Meet here in Babylon a week from tonight.*

CHAPTER 20

Edvin sat in the Ziggurat of Knowledge penthouse once again while going over all project reports. He came early to be sure he understood them before the President arrived. Over the last few days, new reports from Dr. Apama Bhattacharya of the environmental project were coming in, and things were not looking good. Edvin glanced at his watch. Time to see what Hatim thought of all this.

Edvin descended one floor to the seventh tier. Everyone met in the large conference room there. As he entered, Conrad, Lisa, and Apama stood on the opposite side of the table talking. Just behind him came Ty.

"Ty, glad to see you. I wasn't expecting you."

"Hi, Captain. Yeah, I received the same text. It's good to see you again too."

Everyone took their seat, and shortly after Hatim entered. Everyone stood.

"Please, please, take your seats. We have a lot to discuss."

Anna and Cortez entered behind Hatim. Anna took a seat and Cortez stood at the door. Cortez smiled and nodded when he saw Edvin. Edvin returned the nod.

Hatim began. "It seems every time we get one crisis behind us, another rises up. First, I would like to thank Ms. Bonfield for her excellent work in keeping everything in a proper perspective for the people of the world. We can't let those around the world get too discouraged, and she has done a superb job in keeping spirits high."

Everyone applauded; Anna smiled.

"Now for the crisis before us. Dr. Bhattacharya, please provide us the latest update."

"Well, Mr. President, I'm afraid things aren't good. Dr. Moretti obtained a sample of the meteor from the North American impact site, and its composition contains an element we haven't yet been able to identify. When combined with oxygen, it has a reddish color, is water soluble, and is toxic to both humans and animals."

"Yes," Ty said, "we cautioned people not to drink the contaminated water, but because water is so scarce these days, people are desperate. We advised them to boil the water first, but we found this creates toxic steam. We've had thousands of deaths from people trying to purify the water before drinking it. Even normal filtration doesn't work. Only high-pressure filtration can remove the toxicity from the water. This is very expensive, and it's a slow process. We're setting up several water treatment plants, but that takes time—and people are continuing to die."

"But not everyone who drinks the water is affected," Hatim said. "Is that right, Dr. Moretti?"

"Yes, Mr. President, that seems to be correct, but it is not completely substantiated. We have rumors some drink the water unfiltered and are fine, but when questioned, these individuals deny the allegations."

"Have you forced them to drink the contaminated water?"

Ty's eyes grew wide. "No, Mr. President. What if the rumors are wrong?"

"Well, Dr. Moretti, desperate times call for desperate measures. If they are immune, we need to find out how and why. Time is of the essence."

Ty looked reluctant, but answered, "Yes, sir."

"I've heard these individuals have proclaimed allegiance to someone called Yahushua Ha-Mashiach ben Elohim, who they claim to be the Jewish Messiah," Hatim said. "Is this correct?"

Ty looked uncomfortable. "Those are the rumors."

"We can't let these people destroy the unity we have so carefully built. Dr. Bonn, I believe this is in alignment with your specialty. Have a group of these individuals gathered and brought to your lab for further investigation. We must get to the bottom of this."

Bonn nodded. A smile—which struck Edvin as pure evil—spread across his face.

Hatim looked at Cortez. "Lieutenant, please come to the table and present your idea. We must look to all fronts to protect our citizens."

Cortez sat down. He looked completely around the table and smiled. "Well, my idea is to limit those not loyal to the President."

The statement made Edvin wary. "And how do you plan to do that?" he quickly asked.

Cortez smiled. "I suggest we don't let anyone make any type of transaction without an implanted chip that can be scanned when they buy something, sell something, or attend any public gathering."

Edvin tried to keep his anxiety hidden. This would definitely be a game changer. He had no idea how he would be able to stay under the radar if this plan ever rolled out.

Bonn drummed his fingers. "How long would it take to get something like this up and running? We have a project similar to that already ongoing."

"It shouldn't take too long," Cortez replied. "I can work

with you on the details. It's just getting a device together and then deploying it to everyone. There's another upside to this. Once automated, we can keep track of what's purchased, by whom, and where. We can target the right goods and services for the right areas. This could help us to use our resources more wisely."

"Very impressive, Lieutenant. But I suggest we deploy this on a staggered basis," Ty suggested. "Although it sounds simple, we want to be sure there are no side effects before we deploy this to everyone."

"OK," Hatim said. "I want the three of you to turn this into a high-priority project."

"Great," Cortez said with a broad smile. "And I'm willing to be the first to try it."

"Thank you for your loyalty, Lieutenant." Hatim turned to Apama. "Anything else, Dr. Bhattacharya?"

"Yes, it seems this mysterious compound is taken up by plankton, making them red and causing them to bloom and remove oxygen from the water," she said. "Many fish have already died in the Great Lakes region, and the compound seems to be moving downstream and into the rivers. This is also happening in the Nile and other small streams in northern Europe and Asia where meteorites landed."

Edvin thought of some of the prophecies he had heard. "Are the oceans in any danger?"

"Currently, no. The lack of rain has increased the salinity level, and this seems to inhibit their growth. However . . . " She looked at Lisa.

Jensen picked up the narrative. "We have received word another asteroid is headed our way."

"What?" Hatim leaned forward in his seat. "When will it be here?"

"Within two and a half months. This one was behind the

sun and unnoticed when we focused on the previous one. This one may even be the parent of the former—it's five times larger than the previous one. We have more notice on this one, but I'm not sure that really helps us."

Conrad looked at Lisa. "And how close to earth will this one come?"

Lisa paused. And then a large sigh. "It's likely to be a direct hit."

Around the room, everyone gasped.

"A direct hit?" Hatim's gaze darted between Lisa and Apama. "Do we know where?"

Lisa looked extremely nervous bringing this news to the President.

"Don't worry, Dr. Jensen, we're not going to shoot the messenger." Hatim gave a small smile.

His words seemed to ease some of the tension. With a slight smile, she continued. "Thank you, sir. It's hard to predict, but we feel it will be somewhere in the arctic."

"Well, at least that's a nonpopulated area," Edvin said. "That should be a good thing, right?"

"Not necessarily." Apama tapped her pencil on the table. "It's possible this will melt a tremendous amount of polar ice. This, along with the active volcano in Antarctica, may melt enough ice to change the oceans' salinity level, which could be just enough to cause the plankton to bloom into the oceans. Also, though we're not sure, if this is the parent to the previous asteroid, it will bring more of this red element, which the plankton seem to love."

A sigh could be heard from Conrad. "So, how bad would it get?"

"I've brought a computer model," Ty said. "I had some of our modelers take the data Doctors Jensen and Bhattacharya provided to see the potential impact."

Ty pressed a button on the table console. The lights dimmed and a projection of North America displayed. “Based on Dr. Jensen’s projections, the likeliest place for the large asteroid to hit is slightly north of Greenland. This impact could melt as much as one-third of the polar ice. If we take the impact on sea level and salinity into account . . . ”

“Don’t forget the effect on Antarctica,” Apama said.

Edvin raised his eyebrows. “What do you mean?”

“The impact will probably cause many earthquakes to occur and volcanoes to erupt. Therefore, even more ice may melt in the southern polar region.”

“Yes,” Ty said, “if we take all this into account, consider how quickly the effect will spread down the Mississippi and Lawrence rivers, and assume the same amount of this unidentified element will be dispersed by the new impact, the plankton bloom will occur in a matter of days in the Gulf and eastern coastline. The model predicts the bloom will be so heavy and deep no ships will be able to travel through it.”

“Don’t forget,” Apama said, “the Gulf Stream, if not weakened, will carry it into northern Europe shortly thereafter. We’re talking about a global problem here. Not only a problem in North America.”

Hatim’s eyes widened. “Do we have any idea how long this will last?”

“It’s a good question without a conclusive answer,” Ty said. “We believe it will be at least several months. We can’t be sure when maritime traffic could resume. It’s likely some seaports will be less affected than others.” Ty shrugged. “It’s just hard to predict.”

“So, how do we counter this?” Hatim’s gaze scanned the room. “Any ideas?”

“We have to let these areas know we’re looking out for them,” Conrad said. “If nothing else, we should provide enough fuel so they can last through these months and not experience panic because of potentially low fuel reserves."

Edvin shook his head. "But if we send more tankers there now, they may get stuck, or if we get fuel to them too early, it may destabilize their economy."

"There's another alternative," Bonn said. "We can fly the fuel in just when needed, and this will then have a positive effect on the economy. It will demonstrate the President is looking out for the people, and it will carry them over until the crisis is resolved."

"Your plan makes a lot of sense, Dr. Bonn," Hatim said. "Dr. Bhattacharya, can you coordinate this?"

"Yes, sir. I have the appropriate contacts to make it happen."

"Since the Middle East is under my jurisdiction now, I don't foresee a problem in providing the resources," Hatim said.

Apama nodded. "Very good, sir."

"Does anyone have any other news to report?" Hatim looked around the table. No one stirred. "I take that to mean no one is aware of any other crises?"

Again, heads were still.

"OK, let's summarize. Ms. Bonfield, contact the American Territories and let them know our plan. They can help keep any panic at bay." Anna nodded. "Cortez, Dr. Bonn, and Dr. Moretti, I want the electronic implants to be ready within the month and deployed to the first ten thousand test subjects. Start in Europe and Asia. That will also test for any ethnic differences.

"If all seems OK, you may deploy worldwide. Ms. Bonfield, I want you to coordinate how these will be implanted and read by businesses. Then, Dr. Bonn and Dr. Bhattacharya, coordinate the fuel to the Americas and other places as needed. And Dr. Jensen, work with Ms. Bonfield as to how to communicate this next asteroid impact." He looked around the table. "Any questions?" His pause lasted only a second. "Oh, and I want each of you to keep your updates posted so Captain Isakson can monitor them. Captain, I want you to alert me if anything goes off target timelines."

"Yes, sir. I'll also be sure everyone provides timely updates."

"Very good. Thank you all for your efforts and helping to address our crisis." Hatim stood and left, accompanied by Cortez and Anna.

Everyone else stood. Edvin headed toward Lisa to ask her additional questions about the asteroid. Instead, Conrad interrupted. "Excuse me, Captain. Could I speak with you a moment?"

As much as Edvin wanted to say no, he didn't. He had to be sure Conrad had no suspicions. "Sure, Conrad. What's up?"

"Since you're here, I was wondering if you wouldn't mind donning the helmet again." Edvin started to make an excuse; Conrad jumped in. "Just for a brief time. It would really be helpful."

Edvin didn't want to spend any time with Conrad's project, but then a thought occurred to him: could he use this chance to communicate with Lars about his newfound information concerning the Messiah? All could be done via thought, and he might not ever have a better chance. Edvin smiled. "Sure, Conrad. I would be happy to help. Would later this afternoon work?"

Conrad looked stunned but happy. "Oh, yes . . . that would be great. I'll set everything up. Will 3:30 be OK?"

"Sure. I'll stop by your lab then."

Edvin walked over to where Lisa and Apama were talking. "Lisa, do you have a more definitive time on the asteroid's arrival?"

"To the best of my knowledge, it will be ten weeks from today."

"Apama, do you have an idea what type of planes you plan to use to transport the fuel—and when?"

"I'm going to check to see if we can use Boeing 747s. Since we have a couple of months, I think I can get a number of them ready in time."

"Any idea how many you need?"

"Probably at least ten, I would think. Five to the Americas, three to Europe, and perhaps two to Asia, as it's likely the bloom will also occur in the Yellow River based upon data we have to date. I would probably have the fuel delivered just before the asteroid—or, I guess, in this case, the meteorite—hits so the blast doesn't interfere with delivery."

"OK, keep me posted."

Both nodded.

As Edvin turned, he saw Ty heading out the door. Edvin hurried to catch up. "Ty, can I talk to you over lunch?"

"Sure. What's on your mind?"

As Edvin entered the elevator, he pressed the down button and turned to Ty. "I wanted to see if you would consider coming back as Head of Research here."

Ty looked at Edvin and gave a smile. "Still having trouble with Conrad? I assumed you two made up. He told me you were going to help him this afternoon."

Edvin shook his head. "I still have to play nice—even if I don't want to."

"I can't come back. I'm too deep into my research in Washington." Ty gave Edvin a slap on the back as they stepped from the elevator. "Come on, Captain. Conrad can be a pain, but he isn't that bad."

Edvin shrugged. "Maybe."

They grabbed lunch and discussed current events a while longer.

Finally, Edvin checked the time. "Well, I've put off the inevitable long enough," he said. "I guess it's time to see what Conrad wants me to do."

Ty stood and shook his hand. "I'll be in touch."

Edvin nodded and headed to the elevator. As he reached Conrad's lab, he took a deep breath and opened the door. He really didn't want to see Lars in his condition—whatever this condition was. But if he could get Lars to see the truth, it would be worth it. He wondered, though: would Conrad even want him to work with Lars again, or work with someone else?

"Hi, Conrad. I guess I'm ready. What do you want me to do?"

"I want you to try with the same individual you had some success with before."

Edvin breathed a small sigh of relief. He would at least have his chance with Lars. As Edvin went to the helmet, there sat Lars again. Edvin's heart sank. *Will Lars be upset that I've returned?* He wanted to ask what Conrad did to Lars to keep him in this zombie-like state, but Edvin realized he really didn't want to know. It would be too hard to take.

Edvin sat in the opposite chair and donned the helmet. Lars remained expressionless.

"OK, now I'm going to put the frequency up to where Sean had it last time," Conrad said.

Lars. Lars—are you there? Can you understand me? Edvin hoped deeply that Lars would respond.

Within the next few minutes, Lars blinked and his eyes met Edvin's. It was the same freaky stare he had given Edvin the last time.

Lars. This is Edvin. Can you hear me?

Go.

Did Lars think that? It had been so brief. Edvin glanced at Conrad. His attention was distracted as he made notes regarding the displayed frequencies. *Lars, I have to talk with you. I've found the Messiah. Adelina is with him! I have trusted in him. I want you to also. Just put your faith in him. He's the one who came to die for our sins. Please, Lars, trust in him too.*

Edvin wasn't sure if he was making sense or if Lars could understand him.

Go.

Lars. Did you hear me?

Go . . . Edvin . . . go . . . don't . . . come . . . back.

But—Lars . . .

Go.

Lars began to shake. He shrieked at the top of his lungs. "Go, go . . . *goooo*!"

It was deafening. Edvin grabbed the helmet and threw it down in horror. Seeing Lars like this unnerved him. He didn't know what to do. Conrad stood, excited, a big smile on his face. Edvin was repulsed. Lars wouldn't stop yelling. Edvin put his hands over his ears and ran from the lab. He stopped in the hall, eyes watering, bent over, trying to catch his breath. He felt nauseous. *Horrible, just horrible. This was a bad idea.*

Conrad burst through the door. "That was remarkable!"

"What? What? . . . *How* was that remarkable? That was awful. Is he still yelling?"

Conrad shook his head. "No, he stopped yelling after you left. This is exciting stuff. We need to see if we can duplicate the response."

Edvin looked at Conrad with disgust. "There is no 'we.' I'm never setting foot in your lab again. I shouldn't have listened to you." Edvin began to walk away.

"But, Captain, this is progress. We need to continue."

Edvin turned back to Conrad and put his finger in his face. "Don't you *ever* ask me to help you again. *Ever*. Do you understand?"

Conrad held up his palms. “OK, OK. Calm down. It was only an experiment.”

Edvin turned and left. As he entered the elevator, he pressed the top tier and entered his thumbprint. He leaned against the side of the elevator and put his palms over his eyes. *Oh, Edvin, that was a stupid, stupid idea.* His eyes watered again. *Is Lars lost forever?*

Edvin closed his eyes and said a brief prayer. Hopefully, God would use the little he said to help Lars find the truth. There was nothing more he could do.

He couldn’t wait to get back to Israel.

CHAPTER 21

Once back in Israel, Edvin invited Elsbeth, Mik'kel, and Jeremiah to his apartment and told them what he learned in Babylon.

"Edvin, we have to do something." Elsbeth sat back, tapping the chair arm, thinking. "There are so many people who will be killed for no good reason."

"I don't disagree with you, Elsbeth, but what can we do?" Edvin asked. "And even if we saved them all, Israel isn't large enough to take in everyone. On top of that, Afrom isn't letting in any Gentiles unless they have confirmed exit dates."

Jeremiah leaned forward. "I may be able to help."

"Really? How?" Edvin looked at Jeremiah with raised eyebrows.

"Scripture states there will be two main places where followers of the Messiah will be located. One is Israel. The other is in southern Jordan. Many believe this second place is at or near Petra. This would be a good place for Gentiles, and, later, for Jews who will have to flee Israel."

Edvin shook his index finger with newfound excitement. "Jordan is still neutral territory, so that may work. King Nazari's not exactly happy with the President, so he may not care if those who are against the President find safety in his country. While he wouldn't protect, he may not persecute either."

"And," Mik'kel added, "Israel gives Jordan some of its reserve electricity, so that should help them look the other way—at least for a time."

Edvin's head jerked back slightly. "How does Israel have reserve electricity? Hatim doesn't just give that away."

"We've never relied on him," Mik'kel said. "The burning of all the weapons from the pre-treaty war has been supplying our country with power ever since. Some of our scientists have made the process very efficient. This has given us leverage with King Nazari, who has treaded lightly at the temple, and with passage of Israeli forces inside Jordan. The downside is this arrangement has increased persecution in other countries." Mik'kel shrugged. "Just because of jealousy, I guess."

Edvin nodded.

"But back to this crisis." Mik'kel turned to Jeremiah. "You said the prophets are protected, right?"

Jeremiah nodded.

"So, Edvin, if you can get the plan from Cortez as to who's being tagged when . . . and, Jeremiah, if you can find out all who the prophets feel are true to the Messiah, then we can head them off in their plans and get as many as possible to safety."

Edvin tapped his chin with his index finger. "That may work, but it will definitely be risky. We may lose many getting others to safety."

"Safety is never guaranteed," Jeremiah said. "And speaking of safety, I've obtained an encryption app for my phone. I'll send it to each of you." He looked at Edvin. "I think this is an upgrade to the one you already have, and it will better prevent any calls you make to any of us being traced."

Edvin nodded. "Good plan. Also, I'll ask Cortez to keep

me apprised of the schedule for tagging, and I'll pass that along. You three need to find others in various places around the earth who can pilot, hide, and transfer people. Then, Mik'kel, you and I can check on how to get to Petra. We need to plan how to smuggle supplies there that can support a large population."

* * * * *

Over the next several weeks, the four did further planning and made contacts based on information Jeremiah obtained from other prophets.

In further contact with Cortez, Edvin found that Hatim's plans were coming together quickly, even ahead of schedule. Edvin decided to hold a conference call with the key Hatim lieutenants to get everyone on the same scheduling plan.

"Cortez, you said you're ahead of schedule?"

"Absolutely, Captain. We've even deployed to the first set of subjects."

"Really? I didn't expect things to happen so quickly."

"Well, the President and I previously worked on a prototype, so getting them ready didn't take too long. The devices are paper thin, so some place them just under the skin in their hand and others on the forehead. It's becoming the new fashion trend to put it so close to the skin that it looks like a tattoo. Of course, some do plant it deeper."

"Any adverse effects, Ty?"

"None have been reported except for a minor rash by some, but it goes away after a couple of days. As you know, we asked for ten thousand volunteers and received way more offers than needed. People were disappointed we had to turn them away."

"What do you have to report, Anna?"

"Every business we've contacted seems supportive. When

fully implemented, some stores will scan patrons at the checkout before they scan their purchases. However, many are choosing to have a scanner at store entry. That way, a person won't be able to enter without the chip. We can then link scanners at checkout to our network database for better proactive distribution of goods, as well as capturing the picture of those who don't have the chip at store entry. Once rolled out completely, it seems everything will work smoothly."

"So, Cortez, what's your deployment plan from here?"

"We feel we'll continue with volunteers first since we had such a positive response. Then, I have it broken down by territory and region when we make it mandatory."

"OK. Can you send me your plan so I can monitor progress?"

"Roger that, Captain. I'll post it with the next scheduled update."

"Looks like you'll get back to your research project earlier than expected, Ty."

Ty laughed. "Yeah. Heading back to Washington tomorrow. I think Cortez and Anna have everything well under control now."

"Very good, everyone. I look forward to your updates."

Edvin disconnected the call and let out a big sigh. Things were going way faster than he expected. The sooner he and Mik'kel got to Jordan, the better. Edvin headed down the hall to Mik'kel's apartment.

Mik'kel opened the door. "You know, I'm beginning to regret my decision to have you so close."

"Very funny. How soon can you get to Jordan?"

"Well, probably sometime next week. Come on in."

As Mik'kel prepared tea, Edvin updated Mik'kel on what he had just learned.

"I'll have to come up with a cover story in case this gets

back to Hatim. The only one I can think of is one that gives away some of the details."

"How so?" Mik'kel asked.

"Well, I would need a good excuse to travel into Jordan. I don't think 'sightseeing' works at all, especially since all tourism into Jordan was canceled after the attack on Israel two years ago. Unless you have a better idea, I'll need to say I heard rumors of people hiding out in southern Jordan, and I want to investigate."

Mik'kel shrugged. "I don't see that as a problem. You're not stating they're there, but that you're investigating. If questioned, you can say you're still looking into it." Mik'kel paused in thought. "Or, of course, we could try and sneak in."

Edvin shook his head. "No, I don't want to do that. At least, not this time. We first have to be sure this is even viable. What do you know about Petra?"

"Not much. I guess we'll find out together."

* * * * *

Mik'kel was away for a week helping Afrom plan for how Israel could support additional Jews and Israelis entering the country. Edvin spent his time going over all projects and ensuring all were going as Hatim expected. It looked like the tagging project was progressing much faster than Edvin hoped. This made Edvin even more anxious to get to Jordan and get plans in place.

The day before their planned departure to Jordan, Edvin and Mik'kel spent several hours preparing. Since it would take about four hours of travel by jeep, and they wanted to encounter as few people as possible, they took provisions and gear for an overnight stay.

They started out early in the morning so they would have

several hours of daylight to look around once they arrived. The Jericho pass into Jordan had recently opened, so they decided to cross there, take Highway 15 to the south, and then head west toward Petra once they reached the town of Al Muḩammadiyah. Edvin found his fears about the border crossing unfounded. Since he had World Forces credentials, and Mik'kel was authorized to be traveling with him, there were no questions.

Once they headed west, they found out the reason the area had been closed. Potholes were everywhere—as well as rock debris.

Edvin groaned. "This is going to slow us down significantly. It's a good thing we left early."

"It's surprising to see how far south and east the eruptions and damage occurred during the invasion. I guess this area had lowest priority for restoration."

Edvin nodded. "But that could be a blessing in disguise. It could make this area even more secluded. A better place to hide out."

Nearly two hours behind their schedule, the two arrived at Petra's visitor center.

Edvin let out a low whistle. "Look at all the damage." He pointed to the building in front of them. "The visitor center is totally destroyed."

"All the debris over here," Mik'kel added, pointing. "It would take a massive amount of work to clean all this up. You're right on about this area remaining secluded."

Edvin drove slowly through the area, avoiding the rock debris and fissures that spotted the area. "I never knew how big this area was. Did you?"

Mik'kel shook his head. "No. I remember seeing information about Petra on television, but I never knew it was so large.

This area could hold hundreds or even thousands of people."

"Provided we can get enough supplies here."

Mik'kel nodded. As they passed one of many structures, he jerked around.

"What is it?"

"Thought I saw something."

Edvin rolled the jeep to a stop. "Where?"

"In that cave structure. Over there." Mik'kel pointed to a doorway-like entrance into the mountain's side.

"You saw what?"

Mik'kel was quiet. Edvin looked at him, a little annoyed. *What is his problem?*

"A little girl," Mik'kel said, almost inaudibly.

Edvin thought he misunderstood. "*A little girl?* Mik'kel, do you realize that doesn't make any sense?"

"Yes, I do." Mik'kel's tone was a bit defiant. "But I know what I saw."

"OK. Let's calm down. Let's check it out."

Edvin pulled closer. They got out and slowly walked toward the structure, each pulling out a pistol and small flashlight. Once past the opening, Edvin trained his flashlight, but its light beam revealed nothing. Edvin swallowed hard and continued deeper into the cave. Mik'kel followed. It took some time for his eyes to adjust to the darkness. His flashlight only revealed the area directly in front of him.

"Do you smell that?" Edvin whispered back to Mik'kel.

"Yeah. It smells like smoke. I think someone's here."

As his eyes adjusted, Edvin could see shadows, but nothing specific. He got an eerie feeling he was being watched. His heart raced; his mouth went dry. He heard something like a twig cracking and turned quickly toward the sound—but didn't see anything.

"Did you hear that?" Mik'kel's voice was a whisper.

Edvin nodded, but then realized Mik'kel couldn't see. "Yeah," he whispered.

Edvin heard a loud click to his left. He turned. His flashlight revealed a face with piercing blue eyes directly in front of him—and a rifle five centimeters from his chest. Edvin slid back by about a foot. When he did, he felt another rifle in his back. Edvin held up his hands and someone stepped forward and took his pistol. They did the same with Mik'kel.

"He's coming." The blue-eyed man with the rifle half-whispered the words as he stared at Edvin.

Edvin wanted to ask what all this was about but knew that would be a mistake. It had to be code for something. Edvin tried to think quickly. *Who are these people?* Would they have figured out Scripture and become the first to arrive here? Then something hit him. *The Messiah is coming.* Yes, that must be it—a test. Could he come up with the correct reply? It needed to be something affirming of the question and affirming his belief in the same.

"He's coming again," Edvin replied.

The man stood transfixed; Edvin worried he had said the wrong thing. The man lowered his rifle and a smile spread across his face.

"Sorry about that," the man said. "Can't be too careful, you know."

"Truman, look at how he's dressed." The other man raised his rifle again.

The blue-eyed man—who was apparently Truman—also raised his rifle again. "Want to explain yourself? What's someone from World Forces doing here?"

"Easy, easy," Mik'kel said.

"And you. What's an Israeli doing with a World Forces officer?"

"I can explain," Edvin said.

"Then get on with it." The man behind Edvin used his gun to poke him in the back.

"It's pretty simple. Both of us are followers of the Messiah, which I assume you are as well."

"And how did a World Forces officer come to be a follower of our Messiah?" The blue-eyed man gave a hard stare.

"Through a good friend like Mik'kel here—and a prophet in Jerusalem named Jeremiah."

The man lowered his rifle again and stuck out his hand. "My name is Truman. Truman James."

Edvin shook his hand. "Edvin Isakson. This is Mik'kel Cohen."

Truman shook hands with Mik'kel. "Iris, turn the lanterns back on," he shouted. "I think we're among friends here."

Several lanterns came on, and Edvin looked around to see the cave held more than two dozen people. A little girl peeked out from behind a woman. Edvin's eyes widened. He turned back to Truman.

"You have a child here. Explain."

Truman laughed. "Well, it seems the ban on children has led to memory failure."

Others around him also laughed.

Edvin shook his head, ignoring the laughter. "But it's impossible because of the food. It has chemicals to prevent procreation."

Truman nodded. "Yes. And that's the reason we don't eat that food. After one of the prophets helped us see truth and accept the Messiah, we began growing our own food. We realized the other food had something in it. Once we did, Iris, my wife, got pregnant. That, of course, made us a target for the government. We've been on the run for some time. We later heard one of the prophets state that, according to Scripture, this area would be one of the places to which the Messiah will return. So we headed here."

Mik'kel nodded. "Where are you from, and how long have you been here?"

"We came from Great Britain, and about a month. We're fine with water. There's a large cistern in one of the caves here. Food is our main concern. Two families with us know some Arabic, so they periodically go to nearby towns to get supplies. But they can only get a little at a time to avoid suspicion."

Edvin decided he needed to jump in with the reason they were here to begin with. "Mik'kel and I came here to see if this is a good place to bring followers of the Messiah. Fairly soon, anyone who doesn't pledge allegiance to President Hatim will be incarcerated. That will likely mean death, so we're looking for alternatives for them. We've formulated a plan. Can you help integrate others as they arrive?"

"Sure. As you can see, this place can handle quite a number of people—as long as we have supplies."

"How are you generating your power?"

"We have a generator in another cave in the back. We close it up when the generator is on. The cave has several holes leading to the outside, and this helps ventilate, and being in the back cave does help cut down the noise. We try to use it as little as possible. We use it to recharge batteries and sometimes to provide needed light."

"Looks like a strong setup," Edvin said.

Truman smiled. "We're proud of it."

After a tour of the place and discussing with Truman what could be used for shelters and supply depots, Edvin and Mik'kel discussed their plans and ideas with him. They stayed for dinner and the night.

The next morning, Edvin and Mik'kel took the supplies remaining in the jeep and left them with Truman and his small clan.

On the way back to Jerusalem, Edvin and Mik'kel made additional plans for how to make Petra a survivable place for hundreds. Mik'kel said he would tell the Prime Minister about the hazards of the food supplied by Hatim's administration. Once the Prime Minister declared it non-kosher, most Jews would avoid it.

Back in his apartment late that day, Edvin collapsed on the sofa. He was tired but not sleepy. His mind was still swirling with ideas. His phone beeped with a text message: *Important meeting. Head to Babylon immediately.*

Edvin threw his head back in frustration. *No rest for the weary.* He grabbed a few things, along with his tablet, stuffed them in a duffel, and headed out the door.

CHAPTER 22

On the plane, Edvin checked his newsfeed. He checked the news every day even though he knew it was slanted to what Hatim wanted the masses to know. But it also provided vital information he needed to understand. It had been a couple of days since he had reviewed the news due to his trip to Jordan. There was one curious tagline: "Lopions attack." That seemed like a tabloid tagline, as they were supposed to be docile creatures, especially to humans.

Edvin sat stunned as he watched. The video was from one of the tagging centers in Europe. He couldn't believe what he was watching. An entire swarm of lopions flew into a building and stung nearly everyone in sight. The video zoomed to a close-up of Cortez as a lopion attacked. The creature landed on his shoulder and stung him in the neck. Cortez fell to the floor grabbing his neck, screaming in agony. He writhed on the floor. Edvin knew Cortez and what a high pain tolerance he had. This pain must have been excruciating. The screaming reached high decibels, and the camera showed many people writhing in agony and screaming on the floor.

As Edvin watched, he noticed several people were still standing unharmed, including the cameraman. *What made the difference?* This event had to be why Hatim called the meeting. Poor Cortez. He wondered how he was doing.

Once back in the Ziggurat's seventh-tier conference room, Edvin, first to arrive, waited for the others. Dr. Lyle entered first.

"Dr. Lyle! Great to see you. But what are you doing here?"

Lyle came over and shook hands with Edvin. "Good to see you again, Captain. Please, call me Margaret. Dr. Hatim asked me to provide a medical perspective."

Edvin wanted to ask for more details, but Hatim and the others arrived within moments: Ty, Anna, Lisa, Apama, and Conrad. This time Ranata entered rather than Cortez. It seemed she was Cortez's replacement on the President's detail.

"Everyone, please take your seats," Hatim said. He seemed direct, wanting to get to business. "Dr. Moretti, can you explain what happened with the lopions? How did they go from docile to hostile?"

Ty stood. "It actually has to do with the chips used in the tagging process."

Hatim turned his head; it was clear this was news to him. "How so?"

"Every electronic device gives off a frequency," Ty said. "In this case, a faint one, but one near the frequency of an insect swarm. Lopions would normally be confined to desert regions, but because of the lack of rain, the drought-resistant plants were used more widely than first planned. Lopions were deployed wherever these plants were distributed. Having so many individual chips emitting their frequency simultaneously made the lopions think an insect swarm had started, and they attacked whatever—whoever—emitted the frequency."

Hatim then turned to Margaret. "Dr. Lyle, how does this affect people. Will they recover?"

"Mr. President, we're still studying this," she said. "We've never experienced anything like it. However, from what we've found to this point, the venom of the sting seems to affect the body's ability to distinguish between pressure and pain. It's as if the body is treating its pressure receptors as pain receptors. Every movement and touch seems to be sensed as pain."

Edvin thought back to the first time he viewed the lopion in the lab. "But that's not how they were designed," he interjected. He looked at Ty, who shook his head.

"It seems," Margaret said, "the element from the meteorite somehow got incorporated into the venom and is the real culprit here. We don't know how long this element stays in one's body, so it's wait and see. But my guess is it may be months of agony for these people."

Hatim nodded. "So, how do we move forward with the chips?"

Ty jumped in. "Well, I think we can modify the frequency the chip emits, and that should mitigate the problem. The biggest drawback is making the modification."

This made Edvin wonder if that action would provide another window of opportunity. "And how long will that take?"

"A couple of months. At least."

Edvin felt relief and concern at the same time. This news provided a window, but not much of one.

"If that's the case," Hatim said, "we have to skip the volunteer state and go straight to mandatory. I want this implemented as quickly as possible." He turned to Anna. "Do we have the database in place to handle this shift?"

She nodded. "Absolutely, sir. All is in place."

"OK, then. Let's get this done."

"What about the chips already deployed? Are those people still in danger?" Edvin wondered if still another window of opportunity could be gained.

Ty shook his head. “All the lopions that attacked were killed, so there’s no danger from those. The people with the chips already deployed will be dispersed enough that they pose no problem.”

Edvin nodded. He felt disappointment more time couldn’t be gained, however.

Hatim shifted the meeting’s focus. “While we’re here,” he said, “let’s go ahead and address the other crisis looming on the horizon. Dr. Jensen, anything to report?”

“It looks as though our predictions are still on course. We still believe the meteorite will hit the arctic, and it should arrive the end of next week.”

“And,” Anna said, “we have the planes ready to roll. All we need is your go-ahead, Mr. President.”

“OK. Let’s do it. Anyone: anything else to add?”

The room was silent.

“Then you are dismissed.”

Everyone rose. Hatim walked around the table to approach Edvin.

“Captain Isakson, I have to travel to Israel to speak with Prime Minister Afrom. You can ride with us if you wish.”

“Thank you, sir. That would be appreciated.”

As they headed to the bottom tier, Edvin hung back to talk with Ranata as the others walked more briskly toward the plane.

“Hey,” Ranata said, “I haven’t seen you in forever.”

“I know. Seems the same,” Edvin said.

“Thanks, by the way.”

Edvin looked at her, eyebrows raised. He couldn’t think of what he had done.

“The tickets to Gwen Sheridan’s concert!” Ranata said with a short laugh. “It was a totally epic performance.” She seemed to dance with excitement just recalling it. “I’m a huge fan, but this particular concert was above and beyond anything she's ever done."

"Well, glad you liked it. Sorry I missed it."

Ranata grinned. "Well, I'm only halfway sorry you missed it. If you hadn't, I wouldn't have been there. It was a sold-out performance."

Edvin laughed. "Well, at least I know where I stand."

She slapped him on his shoulder. "That's payment for the time you pulled me into that stupid bathtub."

Edvin laughed again. "I totally forgot about that. But I see it made a big impression on you."

Ranata slapped him again, then laughed. She pointed a finger at him, "You . . . "

It was then that her face paled and turned to a look of terror.

"Ranata, what is it?"

She kept pointing, but now at something behind him. Edvin turned to look—but saw nothing. She backed up, terror still on her face.

"What . . . what is that?" She pulled her gun and pointed it.

Edvin looked behind him again. "What is what, Ranata? There's nothing there. What are you pointing at?"

She glanced at Edvin in disbelief. "You . . . you don't see that? How can you not see it?"

Edvin slowly put his hand on her gun, lowered it, and took it from her. "There's nothing there, Ranata."

Ranata's disposition suddenly changed. She went from a soldier to a frightened woman. She jumped behind him. "Oh my God, it's getting closer. It's . . . it's hideous-looking. It's like a horse, but with a lion's head breathing fire and smoke. And its tail moves . . . like a snake."

Edvin grabbed onto and held Ranata. She was shaking uncontrollably. "Ranata, you're OK! There's nothing there!"

"Don't you smell it?" She was whispering in horror. "It's

overpowering."

"Smell *what*, Ranata?"

"Sulfur. It's . . . horrible. It's stifling."

He shook his head. He felt so sorry for her. "Ranata, there's nothing. Nothing's there."

She grabbed his arm and looked at him with eyes wide, shaking her head. "No, Edvin. No. It's coming for me. It's going to kill me." Tears streamed down her face. "Help me, Edvin. Help me."

Edvin didn't know what to do. He could see nothing, but apparently Ranata did—or thought she did.

She fell to the ground trembling uncontrollably. Edvin tried to help her up. He looked around for assistance, but the others had already boarded the plane. She grabbed his arms with a vice-strength grip. Tears streamed continuously down her cheeks; she looked into Edvin's eyes, lips and voice trembling. She cried, almost inaudibly. "Help me, Edvin, please. Please help me."

She put her hands over her face and screamed a horrible scream. Then Ranata went silent.

Edvin was in a total fog, his mind confused. *What just happened?* "Ranata! Ranata!" She was limp in his arms. He laid her flat on the ground and checked for a pulse. He felt none. He started CPR immediately. "Ranata! Ranata!" Edvin was screaming, trying to will her to consciousness. "You can't leave me. You can't!" He continued chest compressions.

"Somebody, somebody! Help!" he yelled, looking around the airport tarmac.

Someone from the plane ran out, along with Hatim. The man checked Ranata, looked at Hatim, and shook his head. He pulled out his phone and called someone. Hatim pulled Edvin up from the ground. Edvin looked from Ranata to Hatim, shaking his head. "No. No, this can't be happening."

"Captain. Captain, she's gone," Hatim said.

Edvin just shook his head.

"Captain. She's gone."

Dr. Lyle came running across the tarmac. "Oh my God. It's another one." She bent down and examined Ranata's body.

Edvin couldn't believe what Margaret had said. "What do you mean, 'another one'?"

Lyle looked up. "There's at least a dozen or more dead inside. Did she claim to see something horrifying, something you couldn't see?"

Edvin nodded.

"Same thing with the others. They kept screaming something was coming after them, but those around them couldn't see anything. They went hysterical and collapsed."

Others came and carried Ranata's body back to the ziggurat.

Lyle looked at Hatim. "I'll have Dr. Bonn examine the victims. I'll assist, but I'm not hopeful of finding anything."

The thought of Conrad examining Ranata made Edvin's skin crawl. He shook his head. "No, you do it," he said, turning to Lyle.

She was quick with an answer. "Dr. Bonn is best-qualified for this type of examination." She turned to go, but then turned back. "I'll keep you apprised of our findings."

Edvin nodded.

"OK," Hatim said. "We have to go."

Edvin reluctantly followed. He took a seat on the plane. The memory of Ranata's actions and death kept going through his mind. His eyes watered. He blinked several times to try to keep his tears at bay. The pain was too great. After the plane took off, he looked out the window and saw the Ziggurat of Knowledge grow smaller and smaller. He couldn't wait until he reached Israel. He said a short prayer: *Father, give me strength. This is all getting way harder than I ever thought.* He closed his eyes and tried to clear his mind . . .

. . . Edvin was wakened by his phone beeping. Disoriented, he looked around trying to get his bearings. He heard the phone beep again. Reality slowly came back. He sat up and took out his phone.

"Captain Isakson."

"Captain, this is Lisa Jensen. We have a problem."

He unbuckled and walked to where Dr. Hatim sat. "Dr. Jensen, I'm putting you on speaker."

"It's the asteroid, sir."

Hatim sat upright. "What about it?"

"We surmised this one was the parent of the previous one."

"Yes. You've already told us that."

"Yes . . . but . . . we failed to see there were other smaller asteroids between the two."

Edvin contorted his face. "How did you miss them?"

"The parent asteroid dwarfed them, and our focus was on it, I'm afraid."

Hatim looked from Edvin to the phone. "When will they hit?"

"Sir . . . they're hitting right now."

Edvin and Hatim looked at each other wide-eyed.

Hatim pinched the bridge of his nose and shook his head slightly. "How many?"

Edvin added, "And where?"

"There are dozens, and they may hit anywhere," Jensen said. "This will look like a meteor shower from the ground. Many will burn up in the atmosphere, and some may hit, but being in the air—you're in danger."

Edvin gasped. "The fuel planes, too." He turned to Anna. "Are they in the air?"

Anna nodded.

Edvin swallowed hard. "We have to get them to land—now."

"The control tower where they took off was one of the first casualties of a meteor hit," Lisa said.

"How do we warn them?" Edvin asked.

"We're contacting other locations to try and make contact. But, gentlemen, you also need to land as soon as possible," Lisa said.

"Thanks, Dr. Jensen. We'll contact you as soon as we land. Let us know when you find out more," Hatim said.

"Yes sir, Mr. President."

Hatim put in a call to the pilot. "Jacobs, land this bloody thing as quickly as possible."

"Yes, sir. Israel has the closest airport."

"Get it there as fast as possible."

Edvin headed back to his seat. As he sat down, he saw a flash go by; it just missed the plane. He buckled in and said another prayer. Another flash went by. He glanced at Anna. She looked terrified and had a vice grip on the arms of her seat.

The plane jerked. Edvin saw the wing outside . . . now broken in half and in flames.

The pilot came on the speaker. "We've been hit. Buckle up. Prepare for impact."

CHAPTER 23

Edvin woke with his mind in a fog. He couldn't register his surroundings. He moved and pain shot through his body. His head ached. When he put his hand where his head throbbed and pulled it back, there was blood. He realized he was strapped in a seat. *The plane. The crash. Where is everyone?* He looked around but saw only open desert in front of him. He unbuckled, but as he attempted to get up, the pain made him sit again.

He looked down. Under his seat, the bar designed to keep under-seat baggage from moving around was bent and wedged, holding his ankle in tight. There was a steel bar of the airplane hanging not far from him. He pulled it free and used it to pry apart the bar below his seat that trapped his ankle.

Once free, he breathed a sigh of relief, then winced from the pain.

He looked around. Only he was inside this piece of the wreckage. Other pieces of burning wreckage were visible farther ahead. He stood slowly and hobbled on his hurt ankle even though the pain made him dizzy each time he put weight on it. He grabbed the steel rod he used before and utilized it to relieve some of the pressure on his ankle as he walked.

After exiting from this piece of the wreckage, Edvin looked

up at a full reddish moon, and it helped provide light, though it was muted. As he looked around, there were burning pieces of wreckage everywhere. *How did I survive this?* He turned to his right and caught something out of the corner of his eye reflecting the moonlight. He walked over and saw a hand with a bracelet extending from another piece of wreckage. Anna. He hobbled her way as quickly as possible. She was breathing but unconscious. He saw some of her hair matted with dried blood. Likely the wound wasn't too deep. He bent over and lightly patted her cheeks.

"Anna. Anna. Can you hear me?"

Anna moaned but didn't fully wake. He could see no other wounds on her, so he decided to leave her for now and look elsewhere. As he stood, he heard another moan. He hobbled around another piece of wreckage and saw the nose of the plane with the pilot still strapped in his seat. The cockpit door had somehow been knocked open.

"Jacobs. Jacobs! Are you OK?"

Jacobs moaned. "Yeah, I think so. I have a few gashes, but somehow I'm OK."

"How's your copilot?"

Edvin saw Jacobs look over and shake the man to his right. "Bill. Bill, are you all right?" There was no movement.

Once Edvin stepped around debris to reach Bill's side, he turned away quickly. He could feel the bile rise in his throat; he tried to keep it down. Bill's face had been crushed by something smashing into it. A tiny meteor, perhaps. There was a hole in the windshield where something came through.

Jacobs wasn't able to keep his reflex in check. Once he saw Bill's face, he wretched and vomited. "Oh, my God." He shook his head. "Bill, oh Bill."

Edvin patted Jacobs's shoulder. "I'm so sorry, Jacobs."

Jacobs nodded but didn't say anything.

"Can you help me look for the President? I found Anna, but no sign of him."

Jacobs nodded. "He shouldn't be too far from Anna, should he? They were sitting next to each other, weren't they?" He moaned again as he got out of his seat and headed to help look. "Maybe he was thrown farther."

"Maybe. Let's go back to Anna and look from there."

Anna was now moaning more and starting to move. Edvin bent down to check on her as Jacobs looked for Hatim.

"Anna, can you hear me? Are you OK?"

She gave a slight nod and tried to sit up. "I . . . I think so. Is everyone else OK?"

Edvin helped her sit up. She looked dazed, but he couldn't see any injuries except for the gash on her head, which had apparently stopped bleeding.

"How's your head?"

She touched the spot gingerly. "It really hurts. But I think it's OK."

Edvin heard Jacobs yell. "Captain! Captain, come quick!"

"Stay here, Anna. I'll be back in a minute."

She nodded, waving her hand. "Go, go. I'll be fine."

Edvin ran to where Jacobs knelt. Jacobs looked at him. He was wide-eyed and looked concerned.

"What's wrong? How is he?"

Edvin froze as Jacobs revealed Hatim's body, which appeared face up with a large piece of glass buried deep into the side of his forehead. Edvin's eyes widened as he looked at Jacobs, whose expression mirrored how he knew his must look. Edvin bent down and checked Hatim's pulse. Weak. But there. He examined the glass. The wound had a little blood, but it was as if the glass had sealed the wound shut.

Jacobs stood, dumbfounded. "What should we do for him?"

Edvin shrugged. "I don't think there's anything we *can* do.

His wound's not bleeding much at present, so I would say leave it there until we can get more professional help. His pulse is weak but steady."

Edvin heard a gasp behind him. He turned. Anna had her hand over her mouth. Tears were trickling down her face. Edvin went and held her. She sobbed in his arms.

"He's alive, Anna. He's alive. There's a good chance he'll make it. We have to get help."

Anna nodded and sniffed while trying to regain control. She wiped her eyes. "Does anyone have a cell phone? I can't find mine."

Edvin and Jacobs patted their pockets. Both shook their heads.

"Mine must be back in the wreckage," Edvin said. He remembered he had used it just before the crash. It had to be back there somewhere.

Edvin hobbled back to the wreckage he had crawled out of. Anna went with him as Jacobs stayed with Hatim. Both looked over the wreckage. Edvin found his tablet, but not his phone. Anna went deeper into the wreckage on her hands and knees looking in each and every crevice she could find.

"I see it. I see it!" Anna called. "It's in the back corner wedged between where the seat is attached to the floor and the wall of the plane. See if you can find something like your walking stick, but much skinnier."

Edvin pulled another piece off the plane wreckage and handed it to Anna. After about a minute: "I have it." She came out from under the seat and handed the phone to Edvin.

"It still has power, but not much." He hit the callback button so he would reach Lisa, who had called him last.

"Lisa?"

"Captain, is that you? Is everything all right?"

"Lisa, we crashed. My cell phone is almost out of power.

The President's in very bad shape. Can you get someone here as fast as possible?"

"Where are you?"

Edvin felt like an idiot. He should have checked that first. "Hold a sec." He accessed his location as the phone overlaid his GPS coordinates on the map. "It looks like we're slightly northwest of Eilat."

"OK. I'll contact the airport there and have them send a chopper to pick you up. I'll have Lieutenant Amari fly to Eilat as soon as possible. I'm sure the President would want to be brought back to Babylon. We have some of the best specialists here."

"Great. Thanks, Lisa. I'll try to conserve power in case you need to call us back."

"OK. If your tablet still has power, check the latest news-feed. Otherwise, I'll update you after you get to Eilat."

"Very good. Thanks, Lisa. Bye."

Edvin looked at Anna. "A chopper will be here soon."

Anna sighed and gave a tired smile. She patted Edvin on his shoulder. They both headed back to be with Jacobs and Hatim.

While they waited, Edvin checked his newsfeed since his tablet still had power and satellite connection. The first tagline caught his attention: "Forest fires ablaze."

Edvin kept shaking his head. It couldn't have been worse. Not one plane made it to its destination. Each crash spread fuel over large areas, and this incinerated the dry foliage in those places as the crash ignited the fuel. Due to the dryness of the forestry, the fires spread rapidly. There were five crashes: in Europe, Southern Russia, Southern Africa, one in the Indian Ocean, and the other in the Mediterranean. On top of that, the meteors started fires in the Amazon, American Midwest, Pacific Northwest, and Australia.

Each fire spread quickly. World Forces could likely help with a couple of the blazes, but not many. With no rain in sight, the devastation would be enormous.

The chopper arrived as promised. The medics agreed Hatim's wound should remain as it was until he reached the operating room. They reached the hospital at Eilat within forty-five minutes. Edvin wanted to call Elsbeth, but knew it wasn't a wise idea to potentially let others know his girlfriend was Jewish.

The physicians at the hospital stabilized Hatim but didn't operate as they received word to transport him to Babylon as soon as Saeed's plane landed. After being stabilized, he was taken to the airport to meet Saeed's incoming plane. Only minutes after they reached the airport, Saeed landed.

Conrad and Margaret ran to meet them. "How's he doing?" Margaret, out of breath, asked.

"Stable for now. But he needs to be operated on as soon as possible," the attending physician who accompanied him said.

Margaret nodded. "Conrad, let's get him on board."

Saeed ran up and shook Edvin's hand. "Cap. You coming with us?"

"Not yet. I need to do some things in Jerusalem. I'll come later."

Saeed nodded. "Anna, Jacobs. Ready?" Both nodded.

"Hey, Jacobs," Saeed said. "Care to be my copilot on the way back?"

Jacobs smiled. "Sure. I hate being a passenger."

Saeed gave him a thumbs-up.

"Saeed, I'm really sorry about Ranata," Edvin said.

"Thanks, Cap." His eyes looked misty. "I'm glad you were able to be with her in the end. At least she was with a friend." He paused. "You heard about Chong, Masaki, and Mrs. De Voss?"

Edvin shook his head. His heart sank even before he heard the news.

“They’re all gone—the same way as Ranata. I heard the death toll is up to the hundreds of thousands.” He paused. “And that’s just in Europe alone.”

Edvin shook his head. “I’m sorry, Saeed. I know you were closer to Chong and Masaki than me. I’ll have to call Dr. De Voss.”

Saeed nodded. He turned to go, but then turned back and suddenly gave Edvin a hug. He patted him on the shoulder and jogged back to his plane.

Edvin managed to get a ride back to Israel on a military chopper headed that way. He couldn’t wait to get back and see Elsbeth. He wanted to rest, but knew he had to prepare for the largest meteor to hit earth in millennia.

CHAPTER 24

Edvin looked around. He saw the Ziggurat of Knowledge in the distance. *How did I get here?* He walked toward the ziggurat but soon came to a pit with smoke coming out of it. He peeked over the edge but could see no bottom. More and more smoke came from the pit and rose into the sky.

He heard a noise coming from the pit that grew louder and louder; it sounded like an advancing army. Edvin saw a swarm of . . . *something* . . . rising. As the swarm flew up out of the pit, Edvin stumbled and fell backward. Lopions—by the thousands—flew from the pit into the sky.

He heard a voice coming from somewhere—and yet nowhere. *Go. Possess your counterpart. Target those without my seal. Harm not the earth—only those who refuse the truth.*

Edvin stared in amazement as so many lopions flew from the pit. One flew out of the pit, turned, and headed straight toward him. He stood up and walked backward. The lopion kept coming toward him. He turned and ran. He could hear the lopion gaining on him. Edvin knew the pain that awaited him. His heart raced with the adrenaline surge, and sweat from the anxiety bled through his shirt. He glanced back. . . . It was almost on him. He ran with all his might. He glanced back again. . . . It landed on his shoulder. He waved his hand over his shoulder frantically trying to prevent it from landing.

When he looked ahead, he came to an abrupt stop. The lopion touched him—and then vanished.

Before him stood one of the most hideous creatures he had ever seen. It appeared black as midnight with highlights of deep purple. The body looked like a horse but had a lion's head breathing out dark smoke. Its tail seemed to have a mind of its own. It moved more like a snake than the tail of a horse. The smell of sulfur coming from the creature was pungent and thick. It became difficult to breathe.

Is this what Ranata saw?

The veins in Edvin's neck were throbbing with the beat of his heart. He wanted to run, but his body seemed to be transfixed. The creature slowly turned toward him. Its deep black eyes locked with his, and it slowly began advancing toward him. Although his feet felt like stone, Edvin backed away from the advancing creature. He heard the voice again. *Go. Kill. Target those who refuse the truth.*

The creature kept advancing toward Edvin—now more quickly. Edvin didn't know what to do except try to run, even though he somehow knew escape was impossible. He turned, but again stopped short. There stood Ranata! Her pale complexion, expressionless face, and empty stare made Edvin shudder. The index finger of her outstretched hand pointed directly at him.

"You, Edvin. You knew the truth and didn't tell me. Why didn't you tell me?"

Edvin's voice caught in his throat, regret sinking into his soul. "I . . . uh . . . Ranata. I'm . . . I'm sorry. I'm so sorry." Tears formed and trickled down his face. He reached for her, but she remained resolute in her hard stare and pointing finger.

"You killed me, Edvin."

Edvin shook his head; his vision blurred with his tears.

"No, Ranata. No."

"You knew the truth but didn't tell me. You. It was you who killed me."

Edvin's heart sank. He felt as heavy as concrete. *Is she right? Is it my fault? . . .*

. . . "Edvin. Edvin!"

The voice was not Ranata. And it wasn't the looming voice from before. It seemed to be from far away. He felt his body being shaken.

"Edvin! Wake up. You're dreaming. Can you hear me?"

Edvin opened his eyes. Slowly the form of Elsbeth came into focus. He grabbed her and held her tightly.

"Edvin, are you OK?"

Edvin released his grip and ran his hand over his face. "I've never had such a horrible nightmare."

Elsbeth sat beside him and ran her fingers through his disheveled hair. He gazed into her eyes. He felt so fortunate to have her in his life. "I think I just dreamed what Ranata must have seen."

"Really? It must have been terrifying the way you were acting in your sleep."

Edvin nodded. "Yeah, it was." He looked down at his hands. "But that wasn't the worse part."

Elsbeth pulled Edvin's face back to hers. "What happened?"

"Ranata was there, looking quite pale—like she came back from the dead just to talk to me."

Elsbeth gave him a concerned look and ran her hand over the side of his face. "What did she say?"

"She said her death was my fault."

"Oh, Edvin." Elsbeth's tone was loving. "You know that's not true."

"Do I?" His eyes watered as he looked at Elsbeth. "Did I ever tell her about the Messiah? Did I ever tell her about the truth I learned and knew?"

"Edvin, you know everyone is responsible for their own standing. You know you had to be careful. If you went and talked to everyone, then you wouldn't be as effective as you've been. From the beginning, you knew you would have to stay in the background. That was the price of doing what you knew God wanted you to do. You can't blame yourself."

Edvin nodded. He looked at her and gave a weak smile. "I know you're right, but I want to be able to help others find the truth we've found."

"You will, Edvin. You know you will." She kissed him on his cheek. "I've been doing some researching while you and Mik'kel have been off gallivanting around the desert."

"Oh, really? Miss Ambitious, what have you been up to?"

She sat up and smiled. "Well, I can't take all the credit. Jeremiah was extremely helpful. But I managed to find us two pilots to drop supplies, and I've found twenty-five safe houses to help hide people. That's not much, but it's a start. I haven't yet figured out how to get the people from the safe houses here."

Edvin sat impressed, even amazed. *What a dynamo.* "Elsbeth. That's awesome. It's more than a start. It will supercharge our efforts." He hugged her.

She laid her head on his shoulder. "It will take a lot of coordinating. I would like to do that."

"I think you'll be good at it."

"Really? You're not just saying that?"

He moved her head slightly and looked into her eyes. "I think you're the most capable and awesome person I know." He pulled her in and gave her a kiss. As he pulled back to end the kiss, she leaned in and prolonged it. He returned her kiss with passion.

She rested her cheek on his chest and put her arm around

him. He ran his fingers through her hair, which felt soft to his touch. There was silence between them for several minutes.

"Edvin," she said quietly. "Is there a future for us?"

He paused a moment and looked down at her. "What makes you ask that?"

She shrugged. "I don't know. We're in the throes of all this chaos. There's so much work to do before this tribulation period is over. Do we—should we—take time for ourselves?"

Edvin thought about that for a few moments. "Does God want us to be happy?"

Elsbeth sat up and looked at him. "Yes, of course. What makes you ask that?"

"Just asking."

"So, what would make you happy?"

Edvin smiled. "You."

Elsbeth blushed slightly. The tinge of red made her even more beautiful. "No, be serious. What would make you happy?"

"No, I really am being serious. Why don't we get married?"

Elsbeth stared at him, her eyes darting over his face as if searching for a clue of insincerity. "What?" She asked this in a hushed, barely audible voice.

"If we can do what God desires us to do and we can be happy in the process, why not?"

"Well, what about all the logistics? It's risky even *now* for us to be together."

Edvin sat up even more straight. "OK, hear me out. This is not a rash decision on my part. I've really been thinking about this. There would, of course, be some concessions we would have to make."

"That's an understatement. I get no ring and no marriage license."

"Well, yes and no."

Elsbeth turned up her brow.

Edvin took her hands. "We can still make it meaningful and beautiful. You said you have your mom's wedding ring."

Elsbeth nodded. "Yes, but . . . "

"Well, we can use it in the ceremony, but then you can put it back where you keep it."

Elsbeth opened her mouth to reply, but Edvin held his index finger to her lips.

"I promise, though, I'll give you something special, something that will be meaningful."

"What about for you?"

"I was thinking of—well, hear me out—getting a unique tattoo that would involve your initials. Then, every time I look at it, I'll think of you. And once we're married, your initials will be the same as mine, so only we will know what the tattoo really stands for."

"Wow. I see you *have* really thought about this."

Edvin smiled and nodded. "So, what do you think?"

Elsbeth kissed him on the cheek. "Edvin, I'd love to marry you."

She put her head back on his chest. "There's only one other detail to work out."

"And what's that?"

"My father."

Edvin gave a big sigh. "Your father." That was a detail he hadn't thought through. He wrapped his arms around her and leaned back on the sofa.

They fell asleep in each other's arms.

Edvin's watch woke him at 11 p.m. He gently woke Elsbeth.

"It's time. Ready to go to the roof?"

Elsbeth yawned and nodded.

Mik'kel and Jeremiah were already on the rooftop when

they arrived.

Elsbeth scanned the sky. "Can you see anything yet?"

Mik'kel shook his head. "Not yet."

Edvin turned on his tablet for his newsfeed. Dr. Jensen was again assisting the newscaster reporting the event. " . . . We now believe the meteor will hit almost dead-on the Arctic Circle between Greenland and Svalbard Island." She used the map displayed behind the newscaster to show the area.

"And what can we expect once it hits?"

"Remember," Jensen said, "this will be the largest meteorite on historical records." She smiled. "But I can assure you it will not be an extinction event."

The newscaster gave a small laugh. "Well, that's good to know. So, what kind of damage will it cause?"

Lisa turned serious. "Since nothing like this has happened, we're not entirely sure what will happen, but we have a pretty good guess. The first thing is, it will melt up to one-third of the polar ice. This can cause flooding as well as tidal waves in coastal areas. It can trigger some earthquakes and volcanic eruptions. It is expected the Erebus Volcano in Antarctica will erupt and melt even more polar ice. Oceanic salinity will decrease and likely fuel the plankton bloom we have already seen in other areas."

She held up an index finger. "But there is one ray of hope."

"And what is that?"

"As you know, we have several forest fires occurring right now which have destroyed about one-third of the earth's vegetation. The meteorite will create a great deal of water vapor that will ascend into the atmosphere and probably cause, or lead to, rain sometime after the blast."

"Really? We will all look forward to that."

Lisa nodded. "Absolutely."

"Wait a minute," Elsbeth said, turning to the others. "That's what the Witness said to President Hatim."

Edvin turned his head. "What do you mean?"

"The Witness at the temple said one-third of the earth's vegetation would be burned up before it would rain. It seems that will be coming true."

"Here it comes!" Mik'kel said, mouth open, pointing to the sky.

All four looked up and saw what looked like a shooting star, but it didn't go out. It steadily got brighter and larger. Each of them stood transfixed. The sight was mesmerizing. The blaze in the sky kept getting larger. Edvin didn't say anything; he simply reached for Elsbeth's hand. They held hands until the meteorite hit. There was a bright flash when it hit, and a delayed, muffled boom could be heard. Edvin felt a rumbling through his body. The building itself swayed briefly, an urn fell off the roof ledge, and several car alarms went off.

Edvin looked back at his tablet's newsfeed. The newscaster was reporting. " . . . We just heard the Bardarbunga Volcano in Iceland has erupted. We're getting reports the impact was felt as far as southern Africa. Various earthquakes have already been reported . . ." He kept looking down and back up, reading, but the four on the rooftop turned to one another.

Edvin squeezed Elsbeth's hand. She turned and looked at him.

"It's time for me to go," he said. "I need to get to Brussels by early morning."

Elsbeth nodded. "I'll miss you." She gave him a kiss. "I'll break Dad in for you."

Edvin chuckled. "I'm sure anything you can do will be helpful."

Edvin said goodbye to Mik'kel and Jeremiah and headed down the stairs.

. . . As he did, his dream of Ranata returned to his mind.

Was there anything he could say to Dr. De Voss and still keep his cover? He'd been such a father figure to Edvin. Surely, he could say *something* to get this wonderful man thinking about his eternal future.

Edvin said a quick prayer as he jumped into a waiting limo.

CHAPTER 25

As Edvin stepped off the plane, Phillips was standing next to a limo.

She saluted as he approached; he returned the salute. She opened the door to the limo for him. "It's good to see you again, Captain."

"Same here, Corporal."

As she pulled the vehicle away, she looked at Edvin in the rearview mirror. "Sir, I hear you were with Lieutenant Edstrom when she died."

Edvin nodded.

"I miss her. I know she was close to you, but she was a terrific friend to me."

"I knew her for many years. She was a great friend." After a pause, Edvin added, "Phillips, when it's just us, I would like for you to call me Edvin. Protocol is important, but in these chaotic times, I think a personal touch is needed at the right times."

"Thank you, sir. I'd like that. You can call me Myrka."

"That's a lovely name. I apologize I never knew that. However, I wouldn't have expected such a name to go with your reddish hair."

Myrka laughed. "Yes, I have an interesting mixed heritage.

My grandmother is Polish, my father English, and my mother Irish. I was named after my grandmother."

"All I can say is, the women of your family have lovely genes."

"Thanks—I think." Her eyes met his and his smile in the rearview mirror. She shook her head. "I've missed your unexpected comments."

Edvin chuckled, then turned more serious. "How is Dr. De Voss holding up?"

"Not very well, I'm afraid. I don't think I've ever seen two people so tight with each other." She shook her head slightly. "Some thought he doted on her, but he really didn't. He really valued her opinion. She was politically savvy and had a way of getting to the heart of a matter even when others tried to pull the wool over everyone's eyes. Dr. De Voss is very knowledgeable in the political arena, but she was the one who ensured he looked good in everyone's eyes."

"Yes, she was a lovely woman. Both outside and in." Edvin thought back to Claire. He could look back and see where she got her infectious charm. She had her father's smarts but her mother's savvy.

"Dr. De Voss talks about you a lot," Myrka said. "I think he thinks of you as the son he never had."

"Well, I've always admired him. He almost became my father-in-law, you know."

Myrka nodded. "Yes, he talks of you and his late daughter often as well. So did Mrs. De Voss."

"So, what are your plans now? Will you be staying on with Dr. De Voss?"

Myrka shook her head. "It looks like I'll be going to Babylon under Dr. Hatim's service and helping out Saeed."

"Oh?"

"Yeah, it seems Dr. De Voss wants to bow out of politics

now. He keeps talking about keeping a low profile and feels my services won't be required."

As Edvin thought about this, he saw Myrka had pulled the limo up to the De Voss's magnificent house.

"We're here." Myrka turned the car off.

De Voss met them at the door. "Edvin, I'm so glad you were able to come." Edvin shook his hand, but De Voss pulled him in for a hug.

"I know it's been a long trip. Please come and get a bite to eat. We have some sandwiches. Myrka, would you please bring a platter to the table?"

All three sat and ate at the dining table. Edvin recalled sitting at this very table when De Voss announced his pledge to Hatim. Now his mentor was bowing out of the picture altogether. They sat and talked easily for a couple of hours. It was obvious Myrka had become more than a bodyguard to him. He spoke to her in an almost fatherly tone.

* * * * *

Many people attended Mrs. De Voss's funeral, which was held in an ornate church with large and beautiful stained-glass windows in downtown Brussels. Several of those attending gave loving eulogies for Mrs. De Voss; she was well-liked and involved in many charities and societies for various social causes. Every speaker said her death was a huge loss to society.

In the past, Edvin would have considered such a funeral lovely. Although extremely touching, Edvin found it somewhat hollow as everyone talked about her life and the contributions she had made—but no one said anything about where she would reside eternally.

Once back at the De Voss house, many stopped to pay their respects and sympathies. It was late when only De Voss,

Edvin, and Myrka were left in the house again.

"Dr. De Voss," Edvin said, the house suddenly much quieter, "Myrka said you want to bow out of the political scene. Is that really what you want?"

De Voss smiled, nodded. "Yes, Edvin, I really feel it's time." He held up his hand. "Don't worry. I'm not destined to be a hermit." He laughed lightly. "I'll be involved with local things, but I'll no longer be on the national or international scene. That's why I think Myrka will be better served by working with President Hatim." He turned and gave a big smile to Myrka.

"You don't feel you still need a bodyguard?"

De Voss shook his head. "No. Sure, I would love to have Myrka stay. She has become almost like family to us. But she's young and needs to advance her career. She can't do that by staying tied to me. My biggest concern had been threats to my wife since I was in the international limelight. Now she's gone . . . " He choked up, and it was obvious he had a challenging time continuing. He smiled weakly. "With her not here and my change in political endeavors, I need to let Myrka pursue other opportunities. Her working with the President will open many doors for her."

His dream with Ranata still firmly on his mind, Edvin tried to think of how to turn the conversation to spiritual matters.

"Dr. De Voss, as you know, I've been living in Israel."

De Voss nodded. "That has concerned me."

Edvin smiled. "It hasn't been a burden. I feel it has allowed me to be at the heart of things. I've heard some of the prophets and the two Witnesses at the temple. They tell of the Messiah and what he did for the world centuries ago . . . "

"Don't tell me they've gotten to you," De Voss said. Both he and Myrka laughed lightly.

Edvin felt heat rush to his cheeks, but also knew he had to at least try to get them to understand. Edvin smiled back.

"Well, what impressed me most was the many things the Witnesses and prophets have been saying are also noted in the Scriptures they read to the citizens. And . . . these things are all coming true."

De Voss had a concerned look on his face. "Edvin. I knew that place would not be a good environment for you. Anyone can take these vague scriptures and wield them into whatever they want others to see in them. It really isn't much more than how magicians use sleight of hand. They make their sayings appear as truth, but we know logically it can't be real truth after all."

"Have you read these Scriptures?" Edvin smiled, but his question was obviously direct.

De Voss seemed a bit agitated. "Let's not get caught up in such things during your short visit here. I feel I'm too tired for any debate at such an hour."

"Of course, sir. That wasn't my intent."

De Voss smiled. "I know. Let's retire so you and Myrka can get an early start. It's a long flight back to Babylon." Each stood. "I hope the two of you won't think me rude, but I'll say my goodbyes tonight. I feel I'll need to sleep in tomorrow to recuperate."

"Of course," Myrka said. She gave him a big hug and headed upstairs. "See you in the morning, Edvin."

Edvin nodded and turned to De Voss. "Call me if you ever need anything."

De Voss smiled. "Even if I make something up?"

Edvin smiled back. "It can be for any reason, or no reason at all."

They hugged and Edvin turned to head upstairs. De Voss called him back.

"Edvin, one more thing. I want you to take control of my jet and use it as you see fit."

Edvin's eyes widened; he knew his mouth was hanging open. "But, sir. You'll need it."

De Voss shook his head. "I'll rarely need it. If I do, I'll let you know. It will sit idle too long to be useful to me. I'll be sure the upkeep is taken care of."

"Sir, you're way too kind."

De Voss smiled. "Good night, Edvin."

As Edvin headed upstairs, he was saddened his attempt to talk with this great man had failed. If a good heart and good deeds were enough, Dr. De Voss would certainly have a secured place in Heaven. But still, Edvin knew, De Voss was blinded to the most important thing. Edvin hoped that would change before time ran out.

* * * * *

On the flight, Myrka deflected discussion about anything other than what to expect once she arrived in Babylon. She said she wanted to impress to secure her future in Hatim's employment; she asked Edvin for as much information as possible so she could make a strong impression. Edvin decided this flight wasn't the appropriate time to discuss spiritual things, so he filled her in on as much as he knew.

Her mouth fell open hearing of the President's potentially lethal head wound. "So, no one else knows?" she asked.

"There are a few who do, but it's kept out of the news. Until we know the outcome, we have to ensure political stability."

Myrka remained quiet after hearing the news. She likely was contemplating what all this meant for her, and how she would fit in.

Just before landing, Edvin received a text from Anna: *Come to tier seven as soon as you land.*

As they landed, Myrka was impressed with the city lights. "I can't believe the city is this large. And what is that tiered building in the middle of the city? It's gorgeous."

Edvin smiled. "The city grew rapidly. That gorgeous building, as you called it, is where we're headed. It's called the Ziggurat of Knowledge. You'll love it. There are many kinds of research going on there."

With big eyes and a larger smile, Myrka looked at Edvin. "I can't wait."

After arrival at the ziggurat, Edvin introduced Myrka to Donna, who asked a few questions and said her badge and credentials would be available after the meeting. Edvin brought her with him to the meeting in Tier Seven.

As they entered, there were many present, as expected: Ty, Conrad, Margaret, Anna, Lisa, and Apama. This time Saeed also was in attendance, and his eyes lit up when Myrka entered.

Edvin wasn't prepared for who was sitting at the head of the table: Reverend Duarté.

"Come in, Captain. And Corporal." He gestured for them to sit.

Edvin took his seat wondering what was about to take place.

"Thank you all for coming," Duarté said. "Anna and I thought we needed a meeting to discuss our actions moving forward." He gestured toward Margaret. "Dr. Lyle, can you and Dr. Bonn provide an update to the group on the President's condition?"

"He's in stable condition," Lyle said. "But he hasn't yet regained consciousness."

"And the glass?" Edvin asked.

Margaret looked at Edvin and nodded. "We were able to remove it, and I was able to use 3-D tissue printing to help heal his wound. Still, since he hasn't regained consciousness, I don't know the degree of damage, if any."

Edvin turned toward Duarté. "I assume you have some type of plan, or we wouldn't be here."

Duarte was quick to respond. "Captain Isakson, I assume you remember what the President said at our last visit?"

Edvin thought for a minute. "He . . . wanted you to make him the object of people's worship."

Duarté smiled. "Very good, Captain. That's why we're here. We're going to make the world worship President Hatim."

Edvin opened his mouth to ask how, but decided not to; he was unsure what would be proper to ask. But his curiosity quickly got the better of him, and he asked anyway. "And how are we"—Edvin twirled his index finger, pointing to those around the table—"going to make that happen?"

Duarté looked at Margaret. "Dr. Lyle, wish to fill the Captain in?"

Margaret looked at Edvin. From her expression, he could tell she knew no more than he did.

Duarté chuckled. "Doctor, surely you know all the work you've been doing was not for naught?"

Margaret looked to be in thought. "The tissues?"

Duarté nodded. "And how many tissues do you have?"

"Practically every . . . " Her eyes brightened as if she hit an aha moment. ". . . one in the human body. . . . You . . . want to build a living image of the President?"

Edvin was speechless. From the expressions on the faces of those around the table, they were finding it hard to comprehend as well.

Duarté ignored them and continued. "Dr. Bonn, how far have you progressed in memory transference?"

Bonn swallowed hard. "Well, we've made progress, but to transfer all of one's memory . . . " He shook his head. "I . . . I don't know if my current technique can do that."

Duarté turned back to Margaret. "How long would it take to 3-D tissue-print a body?"

"Well, uh, let me think a minute. If it operates twenty-four/ seven, then probably four to six weeks. I would have to get my lab ready first."

Duarté shook his head. "No. We have to do this in Jerusalem."

Margaret nearly shouted. "Jerusalem!?" She looked around realizing what she had done. "Sorry. It's just . . . why Jerusalem? *Where* in Jerusalem?"

"Why, at the temple, of course."

Margaret shook her head. "But I need a great deal of technology from my lab to make this happen."

"Then, let's move your lab to Jerusalem. How long to recreate it at the temple?"

Edvin found all this hard to comprehend. "Why go to all this trouble if Dr. Lyle can do this right here in her lab?"

"Because we want the world to see it formed and then come to life." Duarté smiled. "What better place to do that than in the land of miracles? We will then show the world the fraud of Israel." He turned back to Margaret. "So. How long to set up in Jerusalem?"

Margaret shrugged. "Six weeks?"

Duarté turned to Conrad. "So, Dr. Bonn, you have your answer. Six weeks to start and six weeks to do the tissue printing. You have three months to get the memory transference to work successfully."

Conrad looked stunned. "That's not a lot of time."

Duarté gave Conrad a cold stare. "But that's how much time you have. The success of the President and his dream is in your hands."

Conrad nodded but looked nervous.

"Now, Ms. Bonfield, we'll need to ensure we have this information broadcast around the world."

"Wait a minute," Margaret said. "I can't have news cameras in my lab."

"Not to worry," Duarté said. "Only a small camera will be installed to show the 3-D printing process of the President's image, and this will be displayed on a large column showing his image on all four sides." He smiled, then chuckled. "We don't want anyone to have to strain to see the magical wonder, now do we?"

Duarté looked around the table. "Now for a few details. Lieutenant Amari and Corporal Phillips, I want you to help Dr. Lyle set up her lab and fly in the equipment she needs."

Both nodded.

"And Captain Isakson. I need you to make peace with the Israeli Prime Minister. He's not going to like this, but you need to help make it happen. Can you do that?"

Edvin knew this request was not a good thing, but he also had the feeling this was what should happen. "I do have a good rapport with Prime Minister Afrom. I'll do my best."

Duarté smiled. "Well, let's hope your best is good enough."

Edvin smiled back, but inside he wanted to wipe that smug grin off Duarté's face. Everything about him was grating.

Duarté looked at Saeed. "I would like you to take the first load of equipment tomorrow."

Edvin felt that was rushing things with Afrom. "Let me first prepare Prime Minister Afrom before we start bringing in equipment," Edvin suggested.

Margaret jumped in. "I think that's a good idea," she said. "It will take me a couple of weeks to prepare the first shipment. It shouldn't hold up things, as we can be setting up as additional equipment is transported."

"OK," Duarté said. "Lieutenant Amari, perhaps you can

take Captain Isakson back to Israel tomorrow for him to get things started?"

"Certainly, sir."

After they dispersed, Edvin headed to the penthouse for the night. His head spun with thoughts. He still had so much to do in a short amount of time. How was he going to get Afrom to agree to Duarté's plan? And how was he going to get High Priest Cohen to agree to him marrying Elsbeth? The second would likely be more difficult than the first.

CHAPTER 26

As soon as the plane landed, Edvin headed straight to take care of his top priority. He said a quick prayer before he entered to meet the Prime Minister.

Afrom's aide nodded to Edvin and opened the door for him. Afrom rose from behind his desk as Edvin entered. They shook hands and Afrom motioned for Edvin to join him at a desk with two chairs.

"So, how's my favorite/least favorite Israeli resident?" Afrom smiled when he said it, but Edvin knew there was a lot of truth to the implication.

Edvin chuckled. "I'm fine, sir. Thank you for seeing me on such short notice."

"Well, I suspect it's something important." His tone was matter-of-fact. "And likely something I'm not going to like."

"I've always found you to be very astute, Prime Minister."

"Now you're just brownnosing."

Edvin laughed. "Just trying to soften the blow."

"OK. Now I'm afraid to ask. What does President Hatim want now?"

"He wants you to allow Dr. Margaret Lyle's lab to be recreated at the temple site."

Afrom looked flabbergasted and tried to say something but

couldn't seem to formulate a response. Edvin held up a palm.

"I think I can help with this, though. You have rooms under the temple, right?"

Afrom sighed and nodded.

"I think I can persuade them to have the lab in one of those rooms so it will not be visible from the outside."

"But something will be visible, right?" Afrom asked.

Edvin took a deep breath and nodded. "I can ensure it will be in the Court of Gentiles, though."

"OK. Thank you. But what is expected to be there?"

"A replica of the President." Edvin paused. "A replica using living tissue."

"What?" Afrom looked like someone had slapped him in the face.

Edvin nodded. "I know. I know. It's crazy."

"What if I refuse? How can this not compete with the purpose of the temple?"

"But, sir, the alternative is worse."

Afrom gave him a hard stare. "Was that a threat?"

Edvin shook his head. "Mr. Prime Minister, I'm merely stating the obvious. Believe me, I understand your concern, and I would have the same reaction if I was in your place. Yet we both know the power President Hatim has wielded. Going against him at this point is a no-win situation."

"Even if I agree, it will spark civil discontent at the least. It could escalate to something worse."

Edvin cleared his throat. He continued. "I really need your commitment to try and keep everyone calm while this is going on."

"I have to be honest with you here. I feel betrayed. President Hatim stated we have seven years. It hasn't even been four."

"I hear you, Mr. Prime Minister. Yet, you know the President is keen on nuance. He stated it was seven years to get you in alignment with his plans. I guess he feels it will take the rest of the time of the treaty to accomplish that."

Afrom sat stoically for a few moments. "Captain Isakson, I've known you for several years now and have been impressed with how you support the President and yet still seem to support us as well. I know you're trying to soften the blow, but you're really delivering an ultimatum. What's the expression? A rose by any other name? Yet, this smells nothing like a rose."

"I'm sorry, sir. It's hard to turn a negative message into a positive one."

Afrom stood. Edvin followed suit.

"Well," Afrom said, "I'll support where I can. Let's hope we can do decent damage control."

"I will do my best, sir."

Afrom walked Edvin to the door. As he exited, Edvin let out a long breath. *That was hard.* In a large way, he felt like he was betraying people he liked, but he knew God still had work for him to do. Now came the bigger challenge—facing Elsbeth's father.

Edvin decided to head to his apartment first and get his thoughts together.

When he arrived, Elsbeth was waiting outside his place.

She greeted him with a smile, a big hug, and a kiss. But, at the same time, something seemed off to Edvin.

"Hi, Sweetie. It's really great to be back. Did you misplace the key I gave you?"

Elsbeth shook her head. "No, I still have it." She gave a small smile. "I wanted to prepare you before you walked in."

Edvin furrowed his brow. "I'm not following you."

Elsbeth sighed. "Edvin, my father is in your apartment."

Edvin turned his head while trying to process this information. "Why . . . is your father in my apartment?"

"While you were gone, I talked to him about us. He insisted on talking to you the minute you arrived."

"And you let him in my apartment?"

"Oh, Edvin. It was either let him in or he would be standing here waiting for you. I wanted to at least let you know before the inquisition."

This was the scenario Edvin had hoped to avoid. He reached for the doorknob. Elsbeth grabbed his arm. He turned to look at her.

"Just want you to know: my father asked Mik'kel and Jeremiah to be here also."

Edvin squinted his eyes in question but didn't pursue it further. He had no idea what to even ask.

As he opened the door, everyone inside was standing, waiting for him. Elsbeth entered behind Edvin.

"High Priest Cohen. It's nice of you to welcome me home." Edvin went over and stuck out his hand. He felt good that Cohen took his hand and shook it. He glanced over at Mik'kel and Jeremiah. Both of them were standing next to Avraham, but with blank expressions. He knew that wasn't good.

"Elsbeth has been talking to me about the two of you," Cohen said.

Edvin nodded. "Yes, sir. I was going to come see you personally when I got back."

"So, what are your intentions?"

"My intentions?" He looked at Elsbeth and then back at Avraham. "Sir, I love your daughter. I want to marry her."

"Why should I let a Gentile marry my daughter, a descendant of Zadok, whose offspring would be part of the priesthood? Should I jeopardize that legacy?"

Edvin saw Elsbeth roll her eyes. It was obvious they had already undergone a similar conversation.

"Sir, if my conversion to Judaism would preserve that legacy, then I would gladly convert—with one provision."

Avraham's eyes widened, and his eyebrows rose.

"I must be a Messianic Jew."

"Most Jews consider that statement an oxymoron."

"Maybe, sir. But not your daughter."

Avraham looked at Elsbeth, who gave a hard stare back.

"Well, I see you are not intimidated. That's a plus."

"Thank you, sir."

Avraham held up his index finger. "But, are you willing to go through brit milah?"

"Abba," Elsbeth said sternly.

Avraham held up his palm. Elsbeth crossed her arms in exasperation.

Edvin glanced at Elsbeth, who shook her head slightly. He focused his eyes back on Avraham.

"Sir, I'm willing to do anything you ask to get your approval for Elsbeth's hand in marriage."

"Very well. That will prove to me your sincerity and dedication to her happiness."

Elsbeth threw up her hands with a loud "huh!" and walked out of the apartment.

Edvin looked at Mik'kel while trying to understand what had just happened.

"Avraham, I'm not sure Edvin knows what he has committed to. We should explain it to him."

Avraham seemed to ignore the comment. "Jeremiah here is a physician and a prominent mohel."

Edvin looked at Mik'kel again. "Does that mean what I think it means?"

Mik'kel nodded. Edvin swallowed hard.

"Second thoughts?" Avraham showed a slight grin.

Edvin shook his head, but inside his mind screamed, *You idiot.*

Instead, he asked a simple question. "So, what do I do?"

"Take a shower," Jeremiah said, "and then come to Mik'kel's apartment in your bathrobe."

Edvin squinted at Jeremiah. "Why Mik'kel's apartment?"

"Well," Mik'kel said. "Think about it. What will you be able to do after you're circumcised? I'm your nursemaid for two weeks."

"And you and Elsbeth are off-limits until the wedding," Avraham said. "I don't want her marrying you by feeling sorry for you."

Edvin resisted the urge to roll his eyes. *More like keeping her from being mad at you for making me suffer.*

But if all this meant even a couple of years with Elsbeth, it was well worth it. Edvin wanted to get it over with.

While embarrassing, the procedure wasn't as bad as Edvin thought it would be. He knew that was likely due to the anesthetic Jeremiah used. Even before it wore off, he knew he had to produce a cover story. He called Saeed.

"Saeed, can you cover for me for a couple of weeks?"

"Anything wrong?"

"No. But I feel that if I can get on the good side of the high priest, we might get this project done with less resistance at the temple. I've made inroads with the Prime Minister. Now I need to do the same with the high priest."

"And you think it will take that long?"

"Probably. I need to get both the Prime Minister and the high priest on the same page. Call me if anything comes up. I'll still be keeping tabs on everyone."

"OK, Cap. You do the politics, and I'll keep things moving."

Edvin ended the call and breathed a deep sigh of relief. He told himself it wasn't really a lie. But he also wasn't sure if he had either man on his side yet.

*****

Since he had no place to go, Edvin spent much more time on his tablet keeping up with the projects in Babylon and the progress of Dr. Lyle's lab at the temple. And, fortunately for him, it seemed Duarté liked the idea of the lab being unseen; it would yield a better visual effect for the image to be displayed on an erected column in the Court of Gentiles.

He also looked at issues from around the world and viewed a news video interview of Apama . . .

. . . "Dr. Bhattacharya, thank you for being with us today. I understand you have some remarkable news for us."

Apama smiled. "Yes, while the plankton bloom has been catastrophic, we've found we can turn it into a positive."

"Sort of like lemons into lemonade."

"Exactly. Getting raw materials for clothing is becoming harder and harder to get, and the price of clothing has skyrocketed."

"So, what answer do you have for our viewers?"

"We've found the plankton in our harbors can be harvested and made into a fiber which can be used to make clothing," she said. "Because it's so plentiful, it becomes a very inexpensive commodity. A blouse made from plankton will cost the consumer one-fifth that of regular clothing."

"Well, that is certainly wonderful news, Dr. Bhattacharya. But I understand you have a precaution for people as well."

Apama nodded. "Yes, a very important one. Clothing can, of course, be made even cheaper, but there is a very important step in the process which should not be short-circuited. There's a needed process to remove the raw element that gets entrapped in the plankton. We have named this element apollyonium. The word *apollyon* is Greek for 'destroyer,' and that's what this element has done ever since the meteorites hit. I won't get geeky as to how unreacted apollyonium gets into the plankton, but if apollyonium gets incorporated into the clothing and is oxidized, it becomes reactive and can cause tissue damage. Therefore, *caveat emptor* is very much needed here. Read labels carefully."

"Thank you, Dr. Bhattacharya. We're happy to know the President's team of scientists is always looking out for our well-being, both financially and physically."

Edvin continued scrolling and went through other reports. One discussed the effects of the meteorite. It stated the large meteorite had caused flooding in many coastal areas. Despite preparations, many people were killed. Insufficient manpower in World Forces to handle the devastation had led to disease, pestilence, and still more death. The decreased salinity increased the plankton bloom and either hindered ships from embarking in ports or stranded them there. This prevented needed supplies from getting to areas that were in most need.

Along with the meteorite impact came many earthquakes. One occurred in the Gulf of Aqaba along the fault line on the sea floor. This caused the water in the gulf to drop, and this caused the port at Eilat to drain substantially. Yet the melting of polar ice countered this with an increase in the water table and brought the gulf water level to near previous levels. While other ports flooded, Eilat again functioned normally. In addition, none of the ports of Israel suffered from the plankton bloom.

After several weeks, the bloom in some ports had subsided slightly, allowing ships to at least move again, even if slowly. Ships had to start and stop often to keep their turbines from overheating due to the increased friction in the plankton-thick waters . . .

. . . The more Edvin read, the more excited he became. He looked up and called Mik'kel over to sit down.

"Mik'kel, I think I've found something important. We've been trying to get people out of countries via air travel, right?"

Mik'kel nodded.

"What if we get them to Israel via ship?"

Mik'kel turned his head slightly. "What do you mean? I thought ship travel was suspended because of the red plankton bloom."

"Yeah." Edvin nodded but tapped his tablet in excitement. "But this says some of the ports are starting up again. Because ship trade has been down for so long, they're rushing to get ship cargo loaded. Eilat is one of the very few ports without a plankton bloom! Although out of the way of much travel, Eilat is becoming an important port as it's one of the few ports where cargo can be transported to other ships."

Mik'kel continued to look at Edvin and shake his head. "So, how does that help us?"

"We get the people into large shipping containers from various ports and then get them out when they get to Eilat. With all the congestion and traffic, it should be easy to smuggle people on and off. Eilat is not that far from Petra. This could be the key to getting a significant number doomed for execution out and to safety. And with all those supplies coming through, maybe we can secure some supplies from there as well."

Mik'kel's eyes lit up. "That's a great plan, Edvin. Let me tell Elsbeth so she can start coordinating. You won't believe all the networks she's been able to set up."

"Yes, I would." Edvin smiled.

Mik'kel slapped Edvin's leg as he got up to head for the door. "Way to go."

Edvin doubled over in pain. "Yow! You did that on purpose."

Mik'kel cringed. "Oh, sorry. My bad."

"You bet it is. Once I'm able to move around, you'll regret that."

"Can't wait, old man."

Mik'kel shut the door just in time to keep a pillow from hitting him. At the same time, Edvin yelped in pain again, this time from the force of his pillow throw. Edvin could hear Mik'kel laugh from the other side of the door. Edvin couldn't wait until he was able to move around again without pain—and see Elsbeth.

Edvin went back to reading more news feeds. He found many blamed the two Witnesses for all the wrong in the world. This hatred got transferred to anyone of Jewish or Israeli descent. Many said in interviews that they hated the prophets and anyone who followed them. It made Edvin sad to think people—whether Christian, Jew, or Israeli—could become targets of persecution without any recourse or protection.

These were the ones he was determined to help.

The next news feed told of another concert by Gwen Sheridan. The picture showed both she and Reverend Duarté on stage together. Evidently, Gwen used her concert to help Duarté turn people's thoughts to Hatim, who he called the world's savior—the one who should not only be honored but worshipped.

Duarté's concert message was subtle but clear: as Hatim is a real person and savior to the world, he is more approachable and personable than an intangible god who is not approachable. Something else caught Edvin's eye. Duarté said the world would soon be able to make that choice.

What did Duarté have up his sleeve next?

CHAPTER 27

Edvin walked back in Mik'kel's apartment, his friend following behind him.

"Thanks for letting me out for a few hours."

"Well, the agreement was two weeks." He pointed to Edvin's hand. "Want to explain that tattoo you got?"

"Sorry. I promised I would share it with Elsbeth first. I'll explain it next week."

Edvin sat on the sofa. It was great to finally sit and not experience pain or discomfort. Good timing, too, as his wedding was in just a few hours.

"I suppose you aren't going to explain the necklace either?"

Edvin shook his head and smiled. "Sorry."

"Well, I'll hang your tux in my closet until you're ready to change."

There was a knock at the door. Edvin got up to answer, but Mik'kel rushed back in. "Wait. It may be Elsbeth."

"So?"

Mik'kel gave Edvin a hard stare. "You have to ask? You don't want to start out on Avraham's bad side, do you?"

"Good point." He stopped and let Mik'kel answer the door.

When Mik'kel opened it, Edvin saw a man and woman standing there.

"Iris?" Mik'kel's announcement was one of surprise. "What are you doing here?" He asked the two to come in, then stuck his head out the doorway to see if anyone had noticed their arrival.

"This is my nephew, Daniel," Iris said.

"Call me Dan."

Mik'kel shook his hand and Edvin came forward and did the same, then gave Iris a hug. Immediately, he had a question for her. "Iris, what are you doing here? It's dangerous to be away from Petra."

Iris's cheeks reddened slightly. "That's why I have Daniel with me. He's one of our stealth investigators, as we call those who go out and gather supplies for us."

Edvin still wasn't sure why they had come. "Do you need anything?"

Iris shook her head. "No, but your fiancée does. No bride should have to get dressed on her own." She looked around. "Where is she?"

"Let me take you to her." Mik'kel pointed toward the door. "She's in her apartment. I'm sure she'll love to see you."

"Thanks. She's been so helpful to us and has given us so many ideas and contacts."

Mik'kel looked at Dan. "You stay here with Edvin. I'll be right back."

Dan nodded as Mik'kel and Iris left.

Edvin motioned for him to sit. "Care for something to drink?"

Dan shook his head as he sat down. "No thanks. I'm fine."

Edvin sat to face him. "So, how's Truman?"

"He's fine. He wanted to come but couldn't. The population there has exploded. Everyone looks up to him for guidance. I guess because we were some of the first to arrive."

Edvin nodded. "Well, he seems to be a take-charge kind

of guy."

"You have no idea."

Edvin laughed, then turned more serious. "Have you gotten anyone coming through Eilat yet?"

Dan nodded. "That was a brilliant plan, by the way. We've gotten two groups so far. One from Hong Kong and one from Mumbai. They've acclimated well. Most speak some English, but even those who don't seem to feel comfortable with us."

Edvin smiled. "I'm amazed how Ruach HaKodesh creates such unity amid differences."

Dan chuckled. "Yeah, that he does. I've gotten to know one of the guys from Hong Kong, Bo Tai."

Edvin gave Dan a double take. "Did you say what I thought you said?"

Dan laughed. "Yeah. I tease him a lot about his name, but he's a great guy. Everyone was afraid of him at first. We thought he was a spy."

Edvin furrowed his brow. "Why's that?"

"He has the mark on his forehead."

Edvin sat up straight. "*What?* Are you sure he's a Christian?"

Dan nodded. "Once we heard his story, we embraced him, and he's proven quite helpful to us. He's originally from a small village north of Hong Kong. It sounded like the government there made extra efforts to get noticed by President Hatim. They took his mark to an extreme. Everyone in his village was to be executed unless everyone had received the mark. He attempted to run away since he was a follower of our Messiah. But he was caught by some of the townsfolk and forced to receive it."

"Then what happened?"

Dan raised his eyebrows and smiled. "This is where it gets interesting. A lopion attack occurred in his village, but he was the only one who didn't get stung. That's when he escaped and fled to Hong Kong."

Edvin tried to process all this. "But I was told the lopion attacked those with the mark because of the frequency the mark emitted."

"Well, it goes to show God's Scripture always rings true. His Word tells us those who belong to him would not get stung—and it seems that held true."

"That's amazing." Edvin furrowed his brow. "But why did he come since he could buy food without persecution?"

"He said he couldn't stand aside and do nothing when other Christians around him were being persecuted. One of the prophets told him of the plan to come to Eilat via ship cargo, so he formed a large group to make the trip. Since he has the mark, he helps us get supplies we would have difficulty getting otherwise. He's now one of my best friends."

"I can't wait to meet him."

Mik'kel reentered. "Edvin, Avraham will be here soon. You'd better go ahead and get ready."

Edvin looked at his watch. "Yikes, it's getting late." He got up and headed for the bedroom. "Great talking with you, Dan. Do you plan to stay for the wedding?"

Dan nodded.

"Great. I'll be out soon."

As soon as Edvin stepped from the bedroom, now dressed in his tux, Mik'kel answered a knock on the door. Avraham entered with Jeremiah. Mik'kel introduced Dan; he told Avraham he was a friend but didn't elaborate. Jeremiah nodded and smiled; he already knew Dan.

Edvin went over and shook hands with Jeremiah. "There's my butcher—I mean, physician."

Jeremiah smiled. "Touché. I hope there's no hard feelings."

Edvin smiled back and shook his head. "No. I'm glad it

was done by a friend. I never expected all of us to get so . . . intimate."

Jeremiah laughed. "Well, we'll leave that department to Elsbeth from now on."

Edvin nodded and patted Jeremiah on his shoulder. He went over and shook hands with Avraham. "Good to see you again, sir."

"Truthfully? Or are you just being nice?"

Edvin smiled. "A little of both, I guess."

Avraham smiled and nodded. "Understood." He turned to Mik'kel. "Is everything ready?"

"Almost." He and Avraham set up the chuppa, under which Edvin and Elsbeth would take their vows. Mik'kel then wrapped a champagne glass in a towel and set it next to where Avraham would stand.

Avraham turned to Edvin. "Are you ready?"

Edvin took a deep breath, let it out, and nodded. He hoped he remembered everything Mik'kel had told him to do.

"First, Edvin, you must sign the ketubah, or marriage contract," Avraham said.

Edvin went to the table, lifted the document, and prayed. "Heavenly Father, all I have I pledge to Elsbeth. I thank you for her and for bringing us together."

Edvin signed. Mik'kel and Jeremiah followed by signing as witnesses. Avraham rolled the contract up and set it next to where he would stand.

"OK," Avraham said. "I'll retrieve the bride. Take your positions."

A few minutes later, Avraham entered. "Everyone ready?"

All nodded. He opened the door. Elsbeth walked into the room with Iris behind her.

Time seemed to stand still for Edvin. Everything melted

away except for the sight of his bride. Edvin couldn't believe how beautiful she looked. Her pure white dress looked simple yet elegant with its lace overlay. The scalloped hem, midway between her knee and ankle, added a stylish dimension, while the dress itself seemed to flow with her every move. She had her hair up in an elegant bun with forget-me-nots intertwined. She looked absolutely stunning.

She came and stood next to Edvin under the chuppa. Edvin did everything Mik'kel had said, but it all seemed a blur as he had a tough time concentrating on anything but Elsbeth. As instructed, he gave Elsbeth the ketubah and put the ring on her index finger. They then drank wine from the glass Avraham gave them during the ceremony.

Before Edvin knew it, Avraham had pronounced them husband and wife. They kissed, and Edvin smashed the glass wrapped in the towel with his foot. Everyone yelled, "Mazel tov!" followed by a round of emotional applause.

As Edvin came out of his Elsbeth trance, Iris was hugging Elsbeth and wiping away tears. Everyone gave him a handshake or hug.

Avraham walked directly in front of him. After an uncomfortable, prolonged pause, Avraham threw his arms around Edvin and hugged him tightly. "Welcome to the family, son."

Edvin smiled. "Thank you, sir."

"We have refreshments!" Mik'kel said. "And some champagne to celebrate this auspicious occasion."

Edvin rolled his eyes as he took a glass from Mik'kel. "Nice speech." Both men laughed.

"Congratulations, old man." They clinked glasses.

"Thanks, Mik'kel. Really. Thanks for everything."

Mik'kel nodded and patted him on his shoulder. "You're most welcome."

After eating and talking for about an hour, Edvin made his

goodbye speech.

"Elsbeth and I would like to thank you for being part of our wedding. We love you all. And Iris and Dan, we are very grateful for your attendance and risking so much to be with us."

"It really means a lot," Elsbeth said.

Edvin nodded. "We'll see most of you tomorrow. Iris, Dan, we hope to see you again soon as well. Have a good night, everyone."

Edvin and Elsbeth left and headed upstairs to Elsbeth's apartment. Edvin smiled to himself—now their apartment. Mik'kel had joked that Edvin's apartment looked the same before and after he moved all Edvin's things to Elsbeth's apartment.

Elsbeth unlocked the apartment door and looked at Edvin. He looked deeply into her eyes, leaned in, and gave her a passionate kiss. He felt her go a little weak, but held her tightly and prolonged the kiss.

As their lips separated, Elsbeth whispered, "Care to come in?"

Edvin smiled. "I thought you'd never ask." He picked her up as she gave a short "ooh!" and giggled. He entered the apartment, shut the door with his foot, carried her to the sofa, and gave her another prolonged kiss.

With his face next to hers, he whispered, "I have something for you."

"Oh, really? What's that?"

"I told you I would give you something special."

"It has already been special."

"My plan is to make it special all night long."

"Ooh. I already can't wait."

Edvin retrieved the box with her necklace. She placed her hand on his.

"Before you do, I'm dying to see what's under your bandage."

Edvin smiled. He took the bandage from his left hand, revealing the tattoo.

Elsbeth's eyes got big and she looked closely.

"Edvin, this is a very unique-looking tattoo." It had the top and bottom lines of an E blending into the top and bottom of an I. The middle line of the E had a red star trimmed in gold attached to it.

"If I didn't know they were initials, I'm not sure I would know what it represents," Elsbeth said.

Edvin laughed lightly. "Well, that is part of the point. The initials represent both of our initials. They are connected because we are forever connected. The star represents you, as you are the star of my life. Trimmed in gold because you are my richest treasure. And filled with red because it is the blood of the Messiah, which gives us life and makes us one forever."

"Oh, Edvin, you put so much thought into this design." Her eyes began to tear. "I love it. It will mean as much to me when I see it as it will to you. Thank you. It's even more meaningful than a ring. While I will miss us not wearing one, this is so much more special." She gave him another kiss.

He looked at her with a sly smile. "And now for you."

She smiled. "I can't wait to see what you've come up with."

"Well, as you can see, I did initials for me. I intended to do the same for you, but I found that not only are initials hard to do in Hebrew, but vowel initials are even harder."

Elsbeth giggled. "In old Hebrew, they're nonexistent. So, you got me an empty necklace?"

Edvin gave a surprised look. "Oh, I should have talked to you earlier. I could have saved a lot of money." Edvin smiled.

Elsbeth gave a pouty face and then laughed. "So that means you have something. What is it?" She leaned in close to his cheek and kept repeating "what is it?" as she gave him a brief kiss between each phrase.

Edvin laughed. "OK. OK. Let me finish explaining the design."

Elsbeth looked at Edvin expectantly.

"So, as I was saying . . . " Edvin gave another smile. "I had to use a couple of Hebrew letters to represent your initials. For your first name, I used 'alef lamed.' Then, to represent Isakson, probably 'segol yod samekh' is the closest. So that is what I used, but I took some poetic license and made the 'segol' symbol—that is, the triangle of dots, to tie all the initials together."

He slowly pulled the necklace from the box and put it in her hand.

She stared at it for a few seconds and then looked up at Edvin. "It's beautiful." Her words came in an excited whisper. She leaned in and gave him a kiss.

"The letters are in gold to represent the gold of the ring you should have. The top two dots of the segol on the corners of the alef and lamed are diamonds, and the bottom dot between the yod and samekh is a ruby. These represent the purity, love, and blood of our Messiah, which tie us together in his love."

"Edvin, I'm so impressed—and honored—at all the thought you put into this. I will cherish it forever. And when I see it, I will always think of you."

"That was the idea." Edvin grinned.

Elsbeth pulled him in for another kiss, which she prolonged for several seconds.

"What now?" she asked.

"Well, I will put this on you." He took it from her hands, undid the clasp, and hooked it around her neck. She looked down at it on her chest and then looked back into Edvin's eyes and smiled.

"Now," he said, "we need to burn the ketubah."

Elsbeth frowned. "This is the part I hate. I know we need to do this to protect ourselves, but it is such a shame."

Edvin nodded. He got a nearby trash can and a lighter and walked back to Elsbeth. "Let's pray first." He held her hands in his and they bowed their heads. "Father, we thank you for bringing us together and allowing us to be joined together in marriage. We recognize our marriage will not be honored by man, but we know you honor our union. We ask you to continue to use us to bring more people into your kingdom and to keep those of yours safe in these troubled times. As we burn this ketubah, please accept this as a burnt offering to you as we devote ourselves and our marriage to you for you to use as you desire."

Edvin took the contract and burned it from the bottom, holding it over the trash can so the ashes would be contained. After over half of it had burned, he dropped the rest into the container as the flame continued to do its work.

Elsbeth kissed Edvin again. Her eyes had tears. "Thank you," she whispered, "for turning something negative into something so positive." Her eyes met his. "I love you with all my heart."

Edvin kissed her hand. "And I, you." He paused. "And one final thing. Where's the box you kept your mother's ring in all these years?"

Elsbeth opened a drawer of the table next to the sofa and handed it to Edvin. He opened his hand and she placed her hand with the ring in his. He bowed his head and Elsbeth followed his lead.

"Heavenly Father, although a ring is the normal token and symbol of the love shown between two people, we ask you to accept my tattoo and Elsbeth's necklace to replace this typical token. May every time we see each of these symbols on our bodies remind us of our love for each other and our devotion to you. Amen."

Edvin took her ring and returned it to the box; Elsbeth

put it back in the drawer. She put on some soft music and Edvin poured champagne. They spent the next several minutes talking and snuggling. Edvin stood and held his hand out to Elsbeth and raised her to her feet. He wrapped his arms around her waist and slow danced with her as she put her head on his chest. He had waited a long time for this experience. Her perfume was intoxicating with its hint of musk and orchid overtones. He smiled. This was a scent that definitely said "Elsbeth." He breathed in deeply to help his mind connect the aroma to this event.

Edvin stopped dancing. Elsbeth looked up and he gave her another passionate kiss. He then scooped her into his arms and gazed into her eyes. "I think it's time I take you to the bedroom," he said as he gave her an Eskimo kiss.

Elsbeth smiled and whispered, "Yes, I think you should."

With her held gently and yet securely in his arms, he headed to the bedroom. He heard his phone vibrate as he walked by the end table next to the sofa. He didn't even look at it. For the first time in a long time, he let a text go unread. If he could help it, nothing would distract him tonight from this time with Elsbeth.

Tonight, only she mattered. Other things would matter tomorrow and other things would vie for his time, but not tonight. Tonight, only Elsbeth existed.

CHAPTER 28

The next morning, Edvin woke with Elsbeth still nestled close to him. He wanted to stay there and make time stand still. Most people got a week for their honeymoon, he thought. Yet, Edvin reminded himself, not everyone had to hide their marriage and keep it a secret. Being off the radar for two weeks, Edvin knew he had to make his presence known or he would be in serious trouble. He buried his head into her soft hair for a moment and again breathed in her perfume. It brought back the memory of last night. Edvin smiled. He hoped every detail would remain in his mind forever.

He forced himself out of bed. Elsbeth stirred slightly and then, once again, went into rhythmic breathing. Donning his bathrobe, he headed to the kitchen to prepare tea. He grabbed his phone and tablet and sat at the table to review the various projects. He noticed some blueberry scones on the counter and grabbed one to go with his tea. Evidently, Elsbeth had been in a homemaking mood yesterday before the wedding. Or maybe Iris made them. Either way, Edvin was glad.

He remembered he had received a text the night before, so he brought up the text on his phone. His heart sank. This wasn't going to be a good day after all. He read the text again: *Need to keep High Priest Cohen away from temple. Duarté is suspending temple sacrifice.*

Just great, Edvin thought. He'd been Cohen's son-in-law less than twenty-four hours and already he had to get on the man's blacklist.

Elsbeth walked into the kitchen smiling. "Morning. How's my favorite husband?"

Edvin chuckled. "Hopefully, your only one. What have you been doing down at Petra anyway?"

Elsbeth laughed. "Certainly no time for flirting." She leaned over Edvin and gave him a kiss. "Anyway, you'll always be my favorite."

"Thanks. Glad to be a priority."

She gave him a hug. "Always. Definitely always. Thanks again for last night. It was wonderful."

He smiled. "I definitely agree with you on that."

She poured some hot water for a cup of tea. "So, what does your day look like?" She took a scone and sat at the table across from him.

Edvin didn't answer. He handed her his phone so she could read the text.

Her expression went from a smile to a frown in an instant. "Oh, Edvin. It's starting already. Jeremiah said this would happen. I didn't think it would be so soon. Dad will be heartbroken." She shook her head. "I wish I could get him to see the truth. I think he's been dreaming of the temple for so long he can't see any other truth even though it's staring him in the face."

"Yeah, and his brand-new son-in-law is the one who has to break this news to him. There go my chances for getting on his good side."

Elsbeth gave a grimace before she sipped her tea. "I'm sorry, Edvin. I'll try and talk to him later as well."

Edvin nodded. "Thanks. Anyway, I need to get going. So

I'll take a shower and need to head out."

"Need help with your shower?" Elsbeth gave a sly smile.

"Mmm, that sounds wonderful. But I'm already late." He gave her a painful look. "I really wish we had more time. Rain check for tonight?"

Elsbeth smiled. "Absolutely. You can count on it."

Edvin took a quick shower, dressed, kissed Elsbeth, and hurried to the temple site. As he approached, he noticed a commotion happening at the temple gate. He saw Saeed and hurried over. "What's going on?"

Saeed gave him a shocked look. "You don't know? I thought the high priest was your project these past two weeks."

"Sorry. I, uh, was also under the weather for a while. What's all the commotion about?"

"You got the text, right?"

Edvin nodded.

"Well, the priests are having a fit not being allowed back onto temple grounds. Duarté wants all sacrifice to cease so everyone can focus on the image to be displayed. Then there are the two Witnesses who keep preaching against Duarté and the image of Hatim being created. I could really use your help on this."

Edvin nodded and walked over to where guards were keeping the priests from the temple. He saw High Priest Cohen doing most of the arguing.

"Excuse me, High Priest Cohen," Edvin said, breaking in. "Can I have a word with you?"

Avraham turned with an agitated look, but it softened slightly when he saw it was Edvin. Edvin motioned for him to step away from the crowd so they could talk more privately.

"Edvin, what's going on here?" Avraham asked in a hushed voice. "This is ridiculous. We must go about our temple duties."

Edvin put his hand on Avraham's shoulder. "Sir, please. Calm down."

Avraham took a step back to remove Edvin's hand. "*How* can I do that? It's one thing to have a vulgar image displayed from the Court of Gentiles, but to prohibit us from our own temple . . . " He pointed his index finger emphatically into his own chest. "It's just . . . just . . . " He threw his hands up in a rage of exasperation. He turned his index finger and now pointed it at Edvin. "If you don't do something about this, I'm going to go straight to Prime Minister Afrom." He looked at Edvin as though this was a clear ultimatum.

"Priest Cohen . . . " Edvin sighed and softened his voice. "Avraham, I have already talked to the Prime Minister. I'm afraid there's nothing I can do. I take orders like everyone else. I want this to not escalate into something nasty. The Prime Minister wants this to not escalate. And I'm sure you don't either. As high priest, you can help these other priests calm down. Probably the best thing to do is for all of you to go home—for now."

Avraham's face turned red; he was about to say something. Edvin held up a palm.

"Avraham, I know this is upsetting. But I can't do anything about it—yet. I promise I'll see if I can get this decision turned around."

For a moment, Avraham had an expectant look.

"But I can't promise anything," Edvin said. "I will try. You know I will."

Avraham took a deep breath and nodded. He looked crushed, to say the least. Edvin felt deeply for him. Avraham walked over to where the other priests were arguing with the guards. Edvin didn't hear what was being said, but after more heated discussion, the priests relented and walked back toward the city. As Avraham walked away, he turned to look back at Edvin one final time.

Saeed came over. "I don't know what you said, but good work."

"So, why is Duarté making them stop sacrificing?"

Saeed shrugged. "I guess he wants everyone to focus on the image of President Hatim and feels this would be too distracting." He looked around to see if anyone was in hearing distance. "I can tell you, though, if he could get rid of the two Witnesses, he would do so in a heartbeat. He and they have been in a shouting match all morning."

Edvin had an exasperated look. "Great. Well, I guess I need to go in and see what's going on."

As Edvin entered the temple area, he heard the Witnesses preaching to the people, who were watching the large column being erected.

"God has been gracious!" one of them was saying. "You need to repent before his great wrath is poured out." A few were listening, but most had their backs to the Witnesses, ignoring them.

Erected in one corner of the Court of Gentiles was a huge column about three and a half meters high and two meters wide. There were cameras mounted on one of the walls so the column could be broadcast and viewed around the world.

Edvin headed to the underground rooms, accessible at the back of the temple area. He found Dr. Lyle's lab and entered. He saw tissues in liquid media everywhere and a large cylindrical container in the middle of the lab with several black bands at the top and bottom of the cylinder.

"Dr. Lyle. How's everything going?"

Margaret looked up. It looked like she hadn't slept in days. "Captain. Well, you *do* exist."

Edvin smiled but decided not to try to explain anything. "Everything all set?"

"As ready as it'll ever be." She stood up from her microscope and donned her glasses. "You know, when President Hatim started me down this road, I thought it was to perhaps repair or replace an organ. Now . . . now I have to recreate an entire person—from scratch." She shook her head. "This is too daunting. If I was smart, I would quit." She smiled. "But, it's so darn exciting, I can't."

"So, you think it will work?"

Margaret shrugged. "In theory, yes. But no one's ever done this before. If it works . . . well, the ramifications will be extraordinary. Heck, I could start my own foundation. Maybe even get the Nobel Prize for medicine." She gave a broad smile. "Wouldn't that be a kicker?"

"I think you would have earned it. You wouldn't even have competition."

Margaret blushed a little and smiled. "Anyway, I really have a lot more to do. We start first thing tomorrow."

"Do you have enough cells?"

"I think so. Using stem cells, we've been growing cells from every biopsy we received. From the President's head injury, we now have some of his brain cells and have been growing them ever since the accident. We've also modified the printing technique. It will print continuously around the cylinder. That should make things go faster, and we'll have several printing heads going simultaneously."

Edvin tried to understand what she was saying, but didn't grasp all of it. "Well, all I can say is, good luck."

As Edvin looked around, he noticed a door in the back of the room. As he opened it and looked inside, he stopped short. There lay Dr. Hatim hooked up to all sorts of tubes and electronics.

"Dr. Lyle, you have President Hatim *here*?"

"Yes, of course I do. If I and Conrad are here, then how

could we keep him back in Babylon?"

"How is he?"

"No change."

"What happens if he doesn't wake up?"

Margaret shrugged. "One bridge at a time, Captain."

"Has Conrad worked out the memory transference? Will it work?"

Margaret looked up, now with annoyance. "That's another bridge, Captain. One at a time, please. One at a time."

Edvin nodded. He took that as his cue to leave and let her work. Being so busy, Lyle didn't even look up when he left.

Once back on the temple surface, Edvin saw Duarté standing next to the column with Myrka. Seeing him, Duarté motioned him over. Saeed approached at the same time.

Duarté seemed overjoyed. "Isn't this all so exciting?" Before either could respond, though, he continued. "I've asked Dr. Jensen to be here today. We'll have a meeting first thing in the morning at the King David Hotel. I would like for both of you to be there."

Both Edvin and Saeed nodded. Duarté didn't provide any details. After tomorrow, Edvin hoped he would better understand the direction Duarté wanted to go. He had a feeling, though, it wouldn't be anything good.

Edvin spent some time catching up with Saeed and Myrka. He said he would see them in the morning, then left for home.

As he entered the apartment, the smell of something in the oven surrounded him, tantalizing both his nose and taste buds.

"Mmm. Something smells good."

Elsbeth turned with her index finger in her mouth from sampling something in a bowl. A broad smile filled her face.

"Hey, you're home early." She dipped her finger in the bowl

and walked over and put it in his mouth. The tangy taste of lemon followed by a delightful sweetness filled his taste buds.

"Mmm, now something tastes good."

Elsbeth giggled, then looked concerned. "Is everything OK?"

Edvin shrugged. "Can we sit and talk?"

"Sure. Let me put this in the fridge."

She came over and sat in his lap. "Want to tell me about it?"

He wrapped his arms around her. "You know, you're making it hard to concentrate on talking."

"Oh, really?" She unbuttoned his shirt. "And why is that?" She pulled the shirttail out of his pants, exposing his torso, and rubbed her hands across his chest.

Edvin put his head back on the sofa and laughed. "Honey, I really need to talk to you about something, and you're making it difficult."

"Oh, I'm here for you, Sweetie. I just think better after a shower. But I have one problem."

Edvin smiled. "And what is that?"

Elsbeth leaned in nose to nose and whispered, "There's a spot between my shoulder blades I just can't reach." She kissed his cheek. "I was hoping you would be magnanimous and wash it for me."

"I think I can be persuaded."

Elsbeth smiled, stood, and headed for the bedroom. Edvin followed quickly behind. *Being married,* he thought, *while risky, is also fun.*

Later, over lamb and rice casserole followed by lemon trifle, Edvin told Elsbeth about his day and his concerns. He appreciated having someone to confide in.

"Things are happening so fast now," Elsbeth said. "How much time do we have?"

"Well, Jeremiah said once the image is in the temple, things will get much worse. So I guess we only have about a month to be sure all our plans for getting supplies and people into Petra are solidly in place."

"I think that's the good news," Elsbeth said. "We now have two ways to get people into Petra. The shipping route through Eilat is working well. Dan told me about Bo Tai—I love that name." She chuckled. "I think he can really be an asset for us there to help with getting some of the harder supplies."

She took another bite and thought for a few minutes. She waived her fork in midair. "All that is not what I'm concerned about, though."

"So, what *are* you concerned about?"

Elsbeth's eyes met his. "You."

"Me? Why?"

"Edvin, I love being married to you and I enjoy our time together. Still, I wonder if I'm putting your life more at risk. What if one of us slips up and says something that gives our secret away? I couldn't bear losing you."

Edvin took her hand. "Nor I you. If things heat up too much, we'll go to Petra ourselves and work from there. It'll be harder, of course, but we can make it work."

Elsbeth gave a sigh. "Then why not go now?"

Edvin gave her a sympathetic look and kissed her hand. "Darling, you know we can't yet. There's too much at stake. We have to keep going as long as possible."

Elsbeth nodded. "I know. Thanks for being the strong one for us."

Edvin smiled. "You run circles around me. Give yourself some credit."

Elsbeth suddenly displayed a wry grin. "I do. I was only trying to make you feel special."

Edvin gave a look of mock shock. "You were, were you?" He

jumped up—and so did she a split-second later. Edvin managed to grab her before she had taken two steps. He picked her up as she gave a yelp and then fell on the sofa with her.

"Are you going to apologize?"

Elsbeth shook her head, trying to hold back her laughter.

Edvin smiled. "You'd better apologize or you're going to regret it."

Elsbeth again shook her head, this time giggling.

Edvin quickly planted raspberries on her cheek and neck. Elsbeth screamed with laughter. "All right, all right. I give. I apologize."

Edvin stopped and gazed into her eyes. "I love you so much."

Elsbeth's eyes darted over his face and landed back at his eyes. "And I you. Now carry me to the bedroom."

Edvin smiled. "Yes, my lady."

Edvin picked her up and headed to the bedroom. He had to be the happiest—and luckiest—man alive.

Tomorrow was an unknown. How long would—could?—this happiness last? Thankfully, God was allowing them to enjoy it for now. Darker days were certainly ahead.

CHAPTER 29

Edvin entered the lobby of the King David Hotel. Despite being here before, the beauty of the lobby still impressed him. He took the elevator to the conference floor and searched the wall placards to find the right room. He passed the placard reading "Jericho I" and entered. Saeed and Myrka were already waiting. He went over and talked with them until others began arriving. Next in the room was Lisa Jensen, who was followed by someone he had only met once.

Edvin walked in their direction. "Good to see you again, Lisa."

"Hi, Captain. Same here. You remember Dr. Jamison McIntyre."

"Of course. It's good to see you again, Jamison. I've been following your updates. It seems the activity in your lab has increased drastically recently."

"My pleasure, Captain. Yes, Reverend Duarté wanted me to increase some of my research efforts."

Edvin wanted to ask why Jamison hadn't included him in the loop and what this meeting was about, but before he could do so, Duarté entered, followed by Anna.

"Good morning, everyone. Let's all take a seat."

Everyone had a seat and waited for Duarté expectantly.

Edvin looked around. It seemed obvious no one else knew why Duarté had called them here either.

Duarté looked around the table and smiled. "Well, I guess you want to know why I've called you here. I didn't want to say anything until now because I didn't want any of this to get out," Duarté began. "Before President Hatim had his accident, I promised him I would help the world worship him. I did that for two reasons. One, I think he deserves it because of all his sacrifice for the world. And second, there is no one more powerful or more deserving than he. The people of the world need to understand how fortunate they are to have him."

Edvin noticed everyone nodding as Duarté talked. He obviously had the power of a charismatic reverend and could carry a crowd on his words. Edvin wondered how he could get Saeed and Myrka to see the truth. He knew he would have much work to do.

"Dr. Jensen, I have a challenging question for you."

Jensen sat up even straighter. "Yes, sir."

"Is it possible to have something come through the atmosphere and burn up almost completely, but still hit the earth without a destructive effect?"

"Well . . . " Lisa tilted her head slightly to the side in thought. "I guess it's possible, but it likely wouldn't occur naturally. Meteors usually burn up completely or explode, which can be devastating. Even small meteorites that hit earth can be quite destructive."

Duarté nodded. "I understand that, Dr. Jensen. But if you had to orchestrate such an effect . . . " He paused. "Could you do it?"

"It would take a lot of calculation, but I think I could make it happen. But . . . why would I need to do that?"

"I want to call fire down from the sky in the name of President Hatim."

Lisa's face looked frozen. She was speechless.

Saeed looked at her and jumped in. "Where do you want it to land?"

"What about the temple altar?" Myrka said.

Duarté pointed his finger at her. "That, my dear, is a great idea."

Myrka looked at Saeed and smiled.

Duarté looked back at Lisa. "Well, Dr. Jensen, can you accomplish that?"

"We have a satellite launch week after next to look for other asteroids that may be headed for earth. I could do my calculations and get something on board." She paused. "I may have to delay launch a few days. This will be tricky. I'll have to build in small thrusters to slow down its descent. It's a matter of balancing the overall weight with what has to get added."

"As long as it's ready within four weeks," Duarté pronounced. He held up his index finger. "And it has to deploy by remote control. How long will it take to reach the ground?"

"Let me see." She did some quick calculations on paper in front of her. She looked back up. "At least half an hour, sir."

"Hmm. OK. I'll figure out how to work with that."

"I'll see if I can make it burn blue until it's closer to the ground so it won't be as conspicuous," Lisa said.

Duarté smiled. "Excellent." He turned to Jamison. "Now, Dr. McIntyre. Tell me about the progress you've made with your nanite technology."

Jamison leaned forward with arms folded on the table. "Well, as you requested, I've built nanites powered by nanobots with the ability to transport oxygen and travel throughout the bloodstream."

"Very good, Dr. McIntyre. Now, a few more questions. One, how long will they last? And two, can they operate even if the heart isn't beating?"

"Sir?" Jamison's eyes got big and his eyes darted around the room as if looking for clarity.

"Don't panic, doctor. I'm just trying to understand all our options. If a person was near death and received this, what would happen?"

Jamison had a confused look on his face. "You can administer these to a well person without much effect. Once a person dies or some tissue becomes anoxic, they will replicate and the nanobots will activate. They run on body heat but should maintain enough power to work for about three days before they completely shut down. Until that time, they will supply oxygen to the various body tissues, but once shut down, decay will begin."

"Thank you, Dr. McIntyre. Do you have them with you?"

Jamison nodded.

"Great. Please give your readied nanites to Dr. Lyle as soon as possible. I'm sure she can also use your help with their deployment."

"Certainly."

"Dr. Jensen, Dr. McIntyre, feel free to leave now if you wish. I need to talk to the others about a few other matters."

Both Lisa and Jamison nodded, rose, and stepped from the conference room.

"Now, let's get down to brass tacks, as they say," Duarté said, chuckling, before turning quite serious. "I want to have a public ceremony as soon as 'the image' is ready. I think that's what I'll call the figure Dr. Lyle is creating. Simple, but informative." He turned to Anna. "Ms. Bonfield, can you go ahead and invite the right people? I'll leave the appropriate list to you, but make it the usual political leaders, celebrities, and those in the know."

Anna nodded. "Certainly, Reverend Duarté. I've done this many times for President Hatim. I already have in mind who we should invite."

"Wonderful." Duarté smiled. "I knew you would have everything under control. Be sure we have important people from Israel there as well."

Anna nodded. "I'll be sure Prime Minister Afrom and High Priest Cohen are present." Anna paused. "I assume you want King Nazari present as well?"

"Absolutely. All these leaders are important, as well as significant international press and news stations."

Anna nodded. "I'll take care of all that."

Duarté nodded. "Now for other details. Corporal Phillips, I would like you and Lieutenant Amari to handle the launch of the fireball."

Myrka nodded. "How will we know when to launch?"

"When I begin talking at the ceremony, you alert Lieutenant Amari, who will be in a plane in the air and remotely launch the drop from the satellite, visually confirm the launch, and confirm it back to you. When I see you nod, I'll know all is on cue."

Saeed nodded as Myrka quickly took notes.

Duarté looked at Edvin. "Now, for you, Captain Isakson. I would like you to do what you always do."

Edvin was unsure exactly what Duarté was referring to. "Sir?"

Duarté laughed. "Troubleshoot, of course. There may be many details or issues that must be done at the last minute. I would like to be sure you'll be on top of it."

Edvin laughed lightly but breathed a sigh of relief. "Of course, Reverend. I'll be there early and stay late."

Duarté smiled. "That's what I wanted to hear."

"Just one final question, sir."

"Yes, Captain?"

"Do you have a date in mind for this ceremony?"

"Thirty days from today." As if anticipating his question, Duarté continued. "We will continue with or without President Hatim. I'm hopeful he will awaken before the ceremony since it's all about him. However, if he doesn't wake up—or worse, passes away, heaven forbid—we will go on. It will still be all about him."

Duarté looked at each of them. "Any more questions? Everyone OK?"

No one said anything.

Duarté smiled. "Excellent." He stood, and everyone else followed.

As Edvin left the hotel, it dawned on him he had a great deal to do in a month's time. He remembered Jeremiah stating that once the image became established at the temple, persecution would get much worse—especially for Christians, Jews, and Israelis.

Edvin decided he needed to talk with Jeremiah about how to get even more people, especially those within Jerusalem, into Petra.

CHAPTER 30

"No, I'm not saying it's a bad idea," Mik'kel said. "Just the opposite. I'm asking: how many you are including in this?"

Edvin took a seat on the sofa with his tea as Elsbeth brought over scones for Mik'kel and Jeremiah. "Well, all of us, of course. And I think Truman should have an encrypted phone as well. Some of us travel to Petra frequently, so being able to stay in touch with them is just as important."

Jeremiah nodded. "And once this image is presented, things will only get worse. So Petra will be more important than ever."

"I'll take the encryption app to Truman when Mik'kel and I go day after tomorrow," Elsbeth said.

"I know I shouldn't say this, but I really get nervous when you leave to go there," Edvin said.

Elsbeth stopped her cup in midair, then set it down. "Edvin, that's exactly how I feel every time you leave. But, we do what we must. These people need someone to help them connect there. Many of these are women and children and . . . " She looked at Mik'kel. "No offense, Mik'kel, but a woman can do that kind of thing better."

Mik'kel held up his hands. "No argument from me."

"I know—and I agree," Edvin said. "But that's how I feel."

Elsbeth smiled. "Well, I do appreciate you caring." She leaned in and gave him a kiss.

Edvin turned to Jeremiah. "So, how many are going to Petra this time?"

"I have twenty ready to go. It may be twenty-two, but two of them are on the fence. They have other family nearby and are having second thoughts."

Elsbeth shook her head. "Did you tell them the risks?"

Jeremiah nodded. "I've shown them Scripture and what they can expect." He shrugged. "But I can't make them go. I only hope they will have another opportunity."

"Well, I hope we'll have several more opportunities before the end of the month," Mik'kel said. He looked at Jeremiah. "And I hope you'll be able to go yourself toward the end of the month. There are several things I have to take care of for the Prime Minister."

Jeremiah nodded. "Sure. I'll make it a point to do so."

"Plus," Elsbeth said, "the people there are really appreciative when you go. Your explanation from Scripture gives them so much hope and encouragement."

Jeremiah smiled. "I really like talking to them and getting to know them." He paused. "But I also have a calling to the people here."

After talking a few more hours and getting plans made, Mik'kel and Jeremiah left. Edvin stayed up as Elsbeth went to bed. He wanted to go over the various projects and ensure everything was in order. Due to the increase in the work Duarté had requested of Lisa, Jamison, and Margaret, Edvin had to make available funds balance across all projects. Because he didn't give them advance notice, he could already hear the complaining the other scientists would give him as he would now have to decrease their funding without warning. He hated this part of his job the most. He found scientists to be extremely friendly—until you started messing with their funding. But Edvin had promised to keep everyone on budget, and he felt obligated to do just that.

He sent everyone affected an e-mail of explanation and hoped for the best.

* * * * *

The month went by quickly. As Elsbeth and Mik'kel made two trips to Petra, and Elsbeth and Jeremiah a third trip—this meant a total of ninety-seven people moved there—Edvin spent his time calming Prime Minister Afrom, overseeing preparations for the guests coming to Duarté's planned celebration, and coordinating the order of events for the day.

Unexpectedly, he also found himself performing crowd control at the temple. The formation of the image was clearly mesmerizing to many. They came and spent an hour or more simply staring at how the 3-D tissue printer worked, putting tissues together to form the image. Duarté became more and more ecstatic with the response of the people.

Then came the time for Hatim's memory transference. Margaret summoned Edvin to her lab below the temple just two days before the ceremony.

Margaret looked up as Edvin entered. "Captain, thanks for coming on such short notice." She motioned for him to come deeper into the room, near where the image stood. It looked complete, extremely lifelike.

"What else has to happen for the image to be complete?" he asked.

"The heart is now beating, and all is intact. All that's needed now is for the memory transference from the President. We're hoping that will enable . . . it . . . to wake, walk, and talk."

"Will the President wake also?"

Margaret shrugged. "We don't know. Conrad's been working with the President all month, but there's been no change. And that leads to this: can you help him bring the President's body in here next to the image?"

"Certainly."

"Go ahead and join Conrad. He's already in there with Jamison."

Edvin entered the room where Hatim lay. Everything looked the same as he had observed before. Hatim was still hooked to many tubes, wires, and machines. Although his head had healed, a prominent raised scar went from just above his right eye, up his forehead, and into his hairline.

Conrad turned as Edvin entered. "Captain."

Jamison nodded.

Edvin nodded toward Hatim's body. "How's he doing?"

Conrad shook his head. "No change. I don't get it. I thought for sure he would have wakened by now. His brain activity seems normal. I just don't get it."

"And the nanites?"

"Administered," Jamison said.

"Ready to move him into the other room?" Edvin asked.

Conrad nodded. "Help keep all the wires and machines intact, please."

Slowly, they moved Hatim's body into the other room and next to the image. Conrad prepared both bodies for the transference. The helmets looked similar to what Edvin used when he tried to communicate with Lars. Conrad placed the helmets on both bodies, and wires connected from the helmets to a box with various dials and lights.

"How do you know this will work? And how will you know it has?" Edvin asked.

"Well, I don't really know it will work," Conrad said. "It

should work based on my research over the last few months. But remember, we've never done this before. I'll know it has worked when the brain waves from the image match those of the President."

Margaret walked over. She looked at Conrad and gave a weak smile. "The time has arrived, Conrad. All our work hangs on these next few minutes."

Conrad nodded. Sweat droplets formed on his forehead and sweat spots became visible on his shirt. "Margaret, monitor the President's vitals." He looked at Jamison and pointed to a machine next to the image. "And Jamison, monitor the brain waves of the image."

Both nodded and stepped to their positions.

"OK," Conrad said, wiping his brow. "I'm going to turn on the transference machine and start increasing the frequency. Let me know when you see any signs of activity."

As Conrad powered on the machine and turned certain dials, a slight whirring sound could be heard, and it became higher in pitch, though not in volume.

"I think it's working," Jamison said. "Brain waves from the image are starting to show."

Conrad looked at Margaret. "How's the President?"

"Everything seems normal."

"Check his brain waves, Margaret. Everything OK there as well?"

Margaret nodded. "Yes, all still seems fine."

Conrad gave a deep sigh, and a smile appeared where great concern had been moments earlier. "I'll leave the frequency here until the transference seems complete."

After a few minutes, Jamison announced, "Conrad, it appears complete. All brain waves appear to mirror those of the President's."

It was then that Edvin noticed it: a twitch in Hatim's hand.

Before he could say anything, machines started beeping. The President's body began to enter some type of seizure.

"What's going on, Margaret?" Conrad hurried over to check.

"I . . . I don't know. Everything was fine and then . . . boom. Everything went wrong."

Jamison responded, panic in his voice. "The image is also convulsing."

Conrad turned and seemed torn between the two—uncertain which to assist. Then, just as quickly as the seizures began, they ceased. Conrad kept looking back and forth between the two.

"Vitals are stabilizing," Margaret said. She sighed, put her hands on hips, and shook her head. "That was scary." She looked at Edvin and gave a weak smile.

"How's the image?"

Before Jamison could answer, Hatim's machines started going haywire again. Conrad jerked around to see what was producing the noise.

"He's flatlined," Margaret yelled. "Conrad, get two cc of epi." She turned to the defibrillator. When she turned back, Conrad had not moved.

"Conrad!" she shouted. Then, with more force, "Conrad!"

He turned toward her. A defeated look was spread across his face. He pointed at the EEG machine.

Margaret dropped the defibrillator pads and gasped.

Edvin looked between the two. "What's the matter?"

Margaret looked at Edvin and then back at the EEG. "His EEG. It . . . also flatlined."

"What does that mean?"

Margaret stood staring at the EEG.

"It means . . . he's dead," Jamison said.

"What?" Edvin tried to process everything. He reminded

himself Jeremiah had predicted this scenario, but it was still so surreal.

Edvin walked to his phone and punched Duarté's number.

"Reverend? Isakson. You need to get to Dr. Lyle's lab fast."

"What's the matter?"

"It's the President, sir. He's dead."

"What? That's impossible."

"I'm afraid not, sir."

"I'm upstairs. Be there in two minutes."

Edvin could hear Duarté before he arrived. He burst into the lab out of breath.

"What . . . what happened?" He was gasping, trying to catch his breath.

"All was going fine," Conrad said. "And then he flatlined."

"Why?"

"We don't know."

Duarté looked from Conrad to Margaret.

"Reverend, both the ECG and EEG flatlined. There was nothing we could do." Margaret's eyes moistened.

Duarté's eyes darted about as if trying to decide what to do. He put his hands to his temples.

"OK. OK. This is certainly not ideal," he said. "But I'm still determined to make this work."

He looked at Jamison. "You injected him with the nanites?"

Jamison nodded.

"Now, we need to find a glass case his body can fit in," Duarté said, turning to Margaret. "Dr. Lyle, do you have a case that large?"

Margaret stood staring at Hatim's body, tears trickling down her face.

Edvin stepped over and touched her arm. She jumped slightly. "Margaret, are you OK?"

She nodded slightly, wiping tears from her cheeks. "I'm

sorry. What were you saying?"

"Do you have a glass case," Duarté repeated, "the size of the President's body?"

Margaret nodded. "There's one in the back corner. But I don't quite understand."

"It's important the public be able to see his body," Duarté said. "The nanites will ensure he maintains his color, and he will appear as if he's just sleeping." He looked in the lab's back corner. "Captain, can you and Dr. McIntyre place the glass case on that gurney?"

Duarté retrieved the President's suit that Margaret had put away. Conrad detached all wires from Hatim's body; Duarté dressed the corpse. Edvin and Jamison put the body in the glass case, sealed it, and pumped it full of pure oxygen.

"OK, we're set here," Duarté said. "The oxygen will keep the nanites working longer, and when the oxygen is used up, there will only be a vacuum left, which will help prevent decay. Now, I need to go find Ms. Bonfield and formulate how best to get the word to the international press."

"Does the agenda change?" Edvin asked.

Duarté shook his head. "No, Captain. Not really. We will display the body and perhaps have a eulogy. But everything else will go as planned."

Duarté turned and left. Edvin walked to where Jamison stood next to the image. "Is everything OK with the image?"

"It seems that way. Vitals look fine. EEG looks fine. Yet, I don't know how to make him actually sentient."

"Is that what the transference was supposed to do?" Edvin was struck by the simplicity of the question, and yet how important it was.

Jamison nodded. "At least that's what we thought would happen. No one really *understands* sentience. We thought if their two brains matched, that would trigger it. Although the organs of the image were obtained from others, the brain is an actual match of the President's." He shrugged. "I guess we still have a lot to learn."

Edvin nodded. His phone beeped with a text from Duarté: *Newscast prepared. Will be on in a couple of minutes.*

Edvin pulled out his tablet. "Conrad. Margaret. Announcement about the President is coming on. Want to see?" He looked at Jamison also, and he nodded.

Margaret gave a scrunched-brow look. "You mean Anna has it prepared already?"

"She must have had something prepared beforehand, just in case," Conrad said.

"Let's find out." Edvin tapped on the newscast and everyone gathered.

"We have important news today . . . " The newscaster's countenance changed visibly although she tried to hide it. Her complexion paled. "I'm . . . I'm afraid I have some very devastating news. This is a sad time for the world. I have just learned President Hatim was in a plane crash and . . . did not survive. There's no word yet as to other details. Many VIPs of the world are already in Jerusalem for the unveiling of The Image many of us have seen created over the last month. We'll be coming to you live from Jerusalem for that event if it will still be held."

She put her hand to her ear. "Ladies and gentlemen, we are told the body of the President will be presented for viewing at The Image unveiling, and the event will be held as scheduled. We'll continue to update this story. And now let's go live to . . . "

Edvin turned the tablet off. Everyone was transfixed. He knew he had to break the tension and get those around him refocused. "OK, everyone. It seems we have a meeting to get ready for. Let's get things ready."

Everyone nodded and turned to their duties. Edvin headed upstairs. He knew the number of people coming to the gathering would now likely be even larger than expected. He would need to get more seating as well as more guards to help keep the crowds under control.

As he walked by the erected column in the Court of Gentiles, there stood the image—looking quite serene.

He looked over and saw the two Witnesses. Edvin wondered what exactly would take place day after tomorrow.

CHAPTER 31

Edvin barely slept as he turned his focus toward getting everything ready for the ceremony. Based on Anna's educated guess, he had prepared for an additional fifty VIPs. As expected, the announcement of Hatim's death led to even more people accepting the invitation.

Edvin arrived very early the morning of the ceremony to coordinate and address issues. He made sure the setup for all seating, including those for VIPs, took place in the Court of Gentiles to avoid additional controversy with either his new father-in-law or the Prime Minister.

The large column showed the completed image of Hatim. Opposite the VIP seating sat the glass casket with the President's body. It was positioned at a slight angle for better viewing. In addition, a large screen, almost the size of the image itself, and erected above the casket, allowed better viewing of the President's body from a distance. Edvin looked at the image and the screen projecting the President's body. If not for the scar, the two would be identical. As Duarté had said, the President looked to be asleep, and his color remained normal. The nanites, thanks to Jamison, were working.

About two hours before the ceremony, people began gathering. The VIPs walked past the casket for a viewing before taking their seats. Dignitaries, like King Nazari with his wife and son, Prime Minister Afrom, several kings from various world territories, and Dr. De Voss all paraded past the casket. It was strange to Edvin: only De Voss appeared distraught. Edvin's heart went out to him.

Several entertainers also came. Gwen Sheridan dabbed her eyes with a handkerchief, and Ken Colston looked solemn. Many of the leading scientists from the Ziggurat of Knowledge—Lisa, Apama, and Ty among them—arrived. Conrad, Jamison, and Margaret were also in the audience. Many appeared to be holding back tears. High Priest Cohen arrived with Elsbeth, both looking reluctant to be present. There were many news anchors, journalists, and photographers present.

Once everyone had arrived, Edvin followed behind Duarté with Myrka. Duarté went to the podium in front of the President's casket. Edvin and Myrka stood to the side in an at-ease stance.

"Honored guests, I am glad you are here to honor one of the greatest men our world has ever known," Duarté began.

Edvin saw Myrka touch her ear and begin to speak. He had given her and Saeed earpieces so they could communicate with each other and him. "Amari, the ceremony has begun," she said.

"Roger that. Initiating the laser now to activate launch from satellite," Saeed relayed.

Duarté continued. "I'm sure we each have stories we can tell as to how President Hatim has helped us and enriched our lives. I want each of you to think about the first time you met him. Think about where you were then and where you are now. I think you'd agree your life is now more enriched than when you first met him."

Edvin scanned the crowd. Many were nodding as Duarté talked; there were some, however, who weren't.

"Now, to honor the President, an image of him has been created. This is not an ordinary image. One like it has never before been created. We call it The Image because it is unique—one of a kind. Not only is its likeness that of the President, it's a *living* image. It's a tribute not only to him, but to you as well. I would like to ask Dr. Margaret Lyle to come forward and explain her incredible work."

Edvin's earpiece sprang to life. "Phillips, this is Amari. I confirm the sighting of the fireball."

As Duarté stepped from the podium and made way for Margaret, he looked at Myrka. She nodded. He looked at his watch and nodded in return.

Margaret approached the podium and smiled. "This is a bittersweet moment for me." Her eyes watered; her voice cracked. She swallowed and cleared her throat. "I'm sure many of you experienced how President Hatim seemed to always be a step ahead of everyone." She smiled. "That's how he was with this project as well. Many of you have donated, at his request, a part of you that has now been used to create his image. He is responsible for the creation you are about to see, and he made *you* a part of this creation as well. You gave him a part of your life. Now he has given back life itself . . . "

"There is only one true giver of life!" yelled one of the Witnesses, who stood stoically at the edge of the Court of Gentiles, remaining in the area where only Jews were allowed access.

This threw Margaret off; she stammered while trying to complete her thoughts. She glanced at the Witness and back at the crowd several times. "Today . . . today we honor the one who has allowed mankind to reach a new plateau of knowledge." She glanced back at the Witnesses, who were pacing back and forth but remaining quiet. "Now I present to you—The Image! And I turn the podium back to Reverend Duarté."

She stepped from the podium and headed back to her seat, still flustered from the interruption. The crowd looked to its left as everyone heard noise from the large column projecting the image of Margaret and Hatim's creation. The column descended into the temple floor while something inside the column *ascended*. Soon it became evident to all: the image *itself* rose into view. Applause erupted. The image remained motionless.

Duarté returned to the podium. "Honored guests, what President Hatim and Dr. Lyle have accomplished is truly amazing, truly monumental. This day will go down in the history books, and you are the ones to bear witness of it. Now . . . " He held up his hands and looked to the heavens. Some in the crowd began to follow his gaze. "Now, in the name of President Hatim . . . I call fire from the sky to bear witness to this truth, and to show the world he alone is worthy of our worship and praise!"

Almost on cue, the fireball burst into visible flames as it descended. Everyone gave a gasp and pointed at the sky. Edvin looked as well. The fireball, mesmerizing to watch, continued its descent.

Myrka poked Edvin. He turned and saw a shocked look on her face. She nodded toward the President's body in the casket. "The scar."

"What? What are you talking about?"

"Captain. The President's scar. It's fading."

Edvin looked and, sure enough, the scar was losing its prominence.

Someone in the crowd saw it as well. "Look! Look at the President. His scar is vanishing!" a male voice shouted.

This created a stir. Some pointed, others gasped. Many

looked from the sky to the President and back again. People whispered to each other wondering what to make of it all.

Edvin watched the fireball descend. Its path looked dead-on, but he wasn't sure Lisa's calculations had been entirely accurate. It looked too large in size for where it should be in its descent. By the time it reached earth, there should only be enough of the fireball left to light the wood on the altar. But it looked too large to dissipate before landing. It didn't look as though its thrusters were slowing it down enough either.

The fireball descended and smashed into the altar, but with more force than predicted. It engulfed the altar in fire with a boom that startled the crowd. Shrieks were heard. The altar burst into flames as the rest of the fireball dissipated, but in the process, it sent flaming pieces from the altar flying. One of the larger pieces hit one of the legs holding up the bottom section of the casket. The glass casket slid off the now tilted table and made a loud crash onto the temple pavement. The escaping oxygen created a pillar of fire which ignited—and then vanished. More shrieking from the crowd could be heard; some recoiled from the event. Others stood and seemed to be scanning the area looking for a safe exit.

The President's body lay motionless on the temple pavement with shattered glass all around. And then Hatim . . . suddenly opened his eyes, sucked in a large breath of air, and came to a sitting position.

Many gasped. Many froze, but then turned in amazement as the image also opened its eyes, sucked in a large breath of air, and breathed heavily for a few moments.

The crowd showed signs of wanting to flee but being transfixed at the same time.

Edvin stood glued, eyes wide, unsure what to do—but then walked over to the President and helped him to his feet.

Hatim acted as if virtually nothing had happened. Edvin

noticed his scar had completely healed; there was no sign it ever existed. But his eyes. They looked different. They looked *colder*, as though all the caring was gone.

Hatim smiled. "Thank you, Captain."

Hatim walked to the podium. He raised his hands to quiet the crowd. This took several moments as chaos had been everywhere. Many were wide-eyed, and many looked ready to flee any second.

"My dear friends. Please, please. Take your seats." Hatim gave a reassuring smile. Slowly the crowd settled in. Some kept looking from the President to the image.

"Thank you all for coming to honor me." He put his hand to his chest. "It really moves me that you care so much about me." He made eye contact with Margaret. "And Dr. Lyle, what you have accomplished with The Image . . . " He looked at Duarté. "That's what you're calling it, correct?"

Duarté nodded.

"Excellent. I think that's a very appropriate name. Straight and to the point. Dr. Lyle and Dr. Bonn, I owe both of you a debt of gratitude."

Both smiled. Conrad looked quite smug in this moment of recognition.

Hatim looked at the image. "Image, now that you are with us and have taken your first breaths, what do you have to say?"

The Image looked at Hatim. "I am here to serve Malach Ebano Sahir Shen Ignado Ahmed Hatim—my Messiah."

One of the Witnesses called out: "Beware the abomination that causes desolation! The Messiah warned you of this."

Hatim walked from the podium and gestured toward the Witness. "Well, I see we have a dissident. Someone who denies reality." Many in the crowd laughed as Hatim chuckled.

"Let me ask the distinguished gentlemen in the, uh, stylish sackcloth garment . . . " More laughs were heard. " . . . how these events compare to *their* Messiah." Hatim turned and addressed the Witnesses. "You claim your Messiah died and rose on the third day. I died and rose on the *second* day." He glanced back at the crowd and then to the Witnesses. "Tell me, what took him so long?" More laughter could be heard. "Now, let me ask: did your Messiah ever create life when he stood on the earth?" Hatim waited a few seconds. The Witnesses said nothing. Hatim cupped his hand behind his ear. "I'm not hearing anything. Does that mean you finally have nothing to say?" He laughed. "Well, that *is* a first." He looked back at the crowd and others laughed with him. He raised his hands in the air. "So, that means I've done something your Messiah never did."

"Our Messiah *created* life itself," one of the Witnesses said.

Hatim began playing to the crowd and goading the Witnesses. "Oh . . . " He put his fingers to his mouth. "I forgot. Your Messiah was from the beginning of time." Hatim rolled his eyes in an overly exaggerated manner. The crowd laughed still more. "Well, I disagree. What's going to happen? Am I going to be struck down?"

"You've already been cast down."

Edvin saw Hatim's face, for a brief moment, flash a look of pure hatred. The crowd didn't see it as he had been facing away from them. Edvin was having a hard time processing this change in Hatim. He had always been a little arrogant, but his mannerisms were usually clothed in charm. Now they were clothed in sarcasm.

Hatim turned to the Witnesses. "It sounds like you want a showdown. OK. I say we have just that. Let's ask the crowd." He turned to the large audience. "Would you like to see which Messiah wins: The Messiah of the Witnesses, or the Messiah of The Image?"

Most of the crowd applauded.

Hatim smiled. "Excellent. It looks like everyone wants to see a showdown." Hatim turned to the Witnesses. "Let's see if you can send fire to me before I send fire to you."

Hatim lifted his hands toward the altar and twirled his body. Two fireballs leapt from the altar and flew into the two Witnesses. The fire didn't consume them, but burned a hole in their chests. They crumpled to the ground like marionettes with their strings cut. It happened so quickly no one had time to react. Mouths dropped open; people were stunned.

Hatim turned to the crowd and bowed. A few started to applaud and then more and more followed.

"Bravo!" someone yelled.

"No more depressing prophecies!" another called.

Hatim smiled. "Let the next three days be for merriment! Give gifts in memorial of this momentous day. We have seen an end to all this doomsday prophecy."

There was still more applause from the crowd.

While this went on, Edvin whispered in Myrka's direction. "Did you or Lisa rig the fire to do that to the Witnesses?"

Myrka shook her head. "No. Even if we did, how would the President have known about it?"

Edvin thought about that. *So how was all this possible?* Maybe Duarté rigged all this without him knowing. But Hatim would have had to be in on it. *Was this Hatim's doing?* Edvin remembered Hatim's eyes. Those were not his eyes. They were those of someone else. Jeremiah's words came back to him: the true Messiah's Adversary would possess him. Edvin shuddered. *Is Hatim now possessed?*

Hatim returned to the podium. "Now we must attend to other matters. We need to speed up the acceptance of the mark. The rest of the world has embraced it." Edvin saw some in the crowd nod their agreement.

Hatim looked over the audience and smiled. He grabbed

the edges of the podium and leaned forward. "And it's time for Israel to do the same."

The Prime Minister stood defiantly. "You gave us seven years," he said from his seat near the podium.

Hatim stared hard at Afrom. "Yes. But you have made no attempt to join the rest of the world. You remain resolute in your obstinate rituals. That stops—today."

"You have no right—"

"Don't you dare tell me what right I have," Hatim said, his voice escalating. "You signed the contract as well as I, which clearly states you will lead your people to join the rest of the world. Sit. Back. Down."

Afrom clenched his fists and his face turned beet red. But he took his seat.

Hatim whispered something to Duarté, then turned back to the audience. His response was now softer. "Let's ask the image what he thinks should be done." He turned to The Image. "Image, how should the people obey?"

"I serve the wishes of my Messiah." The image genuflected. "Everyone should serve my lord." He stood and remained still.

"Does anyone disagree with The Image?" Hatim slowly scanned the crowd. A sound could not be heard.

A smile slowly crept across Hatim's face. "Very well. The Image will make his dwelling in the inner sanctum of the temple."

High Priest Cohen attempted to stand in protest, but Elsbeth pulled him back down. She said something to quiet him. Edvin wasn't sure what, but it worked, even though her father kept shaking his head.

"Everyone in Jerusalem will meet The Image in the temple. He will come to know you," Hatim said, smiling. Some in the crowd snickered. The expressions on the faces of Afrom, Elsbeth's father, and those in their entourage were ones of horror. "But how should we start? Maybe someone already here."

Hatim's eyes scanned the crowd. They landed on Elsbeth. "Let's say, for instance, the daughter of the High Priest."

Edvin froze. His heart sank. *No, no, no. Not this.* He forced himself to take inconspicuous, determined breaths to remain calm. He tried not to look at Elsbeth; that might give their secret away. Still, he couldn't help but glance at her. She shook her head, and tears trickled down her cheeks as Avraham put his arms around her.

Elsbeth's father blurted out, "You're a monster."

Hatim laughed. "Who's the monster? The one who refused to side with the world? The one who clings to outdated rituals and puts one's whole nation at odds with the world, placing all their lives in peril?" Hatim smiled. "I'm actually doing you a favor. Once your people see the high priest's daughter joining with the rest of the world, so will they."

"And if we refuse?" Afrom's eyes displayed hot anger.

More World Forces soldiers had arrived and now stood at all temple entrances.

Hatim displayed a wicked grin. "Oh, I have to say, I must insist." He turned to Edvin. "Captain, please take High Priest Cohen's daughter and wait at the temple entrance until The Image is ready."

Edvin did as ordered, yet inside he was completely distraught. He tried to think of many things he might do, but he knew all of them would end badly. He stood at the end of the row until Elsbeth had walked down. Tears were still running down her cheeks. She looked at him, but he deflected the gaze. He took her arm and walked toward the temple itself. He didn't let go until they were on the other side, out of sight.

When he reached a spot where no one could see them, he let go and wrapped his arms around her with a tight hug. "Sweetie, I'm so sorry you had to go through that. I'm sorry."

After he let go, she wiped tears from her cheeks. "Edvin, what are we going to do?"

"There's only one thing to do."

Elsbeth gave him a puzzled look. "What's that?"

"You have to hit me in the face—hard. You then have to flee out those side doors, stay hidden, and head to Petra as fast as you can. I'll catch up with you later."

Elsbeth shook her head. "Edvin, I can't hit you like that."

"Elsbeth, you have to. We have to make it convincing." He stuck out his chin. "OK, go ahead."

Elsbeth closed her eyes and balled her fist. She shook her head. "I can't do it."

"Elsbeth, you said it earlier. We have to do what we have . . ."

Edvin sensed someone coming from behind him. He turned but felt an excruciating pain in his jaw and then his head; the blow knocked him off his feet. He hit the ground hard. The blow dazed him, and his vision blurred, making it hard to see who hit him and what they would do with Elsbeth. He shook his head wildly trying to restore his distorted hearing. He heard only bits of conversation: "You have to leave now" . . . "Don't worry, he'll be OK" . . . "I'll see you later."

When Edvin's senses returned to nearly normal, he was all alone. He saw no sign of Elsbeth, nor whoever attacked him. He tried to stand, but his dizziness caused him to stumble. He put his hand to his jaw but winced as more pain shot through him. He found blood coming from the corner of his mouth and nose. Somebody really packed a punch. He stumbled back to the other side of the temple.

Saeed had returned and was talking to Myrka. They stopped when they saw Edvin and rushed to him.

"Are you OK?" Saeed asked.

Edvin nodded slowly as he saw Hatim and Duarté also

walking over.

Hatim scrunched his brow. "Captain? What happened?"

Edvin rubbed his jaw gingerly. "She's stronger than she looks. Sorry, sir. She got away."

Hatim sighed. "It would be better if we had her, but no matter." He turned to head back. "It still fulfilled its purpose." He stopped and turned once again to face them. "I want all of you to come back to Babylon with me tonight. We have things to discuss. Reverend, tell Anna to stay here and coordinate the meetings with The Image. We'll let him decide what happens to those who don't take the mark."

All nodded. Duarté walked back with Hatim. Duarté did his magic to close out the ceremony, just as he had done at Gwen's concert. By the end, he had everyone—or almost everyone—feeling uplifted, as though a part of something larger than themselves. Afterward, many talked about how special the ceremony had been and how happy they were the President was back among them.

* * * * *

On the plane ride to Babylon, Duarté and Hatim were in discussion nearly the entire time. Saeed and Myrka sat with each other, and it appeared their discussions were going a good bit beyond merely professional. *Good for them,* Edvin thought. Seeing them, though, made Edvin think about Elsbeth. He had no chance to communicate with her, or anyone, before he left.

He prayed she was fine and made it to Petra.

Whether just in a good mood or for other reasons—Edvin was unsure—Hatim asked all of them to stay in the Penthouse that night. Edvin had a difficult time sleeping; he felt horrible he enjoyed a place of luxury while he had no idea what

Elsbeth had to experience that night, or even where she was. He wanted to call but believed it would be too risky. Eventually, he nodded off . . .

Edvin woke to a knock on his door. He glanced at the clock: 9:30 a.m. He couldn't believe he had slept that long. He assumed it would be Saeed telling him to get moving.

He opened the door and, to his surprise, there stood Cortez.

CHAPTER 32

After the shock wore off, Edvin stuck out his hand. "Cortez, how are you feeling?"

Cortez shook Edvin's hand, but there was no warmth there. Edvin thought that strange since it had been more than five months since the lopion attack, and they had not talked once in that time.

"It's really great to see you. I could almost hug you." Edvin laughed.

"That would really be inappropriate, sir. Would you please follow me? The President wishes to see you."

Edvin squinted; it seemed odd Cortez would act so coldly about their meeting again. And his eyes. Cortez's eyes reminded him of Hatim's. They no longer had the same sparkle they had before. Was that because of the lopion sting, or something else?

Edvin dressed quickly. As he walked from his room, he saw Saeed and Myrka standing nearby as well. He gave Saeed a questioning look. Saeed looked back and gave a small shrug. Cortez said nothing as they traveled down to Tier Four. He escorted them to just outside Conrad's lab and asked them to wait until called. Cortez entered the lab.

Edvin looked at Saeed. "Can you explain what is up with Cortez?"

Saeed shrugged again. "I have no idea. When I saw him, I patted him on the shoulder and he looked at me like I had violated his space. Weird."

"It's like it isn't him anymore," Myrka said. "Is this what the lopion sting does to people? Does it alter their mind or their memories?"

"Maybe," Edvin said. "I don't think I've met anyone who recovered from that sting."

"Does anyone else get the feeling they've been called to the principal's office?" Saeed looked between Edvin and Myrka. "Why would we have to wait before we see the President?"

"Yeah," Myrka said. "We serve him all the time. Suddenly, it's like we're outcasts or have to prove our worth or something." She folded her arms. "It's just . . . just . . . "

"Weird," Saeed said.

Myrka nodded. "Exactly."

Edvin glanced through the glass in the door. "Well, I guess we'll find out. Here he comes."

Face expressionless, Cortez opened the door. "The President will see you now."

Cortez turned and led them into the lab. Saeed shook his head and whispered to Edvin, "This is not normal." Edvin nodded.

At the other end of the lab stood Hatim, Conrad, and his assistant Sean. Edvin noticed someone sitting off to the side in a chair. *Lars*. Edvin's heart did a flip-flop. The poor guy looked awful: unkempt hair, wrinkled clothes, and it looked like he hadn't slept in days. He stared straight ahead, just as he did the last time Edvin saw him. Edvin almost choked up but forced himself not to show any emotion. Edvin wanted to run over, hug him, and ask forgiveness. He reminded himself it was Lars who made him promise to leave him here. But, should he have listened? Edvin forced himself to stop thinking about that and focus on this moment and whatever was about to take place.

Edvin now found himself disagreeing with Saeed. This felt more like the beginning of an inquisition rather than meeting the principal.

"You wanted to see us, sir?" Edvin tried to remain as calm as possible.

"Yes, Captain, I did." Hatim pointed to Lars. "Do you know this man?"

Edvin became nauseous. *He knows.* "I believe he is one of Dr. Bonn's subjects. I met him the last time I visited here."

"You made a . . . connection with him. Is that right?"

"Well, sort of. I guess. Mr. McElhaney here stated something happened. But I'm not sure anything significant happened."

Hatim's eyebrows went up. "Oh, is that so? Well, it seems your definition of significant is much different than that of Dr. Bonn's and Mr. McElhaney's." He turned to Conrad. "Care to explain it to him, Dr. Bonn?"

Saeed and Myrka kept looking from Edvin to Hatim to Lars. They had the most puzzled looks on their faces.

"Captain, when you first donned that helmet"—Conrad pointed to the one on the table next to him—"Sean, here, saw an important change at a certain frequency. He ran to get me. While you were not here, after we returned, the machine recorded several minutes of a connection—more than coincidence or something transient. A true connection. Actually, it became the breakthrough we'd hoped for. Yet we couldn't understand how such a connection occurred. Not until we had a pair of siblings in our study did we discover the same phenomenon with them. That breakthrough actually allowed me to make the memory transference between the President and The Image."

"So, you see, Captain . . . " Hatim smiled again, but this time wickedly. "This means you've been lying to us."

Edvin shook his head. "Sir? I've never lied to you. I may not have been forthcoming about everything, but I haven't lied to you."

"Are we now going to quibble over semantics?"

Hatim nodded to Cortez, who walked over and removed the weapons Edvin, Saeed, and Myrka carried.

"See, I always wondered about your last name. Isakson just screams Jewish, doesn't it? But records indicated you had not a trace of Jewish or Israeli blood in you. Very curious, wouldn't you agree? Yet, when I was told records stated you were adopted, well, naturally I thought that explained it. I had no reason to investigate further. You were a pure blood, you were likeable, and you were loyal."

A frown dropped over Hatim's face. "Or so I thought."

Hatim pulled Cortez's gun from his holster and pointed it at Edvin. Edvin instinctively raised his hands in the air. Saeed and Myrka took a step back.

"Imagine what a shock it gave me to hear this report from Dr. Bonn. You, a sibling of one of his subjects. A sibling who has a significant amount of Israeli DNA. Now, tell me—*Captain*—how is that physically possible?" Hatim now spoke through his teeth and his eyes were like daggers pointed at Edvin.

Just as quickly, Hatim's voice changed back to normal. "And guess what we found when we dug even deeper?" Hatim flashed that wicked smile again. "Your altered birth certificate. While legally you and your brother here had different last names, you were still blood brothers born of the same mother and same father." He spoke through his teeth, again with rage, his face getting more and more red as he spoke. "So I ask you again, Captain. How do you explain all this? How do I trust your loyalty? You haven't even taken the mark. Are you willing to take it now? Are you going to show your loyalty?"

Edvin tried to think of what options he might possibly have.

Nothing looked good. He had to keep them talking until he could think of something.

"But sir, my name hasn't come up on the list yet."

"Yes, and why is that? Why is it most of those closest to me haven't been on the list yet?"

Edvin looked at Cortez with raised eyebrows. Maybe this would be a way to deflect the hatred exuding from Hatim.

Hatim turned to Cortez, whose face turned red as he swallowed. "Sir . . . sir, I thought it best to deal with the masses first. I didn't want to take the time—or think it necessary—to tag those most loyal. Of course, I was the first."

Hatim patted Cortez on his shoulder and rubbed his back. "Yes, Cortez, you've been most loyal. Your logic is sound." He turned back to Edvin, hatred again flaring. "Cortez volunteered. You should have done the same. Now . . . now you will be made to comply—or else."

"But sir." Saeed jumped in. "We all have been loyal to you. The captain has done everything to keep your projects going while you were . . . away."

Hatim pointed the gun at Saeed. "So, Lieutenant. You side with your captain over me, do you?"

"What? No. I mean . . . Sir, I'm saying there *aren't* two sides here. We're all on your side."

"All on my side?" Hatim laughed. "Cortez is on my side. I don't see all of you, as you state it, on my side. Maybe the best thing is not to force you to take the mark, but to eliminate the threat entirely. How can I ever trust you again?"

"But what have we done," Myrka asked, "that makes you doubt our loyalty? I've always been loyal."

Hatim laughed. "You—both of you—have always been loyal to your captain here. If he isn't loyal to me, then neither are you."

Edvin's eyes darted around to see what could get him out

of this mess. He had always prided himself on thinking clearly in tough situations. Now he couldn't think of a single option. He glanced at Lars. Lars was visibly trembling. Was he about to have a seizure? He glanced back at Hatim. No one noticed Lars; everyone in the room was focused on Hatim and Edvin.

"Mr. President, we've all had a very emotional week," Edvin said, trying to talk calmly, slowly. "It's really easy to see how things can get blown out of proportion. Can you lower the gun so we can talk rationally?"

Hatim shook his head. "No, Captain Isakson, you won't be able to negotiate yourself out of this one. There's only one option here. When there's a threat, it has to be eliminated."

Edvin saw movement out of the corner of his eye. Before anyone could react, Lars came rushing forward like a linebacker. He ran into Hatim, who fell into Cortez, causing the gun to fire into the air. Cortez hit Conrad, which forced Sean into the table, hitting his head. At the same time, Lars screamed at the top of his lungs, over and over: *"Ruuuun!"*

Edvin took advantage of the situation and grabbed Saeed's arm; they headed for the door. Myrka stood transfixed. Saeed grabbed her hand as Edvin pulled his arm. She lost her balance from the sudden jerk. Saeed grabbed her jacket at the nape of the neck and pulled her back to her feet. All three bolted for the door. Edvin pulled a concealed handgun from his sock and shot the intercom. As soon as the door closed behind them, he shot the locking mechanism.

Myrka's eyes went wide. "What are you doing?"

"Trying to get us a little more time!" Edvin pushed them forward.

They headed for the stairs. Edvin looked behind and saw Cortez's face at the lab door window, pounding on it with his fists. Thank goodness the door walls were quite thick. All three raced down the stairs to the First Tier. There they walked fast and yet as casually as possible. Once out the door, they sprinted to the nearby hangar where the plane De Voss had given Edvin was stored.

Edvin turned to Saeed as they ran. "Can you fly us out of here?"

"Just try and stop me," Saeed said.

Saeed jumped in the cockpit while Edvin and Myrka boarded the passenger area. Saeed started the plane and taxied down the runway as quickly as possible. In only a few moments they were in the air. All three let out a sigh, took in a gulp of air, and looked at each other.

"What on earth was that all about?" Myrka looked at Edvin. "Captain, I think you owe us an explanation. We're tied to your fate whether we want that or not. So, please. Tell us what just happened."

Edvin nodded. He said a quick prayer and hoped what he said would be accepted. He wanted it to make the right impact on these two good friends. He didn't want to lose them.

"OK. President Hatim was right. Lars is my brother," Edvin began.

Myrka gave him a horrified stare. "What? He's your brother and you left him there?"

Edvin felt deflated. *This isn't starting well.* He waved his hands. "Wait, wait. Let me start from the beginning."

As quickly as he could, Edvin went back to what happened with Lars in Stockholm: Lars's fears about what would happen, how he found Lars in prison and tried to divert him to Israel, how he later found him in a semi-vegetable state, and how he communicated with Lars but how Lars wouldn't at least try to leave.

"Wow, that's quite the story," Myrka said. "But doesn't that mean you did lie?"

Edvin shook his head. "No. I never corrected what Lars

did. But until today no one ever confronted me on this issue. I've been as loyal to the President as the two of you."

Myrka thought for a minute. "Until today, he always appreciated you. So what caused such a change? He didn't just not like you just now. He really, really *hated* you."

"Think about it, Myrka. Doesn't the world seem like it's gone crazy? Not just this, but everything?"

"Yeah," Saeed said. "We were talking about that the other day. Even Cortez—acting so strange. There's no way he would have greeted us like that a year ago."

"I think I have the answer," Edvin said.

Myrka furrowed her brow and tilted her head in puzzlement. "Like what?"

"OK. Don't freak out on me. I want you to read something."

Edvin unlocked a file on his tablet and handed it to Myrka.

She glanced at it, rolled her eyes, and handed it back to Edvin. "Really? You've really gone off the deep end here. I'm not reading that."

"What is it?" Saeed asked while still focused on the controls.

"It's the Bible, Saeed. Edvin wants me to read from the Bible."

"What's that got to do with anything? What's going on, Edvin? Maybe you are the enemy."

"No, I'm not. I'm your friend. And I will always be your friend. Hear me on this one thing. What have you got to lose? You've got a couple of hours to kill anyway, right?" Edvin pleaded with the most sincere look he could give.

Myrka rolled her eyes again and snatched the tablet from Edvin. "All right. What am I supposed to read?"

"Read chapter 9 of Revelation—here it is—and let me know what you think."

"But Edvin. That's just a fantasy story."

"Read it. And then tell me if we're in fantasy world or not."

Myrka gave Edvin a dubious look but started reading. Her face went from doubtful to interested to glued to what she was reading. Periodically, she glanced up at Edvin with eyes wide—then read more.

"Edvin, this is . . . this is unbelievable. This last part here, this is exactly what Mrs. De Voss described to me in her panic state just before she died. How . . . how is this possible?"

"Fill me in, fill me in," Saeed said. He put the plane on autopilot and turned to snatch the tablet away from Myrka. He had the same reaction. "Who wrote this?"

"This was written around 95 AD," Edvin said.

Saeed looked at Edvin, mouth open. "No way. Really?"

Edvin nodded. "Now turn to chapter 11 of Revelation and read the first half of that chapter."

Saeed ran his finger across the screen a couple of times and began reading. He would read a few sentences and then look at Edvin. "It's like someone wrote this yesterday." Saeed gave Edvin a sly smile. "You're not trying to pull one over on me, are you?" He pointed his index finger at Edvin. "That is just like something you'd do."

Edvin shook his head. "Saeed, no. There's too much at stake to pull any punches now."

Saeed nodded. "You're right. But this . . . " He ran his hand through his hair. "This means . . . if this is true . . . then the rest of it is true."

Edvin nodded.

"I . . . I don't know about this, Edvin," Myrka said. "It goes against everything I ever thought."

"So, everything we've been going through is in here?" Saeed asked.

Edvin nodded again. He didn't want to push, but he wanted the truth to sink in. He prayed his two friends would be open to the truth.

"I need time to process this," Myrka said. "This is pretty heavy."

Saeed simply nodded. It was obvious he was having the same emotions.

"OK. I'm not going to pressure you, but think about it. What's the most logical step?"

"I hear you," Saeed said. "But give me some time. OK?"

Edvin nodded and patted him on his shoulder. "Sure."

Saeed turned back to his control panel. "OK. We have a decision to make. We're coming into Israeli airspace soon. Where are we going to land?"

"Eilat," Edvin said. "I know just the place for us to hide out."

Myrka looked at Edvin. "Is *that* in there, too?"

Edvin smiled.

CHAPTER 33

Just before reaching Eilat, Saeed spotted an abandoned airfield. "I have an idea. Let's land here. There, no one will have a record of where we landed. It could buy us more time."

"Roger that," Edvin said.

As they landed and taxied toward what appeared to be a deserted, half-torn-open hangar, Myrka looked out the cockpit window. "What on earth happened here?"

"I think this airstrip was one destroyed by the hail and burning sulfur several years ago."

"Lucky for us," Saeed said. As he looked out the cockpit window, he whistled. "Man, something did a number on that hangar. It may hide the plane—until someone is really looking. It could still be spotted."

"That's a chance we'll have to take," Edvin said.

Saeed shut down the engine. They stepped out and looked around.

"Now what?" Myrka rubbed the back of her neck. "I see some jeeps, but most look in bad shape."

"Well, let's see what we can get done. Saeed, see if any of these are drivable. Myrka, let's see if we can salvage fuel from any of them."

Both nodded and began their search. Edvin had been

wanting to know how Elsbeth fared after escaping from the temple; he decided now was probably a good time to call her. He dialed her encrypted number and heard a voice on the other end.

"Edvin, is that you?"

"Elsbeth." Her voice made him so happy it brought tears to his eyes. "It's so great to hear your voice. Are you OK? Did you make it to Petra?"

"Yes, yes. I'm fine. I'm here with Truman and everyone else. Where are you? Are you OK?"

"I'm OK now that I know you're safe. We're just outside Eilat at an abandoned airstrip."

"We?"

"I'm with two friends, Saeed and Myrka. We had to escape Babylon. I'll tell you what happened once we're together."

"Edvin." Elsbeth had concern in her voice. "Can you trust them?"

"Don't worry, honey. Yes, I'm sure we can trust them. We had a good conversation on the way over, but that's another story for later. We're trying to find something to drive to make our way toward Petra."

"Look in the back corner of the hangar," Elsbeth suddenly said. "If you look closely, you'll find a trap door on the floor under some junk. There should be fuel there."

"How on earth do you know that?" Edvin asked.

Elsbeth laughed lightly. "That's the airstrip we've been using. Didn't you wonder why the airstrip looked clear but still had so much junk everywhere?"

Edvin was dumbstruck. "Didn't even occur to me."

"I guess that's why we've been so successful," Elsbeth said. "We keep it looking rundown, but we keep it functional. We also keep a couple of jeeps functioning, but again, looking out of commission."

"Yeah, Saeed and Myrka are checking them out."

"You won't find any of them working, and all their fuel has been drained, but don't worry. The jeep right behind the hangar will work if you replace the spark plugs. You'll find those on the opposite side of the hangar from the fuel wrapped in a rag inside an old jar."

"Elsbeth?"

"Yes?"

"You're amazing. Did I ever tell you that?"

"You have a habit of stating the obvious."

Edvin laughed. "I miss you so much."

"Get here as fast as you can."

Edvin ran to tell Saeed and Myrka what he had just learned. They were as surprised and impressed as he.

"Somebody has a pretty special operation going here," Saeed said. "I'd like to meet them."

"Let's go. I'll introduce you."

* * * * *

A couple of hours later, they arrived in Petra. Edvin pulled up to where he and Mik'kel had met Truman before. He felt badly that Elsbeth and Mik'kel had been here many times since, but this was only his second arrival. It now looked like this would be home for a while.

"Are you sure someone is here?" Myrka said, spinning in a three-sixty. "It looks deserted."

Edvin smiled. "Isn't that what a good hideout should look like?"

Myrka laughed. "I guess it would." She then turned with a jerk.

Saeed squinted. "What's the matter?"

"I thought I saw something move."

Edvin turned and saw someone exit the doorway of a nearby building. He grinned. Elsbeth. She ran and threw herself at him. He grabbed her in his arms, held her tight, and kissed her with all his being. He couldn't believe he could love someone as much as he loved this woman. He found her amazing in so many ways.

Her eyes scanned his face. Concern suddenly came across hers. "Oh, Edvin, your face is bruised. Are you all right?"

Edvin smiled. "Now that I'm here, I'm right as rain."

Saeed and Myrka looked at each other in amazement.

"Well, Captain," Saeed said, "you've obviously been keeping something from us."

Edvin gave a wide grin. With his arm around Elsbeth's shoulders, he announced, "Saeed. Myrka. I would like you to meet Elsbeth, my wife."

Saeed's head jerked back. "Your *wife*? What do you mean, your wife? How . . . I mean when . . . did this happen?"

Edvin laughed. "Well, not that long ago."

Saeed held out his hand and shook Elsbeth's. "It's very nice to meet you. Sorry for being so shocked, but I never thought this guy would find anyone willing to have him."

Elsbeth laughed. "Well, he really isn't that bad once you get to know him."

Saeed chuckled. "I'll have to take your word for it."

Edvin gave a mock hurt look. "Wait a minute. I'm standing right here."

Saeed laughed more loudly.

"Hi, Elsbeth. I'm Myrka. I have to put up with this all the time."

Elsbeth smiled. "My pleasure to meet you. We'll have to spend some time together. I'm sure you have some stories I'm dying to hear." She glanced at Edvin. "And I'm sure I have some for you as well."

"Hey, hold up," Edvin said. "I've been here all of ten minutes and everyone is already plotting against me."

"Oh, sorry darling. Were you saying something?"

Edvin rolled his eyes. Elsbeth giggled and wrapped her arm around his waist. "Come on inside, everyone. Let's get caught up."

Before they reached the dwelling, Mik'kel walked out to meet Edvin. They embraced and gave each other a heartfelt hug and pat on the back.

"Thanks, Mik'kel, for taking care of Elsbeth." He noticed bruising on Mik'kel's knuckles. "You. It was you who slugged me?"

Mik'kel smiled. "You're welcome. By the way, your face looks pretty in red and purple."

"Well, your artistic hand is a little heavy, I must say."

"I was going for convincing. How'd I do?"

"Too well, actually." Edvin rubbed his jaw followed by a laugh. "You always did take your work too seriously."

Mik'kel patted Edvin's shoulder. "I'm glad you're here."

"Me too, buddy. Me too."

As they entered the doorway, Elsbeth talked to one of the men waiting there. "Bo, would you mind taking the jeep to the secure spot around back?"

"Certainly, Mrs. Isakson." He ran to the jeep and, in a moment, it was speeding off.

"So, that's Bo Tai?" Edvin raised his eyebrows.

Elsbeth nodded. "He has such a wonderful disposition. Everyone here loves him."

Truman, Iris, and Dan came over and gave Edvin quick hugs. Edvin introduced them to Saeed and Myrka. Truman invited them over to a small fire and gave them something to eat. Each of them recounted the story and their escape from Babylon. Elsbeth told her story of arrival in Petra as well.

"What about your father, Elsbeth?" Edvin hoped he had come around. "Were you able to talk to him?"

"Well, I haven't been able to talk to him in person. I didn't have time to do that before I left for here. Mik'kel has met with him."

Mik'kel nodded. "He's happy she's safe, but I couldn't get him to change his mind about our belief in the Messiah. He still feels saving the temple is more important."

"Mik'kel gave him an encrypted phone," Elsbeth said. "So I've been able to talk with him periodically. The stories he tells are horrendous. He refuses to come here where it's safe. He feels he needs to be there for the people."

Myrka spoke up. "So, what's going on in Jerusalem?"

Elsbeth's eyes watered. "It's horrible. Those who either refuse to be with The Image or refuse the mark are sacrificed on the temple altar."

"What?" Myrka gave a look of horror. "Are . . . are you sure? The President I know would never allow such a thing."

Saeed put his arm on Myrka's. "Myrka, the President isn't the same as before. You saw how unstable he acted toward us. I think he's gone to the dark side."

"There's more truth to that statement than you know," Truman said.

"What do you mean?" Saeed asked.

"Well, Scripture at least implies that Satan himself will possess him," Truman said.

"Like, the devil?" Myrka shook her head. "I'm afraid I don't believe in such things."

"But," Saeed said, "that would explain a lot."

"Maybe that's why it took so long for the President to wake up," Edvin said. "Maybe he had to be convinced to allow Satan to possess him."

Myrka looked at Edvin. "Well, maybe. But it seems too far

out there for me."

"There's something else," Elsbeth said. "My father told us the two Witnesses came back to life."

"What?" Myrka's eyes widened. "Things get more and more odd. I feel like I've entered the twilight zone."

Edvin nodded and looked at Elsbeth. "So, what happened?"

"He said each day since the ceremony, a large crowd of people came to view their bodies. It was bizarre. People came, made a toast to their passing, and gave each other gifts. Dad said it was morbid. He was going to go to the Prime Minister at the end of the week if no one came to bury the poor souls. Then, on the fourth day, around noon, as people gathered, the Witnesses came back to life. He said their wounds visibly healed, they opened their eyes, sucked in a large breath of air, and stood. The people watching were terrified. They heard something sound like thunder. The Witnesses looked upward and ascended into the sky, rising until they were out of sight. At the same time, an earthquake took place. Many in the crowd scattered, but many were killed—as well as others throughout the city. He said at least seven thousand people were killed and several buildings collapsed."

Truman nodded. "Just as Scripture predicted."

"That has really spurred hope back into the people," Mik'kel said. "President Hatim plans to take The Image to other places in a couple of weeks. Prime Minister Afrom has declared that once they leave, he plans to lock Jerusalem down and never allow World Forces back in. This may be the beginning of a war."

Edvin shook his head. "What about the rest of the country?"

"The military is on high alert, but we may not be able to protect the entire country," Mik'kel said. "Prime Minister Afrom states Jerusalem must be preserved at all costs."

Elsbeth nodded. "Dad said he plans to cleanse the temple

and reinstate sacrifices. I tried to explain the futility of that, but he wouldn't listen."

"All this is overwhelming," Saeed said. "I think I need to read more."

Truman smiled and patted him on the back. Myrka had a strange look on her face. Edvin wasn't sure what to make of it. He decided to change the topic. He didn't want the conversation to get too heavy, too quickly, for Myrka and Saeed. They needed time to process all they had heard.

"Truman, Elsbeth said your numbers have grown rapidly." Edvin looked around. "The number here looks about the same as when we first met. Where are the others?"

Truman smiled. "We're now only one small part of the gathering here. There are at least twenty other gatherings like this one around the Petra village. We try to stay hidden during the day and usually walk outside only at night when the moon provides light. We don't want to attract attention."

Saeed looked at Truman. "So, what do we do now? I don't want to go from being busy to just sitting around here."

"Oh, don't worry," Truman said. "I think we can keep you busy. From what you're saying about all you did at the ziggurat for the President, you can do plenty of the same here." He smiled. "It's just done a little more secretively. The skills you possess are not common here. You will be a big asset to us."

Saeed smiled. He seemed to like this compliment. Edvin was glad it appeared he would fit in so well. Maybe Truman would be able to reach him spiritually where he had not yet been able. Edvin looked around for Elsbeth. He saw her walking with Myrka and introducing her to some of the other women. Edvin suddenly felt better about the entire situation. It seemed both of his friends just might fit in here after all.

"Once it gets dark," Truman said, "I'll take you to the other living areas so others can get to know you. I feel both of you will become leaders here, so it's best they all get to know who you are." Truman looked at Edvin. "Many are anxious to meet the husband of Elsbeth. They hold her in high regard."

"Oh great," Edvin said. "No pressure there."

Truman laughed and patted Edvin on the shoulder. "No worries, Edvin. No worries."

Dan and Bo came running in.

"Put out the fire, Dad. Put it out quickly."

Truman dumped dirt on the fire and scattered the coals.

Edvin's pulse skyrocketed. "What's the matter?"

"Drones," Dan said. "Drones."

CHAPTER 34

Edvin and Saeed went with Truman and Dan to the door of the cave and pulled the blanket hanging to the side of the entrance over to a closed position. Truman explained the blanket blocked any light from the cave being seen. They carefully looked out. Two drones could be seen circling above.

Edvin glanced at Truman. "Do these come often?"

"They seem to fly through here more often than they did before. But I guess we can expect that."

Saeed looked confused. "What do you mean?"

"Well, Scripture states once The Image is set up in the temple, things will get worse."

Saeed shook his head. "I can't get over the fact I'm living a story out of a book."

Truman put his hand on Saeed's shoulder. "You have the wrong perspective, Saeed. You're not a character in a book. God has given us a glimpse into his plan. We live in a unique time in history. He's given us the opportunity to get on the same page as him. That's a rare gift."

"Hmm. That actually makes sense. But I'll have to think about it."

Truman looked at Edvin and winked. Edvin gave an approving look. Truman smiled.

Edvin heard one of the drones come back their way. "Truman, how do you know the drones aren't seeing anything?"

Truman shrugged. "I don't. But so far, no one unexpected has showed up."

Dan looked back at them from the cave entrance. His voice sounded as though in a panic. "We have a problem."

"What's wrong?" Truman rushed his way.

"Molly's doll. It was left outside. One of its braids has a metal band. If it reflects the sunlight . . . " He swallowed hard. "Should . . . should I run and get it?"

"No." Truman grabbed Dan's shoulder. "It's in God's hands now."

They each took quick looks from behind the blanket. Edvin could hear the drone getting closer. As they watched, a dirt devil formed and came closer to the cave and increased in intensity as it approached the doll. It paused next to the doll, then churned up enough dirt that it covered the doll. Just as the drone came into view, the dirt devil dissipated.

Edvin heard a hushed "Wow!" from Saeed.

Truman touched Saeed on the shoulder. "Let's head back in. We'll venture to the other dwellings in a couple of hours. The moon should be full tonight."

As they talked, Truman told how people from all types of backgrounds had arrived since his family first came. Most were Christians, but some arrived here just to escape persecution. He seemed excited; all the activity provided plenty of chances to witness for the Messiah, even at Petra.

As they headed out after dark, the light of the full moon gave the desert an eerie red glow. Not far from where they started, they entered another cave. "I think you may find this stop interesting," Truman said.

Edvin gave a questioning look. Truman smiled. As they walked past the curtain covering the doorway, they were met by several men with guns.

"Hey, Monroe. It's just us."

"Sorry, Truman. Can't be too careful, you know."

Truman nodded. "Monroe, this is Edvin Isakson."

They shook hands. "Monroe Grady."

"Monroe's from MIT in America," Truman said. "Actually, many of the people here are scientists in some form or fashion."

Monroe nodded. "Not all scientists are atheists. Some here still are, but we're working on them." He chuckled. "There's a newcomer here I think you will want to meet."

Monroe led them to a small fire. "Jamison, someone to see you."

Jamison looked up. His eyes widened. "Captain!" He stood and shook Edvin's hand.

"Jamison. I didn't expect it to be you. How are you here?"

Jamison motioned for all of them to sit. "I have important news to tell. But first, I'm here because of Dr. Jensen."

Edvin's eyes got big. "What do you mean?"

"Well . . ." Jamison picked up a twig and turned it between his fingers. "After President Hatim's ceremony the other day, I felt everything seemed wrong. I talked to Lisa about my thoughts, and she turned me in as a traitor."

"Lisa?" Edvin found it hard to believe she could be so cold.

Jamison nodded. "Yes, our darling Lisa." He looked at the stick in his hand for a few moments and then looked up again. "Anyway, I ran. By chance, I ran into someone you know."

Edvin raised his eyebrows.

"The prophet Jeremiah." Jamison grinned. "We had a long talk. He's quite convincing. Or maybe I was just ready to hear what he had to say." Jamison sighed. "At any rate, he set me on the right path and had me come here." He shrugged. "I'm jobless and homeless. But this is the happiest I've been in a long time."

Edvin patted him on the shoulder. "Jamison, that's great. Welcome to our family. And call me Edvin. I'm afraid my captain days are over."

Jamison nodded. "Thanks." He brought his knees tighter to his body and wrapped his arms around them. "Now for what I need to tell you." His eyes darted back and forth between them. "I've been listening to what Truman and Monroe have been reading from Scripture concerning what will happen next. I have a theory that may explain some of it."

"I'm listening," Edvin said.

"It talks about the sun scorching the earth. And about darkness and sores."

Truman nodded. "And you think these are connected somehow?"

Jamison nodded. "Cap— . . . I mean, Edvin. You know my lab was located between Lisa's and Apama's."

Edvin nodded.

"We would often talk on breaks about various 'what if' scenarios. Apama found a way to make fibers from the plankton bloom and then a way to make them into clothing, but she had a concern."

Edvin nodded. "I saw a news clip about that."

"Most scientists believed the concern unfounded because the chance of apollyonium ionizing to a great extent was remote. So we talked about possible significant triggers."

Edvin nodded. "And?"

"We came up with only two scenarios which would be catastrophic enough to warrant a widespread concern. One would be a major solar flare, and the other would be radiation from a magnetar. However, Apama believed even if a local effect occurred, it could still cause tissue damage for an individual, so she became adamant about the precaution."

"But aren't solar flares pretty common?" Saeed scratched his head. "So, why the concern?"

Jamison shook his head. "Most solar flares are not massive enough to elicit a radiation threat. That's why the rare ones are called massive solar flares. They produce massive radiation. I did hear Lisa say the solar flare activity has picked up recently."

"And what about the other thing? The 'mag' something?" Edvin asked.

"Magnetar. That's a star that puts out intense X-ray and gamma radiation. However, radiation from a magnetar reaching earth is even rarer than a massive solar flare. I have only heard of this occurring once—back in 2004, I think. It knocked out several satellites and disrupted a lot of sensitive equipment."

Edvin cocked his head. "But you think this will occur?"

Jamison nodded. "I always told Apama she was overreacting, but since I've been here, I've reconsidered. Knowing nature has been pretty freaky recently, and now hearing this prophecy, I think this is describing both of these events occurring simultaneously. It's the only thing that could explain how the event would be worldwide and involve both sun and darkness."

"Is there any way to predict when it will occur?" Truman looked hopeful.

Jamison shook his head. "No, that's the problem. But what it means is, if we have any clothing made from the plankton—unless it has a Pangaea symbol—we should destroy it. We can't be certain, but the huge meteorite hitting the earth likely put a lot of apollyonium into the atmosphere. The volcanoes probably did the same. If this does occur, as I said, any apollyonium not already converted to apollyonium oxide, either in the atmosphere or in the clothing, will react if ionized from the magnetic storm. And that could be fatal if it reacts with human tissue."

"Clothing is already in short supply," Truman said.

"I heard Apama say a major shipment will be coming in sometime the end of this month. They will have to use the port at Eilat as it's still the only port free from the bloom." Jamison's eyes got wide and he slapped his hand to his head. "Oh, I forgot something. I'm so sorry. Jeremiah said to tell you another shipment of people will be coming in at the end of this month as well." He shook his head. "I should have told you earlier. I'm sorry."

"No worries," Truman said. "Looks like we can kill two birds with one stone."

After talking more, Truman introduced Edvin and Saeed to several others. They met people from all over the world. Despite their hardships, most were in good spirits. As usual, there were a few who complained about all the inconveniences, but they were the minority.

* * * * *

Saeed seemed to be in his element. He helped many with organization and doing more with less. Soon, it seemed nearly everyone was singing his praises.

Myrka was a natural with the children. She instinctively knew how to get on their level; children adored her. She and Elsbeth became best friends. Elsbeth had the ability to remember almost everyone and what was important to them. Truman hadn't exaggerated. Everyone loved her.

After a couple of weeks, Jeremiah brought another group from Jerusalem. The group reacted with surprise that everyone treated them so kindly. Many had not accepted the

Messiah and thought they would be unwelcome. They were pleasantly mistaken.

Jeremiah ate with them that evening before heading back. As they sat together eating and talking, Jeremiah handed a flash drive to Edvin. He seemed hesitant to do so, but handed it over.

"Edvin, this is from Mik'kel."

Edvin took it with a questioning look. "What is it?"

"Something you need to see—but won't want to see. It has a disturbing video that he felt you should view. Israeli intelligence found this from some of their hacking." Jeremiah looked at Myrka. "You should see it also."

As Edvin loaded it onto his tablet, Myrka and others gathered around.

As soon as the video began, Myrka gasped. "What is he doing?"

The video showed De Voss tied with his hands over his head. His shirt had been ripped open, exposing bruises and bloody spots. His face looked disfigured as one of his eyes had been swollen shut. The other eye looked bloodshot, like he had not slept in a long time.

Hatim yelled. "Where is he, Ivan?"

De Voss struggled to get words out. "I . . . don't know. Why do you think I would?"

Hatim pointed his finger, his voice stern. "Because you're the one who planted that traitor in my midst from the very beginning. Was that your plan all along?"

"Malach, please."

Hatim turned in a fit of rage and slapped De Voss in the face. "Don't you dare call me that. You have no right."

Blood now dripped from the corner of De Voss's mouth. "Well, I used to. We're friends, Mal—" He paused. "President Hatim. We've always been."

"Or so I thought. I can't believe you would do something like this."

"Like what? Edvin has always been loyal, from day one. I never saw any deception in him."

Hatim pointed his finger. "He never took the mark." He took a step closer, still pointing. His eyes narrowed. "You never took the mark."

De Voss sighed. "President Hatim, please. You're being irrational. I'm on the list for next week. Take a look. You'll see."

"You should have volunteered earlier."

De Voss shook his head. "That's what this is all about? Because I followed the list your team put together?" He sighed. "Malach, please, listen to yourself. Are you well?"

In another fit of rage, Hatim now punched De Voss in the face. De Voss spit out blood. His teeth were tinged with blood as he spoke. "Why . . . why are you doing this?"

"Because I need to eradicate all those not supportive of me."

"But I am supportive. I always have been. I helped you become President!"

Hatim showed a brief tinge of regret, but then his expression turned stern. He turned back to De Voss, raised a pistol, and pointed it at De Voss.

De Voss's eyes widened. "What are you doing?"

"Once people see I will not tolerate insubordination from someone close to me, they will see my resolve, and none will defy me."

De Voss slowly shook his head. "You're not making any sense. Malach, please . . . "

In a now calm voice, Hatim said, "I told you not to call me that." He pulled the trigger. The bullet entered De Voss's forehead. For a brief second, De Voss stared at Hatim, then blood appeared on his forehead, and De Voss's head fell to his chest.

Edvin stopped the video. Myrka and Elsbeth each gasped

and placed a hand over their mouth. Both just stared at Edvin, whose eyes were already watering.

"He's a monster." Myrka turned and walked off. Saeed quickly followed her.

Edvin sat stunned. Elsbeth reached over and hugged his arm. "I'm so sorry, Edvin."

"It's my fault. Dr. De Voss is dead, and it's all my fault."

Jeremiah put his hand on Edvin's shoulder. "No, Edvin. President Hatim has yielded to the Adversary. You can't blame yourself."

Tears ran down his cheeks. He looked at Elsbeth. "He was like a father to me." He shook his head. "Why?"

Elsbeth was now crying softly. "I don't know. These are hard times."

Edvin nodded. "I . . . I don't think he ever believed in the Messiah. I tried once to tell him." His voice caught in his throat. "I had hoped to try again. Now . . . "

Edvin shook his head and let the tears flow.

CHAPTER 35

Later that evening Jeremiah confirmed a group would be arriving from Africa. Truman made plans for five to travel to Eilat and retrieve them: Truman, Dan, Monroe, Edvin, and Saeed. Myrka acted upset that she wasn't chosen, but Elsbeth wanted her to stay and hear Jeremiah speak. Edvin agreed with her plan. He would have liked Saeed to stay and hear Jeremiah as well, but with Truman making significant inroads with Saeed, he wanted to keep the two of them together.

They brought around the jeep stored behind the cave, loaded up, and drove into Eilat under the cloak of darkness. Thankfully, only a small crescent of moon adorned the sky. The mission sounded simple. They were to go to the seaport and find the ship *Mozambique* and, on it, locate a shipping container labeled with a crescent moon but no star. They would get the covered truck stored at one of the warehouses, load everyone, and return to Petra.

Edvin and Truman had another job as well. They somehow had to sneak into the World Forces outpost at the port, find more clothing, and bring it back to the jeep.

They parked the jeep on a side road a couple of blocks from the port. Truman gave each of them earpieces so they could communicate—souvenirs from a previous raid. All managed to get to the port unseen, but for some reason, more World Forces officers than anticipated were present. All five of them stayed in the shadows looking for the right container; they split up to cover more territory faster. Edvin's heart pounded from his adrenaline surge. It had been a long time since he had participated in such a secret operation. He hoped his reflexes weren't rusty.

He heard Dan's voice in his earpiece. "I think I've located it. But we have a problem. Come to the northeast corner of the port."

When Edvin arrived, the others were already there. "Where is it?"

Dan pointed up. Edvin's eyes followed his finger. The container sat atop three other containers—not an ideal location for getting them out. They heard someone approaching. Each of them crouched into a shadow or behind containers. Two guards came by on the other side of the containers from where they hid and talked to each other for what seemed an eternity. They eventually walked on. All five men breathed sighs of relief.

Edvin whispered to Truman. "What do we do?"

Truman looked at the container and the others around them. "It's not ideal, but the other containers next to it are arranged in a step-down fashion. We'll have to help them down from container to container. There's five of us, so we can do it."

Edvin shook his head. "That's going to take a lot of time."

Truman shrugged. "What choice do we have? Moving containers with the crane will only draw attention—way too loud. This is the best—and only—solution we have."

Edvin reluctantly nodded. "OK. Let's do it."

Dan climbed up to the container. Saeed manned the next

tier, then Truman, then Edvin. Monroe kept watch. Dan looked to Monroe for the OK, and once he'd received it, he opened the container door. The opening made more noise than any of them wanted. Everyone froze. Dan waited for Monroe to give the all clear. Just then, a head poked out from the container. Dan quickly put his finger to his lips. The man nodded. Dan looked in with his flashlight, then whispered something to Saeed below him.

When word came down to Edvin, he passed it to Monroe: thirty people. This was going to be tricky.

They helped each make the transition from container to container until they reached the bottom with Monroe and Edvin. Most were adults, but six were children: four toddlers, two infants. The small ones concerned Edvin the most. The toddlers, frightened, remained quiet, but the infants were an unknown. Thankfully, both babies were sleeping. Edvin hoped they stayed that way.

One of the toddlers suddenly pointed to the sky. When Edvin looked, he was mesmerized. The sky became a light show of color that morphed and changed shape like a kaleidoscope. He had seen the aurora borealis when in northern Sweden, but this was like nothing he had seen before.

When everyone reached the ground, Monroe raised his hand, panic on his face. All froze. He motioned for all to move back. Everyone went against the containers to try and meld into the darkness. They heard guards talking. The guards stopped opposite them on the other side of the containers. One of the infants made a noise—a squeal that was something between a cry and a yawn. The mother's eyes got big and she tried to silence the child as best she could. Everyone looked at each other—frozen. The guards stopped talking. Edvin heard footsteps approaching.

The lights in the sky went crazy with their dance at the

same moment the guards startled them with drawn rifles. Both sides had guns pointing at each other. One of the infants began to cry. In an instant, the guards yelled in pain, dropped their guns, and fell to the ground in agony. Sparks shot from their bodies. The guards pulled at their clothes to rip them from their bodies. One of the guards tore off his shirt; multiple large blisters could be seen.

Truman, the first to overcome the urge to stare, motioned for them to go. Everyone moved quickly and traveled the several blocks inland to the warehouse where the truck was hidden. Along the way, they saw many others in agony on the ground. Many were screaming. One lunged at a woman in their group. He clung to her arm screaming, "Help me! Please, help me!" She recoiled in horror. Monroe came by and ripped the man from her arm and let her catch up with the rest of the group. Edvin saw him take a quick moment to rip the shirt from the man and leave him sobbing in the street. Edvin heard a muffled "thank you" as he jogged by.

They found no resistance after that and managed to get everyone in the truck and on their way. No lights were on in the city. Evidently, the power grid had been affected by the magnetic storm. Edvin and Truman ran back to get the jeep. Since it was not running when the magnetic storm hit, it started up and ran. The sky still danced in color. Unfortunately, they had no time to enjoy it.

When they reached the World Forces outpost, they encountered little resistance. Several guards lay writhing in pain. A couple of them tried to put up a fight, but Truman easily overpowered one and Edvin the other. They placed several boxes of clothing in the jeep and were off.

Once out of the city, Edvin breathed a sigh of relief. With Truman driving, he leaned his head back and enjoyed the sky.

"Are all your trips into Eilat like that?"

Truman laughed. "Too much fun for you?"

Edvin turned to look at Truman. "Clearly, your definition of fun and mine are from different dictionaries."

Truman laughed still more. "I have to say, the last trip was not as complicated." Truman glanced at Edvin. "It's a good thing your procurement officers don't listen to your own scientists."

Edvin held up his palms. "That wasn't my department. Good thing, I guess. I would have insisted."

"God knew where not to put you," Truman said. Both men laughed.

Once they got back to camp, Monroe decided to take the thirty new arrivals into his group; he wanted a mix of scientists and nonscientists. He hoped that would help everyone gain perspective and appreciate others. Elsbeth and Myrka greeted the group and fed everyone. Myrka fussed over the children, which helped the women feel more welcome.

That evening at dinner, Elsbeth sat next to Edvin. She had a huge smile on her face.

"Well, someone's in a great mood."

Elsbeth nodded. "I have some great news."

Edvin tilted his head. "Oh?"

"It's Myrka. She accepted the Messiah today."

"Really? I guess her staying here turned into a good idea after all." Edvin felt such relief. Now if only Saeed would do the same.

"It was quite interesting. Jeremiah read Scripture and stated how, today, we have a unique perspective. We have a more detailed knowledge of our future than at any time in prior history. She talked to him afterward and, presto, she believed." Elsbeth was nearly giddy.

"I wish Saeed would do the same."

"Well, let's see what happens. She said she's going to talk to him tonight."

Later that night, Edvin felt his body shaken awake. When consciousness came, there stood Truman. Edvin sat up quickly. "What's wrong?"

Truman smiled. "Not wrong—wonderful. Can you come with me?"

Edvin threw on a shirt and some sweatpants and followed Truman, but couldn't comprehend what his friend was referring to.

They walked outside, and there stood Saeed and Myrka. Edvin still couldn't put the pieces together.

"Hello, Edvin," Saeed said. "Sorry for waking you. But I had to get this straight in my mind."

"No problem." Edvin noticed Saeed acting fidgety, and he kept rubbing his palms on his pants. "What's up?"

Saeed looked at Edvin. "I've known you a long time. I've looked up to you these last several years. I know you've accepted the Messiah for your future hope. I need to know what made you accept him."

"Well . . . " Edvin, still trying to fully awaken, rubbed his chin in thought. "Elsbeth and Mik'kel accepted before I did. I respected them and didn't want to be left out, but for some reason I couldn't do it. I guess I had grown up so skeptical of religious things that I had a difficult time accepting it. Then Jeremiah talked with me. He approached me in a matter-of-fact manner. He didn't preach, and he didn't push. He showed me how Scripture matched the events of the day. I had to allow myself to face my unfounded skepticism and keep an open mind about Scripture, that it could be truth. It took a while for my brain to take that step, but once I decided to do so, it seemed as if a boulder had lifted from my shoulders. I knew I didn't have to worry about my future. I could relax. I was no longer the one in charge."

As Edvin talked, Saeed's eyes got bigger; his nodding became exaggerated.

"Edvin, that's exactly how I feel. I want to, but I don't, at the same time."

Edvin nodded. "It's a decision, Saeed. Your brain must accept what your heart already knows. It's not the normal way of accepting things. That's why it's so hard. It's not by intellect, but by faith. Faith must come first. Once you've accepted it, the intellect of your decision comes later. The order can't be reversed."

Saeed nodded. His eyes were actually filling with tears. His body shook. "I . . . I think I want to take that step. But I don't know what to do."

"Just talk to him. The Messiah, or Yahushua Ha-Mashiach ben Elohim as Scripture also calls him, *died* for your sins. He paid the debt we can't pay. Talk to him. Imagine he's right here. Just speak to him."

Tears now ran down Saeed's cheeks. This was a hard step for someone always opposed to such things. Edvin felt for him. He still remembered how he felt before this step.

Saeed bowed his head. Edvin put his hand on Saeed's shoulder. He could feel him still trembling. "Messiah, I don't know what to say except I'm sorry for all my ways and thoughts where you were shut out. I don't understand everything, but I do believe you died for me and my sins. I don't deserve Heaven, but I know your Scripture promises it to me if I trust in you and your payment for me. It's nothing I do or did, but what you did for me. I do. I trust you. I believe in you. I accept you as my Messiah."

Saeed's trembling suddenly stopped. He opened his eyes and

looked at Edvin. He still had tears running down his cheeks, but his face now showed a smile. “Edvin, you were right. The heavy boulder is gone. I now know my future is secure.” He chuckled and gave Edvin a quick hug. “It’s wonderful.”

He shook Truman’s hand. “Thanks for being patient with me. I really appreciate it.”

Truman smiled. “You did the work. I just listened and answered questions.”

Saeed turned to Myrka. He gave her a big hug. “Thanks for talking with me tonight. I cringed when you told me you had accepted the Messiah. I really didn’t know what that meant. Thanks for pushing me to this decision.”

He gave her a kiss. She blushed, but also looked happy about it. “You’re . . . welcome.”

Edvin and Truman left the two of them to continue to talk. Edvin said a short prayer of thanks as he headed back to Elsbeth. Edvin also felt lighter. Two of his best friends had accepted his Messiah—another burden lifted. Edvin thought he would have trouble sleeping, but the peace of knowing the future for his friends helped him fall asleep in no time.

* * * * *

This became Edvin’s life for the next several months. Sometimes there were planned rescues, either in Jerusalem or Eilat. Sometimes people just showed up. The numbers in Petra continued to grow. Demands were ever increasing as more and more supplies were needed. This became challenging for the first couple of months after the magnetic storm until communications were restored.

One evening, Edvin clicked on a newsfeed that looked interesting: “Dissatisfaction Growing.” A newscaster was interviewing Apama and Lisa.

"This is Bob Rothschild with World News Comment. Today we have Dr. Apama Bhattacharya and Dr. Lisa Jensen from President Hatim's Ziggurat of Knowledge." Both women smiled.

"Dr. Bhattacharya, many are saying the President is not doing enough to protect the world's citizens. How do you respond to that?"

"I assume you are talking about the magnetic storm incident," Apama said. "If you recall, Bob, I was very public about the precautions people should take. We can't police everything or make people do what they should."

"Many people are suing, and many companies in Asia are saying they have been abandoned by the President's government, that their entire economy can be devastated without more assistance."

"I can't really speak to the legal ramifications, but we can't protect people who don't follow our recommendations," Apama said.

"So, you're saying they're on their own?"

"I'm afraid I'm not able to speak to that," Apama said more tersely.

"Dr. Jensen, how rare was this magnetic storm incident?"

"Extremely rare," Jensen said. "We don't usually see effects from a magnetar, and especially one as close as the one we experienced, much less simultaneously with a solar flare—and not just a solar flare, but the largest one we have ever seen."

"So, should companies be held accountable for something that was not expected to happen?"

"Again, that's for the lawyers to decide," Jensen said. "I think this is a matter of ethics, and it's clearly outside of my expertise."

"I want to thank the two of you for being with us today," Rothschild said. He turned to the camera. "Stay tuned as we follow this brewing controversy."

Edvin called Truman over. "Look at this. What do you make of it?"

Truman watched the piece, then said, "Well, I think it's consistent with Scripture. Of course, we don't know how all of this will play out, but I don't think everyone will be eye to eye with Hatim. This seems like the Eastern territory is getting to a place of being at odds with his administration, and there is some Scripture that seems to support that sentiment."

"So, the coming battle could be huge," Edvin said, realization dawning.

Truman nodded. "Absolutely. No doubt. There's nothing that will compare to it."

Myrka walked over. "Edvin, Elsbeth wants to see you. She's in your alcove."

Edvin gave her a confused look. "Is everything OK?"

"All I can say is, she said, 'It's life altering.'"

Edvin's heart raced. *What does that mean?* He looked at Truman with concern. Truman gave a slight shrug and shook his head.

Edvin looked at Myrka for more information, but she said nothing. He raced toward the alcove he and Elsbeth shared.

CHAPTER 36

Edvin rushed past many of the large open areas with alcoves to reach the one belonging to him and Elsbeth, which gave them privacy among so many people now living in Petra.

"Elsbeth." Edvin breathed hard, out of breath. "What's wrong?"

Elsbeth turned with a smile. "Wrong? Who said anything's wrong?"

"Myrka. She said—"

"I think she used the words 'life altering.' And that's what it is."

Edvin looked at her with furrowed brow. "What do you mean?"

Elsbeth grabbed his hands and smiled. "Edvin, we're pregnant."

Edvin heard the words, but they didn't register. His mind seemed stunned, and his muscles didn't respond to his brain. He tried to speak, but words wouldn't come. "Wh—what?"

Elsbeth giggled. "I'm pregnant. We're having a baby."

The words sunk in, and Edvin felt joy growing inside. A smile crept across his face. "Elsbeth, are you sure?"

She nodded. He pulled her to himself and kissed her. "Elsbeth. That's wonderful news."

"So, you're happy about this?"

He nodded. "Of course." He gave her a hug, then pulled slightly back. "How far along are you?"

"Probably a little more than a month." She looked at him and suddenly felt concern over Edvin's expression. "Is anything wrong?"

Edvin shook his head. "No, it's just my conservative side coming out. It's such a dangerous time. I get concerned."

Elsbeth touched Edvin's cheek. "I know. I get a little freaked out myself. But it's also exciting. I know God will take care of us."

Edvin hugged her again and gave her another kiss. "Let's go tell the others."

Elsbeth laughed. "OK, but I bet Myrka already has."

By the time they reached the others, everyone knew. They received so many congratulations that Edvin felt cheated, as though he had no one left to tell. The news spread like wildfire. That evening, probably because of being so well-liked—even loved—by everyone, a burst of activity occurred around Elsbeth. Edvin had to laugh. The activities sometimes included him, but usually not. He was happy to just sit back and see her doted on.

* * * * *

Living in this place became a way of life, and Edvin found himself liking it. Drawbacks existed, but having so many friends made it worthwhile. Local news came from Mik'kel and Jeremiah, who visited periodically. Edvin watched newscasts as well. While the main news channels painted a rosy picture of Hatim's world vision, other websites gave a more realistic view. These sites kept getting shut down—but they would emerge again as different sites.

The picture looked bleak. Multitudes of people died, causing disease and pestilence in many places. This led to a circular problem. The dead weren't buried fast enough, so disease and pestilence caused more death. Food and clothing were short in supply. This caused riots and looting.

Worst of all, the persecution of Christians, Jews, and Israelis became rampant. Hatim's no tolerance policy meant no mark, no life. Bleak stories came in from some who escaped and made it to Petra. Execution centers were set up with people slain by the thousands. Public execution became the norm—as a deterrent, but also as an encouragement to those with the mark to turn in others. Rewards given to those who did so provided incentive for many to do more of the same.

One morning, Edvin's encrypted phone rang. He didn't recognize the number and debated whether to answer. Curiosity got the better of him.

"He is coming," the voice on the other end of the call said.

Edvin, speechless for a second, wondered whether this was a test or if the person on the other end was trying to assure him of his validity.

"He is coming again," Edvin finally decided to answer.

Edvin heard a large sigh on the other end. "Captain, this is Ty."

"Ty? Why are you calling? How did you get this number?"

"Well, that's a long story, but I heard you're no longer employed by President Hatim. I assumed that could mean only one thing. I didn't understand it—but now I do. Praise our Messiah."

"Ty, that's wonderful. I'm so glad you accepted the truth."

"I am too. But that's not why I'm calling."

"What's wrong?"

Ty gave a nervous laugh. "Just about everything. I'm still in D.C., but conditions here are pretty bleak. I've been working day and night at the research center here. Somehow, I never got on Cortez's list for the mark, and being here in the facility almost 24/7, I've been able to survive. But . . . " Ty choked up.

"There's something else, right?"

"Uh, yeah. The President was here about a week ago. He wanted the teleporter online, but we're just not ready. We were getting close. I told you about Brad and his ideas."

"Yeah, I remember."

"Well, it was working—sort of. We had made great strides, but we still weren't ready for prime time. Hatim felt we were too slow. He . . . " Ty stopped in midsentence.

"What happened, Ty?"

"He shot Brad—in cold blood. Hatim became so angry. I never saw him like that before. He stormed out of the lab and said, 'Get it to work, or else.'"

"Why would he do that?"

"He's gone mad. All he talked about was getting 'those Jews.' He feels they are the bane of his existence and the reason for all the problems in the world. Captain, I want to warn you. He's coming to Israel with all the firepower he can muster. He wanted to get everything there using the teleporters. Not having them will slow him down, but not deter him. I just wanted you to know."

"Thanks, Ty. I appreciate this."

"Goodbye, Captain. Godspeed. See you on the other side."

The phone went silent. Edvin thought about that: *See you on the other side.* He had to agree. The end was likely not far away.

Elsbeth rushed over, excited, and grabbed Edvin's arm. "Mik'kel and Jeremiah are here."

There were handshakes and hugs all around. Truman served them coffee and tea. Each side updated the other.

"Congratulations, Myrka. And you, too, Saeed," Jeremiah

said. "It always warms my heart when I hear such good news."

Myrka's eyes watered a bit. "Thank you, Jeremiah. What you shared resonated with me."

Jeremiah smiled. "I can't take credit. Ruach HaKodesh used what I said to help your heart know what your mind couldn't."

Myrka laughed. "That's a good way of putting it."

Elsbeth interrupted. "How's Dad?"

Mik'kel shook his head. "Stubborn as ever. He did get the temple cleansed and has instituted sacrifices again."

Edvin decided he should tell everyone what he just heard from Ty. Everyone shook their heads.

"We've heard the same rumor," Mik'kel said. "We're preparing for the coming battle. Also, the Asian territories are unhappy with the President since the clothing debacle decimated their economy."

"Not that I like the guy anymore," Myrka said, "but can they really hold him at fault when they were warned about the potential hazards of cutting corners?"

Mik'kel shrugged. "Politics is not always logical. I'm sure there's more to it, and this is probably the tipping point. However, we heard they bought off Turkey to block off the Euphrates and Tigris rivers."

"The water levels were already low due to almost two years of no rain," Edvin said. "Even though we've had rain since, it hasn't been much. I know every time we flew over the area traveling to Babylon, the river looked smaller and smaller."

Mik'kel nodded. "Yes, and those waters are some of the least contaminated. Turkey and Syria have been siphoning off more than their allotted amount for a long time now."

Saeed looked confused. "But aren't these countries in the territory under the President's control?"

"Well, Syria is, but Turkey technically isn't," Mik'kel said.

"But word is, he's been so focused on his hatred for us, he's lost a lot of the control he once possessed. I'm not sure he even knows, or cares, at this point."

"Maybe. But he should be concerned an Asian army is plotting against him," Saeed said. "It also works in their favor as they can advance faster over a dry riverbed."

Mik'kel shrugged. "I'm not trying to make sense out of it all. Maybe he feels he can destroy us and them all in the same battle. Despite everything, the army he possesses is still large and formidable."

Elsbeth touched Mik'kel's arm. "Mik'kel, when are you heading back?"

"In the morning. Why?"

"I want to come with you."

Mik'kel's eyes widened. "Do you think that's wise?"

Edvin put his hand on hers. "Honey, with the way things are heating up, and you're almost ready to deliver . . . "

Elsbeth shook her head. "But that's why I need to go." She patted his hand. "I won't deliver for at least another month. But I'm probably the only one who can get Dad to listen."

Edvin tilted his head and shook it slightly. He wanted to be supportive, but this seemed like a bad idea.

Elsbeth glanced at Mik'kel. "You know he won't listen to anyone else." She gave a small laugh. "I'm not sure if he'll even listen to me. But when he sees me pregnant, and knows he has a grandchild on the way, that has to make a difference." Tears welled in her eyes. "I have to try."

Edvin looked at Mik'kel with raised eyebrows, looking for support. Mik'kel gave a half shrug as if to say: She has a point.

Edvin put his head in his hands for a moment and then looked back up. "OK, honey, but I'm coming with you."

"But Edvin, you have so much to do here. I'll be with Mik'kel. I'll be OK."

Edvin shook his head. "No, Elsbeth. If you're going, then so am I."

She patted him on his hand, kissed his cheek, and smiled. "OK."

Jeremiah interjected. "I may have a few more people to get out of the city. They can come back with you, Edvin, if that's OK."

Edvin nodded. "Sure."

Discussions continued, and, after a time, Jeremiah closed with Bible reading and prayer. Everyone settled in for the night.

At breakfast the next day, Edvin noticed Mik'kel glued to his tablet.

Edvin chuckled. "What's so mesmerizing?"

Mik'kel looked up, grave concern on his face. Edvin came around and looked at Mik'kel's tablet. Elsbeth followed.

Myrka followed Elsbeth with Saeed right behind her. "That face can't mean anything good," Edvin said.

Edvin's hand went to Mik'kel's shoulder as he sat next to him, and his eyes went from the newsfeed to Mik'kel and back. "Is . . . is that Babylon?" He wasn't sure why he asked the question. It was obvious. The Ziggurat of Knowledge was ablaze.

Elsbeth gasped. "Did everyone get out?"

"What on earth?" exclaimed Myrka as she came closer. Saeed put his arm around her shoulders, shaking his head.

Mik'kel turned up the volume. The announcer was in mid-sentence: " . . . thankfully, most of the scientists managed to escape to safety . . . "

"Thank God," Myrka said.

" . . . but the city has been decimated from the Asian invasion. They apparently had serious disagreements with the

President, and this will now decimate our entire economy." The camera panned to the newscaster. His face was ashen. "This is bad, folks. Very bad."

Elsbeth shook her head. "Most of the major companies had their headquarters in Babylon."

Jeremiah stood behind them watching. "*Had* is the correct word." He shook his head. "This may be unrecoverable."

The news announcer put his hand to his ear and paused briefly. "I've just received confirmation that Israel was responsible for giving aid to the Asian army to make this invasion possible."

"What?" Edvin looked at Mik'kel.

Mik'kel shook his head. "Lies. Total lies. Afrom hates the President, but there's no way he would condone destroying the world's economy or the mass killing of innocent people."

Jeremiah pointed. "Look at the time stamp at the bottom of the screen."

Mik'kel looked closer. "The invasion occurred more than a week ago."

Edvin looked at Jeremiah. "Why the delay?"

Jeremiah shrugged. "Probably so the President could give an alternate spin and deflect blame. This will only make more countries come to his aid against Israel."

Edvin looked at Elsbeth. "Honey, this changes things."

Elsbeth shook her head. "No, Edvin. It just means it's more important than ever."

Edvin gave a large sigh, but he also knew her mind was made up. "Well, if we're going to do this, we'd better do it fast. Our timetable just got shortened."

They finished breakfast quickly, said their goodbyes, and headed to the jeep.

As Mik'kel pulled off, he said, "I'll head up Highway 90

through Israel. If stopped, I can better talk us through since I'm part of Israeli forces."

Edvin nodded. "Makes sense." Edvin patted Mik'kel's shoulder. "Just make your foot heavy today."

Mik'kel smiled and picked up speed. They all sat back and held on. Along the way, they spotted many planes flying overhead: most were Israeli, but some had the World Forces logo. The increase in activity made Edvin nervous. It took longer than normal to reach Jerusalem because Mik'kel decided to report in at Arad, south of Hebron, to find out the status of developments.

Once Mik'kel got back to the jeep, he looked concerned.

When Mik'kel didn't offer information, Edvin asked, "The report?"

Mik'kel shook his head. "Things are developing fast. There's movement in the Jezreel Valley in the north and there's movement in North Africa." He looked at Elsbeth. "If we're going to do this, we'll need to do it fast. I don't know how long before the storm hits."

"Honey, one last chance to reconsider," Edvin said. "Do you still feel you need to do this?"

She nodded but didn't say anything.

"OK," Mik'kel said. "Here we go."

Once they reached the northern end of the Dead Sea, a sign read: "Victory Memorial Highway 90 North Dead End." Mik'kel took a left.

"What was that sign all about?" Edvin looked back. "I thought Highway 90 led to Highway 1."

Mik'kel shook his head. "It hasn't ever since the pre-treaty war. The Prime Minister had the dead buried here. But the original numbers and the time needed to bury them were grossly underestimated. It took seven months to gather all the bodies, and the numbers grew to be so many the burial ground became a mountain itself and spilled over onto Highway 90. We now have to travel around it to get between Jerusalem and the Dead Sea."

"So, there wasn't a mountain here before then?"

"Nope. Flat as a pancake."

Edvin looked at the mountain's size. While not large compared to other mountains in the area, its size gave a clear representation of the number of people killed during the pre-treaty invasion. "I can't get over how large it is. I assume it's called Victory Memorial because of the outcome?"

Mik'kel nodded. "The Prime Minister wanted some way to let people know our victory didn't come because of World Forces. If you go to where it dead ends, there's a placard that tells the real story of the victory. Sadly, I don't think many people go there."

Edvin thought about that as they headed into Jerusalem. He wondered how many people even thought about why they had to detour.

They got into Jerusalem late. Exhausted, everyone crashed at Mik'kel's and decided to visit High Priest Cohen the next day after the morning sacrifice. Edvin found it hard to sleep. His pulse raced; he couldn't seem to calm it. He couldn't shake the bad feeling he had about being here.

At some point during the night, exhaustion took over and he fell asleep.

Edvin woke to the aroma of something cooking. He looked up from the sofa and saw Elsbeth busy in the kitchen. He sat up.

"Hey, sleepyhead. How'd you sleep?"

Edvin shook his head. "Not that well."

Elsbeth gave a supportive grimace. "I know. Me too." She

smiled. “Maybe some breakfast will perk you up.”

Edvin nodded. “Especially if you have some tea to go with it.”

Elsbeth laughed. “Of course. Does the earth revolve around the sun?”

Edvin chuckled and slowly made his way to the counter. “Where’s Mik’kel and Jeremiah?”

“They each had things to do. Mik’kel had to go in to work and check on further developments. Jeremiah went to get the couples he talked about.”

Edvin was having his scrambled eggs when Elsbeth answered a knock at the door. Jeremiah and three couples walked in. After taking another quick bite and a swallow of tea, Edvin stood to greet them. Elsbeth offered them breakfast, but they declined, so she invited them to the sofa.

However, before they could sit, a horrendous explosion from somewhere outside shook everything. Everyone ducked. The women screamed.

“What’s going on?” one of them yelled.

CHAPTER 37

The apartment quaked from the blast, but it remained intact.

Mik'kel burst through the door with panic on his face. "It's started. Hatim's forces are bombing the city. Troops are advancing. We're countering, but it's all happening too fast. You guys have to leave the city."

Elsbeth shook her head. "No. I have to see my father."

"Elsbeth, be reasonable," Mik'kel said. "I'll go talk to him. You go with Edvin and these good people. Help get them to safety."

Elsbeth's eyes filled with tears. She looked at Edvin. "Edvin, I'm sorry. But I have to see my father. It's his only chance." Tears trickled down her face. "It's his only chance."

Another bomb hit the city. A couple of the women screamed. The apartment shook, causing plaster to fall from the ceiling. Edvin knew how stubborn his wife could be, but he didn't want to leave her.

"Elsbeth, I can't leave you here."

Elsbeth grabbed his hand. "Edvin, you have to get these people to Petra. I'll be with Mik'kel. It'll be all right."

"There are others I need to help," Jeremiah said. "But I'll go with them. Maybe between the three of us we can convince

Avraham."

"We'll be right behind you," Elsbeth said to Edvin. "We'll get Father and then be out of here."

Edvin looked at Mik'kel and Jeremiah. Each nodded. Edvin felt nauseous. This didn't feel right, but he couldn't think of what else to do. The couples were frightened. He couldn't abandon them.

"OK, but we need earbuds." He reached in his jacket pockets. "Here. I happened to bring the ones we used a while back in Eilat." He handed Mik'kel, Elsbeth, and Jeremiah each one. He put the other in his ear. Please, keep in constant contact—no matter what. OK?"

All nodded. "I'll keep my encrypted phone open as well so you can hear everything," Mik'kel said.

Elsbeth gave Edvin a hug. He kissed her. She turned, but he turned her back and kissed her again. He had a sinking feeling things would go awry, and he didn't like it. He felt like he would throw up. He swallowed hard and tried to put that thought out of his mind.

Another bomb hit the city—this time closer, louder. The kitchen window broke. All ducked, and once again the ladies screamed. Two of the women started crying, their husbands trying to comfort them.

"OK. Let's go," Mik'kel said. "We can't stay here any longer."

They exited the building. Edvin and the couples went one way and the others traveled the opposite. Edvin looked back and saw Elsbeth turn the corner of the building. His eyes watered. *Come on, Edvin. Snap out of it. You have a mission to accomplish.*

Edvin got the couples to the jeep and helped them in. "Sorry for the tight quarters, but it's all we have."

"Not a problem," one of them said.

They all managed to get in, and Edvin drove south as fast as he could to get out of the city. Another bomb hit to the right of them. One of the buildings began to crumple, and rubble fell onto the street in front of him. Edvin swerved and made it through before the building itself toppled onto the street just behind them. One of the ladies began to cry again and buried her head in her husband's chest. Edvin gunned the accelerator to pick up more speed.

Thankfully, light traffic on the streets helped. It dawned on Edvin why. Yom Kippur. Hatim was taking advantage of Jerusalem being unprepared on such a major holiday. Although good battle tactics, Edvin felt anger. After several blocked entrances to streets exiting the city, he found an escape route, which led to a major thoroughfare and out of the city.

The earbuds worked for a while. He heard several more bombs go off and Elsbeth scream. Edvin's gut tightened and his eyes watered. *I should be there with her. No,* he told himself. He had to do what he had to do. The people in this jeep were depending on him. He said a quick prayer and kept driving to the south. After a while, his distance from the other three grew too great for the earbuds to continue to work. He had to rely on his encrypted phone. He strapped it to the steering wheel so he could hear better than it laying on the seat.

Edvin and his party were halfway to Petra. Still, Elsbeth hadn't reached her father. He kept hearing more explosions. His heart went out to Elsbeth. He then heard Mik'kel. "World Forces troops are in the city." Edvin clenched the steering wheel. That was certainly not good news. In his mind, Edvin could see them climbing over rubble, trying to hide from the invaders so they wouldn't get caught, and all this would only slow them further.

He heard Elsbeth scream, and then the scream muffled.

"They're animals." That was Jeremiah.

He heard Mik'kel in a whisper. "If you hear us, Edvin, troops are slaughtering anyone they see. Elsbeth just saw a pregnant lady killed and the baby cut out of her on the ground. It's bad, man, it's really bad. Say a prayer."

Edvin's stomach tightened, his eyes wet. What if that happened to Elsbeth? *I should be there.* He shook his head. *No*, he couldn't think like that. Edvin felt nauseous again, like he would throw up. He swallowed several times to prevent that. Tears trickled down his face. *How could anyone hate so much?* Edvin hesitated to say anything. He didn't want to give their position away. He picked up the phone and whispered, "I am."

He heard back: "Thanks, buddy."

Edvin pulled into Petra behind where they usually stayed; he covered the jeep as usual. He couldn't believe it took them this long to get to the temple. Truman came out with Iris, Myrka, and Saeed. They welcomed the guests.

Saeed did a three-sixty. "Where's Elsbeth?"

Edvin could barely say the words. "She's still in Jerusalem."

"What?" Saeed's eyes went wide. "Why?"

"She insisted on seeing her father. Both Mik'kel and Jeremiah had duties in Jerusalem, and I had to get the refugees here. Mik'kel and Jeremiah are with her. They were supposed to go and be right behind me, but the attack was intensifying, and they're still in the city."

Truman put his hand on Edvin's shoulder. "Let's go to the top here. We have a lookout. We've seen troops gather around us as well. Over to the east some fighting has already started. Good for us, I guess. I assume the Asian forces met some of Hatim's. It gives us a little more time before they eventually attack here.

"If you listen closely, you can hear loud thuds—but I can't

make out what's causing it."

Edvin knew Truman was taking him to the lookout so the others wouldn't hear all the bad news. He, Saeed, and Truman sat there listening to what was happening in Jerusalem. Truman would occasionally look through his binoculars to see where the troops were and how close they were in approaching Petra.

Then, through the encrypted phone line, voices began coming in again. Edvin heard Jeremiah: "There's the temple. It's still intact."

"Do you see Father?"

"Wait." Edvin could tell that was Mik'kel. Gunshots were heard . . . "OK, let's go."

Edvin heard scuffling, grunts, gunfire in the background, and another bomb sounded close.

"Abba, Abba." Elsbeth's voice had a tone of panic . . .

"Elsbeth, what are you doing here? And in your condition."

"You have to come with us. You must get out of the city. If you don't, you'll die."

"But child," Avraham said. "It's Yom Kippur. Surely God will save us. He has to."

Edvin could hear Elsbeth crying. "Abba, think back to all the prophets. It's never been about the sacrifice. It's been about the heart. God cares about the heart, not the sacrifice."

"Avraham," Jeremiah said. "The Messiah stated—"

"Don't talk to me about that! Only the Torah matters!"

Edvin sat listening in stunned silence.

"Then listen to this." Edvin never heard Jeremiah speak so sternly. He sounded like one scolding a little child. "You pray Psalms 118. That's your only hope. Pray *baruch haba beshem Adonai*: 'Blessed is he who comes in the name of the Lord.' That's the key to the psalm. If you love your people, if you love your daughter, if you want hope for your grandchild, then pray. Pray, Avraham! Pray like you mean it! Look around you! The city is destroyed, its inhabitants are being slaughtered, and you are sacrificing. Just doing something changes nothing. God looks at our hearts. Change your *heart*, Avraham. For the sake of Israel, change your heart!"

Edvin heard a gunshot and another blast, though not as loud as others, but it still sounded close. Then more gunshots. Edvin couldn't stay silent any longer.

"Mik'kel. Mik'kel! What's happening?"

"It's Elsbeth, Edvin. She's been hit with shrapnel from a hand grenade."

Tears flowed down Edvin's cheeks. He felt helpless. "Is she . . . " He choked up. "Is she all right?"

"For now, I think so."

"Avraham, it's now or never," Jeremiah said.

Avraham began. "*Baruch haba beshem Adonai.*" His voice was merely reciting the words perfunctorily at first, but the more he said it, the more convincing it sounded. Edvin heard Jeremiah join in and turn it into a chant. His voice got louder. Soon, other voices in the background could be heard.

The chant began spreading throughout the city.

Truman looked at Edvin. "I've got to let everyone here hear this. We have many Jews here that need to pray the same."

Edvin nodded and linked Truman to his conversation feed. Truman headed downstairs to the others . . .

Soon, Edvin was hearing the chant throughout Petra as well. The sound was one of desperation, haunting and calming at the same time.

Edvin heard a whirring sound, and a large explosion occurred behind him. He ducked but didn't move. Where could he go? They had rifles, but nothing to repel bombs.

Edvin heard Elsbeth scream. Fear gripped him. He stared at the phone as if willing it to take him to her. He yelled into the phone: "Mik'kel, what's going on?"

"Elsbeth is going into labor. I think the shrapnel is putting her body into shock. The baby's coming."

Edvin's eyes filled with tears, which now streamed down his face. *It's too early. Will it be OK?*

"Elsbeth. Elsbeth! Can you hear me?" Mik'kel's voice sounded forceful. "Your body's going into shock. The baby's coming."

Elsbeth screamed again. Edvin was terrified for both. *Oh God, please. Please let them be OK.*

"Push, Elsbeth, push. You've got to push! Elsbeth! Elsbeth, can you hear me? You've got to push." Mik'kel's voice was sheer panic.

This didn't sound good—at all. "Mik'kel! Mik'kel! What's happening?"

"She's going into shock. We have to get the baby out before she passes out."

Edvin bit his finger waiting to hear the next piece of news. He hated not being there. And then . . . he heard the cry of a baby. Edvin gasped, and tears flowed. *I'm a father.*

"It's a boy, Edvin. It's a boy."

Edvin smiled and tears continued to flow.

Saeed patted him on the back. "Congratulations, Edvin. Congratulations."

Edvin nodded. Then . . . another bomb hit to the right of them. There were screams from downstairs.

"Mik'kel, how's Elsbeth? Is she all right?"

Edvin heard only silence, except for the chanting, accompanied periodically by gunshots and screams in the background.

"Edvin, she's . . . weak. She's lost a lot of blood. I'm . . . I'm not sure if she's going to make it."

Edvin glanced at Saeed. Saeed squeezed Edvin's shoulder. His eyes were watering as well.

"Let me talk to her."

Mik'kel turned the phone to video so Edvin could see her. She looked so pale, and her voice was extremely weak. "Edvin, we have a son. We did good, didn't we?"

The phone then pivoted to show the face of his son, still covered with the vernix and some blood spots from delivery.

Edvin couldn't help but sob and laugh with joy at the same time. "Yes, honey. We did good. You get some rest. OK?"

"Edvin, I . . . I love . . . you . . . very much." Her voice sounded weaker and weaker.

The tears were so many that Edvin really couldn't see. "I love you, too, sweetie. Hang in there. OK?"

Elsbeth didn't say anything more. After a few moments, Mik'kel came back on. The video had been turned off.

"Edvin. I'm . . . I'm sorry. So very, very sorry. She's . . . she's gone."

Edvin bowed his head and sobbed. His whole body shook. Saeed put his head on Edvin's shoulder and cried with him. Edvin felt his heart had been ripped from his chest.

Truman came back to the top. "Look! Look!"

Both Edvin and Saeed looked up, wiping tears from their eyes. "What . . . what is that?"

Toward the north . . . they watched.

. . . Something extremely bright was descending.

"Edvin. Edvin, are you seeing this?"

"What is it, Mik'kel?"

"I think it's . . . the Messiah. He's come. He's finally come."

Edvin was mesmerized as he watched the brightness descend.

Truman patted Edvin on the shoulder while smiling. "No worries, Edvin. You'll see her again real soon."

Edvin nodded. *But why couldn't he have come a few minutes earlier?* Edvin reminded himself he had to trust. That seemed to be so hard—at any point in the history of God's persecuted people.

Once the light reached a point near the earth, they heard an enormous, earth-shattering boom. The sound was deafening. It felt as if the entire earth shook. This felt different from other earthquakes. The boom and reverberations lasted for several minutes. All three of the men on the structure's lookout stared at each other wide-eyed, unsure of what to do or if the lookout would hold them.

"What's going on, Mik'kel?"

Mik'kel's voice sounded as if he was running. "Our Messiah just touched down on the Mount of Olives. The mountain has literally split in two. The earthquake came into the city. The temple is breaking up, but a plain has been created . . . it's a place for us to escape. Jeremiah and Avraham are with me. I have your son. . . . I'll touch back with you later."

Bombs exploded everywhere around them.

"Come on! Let's get down from here!" Truman said.

They scurried down and found the others. Everyone stood in the open. No one knew what to do—there was nothing for them to do. Truman gathered everyone together. So far, the bombs had missed them. Truman prayed and then led everyone in song. The bombs burst around them. Some came close—never close enough to harm them, but certainly close enough to frighten. Mothers were trying to comfort their children, but that proved difficult when they were just as frightened themselves.

Dan pointed toward the north. "Look. The light. It seems to be coming this way."

Everyone looked. Indeed it did. Then, as quickly as the bombing had started, it stopped. Now they heard gunfire and bombs in the opposite direction. Screaming could be heard. The cries sounded eerie as the screams were not just ones of fright; they were painful types of screams. The sound made Edvin's hair stand on end.

Quiet then settled over the area. It seemed so odd to now have everything so still; moments earlier there had been only mayhem. The light grew brighter and brighter, and then it entered their midst . . .

There he was, the Messiah himself, on a white horse which looked splattered with blood up to its neck. The Messiah wore brilliant white clothing, but the edges were also stained with blood. None of this diminished the brilliance of this one person in their midst.

Immediately, everyone fell to their knees and bowed.

And then . . . the Messiah spoke. Edvin had never heard anyone speak like he did. His voice was commanding yet also gentle and melodic. "Rise, my friends."

All stood and gazed at this one in their midst. Edvin found him a complete dichotomy. He appeared awe-inspiring, making Edvin want to run away, but at the same time he seemed gentle, and this made Edvin want to run and hug him.

"I want to thank each of you for your faithfulness. The battle is not yet complete, and I must still face the Adversary. Please head for Jerusalem. I will meet you there once victory is secured."

The Messiah then headed back the same way he had entered. Everyone looked at each other with looks of shock and happiness all rolled into one. Everyone hugged and laughed. Truman ran back to the top of the structure where they had been before. Edvin and Saeed followed.

Truman looked with his binoculars toward the north.

Saeed placed his hand on Truman's shoulder. "Do you see him?"

Truman nodded. He let Saeed look, and then Edvin.

The Messiah seemed to keep a steady pace. Men were falling before him. Although guns were fired, the Messiah didn't flinch or halt his progress in any way. People kept falling like dominoes.

Edvin turned to the west. "Wow," he whispered. "That's incredible."

"What? What?" Both Truman and Saeed asked it at the same time.

"There's water flowing south."

"Really?" Saeed grabbed the binoculars—Edvin didn't care—looked, and passed the glasses to Truman.

Truman smiled. "It's already starting."

"What?" Saeed looked through the binoculars again.

"Scripture states the Dead Sea will become a living sea. I guess the earthquake created a passage for water to flow."

Edvin shook his head. "But won't that drain the sea? Where will more water come from?"

"If I'm right in my understanding, the earthquake extended in the far north to the Euphrates River, and it will now flow into the Jordan," Truman said. "And Scripture states there will be a river flowing out of Jerusalem into the Dead Sea and the Mediterranean Sea."

Truman smiled. "Boys, we're in for quite a treat."

CHAPTER 38

Truman gathered everyone, and they began their trip back to Jerusalem. It felt strange, but good, that no one would be pursuing them on this trip. Edvin had mixed feelings. He couldn't wait to see his son, but now that Elsbeth had died, what would that mean for his future? He knew she had become part of the redeemed, but what did that mean for them as a family?

They came to a place where one truck had overturned, and two had collided, but another whole fleet, maybe two dozen, looked intact but empty. Dead soldiers lay strewn across the ground. There were so many of them. Truman, Edvin, and Saeed walked over, slowly, to investigate.

Truman had the others take the children away from the scene.

Edvin pointed. "Have you ever seen anything like this? It appears their skin is literally melted off their bodies."

Both Saeed and Truman shook their heads.

"I've been in many battles," Saeed said. "But I've never seen anything like this."

"Look at all the hailstones," Truman said. "I've never seen any so large. Look how they crushed so many of them. They're melting now, but I bet I could barely get my arms around one.

That must be what caused the loud thuds we kept hearing earlier in the day."

Saeed went over to try and move one, but found himself straining to barely budge it. "Uhh. It must weigh over forty kilos."

Saeed looked back at Truman and Edvin with a bewildered gaze. "Guys. Come look at this."

There lay a crushed body, with one of the hailstones still over part of it—but the person's head and arm were visible.

"Is . . . is that President Hatim?" Truman looked at Edvin for confirmation.

Edvin shook his head. "No. It's The Image."

Edvin felt no remorse at this sight. He ran his hand through his hair as he stood there observing the gruesome aftermath all around him. "All this is unbelievable."

Truman glanced up and pointed. "Look."

Edvin saw thousands of birds flying into the area.

"Let's get the folks out of here!" Truman said. "Scripture states these birds will gorge themselves on the bodies of these dead soldiers. I don't want the children to see any of this."

"We should head farther west, next to the water," Edvin said. "There's less chance of them seeing anything there."

Truman nodded. "Agreed. Let's go."

They loaded everyone into the trucks. Truman and Dan each drove and found other men to drive the remaining trucks. Edvin and Saeed rode in the cab with Truman. Bo rode with Dan. Myrka rode in the back of a truck to help with the children. After a short while, they reached the Dead Sea. They found a place narrow and shallow enough to cross. After crossing, they followed the western bank of the Dead Sea northward.

"You know," Truman said, "I can almost understand how the Israelites felt long ago as they headed for the Promised Land."

Edvin nodded. "It does have that feel to it. A heightened

sense of expectation."

"Except," Saeed said. "Except . . . we're not on our way to a Promised Land, but to a Promised Kingdom."

Truman laughed. "You're right, my friend. You're very right."

When they reached the northern part of the Dead Sea, Edvin saw what Mik'kel had referred to. There, stretched before them, lay a flat plain that went toward Jerusalem. The plain cut straight through the mountains. The rift, while filling with water, still allowed plenty of room to walk between the forming river and the mountain face.

When they neared Jerusalem, they disembarked and met up with Mik'kel and many others who had escaped the city. All gave their greetings.

"Edvin, I want to present to you your son." Mik'kel placed him in Edvin's arms. Mik'kel had him wrapped in a shirt someone had given. The baby cooed contently. It melted Edvin's heart.

Mik'kel held Edvin's arm and placed something in his hand. "And here's Elsbeth's necklace. I thought you would want this."

Edvin's eyes watered. "Thanks, Mik'kel." He nodded. "Thank you."

Everyone gathered around the baby to get a glimpse and express their congratulations.

Myrka gave Edvin a kiss on the cheek. "Congratulations, Edvin. He's beautiful."

Edvin smiled. "Thanks, Myrka."

"Have you decided on a name?"

Edvin shook his head. "Not yet. Hopefully, I'll have time later to consider options."

Myrka nodded and smiled. "I understand."

Edvin turned. There stood Avraham, his cheeks stained

with tears. He had a weak smile on his face.

"Edvin, your son is beautiful." He slowly stroked the infant's head.

Edvin smiled. "Your grandson, Avraham."

Avraham looked at Edvin, smiled, and nodded. "I'm so sorry for being so stubborn." Tears came to his eyes again. "Elsbeth would still be alive if I . . . "

"Avraham. We'll see Elsbeth again. Soon. She's not gone from us forever. She's with the Messiah in her glorified body. I don't know what all that means yet, but you'll hug her again."

Avraham smiled, though his lips quivered. "Yes, I know you're right. I just hope you can forgive me."

Holding his son in one arm, Edvin put his other hand on Avraham's shoulder. "Abba . . . " Avraham looked at Edvin with deep love and appreciation. "We were all stubborn before we accepted the truth. God had a purpose in how all this unfolded."

Avraham pulled Edvin to him and kissed his cheek. "Thank you, my son."

Edvin gave him a one-arm hug and kissed his father-in-law's head.

"OK, everyone," Mik'kel said. "We should head back to Jerusalem. We have a Messiah to meet."

Everyone shouted and whistled. "Let's go!" "Praise to the Messiah!" "Hallelujah!" And still more shouts could be heard from various people.

Once they neared Jerusalem, the group had to travel north to get to the city proper due to the escarpment that loomed before them and was many meters high. They traveled almost eight kilometers to just outside Geba before the escarpment became low enough to cross. They then turned back south to reach Jerusalem.

Edvin caught up with Mik'kel and Jeremiah. "How did you

get out so quickly if the escarpment is so high?"

Mik'kel shook his head. "It's all a blur, actually. The escarpment must have occurred after we exited the city. I remember the rift going through the mountain making a way for us to travel, but I know the earthquake was still ongoing at the same time."

"Why do you think God allowed the city to be destroyed like that?" Edvin asked. "Isn't Jerusalem supposed to be where the Messiah is to rule?"

"That's a question for you, Jeremiah." Mik'kel smiled. "Or, I guess you can ask the Messiah when he gets to Jerusalem."

Jeremiah laughed. "Well, Scripture doesn't actually state why, except that Jerusalem will be the highest point on earth."

Mik'kel pointed forward. "Look, the light is coming toward Jerusalem from the south. It looks like we'll make it there almost at the same time."

When they reached Jerusalem, the Messiah had reached the Eastern Gate. Many who had radiant bodies rode behind him. Their glorified bodies somehow appeared brighter than those living, but not so bright that it was distracting.

"Amazing," Jeremiah said.

"What?" Edvin looked at him trying to understand what he meant.

"This area used to be a graveyard," Jeremiah said. "It seems the earthquake took care of that."

"Look!" Edvin said. "Both Hatim and Duarté are behind the Messiah."

"Yes. But they don't look very intimidating anymore." Jeremiah's tone had changed to one of certainty. "They put their faith in the wrong person."

"Welcome, my friends," the Messiah said. His voice was mesmerizing. Edvin couldn't understand how a voice could be so commanding and yet melodic at the same time. "This is the gate I exited when I ascended millennia ago. I will reenter the way I exited." He held up his hand. "Open," he commanded.

The stones, placed to seal the gate centuries ago to destroy any hope in the Messiah's return, crumbled. The Messiah rode through. Everyone followed. As they entered the gate, Edvin looked back.

Edvin poked Mik'kel with his elbow. "Look at the sky."

Mik'kel nodded. "Yeah, I noticed that. It's like it's aglow, but not due to the sun. I've never seen anything like it."

Jeremiah chuckled. "I guess we'll need to get used to the unexpected."

Edvin and Mik'kel smiled and nodded.

Although the current temple now lay in ruins, their Messiah went to that spot. Everyone gathered around.

"My friends, I have so longed for this day, as I know many of you have as well," he began. His smile captivated their hearts as he spoke. "As we move forward, we have a lot to do, a lot to share with one another, and a lot to enjoy. I have many special things I look forward to sharing with you." His smile faded.

"Before we go forward, however, there are some unpleasant tasks to perform."

He turned to Hatim and addressed him directly. "The Adversary possesses you. He has always been a deceiver and blinded by his pride. The earth has been his realm ever since being cast out of Heaven. He will now be removed from the earth and confined to the Abyss for the next millennium."

The air next to Hatim began to quiver. Hatim stiffened. He put his hands to his head and screamed. The quivering of the air next to him increased in intensity. Hatim went to his knees. Some kind of being appeared to be pulled *out of* Hatim and into the quivering air. The form, unrecognizable, elongated as the rift seemed to suck it out of Hatim's body and into itself. The rift then looked like a reverse ripple on water as it closed.

Hatim's body went limp.

"Arise."

Hatim slowly rose.

"Malach Ebano Sahir Shen Ignado Ahmed Hatim, your name set you up for greatness. Yet, you let your initials stir your ego rather than revealing the humility needed of someone the world looked up to. Your ego matches that of the one just pulled from you, whose pride doomed him from the time he deemed God Almighty not the Unique One, not the Most Holy One. By pledging yourself to him, you doomed yourself to his eternal fate. Such in life, such in death. You will be with him from this time forward."

The Messiah turned to Duarté. "And you, Mateus Duarté, you neglected the meaning of your name, 'gift of God,' and settled for something inferior in order to satisfy your insatiable ego. You opted for command of an audience over command of your own destiny. You gave yourself to a lesser power in hopes of getting more when a power greater than you could have imagined was always within your grasp. By uniting yourself to the Adversary, you also will be with him from this time forward."

Neither man said anything. Neither tried to argue. They looked solemn and stared straight ahead as they heard this judgment pronounced against them. A look of fear came across their faces with the Messiah's last words.

"Since you never wished to honor me or be with me, I grant your request. You will forever be separated from me and the victors you see here. With the Adversary you aligned. With him you will be. Away with you."

The air around them shimmered briefly and they seemed to be sucked into something like a rift in space-time, and it sealed itself, once again, like a reverse ripple on water. What lingered, for a brief moment, was a whiff of smoke and a smell of sulfur.

The crowd gasped—then burst into loud applause.

The Messiah held up his hands and the applause settled. "My friends, we now have much work to do. As you know, my first coming millennia ago set the stage for what will now occur. Debt for sin had to be paid before other promises could be fulfilled. My promise to King David can now be fulfilled."

There was more applause and praises.

"Many of you who are the faithful have survived and exited the crucible placed upon Israel and the world. I commend you. Wonderful things are in store for you for the next millennium."

Still more applause. The Messiah smiled as he held up his hands again.

"Yet, there are many followers of the Adversary who have also survived. They must be separated from among the righteous and be judged. This will occur over the next several days. After that will come wonderful things. All promises made to Israel over the many millennia will now come true. Israel will lead the world in worship. To do so, a new temple, as shown in Scripture to my prophet Ezekiel, will be built by all who will enter my Promised Kingdom. This will be threefold: moving forward no righteous will die, so the temple will serve as a memorial of the death I paid for mankind's sin; it will perform cleansing needed for objects and people who worship me, their Lord; and it will point to the choice all who are born in my Promised Kingdom must make. The Adversary has been removed, but human nature still remains in you. Going forward, teach these things to your children."

The Messiah looked over the crowd. His eyes locked with those of Edvin, and his smile had a warmth Edvin could almost *physically* feel. The Messiah motioned for Edvin to step forward. He did so, unsure of the purpose, but without any fear.

"Edvin, may I hold your son?"

"Of course, my Lord." He handed his son to his Master.

He smiled at Edvin and kissed the infant on his forehead. "We have much to talk about later. But may I name your son?"

Edvin nodded. "It would be my honor for you to do so." Edvin felt overwhelmed. So many emotions were going through him: excitement, gratitude, thankfulness, awe.

The Messiah smiled as he held up Edvin's son. "My friends, this little one, born even as I descended to the Mount of Olives, is the first one born into my Kingdom. His mother, Elsbeth Cohen Isakson, the final one from the gleaning of the Great Tribulation, is now glorified. Her heritage as a descendent of the priest Zadok of the time of King David, and the heritage of his father, Edvin Isakson from the tribe of Levi, makes this small one appointed for my service. This family forms the doorway into the Promised Kingdom, a blending of the righteous and the glorified.

"I hereby name this one Ya'akov Avraham Cohen Isakson, and his name contains the foundation of the nation of Israel and the worship of the Most High. He is destined to serve his Messiah and will become a key element in my Promised Kingdom." He then kissed the infant Ya'akov on his forehead once again and handed him back to Edvin.

The Messiah raised his hands. His smile remained a most captivating one. "My friends, go now and rest. You have earned it. You no longer need to look over your shoulder or sleep on alert.

"Enter my rest. Once all accounting has been completed, we will reunite and move forward into preparations for our magnificent Kingdom. I will see each of you again soon."

CHAPTER 39

The next two and a half months were a whirlwind of activity. The entire population left on earth was brought before the Messiah. He separated them all into those he called "goats," representing the unrighteous, and those he called "sheep," representing the righteous, or the flock of the Good Shepherd. Many he condemned tried to make excuses for their actions, but he simply stated their actions reflected the true condition of their heart.

Once the task of separation was completed, he called the earth's population together again. He looked across the vast array.

"You have been judged not only by your deeds, but by your heart. Those deemed unrighteous will be held in the place of lost souls until final judgment."

Again, many pleaded for a second chance. He looked at them with deep sadness in his eyes. And then: "Depart from me. I never knew you."

With that, they vanished in a similar fashion as had Hatim and Duarté.

The Messiah stood and held out open arms. "My friends, my children, you are the ones who will enter into my Promised Kingdom and into my rest. But be vigilant. The Adversary is sealed away for only twenty Jubilees. Teach your children the wise choice of accepting me. After the Adversary is released, if they follow him, their fate will be as you have witnessed today: forever separated from me and from you."

He changed his countenance and now smiled. "But today, there is no sadness. Today is only joy and celebration—and a little hard work." He chuckled. "Is everyone OK with that?"

The crowd responded with applause and whistles.

He held up his hands to settle the crowd. "My friends, my glorified church, my bride, will help administrate my kingdom for you through these next years. The glorified righteous prior to my first coming and those out of the Tribulation will assist in this endeavor and will lead and guide you as you live your lives of peace, happiness, and prosperity. The land will be kind and fruitful. The air will be clean and refreshing. All animals will be peaceful and approachable.

"You will have no fear, no want, and no need. All will be freely provided. The time of Refreshing has come. The curse is rescinded, never to return."

Huge applause erupted along with whistles and announcements of praise.

The Messiah smiled and held up his hands. "I give you a gift. Ruach HaKodesh has always been with you. Before today, he had been provided as a deposit, or guarantee, of this day. Now you will receive a full measure of his unity with me and the Almighty."

The Messiah then symbolically blew over the crowd as one blows out candles on a birthday cake.

Edvin had a feeling of increased clarity enter his brain. It came so suddenly and unexpectedly that he gasped. A feeling of serenity flooded through him, and this brought a smile to his face. It was like a conduit directly to the Messiah—as if he knew the Messiah could communicate anytime, anywhere, without being physically present.

He glanced at Mik'kel, who smiled. Obviously, his friend had the same experience.

He heard others gasp. Some giggled, others became wide-eyed, some even cried. Throughout the crowd, expressions of gratitude could be heard.

"Master, I hear you in my mind."

"Thank you, my Lord. It's a wonderful gift."

"Praise be to God. I feel your presence."

The Messiah nodded. "You will forever be connected to me in this fashion. This is what your children will not have until they accept me as their Savior. Teach them these things so they can experience the joy you now have."

The Messiah motioned for several of the glorified to come forward. "My friends, we have much work to do. Once the city is prepared, we will come back together for a coronation and celebration. There is much preparation to be done until then. I ask you to separate yourselves by tribe so your inheritance and duties can be assigned. Those of you who are Gentiles, I have special things in store for you, and special duties for you to hold. Everyone in my Kingdom is special and will be treated as such. Also, there are many loved ones for you to meet and catch up with. Now, go to your assigned places and receive your rewards. Ruach HaKodesh will lead and answer all questions."

Edvin looked at Mik'kel. "I guess we're still stuck with each other," he said, chuckling. "OK. Let's go."

Mik'kel shook his head. "I have to put up with you for a thousand years?"

Edvin threw an elbow in Mik'kel's arm. "Yeah, aren't you a lucky soul?"

Mik'kel laughed and Edvin followed suit. Mik'kel grabbed Edvin's shoulders and gave a squeeze. "There's no one better to spend a millennium with, buddy. No one."

Edvin nodded. "Thanks. I feel the same."

As they headed to their assigned place, someone approached Edvin. He felt like he knew this person even though he felt sure they had never met. In a moment, the realization hit him, and he gasped.

"Adelina? Oh my . . . my goodness. It's you. It's really you."

She looked beautiful. She had some of the features of Lars and Néa, but it was a sense of their spirits connecting in her that made the identification sure. She looked to be in her early to mid-twenties with long reddish hair and green eyes. Her body, now glorified, added to her beauty.

"Hi, Uncle Edvin. I've looked forward to this day." She gave Edvin a hug and looked at Ya'akov. "He's beautiful. Mind if I hold him?"

"Oh, of course not." He gently handed Ya'akov to Adelina. She kissed his cheek.

"Uncle, I have you to thank for this next gift." She motioned for someone to come forward.

Edvin looked—and was left speechless. Tears came to his eyes. "Lars? Lars, is that you?" He didn't look glorified, so, Edvin reasoned, he must have survived the Tribulation.

Lars nodded. He came close, and the two embraced as tears streamed down their faces.

"Edvin, thanks for being there for me and not giving up on me," Lars said. "The things they did to me didn't allow me to respond, but being like that gave me the time to really ponder what you said. In that vegetable-like state, God reached my heart. He could only have done so because of you reaching out to me. Thank you, Edvin. Thank you. Now, I get to meet my daughter as well." More tears came.

Edvin hugged him again. "Come look at your nephew as well."

Adelina held Ya'akov so Lars could see him. He put his index finger close and Ya'akov grabbed it with his tiny hands. Lars smiled. "Edvin, he's beautiful. He must get all his features from his mother."

Edvin lovingly turned a fist into Lars's arm. Lars laughed.

"He's precious, Edvin. Congratulations."

Edvin smiled. "We should head over to our designated place."

They all walked together and got in line for their assignments. As they were talking and waiting, another glorified being walked up.

Mik'kel patted Edvin on his shoulder. He turned—and there before him stood Elsbeth. Edvin looked at her. So many emotions overwhelmed him. He was glad to see her, glad she was fine, but sorry they were now different. He smiled even though his lips trembled. Tears formed in his eyes.

"Elsbeth. Oh, Elsbeth."

She stepped forward and he hugged her with all his might. As he released her, he wiped away tears. "It's wonderful to see you. The added glow makes you even more beautiful."

She laughed and smiled.

"Here is your son. The Messiah named him Ya'akov."

Adelina gently handed the child to her. She looked at him and smiled. "He's so beautiful. I think he has your eyes, Edvin." She glanced up at Edvin and smiled. He caressed her arm and smiled back.

"Edvin, can we talk for a few moments?"

"Sure." They stepped away from the others.

"Oh," Edvin said. "I thought you may want to have this." He took out the necklace and showed it to her.

"Oh, Edvin. Thank you. Would you put it on me?"

He opened the clasp, draped it around her neck, and secured it. She put her fingers over it. "This will always be special to me."

She sighed, looked at Edvin, and gave a weak grin as she put her hand to his cheek. “We need to talk about us.”

Edvin nodded. “What do you wish to say?”

“The Messiah called us ‘the doorway.’ We have a blended family, I guess you can say. We will always be together, but never together, if you know what I’m saying.”

Edvin looked down and then back into her eyes. “I was afraid that would be true.”

Her eyes darted across his face. “I will always love you, but not in the same way as before. My heart and desire is sealed to the Messiah. I won’t have the same capacity for physical love that you will have. I’m sure the Messiah will understand if you should ever want to have someone else.”

Edvin shook his head. “Just having you and Ya’akov in my life is enough, Elsbeth. I too will serve the Messiah and be devoted to him. It will be enough. We will be enough.”

She kissed his cheek. “We will see each other often. There will be plenty of time to talk more.” She handed Ya’akov back to Edvin after she kissed her son’s forehead. “I have some things to take care of. I’ll be back soon.”

Edvin nodded and watched her head in a different direction. He rejoined the group.

“You OK?” Mik’kel had concern in his voice.

Edvin smiled and nodded. “I’m OK.”

Assignments came. Both Edvin and Mik’kel would be working at the new temple assisting the priests in their duties and temple administration. For now, they would help with the construction under the direction of the prophet Ezekiel.

As they headed to their first meeting, Mik’kel asked, “What do you think about our assignment?”

“As long as I don’t have to tell scientists how much money they have to spend, I’m fine.”

Mik'kel laughed. "I see you have some bad memories."

Edvin smiled. "I'm looking forward to creating some new ones."

With so many people available for helping with the cleanup of the city, the construction of the temple, the building of new buildings, bridges, parks, dwelling places, and the palace, everything came together quickly. Although a lot of work, the camaraderie in working together with a common goal made both the city and the temple come together in what seemed almost overnight.

One night at dinner, Edvin and Mik'kel finally had a chance to visit with others they had not seen since getting their assignments. The two were able to pull many of their friends together for a chat.

Edvin noticed Myrka and Saeed to be in unusually good moods. "Saeed, what will be your assignment in our new kingdom?"

"Both Myrka and I have been helping to clean and repair the city. That's now done. I don't really have an assignment, per se." He took Myrka's hand. "I guess my assignment is to be a husband."

"What?" Edvin looked from one to the other. "Are you serious?"

Saeed and Myrka both nodded, their faces beaming with broad smiles.

"Congratulations." Edvin laughed and gave Saeed a slight whack on his shoulder with his fist. "I knew something was up between you two." Edvin held up his glass. "A toast to Saeed and Myrka."

"Hear, hear," the others said as they raised their glasses and clinked them together.

Mik'kel lowered his glass. "So, where will you be living?"

Saeed looked at Myrka. "Well, we've been thinking we would go where Myrka's family originated. She's always wanted to go back there. We have the chance to start our lives together anywhere, so that's where we're going to go."

"Wonderful," Mik'kel said. "I wish you all the best."

"I'm going to miss you both," Edvin said. "Our history goes way back, Saeed."

"Indeed it does, my friend. But we'll see each other periodically, I'm sure. We now have the time to do the important things."

Edvin smiled and nodded.

Myrka reached with her arms. "Edvin, can I hold Ya'akov again?"

"Sure." He gave him to her. "Looks like she's getting some ideas, Saeed."

Myrka's eyes twinkled and she smiled. Saeed looked at Edvin and shrugged. "OK with me."

Edvin laughed and patted him on his shoulder.

Truman and Iris walked by. "Hi, Edvin. Just wanted to say goodbye. Now that things are wrapping up here, we'll be heading back to Great Britain."

Edvin stood and shook Truman's hand and kissed Iris on the cheek. "We'll miss you guys a lot. Keep in touch."

"Absolutely," Truman said. "Mik'kel, all the best to you as well."

Mik'kel shook his hand. "And the same to you. Where's Dan?"

"Oh, he and Bo are around here somewhere. I'm sure they'll stop by before we leave."

Truman and Iris waved goodbye as they headed off.

"Myrka, OK if I take a little walk?" Edvin asked, aware that Myrka looked quite comfortable holding his son. "I just want to take a look around the city."

Myrka nodded and smiled. "Take as much time as you want. Ya'akov and I love to keep each other company."

Edvin smiled and rose to leave the table.

Mik'kel scrunched his brow. "Everything OK, Edvin?"

Edvin nodded. "Just want to walk and think."

Mik'kel nodded. "OK. I'll meet you later."

Edvin walked toward the temple area and then turned south to what everyone now called the Overlook. On the way, he met Ty.

"Ty," he said with surprise. "I didn't know if I would get a chance to see you. How are you?"

Ty smiled. "Much better now."

Edvin chuckled. "I bet. Did you get your assignment?"

Ty nodded. "Believe it or not, the Messiah wants me to head up a Science Center here in Jerusalem. Want to be part of it?"

Edvin held up his palms. "Uh-uh. I have my assignment. I don't want to tell any more scientists they're off budget."

Ty laughed. "I can understand that. But that's one good thing. No more budgets." Ty turned more serious. "I'm really amazed, and delighted, he's so supportive of scientific endeavors."

"That's great, Ty."

"And, what I didn't understand about what Brad tried to tell us is now making more sense. Have you noticed it?"

Edvin looked confused. "Noticed what?"

"Like your mind is getting clearer. I think the Refreshing is rejuvenating us as it is the earth."

"I guess I haven't thought about it. But now that you mention it, I no longer have the aches and pains I had earlier."

Ty nodded. "That's the start. It's only going to get better." Ty began to walk on. "See you later, Edvin. It's only going to get better."

Edvin shook his head and smiled. The vibrancy of everyone enjoying their new duties made him happy. He headed on toward the Overlook. It was a large area that overlooked the valley below. To his left, a river flowed from beneath the temple, cascaded down the escarpment to the valley below, and formed a river flowing between the now *two* Mounts of Olive and on into the Jordan River. It had a branch that flowed into the Dead Sea and another that flowed around the edge of the escarpment. Edvin couldn't see where that branch went, but he knew, innately, that it flowed to the west to the Mediterranean Sea. The valley, already green with lush grass and beautiful shrubbery, had transformed the landscape into something beautiful. He sat and watched for quite some time.

He felt a presence behind him. He looked back and was most surprised to see the Messiah.

Edvin jumped up, genuflected, then stood. "My Lord. I didn't know you were there."

The Messiah smiled and placed his hand on Edvin's shoulder. Edvin felt warmth flood over him and into his very core. Oh, he could get used to a touch like that. It made him want to be in his Master's presence forever.

The Messiah pointed to the valley below. "Do you find this beautiful?"

Edvin nodded. "Very much, my Lord."

He smiled. "This is only the beginning, Edvin. One day soon this entire escarpment will be adorned with shrubbery, trees, and blooming flowers with humming birds and butterflies everywhere. It will be one of the wonders of the world."

"I can't wait to see it."

The Messiah patted Edvin on his shoulder. "Neither can I, Edvin. Neither can I."

They stood there for several minutes looking at the landscape. The Messiah motioned for Edvin to sit and then sat next to him.

"Edvin, I wanted to talk with you since your family is in a unique position. You will all be here in Jerusalem. So I wanted to see what you thought of your situation."

Edvin looked at this one who was the entire reason for his being. "I have to be honest. It does hurt a little. But having them in my life and serving you—that's all I could ever ask."

"I am glad you feel that way, Edvin. I needed someone to help others see there is not a distinction between those glorified and those redeemed. They serve a different purpose, but all are precious to me. Many have relatives on both sides, but none are in as unique a situation as your family. I want to use your family as a symbol of what I want this Promised Kingdom under my reign to represent. Your family will represent the unity of my Kingdom."

Edvin was overwhelmed. He knew there had to be purpose in all that had happened, but he never guessed it would be something so significant. "My Lord. I'm truly honored you have chosen me for such an example. I don't feel worthy, but I'm grateful."

The Messiah smiled. "Remarkable things are yet to come, Edvin. Your family is the doorway to showing what will be and can be.

"You're special to me, Edvin. I just wanted you to know that."

The Messiah stood and left Edvin with his thoughts. Edvin looked back to the valley below and smiled. He could almost see the increased beauty to come.

CHAPTER 40

Jubilee Calendar
00:0:1

Coronation Day had arrived. The excitement in the city seemed palpable. Edvin and Mik'kel helped prepare the temple. Many purification steps and sacrifices were started a week earlier and had continued each day until this ceremony. The articles used in temple worship had to be ready and purified for true worship of the Messiah.

The Messiah came forward in all his true brilliance, his Shekinah glory, which appeared almost too brilliant for anyone to observe without shielding their eyes. He appeared to be on some type of sapphire throne over a multicolored expanse, beneath which were some type of interconnecting wheels with the appearance of fire and lightning between them. The brightness seemed to linger as he advanced, and it looked as if his brilliance elongated behind him as he approached the temple.

He entered the temple complex through its Eastern Gate, then went through the Eastern Inner Gate, and then through the doors of the temple. Everyone knew he would enter the

Holy of Holies.

The priests began the evening sacrifice.

The Messiah next appeared in his glorified, but less brilliant, form on the palace balcony overlooking the temple complex. Everyone roared in applause.

He held up his hands. "My friends. This is a wonderful day for all. All preparations are set for us to enjoy the Kingdom I promised you so many millennia ago. I now have two people to present to you. First, you will have a prince to rule over you and to administrate my Kingdom to all those who will be born into it, and he will be an example to them of how to worship me in their nonglorified state. He comes from you, one of the firstfruits of the Tribulation. He is a direct descendent from King David himself and has been faithful to me throughout the Tribulation Period. I present to you Prince Jeremiah Ranz."

Edvin and Mik'kel looked at each other and applauded, as did everyone else.

"Who would have thought?" Edvin said to his friend. "We entertained royalty and didn't even know it."

Mik'kel smiled. "I'm not sure he did either."

The Messiah continued. "There will be many kings and many nations in my kingdom. I will present each one to each territory. Now, to Israel, as promised to him and to all of you, I present to you King David, who will shepherd Jeremiah and rule over a united Israel."

A glorified one stepped forward. He was a good-looking and muscular man with a neatly trimmed, reddish-colored beard and mustache.

Edvin poked Mik'kel. "I can see why he became a formidable opponent in his day."

Mik'kel nodded. "Or any day."

The King continued. "When Passover is celebrated, no

longer will you celebrate your forefathers coming out of Egypt. You will celebrate Judah and Israel—that is, all of you—coming out of the four corners of the earth during the Tribulation Period to be reunited into a single kingdom—my Promised Kingdom. And I will now drink the fourth cup of Pesach proclaiming I will dwell with you, my people."

Again, thunderous applause.

The Messiah took a crown and placed it on his own head. "This fulfills many prophecies before your eyes today. I am your Messiah, the Anointed One, the true heir of David who has the right to rule forever. I am Emmanuel and now dwell with you, my people, my friends, my children. I am Yahushua Ha-Mashiach ben Elohim, who paid the debt of sin for all mankind." He held up his hands to show his scars. "And I now reign before you as King of Kings. My throne is where my Name has been placed, here in Jerusalem, but my subjects are those who inhabit the whole earth."

More applause, whistles, and shouts of praise could be heard throughout the crowd.

The Messiah did not try and calm them. He waited until the noise died down. He then placed a crown on David's head. "This also fulfills prophecy today before you. I promised through Scripture David would someday rule a united Israel again. Today begins that day. As other kings of other nations will bring their glory into this city to present their gifts to me, so will King David do for you."

David placed a crown on Jeremiah's head. David then spoke. "Jeremiah is one of my direct descendants. As our Messiah spoke, Prince Jeremiah represents those of you who have nonglorified bodies. He has earned this right by being one of the first of my direct descendants to accept our Messiah after the Messiah's bride was caught up in the air to be with him and partake of his marriage supper. Jeremiah remained faithful throughout the Tribulation and the Great Tribulation which many of my prophets referred to as the time of Jacob's Trouble. He will be your prince before you and will lead you in the worship of our Messiah, the rightful ruler of the entire world."

There was more thunderous applause. After a time, the Messiah raised his hands.

"My friends, before the celebration begins, I have a few more things to say. While my throne and glory will be in the Holy of Holies of the temple, I will also have a throne room in the palace so I can meet with you, my subjects, on various matters. These two men here with me will be my representatives who will dwell with you even more closely and will have a palace in the middle of Jerusalem proper. As you know, Jerusalem is where I said my Name would dwell. This is now where it dwells in peace."

After more applause, the Messiah smiled warmly and held up his hands again. "Thank you, my friends, my children. As you have observed, Jerusalem has been divided into three sections. As my Name is triune, so now is my city triune to represent my Name. There is much symbolism represented here. You will teach these things to your children so they also can understand what their Messiah stands for and what he has done for them.

"This time will also be when the former spirit world will be open to you. Soon, for the first time, you will hear my angels singing to you. I have enjoyed them for millennia. I now share that joy with you. This will be the first of many times you will hear them. They will also help guide you. Israel will lead the world in worship, and the angels will lead the world in praise."

The Messiah placed his arms around the two men with him. "Now, my friends, it is time to celebrate this day and this time. The whole earth has now been prepared for you. Go forth, be fruitful, multiply, and worship in the glory of your Lord."

A roar of applause and shouting erupted. Confetti flew, seemingly everywhere. A choir of angels gathered around the temple and began to sing; the spontaneous concert was more glorious than words could express. Following that, another concert of individuals, some glorified, some not, sang to the glory of their King. Dancing took place in the streets. There were vendors distributing food and drink.

The celebration went deep into the morning hours.

Mik'kel and Edvin stood taking it all in. Edvin noticed a change in Mik'kel's face. *Why have I not seen that before?*

"Mik'kel, have you seen your face lately?"

Mik'kel laughed. "What's that supposed to mean?"

"No. Your scar. It's faded."

"What?" Mik'kel put his hand up to feel his scar. "Well, it does feel diminished."

"It's healing, Mik'kel. Healing. The Refreshing has started and is having an effect on all of us."

"I guess it's working," Mik'kel said. "You're starting to actually look handsome."

Edvin tap-punched him in his shoulder with his free hand.

Mik'kel laughed and patted Edvin on the back. He then leaned over and kissed Ya'akov on his forehead. "Or maybe it's *you*—making your daddy look better."

Edvin laughed. He danced with Ya'akov in his arms. He couldn't get over what a contented baby this little boy was. Adelina came over and took Ya'akov, and she also danced with him. Ya'akov giggled as only an infant can. It made everyone around him smile and laugh as well.

Lars and Elsbeth came by. Edvin looked at each of them and smiled. He couldn't be happier. He had a family, although that needed further figuring out, he had a Messiah, and he had a purpose.

And then it hit him: at no other time in history could anyone be assured happiness would last a lifetime, and that a lifetime would last a thousand years.

Ty had been right. The best was yet to come.

I hope you've enjoyed *Promised Kingdom*. Letting others know of your enjoyment of this book is a way to help them share your experience. Please consider posting an honest review. You can post a review at Amazon, Barnes & Noble, Goodreads, or other sites you choose. Reviews can also be posted at more than one site!

This author, and other readers, appreciate your engagement. Also, check out my next book coming soon!

—Randy Dockens

Come Experience the Early Days of the Kingdom!

And tell us what you think at randydockens.com

Advance orders available at
Amazon and Barnes & Noble
September 2019

Can destiny be averted?

Ya'akov, the firstborn into the Promised Kingdom, was named by the King. His family was chosen by the King to be a model to all earth's inhabitants as to how glorified and non-glorified people are to live together. Because of his heritage and birthright, when Ya'akov turns thirty, he will be the first born into the Kingdom to take his rightful place as a priest.

But Ya'akov feels the pressure is too much and wants to explore other options and make his own decision about his future. He becomes infatuated with a woman who he discovers has a negative view of the King. She and her friends try to force him to go against the King. His adventure turns into a nightmare, and hard choices must be made.

Is Ya'akov strong enough to choose the correct path even though suffering likely awaits him? What true destiny awaits? Is all hope lost, or can it be renewed?

Also, please check out:
https://randydockens.com/news/

(BEFORE FINAL EDITING.)

SAMPLE CHAPTER FROM PREQUEL 2 TO
THE MERCY OF THE IRON SCEPTER
A PART OF THE STELE PROPHECY PENTALOGY

HOPE RENEWED

CHAPTER 1

Destiny and heritage are sometimes intertwined.

Ya'akov groaned. Was this his life? Did he have any other choice?

"Hold him down, Ya'akov. I need to immobilize him."

Ya'akov pressed his hands into the soft fleece until he felt the warm body underneath. He could feel the animal's heart beating rapidly, its muscles flinching in fear.

Ya'akov watched his grandfather take the rope and tie the four hooves of the lamb to each other.

"Shhh . . . shhh," Ya'akov whispered as he stroked the lamb's head and rubbed its side to calm the animal as it twitched while trying to kick. Ya'akov had done this many times before. But, *should he? Was it necessary?*

"Is this really that important, grandfather?"

His grandfather cocked his head as he looked at Ya'akov.

"This has been done ever since the first Avraham." He handed Ya'akov a silver bowl. "Is something wrong?"

Ya'akov shrugged. "I guess not."

Avraham took out his knife. Ya'akov saw him feel for the lamb's carotid artery. "Ready?"

Instinctively, Ya'akov placed the bowl approximately three-quarters of a meter from where Avraham had the knife and slightly lower than the lamb's neck. Should it be normal for him to know exactly how far he needed to place the bowl? *Should he have to know?*

Avraham made a quick slice in the lamb's neck. The lamb kicked a couple more times as its blood flowed in a slight arc into the bowl Ya'akov held. The kicks decreased in intensity and stilled. Ya'akov held the bowl closer and closer to the lamb as the arc's length decreased with the force of blood flow. He could feel the bowl's temperature increase from the heat of the blood as it filled the bowl. The cool morning air caused a wisp of steam to be seen rising from the bowl until the blood and bowl equalized in temperature. Not a drop missed the bowl.

Did that mean he'd done this too many times? How many times *had* he done this?

Avraham took the bowl from his hand and, as if reading his thoughts, said, "You've been helping me since you were thirteen. In just two years, you will be thirty, and I will be the one helping you."

Only two more years. Could he see himself doing this for the rest of his life? To what purpose?

"Grandfather, do I have to follow in the footsteps prescribed for me?"

Avraham whipped around, almost spilling the bowl of blood, but recovered quickly. He sighed. "Ya'akov, what a question. Why wouldn't you want to follow your destiny? You're special."

"I don't feel special."

"Wh . . . " Avraham gave an exasperated sigh. He stopped, held the bowl in his left hand, and put his right hand on Ya'akov's shoulder.

"Ya'akov, the Master himself named you. He, himself, stated your destiny. I was standing right here in front of the temple when he did so. Of course you're special. Everyone knows you're special. You're a descendant of Levi, from the family of Zadok, the firstborn of the Refreshing. No one else can claim such a heritage. You're as special as they come, Ya'akov." He patted his shoulder and smiled.

Ya'akov didn't look at his grandfather. Hearing such words only made it seem like a burden rather than a blessing. Finally, he looked up at his grandfather and gave a weak smile. "You're right, grandfather. You always are."

Avraham again patted him on his shoulder. "That's my boy. Now come. Let's anoint the altar and prepare the sacrifice."

Ya'akov followed Avraham and stood in the doorway of the Inner North Gate, holding the bowl as Avraham dipped his fingers into the blood and sprinkled it at the base of each side of the altar. Ya'akov could not yet enter the Inner Court. Only priests could do that. Avraham poured the remainder of the blood on the ground at the altar's base. They both went back and prepared the lamb for sacrifice. Ya'akov carried the lamb on his shoulder, again through the Inner North Gate, and transferred the animal to his grandfather's shoulder. Ya'akov stood there as he watched Avraham slowly ascend the altar's steps and then fling the animal's lifeless body, the morning sacrifice, toward the center of the large altar.

Ya'akov sighed. That would be him soon. Did he really want that?

Ya'akov went to the priests' quarters and washed the remaining blood from his hands. He paused and looked in the mirror. Looking back was a twenty-eight-year-old man with a neatly trimmed pinstriped beard and mustache. He sighed. *I don't think I can do this. Not for the rest of my life.* No. He couldn't be a butcher of animals for the remainder of his days. Life should mean more.

He looked back into the mirror and saw Joel approaching. Joel was five years younger than he and enthusiastic about becoming a priest. Maybe their births should have been reversed.

"Hi, Ya'akov." He stopped and gave Ya'akov a second look. "Are you OK? Is something wrong?"

Ya'akov shook his head. "Nothing, really." Ya'akov turned to walk away.

Joel grabbed his arm. "Ya'akov, we're friends. You can tell me anything. You know that. No judgment."

Ya'akov nodded. "I know. Maybe I'll talk to you later. OK?"

Joel nodded. "Sure. Anytime." He gave Ya'akov a pat on his shoulder. "Anytime."

Ya'akov changed his clothes and met Avraham as he exited the building. He avoided direct eye contact. Avraham caught his arm as he passed.

"What's wrong, Ya'akov? You've been acting strange all morning."

He shook his head. "Nothing. Just a lot on my mind."

Ya'akov turned to leave, but Avraham grabbed him once more, this time at the elbow.

"Ya'akov. Tell me. Please."

Ya'akov looked at Avraham. "Grandfather, I . . . I don't think I can continue doing this."

"What? Can't do what?"

"Sacrificing. I can't continue doing these sacrifices."

Avraham took a step backward, wide-eyed. "You . . . you can't be serious. This is your destiny. You can't deny your calling."

"Calling?" Ya'akov's tone became one of disdain. "You say sacrificing is an honor. It's barbaric."

Avraham leaned forward with a stern look. Ya'akov swallowed hard. He had never talked to his grandfather with such a tone before.

"Barbaric? Well, of course it's barbaric," Avraham began. "It's *supposed* to be barbaric. How else will the King's citizens understand what he did for them? He took on the horror that is due every individual. Only when you understand what he did, what he endured, can you understand and appreciate his love for you."

"Grandfather, I'm not going to debate with you. I . . . I just can't. I can't continue doing this. It all seems so pointless."

Ya'akov now looked straight into Avraham's eyes with determination. Avraham sighed and stepped aside to let him pass. Ya'akov stormed passed him, out the door, and outside the temple complex.

Ya'akov walked through the city, turning right or left without thought. What was he to do with his life? His only study had been to prepare himself to be a priest. But now . . . that seemed so inadequate. He looked up as he turned another corner and realized he was at the Overlook.

The Overlook. A place he had come many times before to clear his mind and think. Was that why his body brought him here—so he could put things in perspective? Was his body telling him what his mind couldn't? He went to the railing and gazed over the edge.

It was always a breathtaking view. The water from under the temple cascaded down the escarpment into a river below. The Ezekiel River—named after the one, millennia ago, to whom God gave a vision of the temple where he now worked. *I should feel privileged.*

Why didn't he?

Movement caught his eye below. As he looked closer, he realized it was one of the landscapers whom the King had commissioned to plant various plant life into the escarpment. Most of the plants came from honoring ceremonies in which people from around the globe presented gifts and talents to their King. After several of these ceremonies, the King decided he would have the various plants from around the world planted into the escarpment for all to enjoy. After twenty-eight years, the entire area was beginning to fill in nicely. There was still a lot more space available for use, but it was obvious the landscapers had a plan in mind as they strategically placed the various greenery based on color array, shape, and texture. Several were already attracting butterflies and humming birds. The Overlook was becoming an extremely popular spot for both visitors and those who lived in Jerusalem. Maybe he should be a landscaper, Ya'akov wondered. It seemed like productive work. Beauty and life came from their work. Not death, like it did from his.

As he looked up, he saw someone approaching. Dad. Evidently, Grandfather had given him an earful, and now he was coming to interrogate. Ya'akov watched as his dad stopped and turned back, talking to someone else approaching. Mom. It seems Grandfather felt he was really going off the deep end. He watched as they approached, hand in hand. Yet, his mother had a glow about her his dad didn't. She was one of the glorified ones. He thought back to the stories told him of the days of transition into today's time of Refreshing. His mother had been pregnant with him and died during childbirth just as the Messiah, the King, was returning to earth. She was known to be the last of the glorified ones, and he the first of those born into the King's Promised Kingdom. Therefore, he and his dad had human bodies, but his mother was a glorified one who helped the King rule the present world. She worked at the

Jerusalem Science Center and his father at the temple assisting the other priests. Because his mother was a direct descendent of Zadok and his father a Levite descendant, Ya'akov was destined to be the first priest in the King's new Kingdom.

It was a nice story. He had heard it all his life. Living it, however, was a different story entirely.

Ya'akov turned back and looked at the valley below, his arms propped on the railing. The river was crystal clear, with one branch traveling between the northern and southern Mount of Olives and on to the Jordan River in the far distance. The second traveled around the escarpment to the Mediterranean Sea. Everything looked lush and beautiful—the antithesis of what he felt inside at this moment.

He felt his dad walk up and put his hand on his back. First came a double pat on his shoulder, and then a slow rub over his entire back. He loved his father and didn't want to hurt him. But he had to tell him the truth.

His eyes met those of Edvin, his father. Edvin smiled. "I hear you're having thoughts about your career."

Ya'akov gave a small laugh. "That's one way to put it. I'm having doubts about having a career."

His father furrowed his brow. "Want to talk about it?"

Ya'akov turned and faced his parents, leaning his body against the railing with his hands behind him. "Not really. But I know you won't let me not talk about it."

Ya'akov looked at his father, who had concern written all over his face. His mother put her arm on his shoulder. "We only want the best for you, Ya'akov."

His gaze turned to his mother. "So, you're OK if I don't enter the priesthood?"

Her mouth fell open in disbelief. Before she could formulate a reply, his father held up his hand. "Elsbeth, let's think before we respond."

Her disbelief turned to Ya'akov's father. "Edvin, so this doesn't take you by surprise? Why am I the last to know?"

Edvin glanced at Ya'akov. "We've had . . . discussions. But I never thought it would come to actual rejection."

Ya'akov held up his hands. "Let's not talk as if I'm not here." He put his hands to his chest. "It's my life, my decision."

Elsbeth shook her head. "But . . . but your destiny."

"Mom, my destiny is what I choose it to be."

"Talk to him."

Ya'akov turned to his dad. "What? Talk to *whom*?"

"The Master," Edvin said. "He'll know what you should do."

"But he's the one who stated my destiny. You think he would change his mind?"

"He wants to talk to you."

He looked back at his mom.

"He wants you to come see him," Elsbeth said. "You would know if . . . "

Edvin shook his head slightly, and she trailed off, not completing her sentence.

"I'm sorry. I didn't mean to be condescending." She grabbed Ya'akov's hand and held it gently with both of hers. "But he does want to talk to you. Please say you'll stop by and see him before you . . . " She shrugged slightly. "Before you do whatever it is you plan to do."

Ya'akov saw the pained look on her face. He nodded. He didn't really want to, but he couldn't disrespect her in this way either.

She gave him a kiss on his cheek. "Thank you." She put her hand to his cheek. "I love you, Ya'akov."

Edvin pulled him close and gave him a hug. "I'm here whenever you want."

Ya'akov nodded. Edvin and Elsbeth joined hands and walked away leaving Ya'akov behind. Before they turned the curve of the path and out of sight, Elsbeth turned and blew him a kiss.

Ya'akov sighed, turned back, and looked out at the scenery. He thought about his promise to his mom.

This next step might be even harder than facing his parents.

The Stele Pentalogy

The next book in this exciting series, *Hope Renewed*, from Randy C. Dockens, will be available October 2019.

The Coded Message Trilogy

Come read this fast-paced trilogy, where an astrophysicist accidently stumbles upon a world secret that plunges him and his friends into an adventure of discovery and intrigue . . .

What Luke Loughton and his friends discover could possibly be the answer to a question you've been wondering all along.

Available Now